# DREAMWAKER SAGA ❶

# lucid
# BODIES

*Lee Gabel*

**FRANKEN**SCRIPT

Frankenscript Press
Box 717, #105 - 1497 Admirals Road
Victoria, BC, Canada   V9A 2P8



Lucid Bodies (Dreamwaker Saga #1)



Cover illustration and design by Lee Gabel

Cover images supplied by DepositPhotos

Body font (ITC Galliard Pro) by International Typeface Corporation
Folios, heads and caps (Zapf Humanist 601) by Bitstream Inc.



ISBN: 978-1-9991856-3-3 (ebook)
ISBN: 978-1-9991856-6-4 (paperback)

Want to join Lee's Reader Group or find out more about Lee and the books he writes? Please go to:
LeeGabel.com/links

DREAMWAKER SAGA 1

# lucid BODIES

*Titles by Lee Gabel*

**Dreamwaker Saga**
Lucid Bodies
Lucid Revenge
Lucid Fate

**Detest-A-Pest Series**
Vermin 2.0
Arachnid 2.0
Molerat 2.0

**Standalone**
David's Summer
Snipped
Tied

For my son.
Good friends can help you through anything.

# Playlist

| | |
|---|---|
| THAT WAS YESTERDAY<br>Foreigner | VENUS<br>Bananarama |
| I'M HER MAN<br>Canned Heat | WE DON'T HAVE TO TAKE<br>OUR CLOTHES OFF<br>Jermaine Stewart |
| WAITING FOR A GIRL LIKE YOU<br>Foreigner | DANGER ZONE<br>Kenny Loggins |
| I WANT TO KNOW<br>WHAT LOVE IS<br>Foreigner | THE HEAT IS ON<br>Glenn Frey |
| TAKE ON ME<br>A-Ha | TIME AFTER TIME<br>Cyndi Lauper |
| STRANGER IN MY OWN HOUSE<br>Foreigner | THESE DREAMS<br>Heart |
| CRUSH ON YOU<br>The Jets | MAGIC<br>The Cars |

Talking In Your Sleep
The Romantics

Little Red Corvette
Prince

You Dropped A Bomb On Me
The Gap Band

She And I
Alabama

Queen Of Hearts
Juice Newton

Here I Go Again
Whitesnake

Hard To Say I'm Sorry
Chicago

Kiss You When It's Dangerous
Eight Seconds

Girls on Film
Duran Duran

Every Breath You Take
The Police

Let's Go Crazy
Prince and The Revolution

A Criminal Mind
Gowan

Another One Bites The Dust
Queen

Against All Odds
Phil Collins

Seek and Destroy
Metallica

With A Little Help
From My Friends
The Beatles

Cruel Summer
Bananarama

Love Is A Battlefield
Pat Benatar

The Winner Takes It All
ABBA

You've Got Another
Thing Coming
Judas Priest

# That Was Yesterday



At that moment under the car, it was hard to tell what was worse, the acrid smell of burning rubber or the searing heat blasting from the engine's undercarriage. Somehow Wynter had escaped the wheels of the black car as it barreled over her.

With her cheek pressed to the hot asphalt, she watched the car's taillights burn red as it screeched to a stop. Wynter looked back and saw the boy again, blond and blue-eyed, but this time he was running, or trying to. The road moved under his feet like a treadmill. He was always too far away and going nowhere.

The boy finally reached toward her just as the car's wheels began to squeal once more. Wynter returned her gaze to the car to see billows of blue-gray smoke pouring out from the back wheels, the car accelerating in reverse toward her. She tried to move but her body refused to obey. In her mind she screamed as the car rolled back over her a second time.

The impact of the rear tires jolted Wynter awake. Thankfully the store was empty. If word of her sleeping on the job had gotten back to Vinny, she was sure he'd fire her on the spot. She pushed aside the issue of *Popular Photography* that she had been reading and wiped away the sleep drool that had collected on the display case.

Her dreams had felt increasingly more real over the past few weeks, more visceral. And they left a lasting hangover that was an unwelcome and stubborn companion today. She rubbed her temples to soothe the relentless pounding behind her eyes.

Wynter had awoken that morning to a clammy sweat, her nightie stuck uncomfortably to her body, her mind still heavy with vibrant leftover images. As the day had pressed on, the morning dream faded and mixed with this latest one, but the pain lingered.

*Maybe, somehow, it* was *real.*

Of course, that was impossible and Wynter shook off the thought. She'd be injured or more likely dead. But the pain was real. She worked her fingers to the back of her neck and ran her fingertips through the roots of her red hair to try to bring some relief. It did not.

Shooters was the only camera store in Newhaven and her shift would soon be over. She imagined crawling into her cool bed to sleep off the rest of the day. Or at least until dinner time. But that meant she might dream again.

Wynter had briefly considered going home early but that meant she'd have to call and ask permission from Vinny, never a pleasant task. She could already hear his reply.

"What's in it for me?" he would say as he wiggled his eyebrows, a lascivious grin spreading across his thin, greasy lips. Vinny was the brainchild behind the store's logo, a sloppily drawn rip-off of the Hooters owl with a pair of binoculars to its eyes and a camera with a long telephoto lens dangling around its neck. Cheap and obvious. In a way it was genius since it captured his personality perfectly.

Vinny may have been a horrible boss, but his saving grace was to rarely show his face around the store. Wynter often wondered how someone with such limited business acumen could keep a photography store profitable, particularly in Newhaven, North Dakota, population 2,328. People weren't exactly beating down the door for camera equipment and supplies.

Stedford Plaza, Newhaven's one shopping mall and home to Shooters, had been deader than usual for a Thursday.

*Small miracles.*

Wynter loved photography and being paid to be around equipment that she could only hope to own someday was certainly a highlight when the days were long and boring. And some of the equipment was top notch. She most coveted the Pentax A* 135mm f1.8 telephoto lens, nicknamed "Speedy Gonzales" due to its fast aperture. Wynter had drooled over it ever since Vinny had brought it into the store, but he refused to let her try it on her old bargain K1000 SLR. With a price tag of over $1,000, she'd likely never get a chance. Vinny didn't believe in "try before you buy."

After rearranging the photography magazines and checking the levels of film stock for the third time that day, Wynter sat on a stool behind the front display case. Locked in front of her was good old Speedy. She hoped the lens would never sell because *she* was going to buy it some day.

Wynter laid her head down on the glass top. Its cool surface soothed her skin, and her head began to feel a bit better.

"Sleeping on the job again?" a voice said from behind. "Wait 'til Vin hears about this."

Wynter lifted her head to see Daytona in front of the stockroom door with her arms crossed. Her skirt and Shooters T-shirt, both black to coordinate, hugged her body and left little to the imagination. With her straightened long blond hair, she could have worked at Hooters for real if she wanted to. That's probably why Vinny had hired her. "Yeah? And what have you been doing?"

Daytona's boyfriend Hunter appeared behind her, his hair sticking up at odd angles. "Doggie-style!" He howled like a wolf.

Daytona whacked his lean chest with the back of her hand. "We've been organizing the back room."

"We've been organizing *something*." Hunter laughed.

Why Vinny had hired these two remained a mystery. Wynter had long suspected hidden cameras in the stockroom to record Daytona and Hunter's sexcapades. "How many times does the back room need to be *organized?*" Wynter gave Daytona a sideways look. "I've been keeping track."

Daytona narrowed her eyes at her instead of answering the question. "I got to go to the bathroom." She trudged out into the main concourse of the plaza, tripping the optical customer alert across the entrance. A soft *ding-dong* sounded inside the stockroom.

Hunter slid up beside Wynter at the counter. "Don't be mad. She won't tell Vinny anything. I'll make sure of it."

Wynter nodded. "I know. Sometimes it'd be nice if you guys did a little work around here."

Hunter smiled. It was one of his best features and made up for his god-awful mullet. "If you had the choice, would you rather be working or... *organizing?*" He motioned to the stockroom.

Wynter shrugged, a delicate shade of pink mixing with her light brown skin. "It's time to lock up."

Hunter gave her a playful shove. "You're hilarious, Wintergreen." That was Hunter's nickname for her. *Wintergreen*. It didn't make any sense. "Got any plans for the weekend?"

"It's still Thursday."

"Doesn't mean you can't have plans."

Wynter closed her eyes. The ache in her head was building again. "I just want to get home. Got a wicked headache."

"Good thing it's almost quitting time."

The clock in the corner of the store read 5:10 p.m. and Wynter could hear the echoes of Daytona's black Converse on the concourse tile.

"Your queen approaches."

"She sure does."

Daytona stepped into the store.

*Ding-dong.*

"Ready to go, Babe?"

Hunter hopped over the counter like an eager puppy.

Daytona directed her gaze at Wynter. "Lock up for us?" She didn't wait for a response.

Hunter ran up and gave Daytona a playful slap on her behind before picking her up and throwing her over his shoulder. "Let's go *organize* somewhere." She pretended to protest between her giggles.

Before the two of them were out of sight, Hunter called back, "Make some plans!"

*Deal with this damn headache,* Wynter thought. *That's my one and only plan.* And if Daytona and Hunter could leave early, so could she, just this one time. After balancing the register, she turned out the lights, pulled the security gate closed, and locked it.

As Wynter approached the exit doors of the plaza, she thought she heard the Shooters phone ringing. Whoever it was, they'd have to try again tomorrow. Her throbbing head took priority now.

She secured the strap of her purse over her shoulder and began her walk home. She couldn't help but wonder if the dream would come back.

○

NEWHAVEN, FLAT AND unmemorable, sprawled smack in the center of North Dakota, divided in half by Interstate 94 and connected on both sides by the Main Street Overpass to the east and the 19th Street Bridge to the west. Both structures crossed the highway, but the Main Street Overpass boasted four lanes instead of two and held the on- and off-ramps to the highway.

To the north lay residential homes and the business center of town, anchored by Stedford Plaza. FoodXpress Supermarket shared the plaza's parking lot along Main Street with Pizza Zip and Golden Palace. Beside the parking lot, Finn's Gas N Go, one of two gas stations in Newhaven, consistently won "Friendliest Full Service" in the annual *Newhaven Register* "Best Of" poll.

The south end of town was a stark contrast to the north. Smaller, cheaper residential homes peppered the area and the only business laying claim across the great Interstate divide was the Starlite SuperSkate roller rink. That arrangement was a match made in heaven since most of the rink's customers were southies anyway.

Wynter wilted under the summer heat. The plaza parking lot was deserted. With an average summer temperature of eighty degrees Fahrenheit, both northies and southies loved to escape to the plaza and its air conditioning even if they had no intention to buy. It was usually Newhaven's gathering place. But not today.

*Why wasn't Stedford packed?*

It was a question that did not stay in Wynter's head for long. Home was fifteen minutes away. She quickened her pace even though it made her head throb more.

She followed Main Street as it curved through the town's business center. Ahead was the overpass. A bridge. Wynter despised bridges. The edges always pulled at her like a magnet to iron. In her mind she'd see herself flying off the edge to certain death in hundreds of ways.

Wynter closed her eyes and took a fortifying breath. Reopening her eyes, it was a surprise to see someone walking toward her, a black hoodie shrouding their face. She stepped onto the overpass's one narrow sidewalk and made sure to stay as far from the outer railing as possible. She could feel the pull of the overpass's edge already.

As the distance between them diminished, Wynter realized the person was close to her age and height. A boy. Curly blond hair poked out of his hoodie. Their eyes met for a second, his blue eyes intense, as they passed each other at the midpoint.

Wynter felt a shiver move through her body.

*Do I know him?*

She continued to walk across the overpass.

*Should I look back? Is he looking back at me?*

The overpass's hold on her faded, replaced with intense curiosity and longing. By the time Wynter reached the opposite side of the overpass, she could stand it no longer. She turned to look back.

The boy with the blond curly hair and eyes like blue sapphires stood on the railing of the overpass, his arms slack at his sides.

"Hey!" Wynter found herself running back towards the boy, her concern for the overpass's edge forgotten. "What are you doing?"

The boy locked gazes with Wynter but said nothing. His left foot stepped into the void.

"No! STOP!" Wynter pumped her legs as fast as they would move her. She reached out with her left hand, open and ready to grab the boy's hoodie and pull him back to safety. But she was too late.

The boy stepped off the railing and plunged toward the highway traffic below.

*If only I had turned around a few seconds sooner, I could have...*

Wynter grabbed the railing and scanned the busy highway, steeling herself for a horrific spectacle below. But there was nothing. No boy. No aftermath. Nothing. The boy was all in her head.

*Am I going crazy?*

From behind, someone yelled at her. Wynter's thoughts melted away. She pushed herself back from the railing, all at once aware of the overpass's edge, stumbled off the curb of the sidewalk, and sat down.

She may not have recognized the boy—*or did she?*—but Wynter knew that voice anywhere. "Quinn?"

Quinn Benoit and Wynter had been best friends since middle school. Quinn worked at the FreshWhip stand at the plaza's food court, practically a stone's throw from Shooters. They had been inseparable all through middle and into high school, but after finishing 11th Grade Wynter had noticed a growing independence in both of them. It was strange and cool at the same time.

Quinn ran up the sidewalk, squatted, and stared back at her with the exotic eyes of her mixed-race parents. She wore a goofy grin behind glasses in rounded tortoise-shell frames and fine black hair cut in a bob. She still had her FreshWhip uniform on, a pink short-sleeved polo top with black shorts, and she held one of their signature drinks in one hand. As her voluminous black leather satchel slid off her shoulder, her grin changed to an expression of concern. "Hey, Bug. You okay? You were supposed to call me." Quinn set her drink down on the curb and helped Wynter to her feet. "What's going on?"

Wynter looked at her and tried to process both Quinn's questions and what she had just seen. "I don't know." She stepped up with trepidation to the railing and looked over the edge. Still nothing but highway traffic below.

Quinn instinctively placed her arm across Wynter's chest as if to prevent her from jumping. She knew Wynter had a history with bridges. It was weird, but hell, everyone had something weird about them. It was the weird things you remembered. "Whoa, girl."

Wynter's eyes cleared as she faced her. "I'm okay."

"You sure?"

Wynter nodded.

Quinn grabbed her satchel, picked up her drink, and took a sip. "Want some? It's orange-strawberry."

"I just need to get home. My head's killing me."

"I got just the thing. Hold this." Quinn handed Wynter the drink and began digging through her satchel.

The cool condensation felt good in Wynter's hand. She closed her eyes, raised the cup, and ran cold droplets across her forehead.

"You're supposed to drink it." Quinn raised a brow. "What's gotten into you?"

"Feels good."

"Tastes better." Quinn found what she was looking for. "Got it! Now this is good shit." She held a small beat up aspirin tin, barely recognizable from all the scratches and dents. She popped the tin open to reveal half a dozen small white tablets and removed two. "Here. Take these."

"What are they?"

Quinn smiled. "Don't worry. It's just generic Tylenol. And it's *not* poisoned." Even though it had been almost four years since tampered Tylenol had killed seven people, a rash of recent copycats had kept the public nervous.

Wynter popped the pills into her mouth without a moment of thought and washed them down with a swig of Quinn's FreshWhip.

"Come on. I'll walk you home."

"But you're a northie."

"So? You're my best friend, Bug." Quinn shoved her satchel out of the way and hooked arms with Wynter. "Besides, we've got much to talk about."

"Like what?"

"Like boys."

Wynter shook her head gently. "I have no time for boys."

"Screw that. We need boyfriends."

"Why?"

"Besides the *obvious*...?" Quinn smirked and raised her brow.

"I hear enough of the *obvious* at the store. Hunter and Daytona are at it all the time. I end up doing all the work."

"Tell Vinny."

Wynter laughed. "Yeah, right. He'd probably join in."

Both girls looked at each other and laughed. "Gross!" they said in unison.

"Hunter *is* hot, though," Quinn said.

"What? Um, no."

"But he is."

Wynter rolled her eyes. "If you go for guys with nothing but air between their ears."

"It's not what's between their *ears* I'm interested in." Quinn sighed. She looked to the sky and a small smile curled her lips.

"You're having a fantasy right now, aren't you?"

Quinn answered with a suggestive grin.

"Jesus. Stop."

"You work with him every day," Quinn said. "Doesn't he make your knees weak?"

Wynter shook her head. "Honestly, no. And even if he did, I can't compete with Daytona."

Quinn stared at her in disbelief. "Hell no. You got the body *and* the brains."

"Change of topic for one hundred, Alex."

"Someone in this go-nowhere town has to pop your cherry."

"Ugh. Stop." Wynter rubbed her temple.

Quinn relented. "Okay, okay. But I'm going to keep my eyes open for *both* of us."

"Whatever floats your boat."

The two girls traversed the overpass and continued down Main Street, straight into southie territory.

Wynter gave Quinn a friendly nudge. "You're on the wrong side of the tracks now, honey."

"Ooo, I'm shaking in my boots." Quinn wiggled her finger at her.

No question about it. Wynter was feeling a bit better. The pills, plus Quinn's energy, had begun to work their magic.

○

A WHOOP-WHOOP sounded from behind. Both girls turned to see a white Chevrolet Suburban following slowly behind them, the Newhaven Police Department logo boldly displayed on the side panel.

Quinn faced Wynter and smirked. "Speak of the devil. Sheriff Hotpants."

"Don't embarrass me, Quinn. I'm serious."

"Have you ever imagined what Anson looks like naked?"

"What? He's like twice our age. And he's practically my uncle."

"So? Last I checked fantasies aren't illegal." Quinn snuck a peek at Anson. "He's wearing short sleeves. And those sunglasses." They were Ray-Bans, the same style worn by Tom Cruise in *Top Gun*.

Wynter whispered through clenched teeth. "Control yourself."

The four-door police SUV rolled up next to the girls. Anson slid his sunglasses down to look over the rims. "Hey there, Wynter, Quinn. Do you need assistance? A ride home perhaps?"

Anson Jacobs had led the McLeod County Sheriff's Office and Newhaven Police Department for the past ten years and worked as a deputy ten years before that. Due to the low crime in Newhaven, Sheriff Anson acted more like a concierge for the town. He knew everyone by name and tried to be as helpful as possible to the citizens of his jurisdiction.

Quinn brought her head close to Wynter's. "Anson wants to give us a ride," she whispered. "It's our lucky day."

"I'm almost home anyway," Wynter whispered back.

"But he's so *hot*."

Anson rubbed his trimmed beard, his biceps flexing. "Did you hear me, ladies? I got places to be, so..."

Wynter shook her head at Quinn.

Quinn licked her lips. "We'd love a ride, Anson." She dug into her satchel, brought out a tube of lipstick, and gave her lips a quick refresh. "Want some?" Wynter declined and followed Quinn into the front bench seat of the SUV.

"I've got a bad headache," Quinn said. "If you could take me home first, I'd really appreciate it."

Wynter pulled Quinn close and whispered into her ear. "What are you *doing*? I'm the one with the headache."

"Giving you more time with this fine specimen."

"I didn't ask—"

"Want something for it?" Anson asked. "I'm sure I've got some painkillers in the first aid kit."

"Actually, I've taken something already," Quinn said. "It just hasn't kicked in yet." She exchanged a glance with Wynter. "Um, it's totally legal, if that's what you're wondering. A generic brand of Tylenol."

Anson called in the ride, pulled a U-turn, and headed back into town toward the northern subdivision of Newhaven. "Don't worry, Quinn. I believe you." He locked gazes with her for a moment. "You're not high. I'd know it if you were." He winked at her.

Quinn turned to Wynter and mouthed "Oh my God."

"Careful." Anson motioned at Quinn's drink. "Spilling FreshWhip in a police vehicle is a felony." His eyes crinkled at the corners as he regarded the blue sky for a moment, before returning his attention to the road ahead. "Beautiful day it turned out to be. Hot."

"*Totally* hot." Quinn glanced at Wynter and stifled a giggle.

Wynter gave Quinn a playful whack.

Quinn spotted two boys ahead, walking on the gravel shoulder of the road. "Isn't that—"

"Cash and Jake?" Anson nodded. "I passed them a few minutes before passing you."

Quinn leaned over Wynter's lap and hooked her elbows on

the SUV's open passenger-side window. Wynter covered her eyes in preparation for an embarrassing display.

"Oh no you don't." Quinn pulled Wynter to the window to join her, their hair mingling in the wind. "Hey Cash! Jake! We've been arrested. You going to bail us out?"

Cash and Jake scrunched their brows in confusion as the police SUV drove by. "What?" Cash said. "What are you talking..." His voice faded out with distance.

"Want me to stop?" Anson had already begun to slow down.

"God no," Quinn said. "They're nerds. At least Jake is. We don't want them to get the wrong idea." She leaned close to Wynter's ear and whispered, "They're probably virgins too."

Wynter looked back at the two boys. Cash, with his short blond hair, blue eyes, a keen fashion sense, and dimples to die for, raised his hand to wave. Tiny butterflies fluttered in her stomach. Cash had always had that effect on her. She had wanted to ask him out on several occasions but always lost her nerve.

Jake on the other hand didn't concern himself with coordinated clothes. Give him jeans, a T-shirt, and a Nintendo baseball cap, and he was good to go. His long brown hair snaked and curled around the hem of his cap.

Cash and Jake made a good pair. They kept each other's styles in check.

Anson glanced at Quinn. "I take it you two already have boyfriends."

"No," Wynter said.

"We're playing the field." Quinn straightened her posture, her reaction almost defensive. "Keeping our options open."

Wynter sat back and watched the reflection of Cash and Jake shrink in the SUV's side mirror. She wondered what Cash was thinking.

"I see." Anson chuckled. "You could do a lot worse. Cash is as reliable as the day is long. I don't know much about Jake, except he's a whiz with technology. If he's a friend of Cash's, that's good enough for me."

Anson turned onto Hobbs Avenue, lined with lush trees and finely manicured lawns. Some yards were separated by the quintessential white picket fences. Every garage could accommodate at least two cars. He turned into the driveway of a raised rancher with white siding and a red brick foundation forming the lower level. A baby blue Volkswagen Bug sat on one half of the driveway. "This is you, right?"

Quinn nodded.

Wynter opened the passenger door to let Quinn out.

"Take care of that head of yours," Anson said.

"Thanks. I will." Quinn rubbed her forehead before stepping almost nose to nose with Wynter. "Enjoy the ride home," she whispered with a wink.

Anson radioed into dispatch before reversing back into the street.

Quinn waved, "Call me later, Bug!"

Wynter raised a "thumbs up" in response.

Anson navigated back to Main Street. "Why 'bug'?"

"Short for shutterbug."

Anson nodded and settled into the drive. "Quinn didn't have a headache, did she?"

"No." Wynter spoke quietly.

"Why would Quinn want to lie to me?"

"It's nothing, Anson. We were just joking around." Wynter paused. "She thinks you're hot. So we—"

"Okay. I get it. Enough said." Anson endured an awkward silence until, "Tell her I'm flattered."

Wynter nodded.

"*You're* the one with the headache."

"It feels a bit better now."

Anson gave her a concerned once-over. "You know you can call me for anything, right? Your mom and I have an agreement."

"I know. Thanks." Wynter propped her head next to the open window. The breeze played with her red hair. "How's Mercy?"

"Pretty great actually." Anson sported a wide smile whenever he talked about Mercedes. "She's thinking about starting her own salon soon, maybe out of Halston."

Mercedes "Mercy" Meadows had been sculpting nails at the Bombshell Salon ever since moving to Newhaven eight years ago. She had been Anson's plus one for the past seven. Apart from her skill with nails, Mercy was known for her always-changing hair color. At the moment it was bleach blond with strawberry tips.

"When are you two going to get married?"

Anson balked. "Soon."

"She's not going to wait forever, you know."

"Yeah," Anson sighed. "I'm working on it."

"Maybe you should—"

"Maybe we should keep our romantic lives to ourselves." Anson crossed the highway into Newhaven's southern, less affluent suburb. Rows of small homes built in the 1950s lined the side streets branching off Main Street, not an attached garage to be seen. "How's that head of yours? Any better?"

"A bit."

"Sure you're okay?"

Wynter almost spilled the beans about the blond boy who was there, then wasn't. She stopped herself at the last moment. Anson would never have believed her anyway. He dealt only in tangible evidence.

"Yeah, I'm fine," she said.

Anson turned into the long entrance of the only home Wynter had ever known. She heard the buzz of the neon sign before seeing it.

Sven Dwarfs Trail'r Park.

The neon tubing in the first "e" in "Seven" had been burnt out for as long as Wynter could remember and removing the "e" from the word "Trailer" had never made any sense to her.

"Dwarves" was spelled wrong, one could only hope by mistake. At the base of the sign was an old, beat up pay phone. She had no idea if it worked. In all of her sixteen years, she'd never had a reason to use it.

*Welcome home, illiterate trailer trash.*

Wynter began to giggle.

Anson raised an eyebrow at her. "What's gotten *into* you? You're really acting weird today."

"I'm just super tired."

Sven Dwarfs was laid out in a circle, with mobile homes lined up perpendicularly around the outside of the central ring road. The inner circle was reserved for recreation, but the grass was knee-high. Maintenance was a low priority.

Anson angled the police SUV next to pad #7 where a beige single-wide trailer sat, a wind chime hanging next to the front door. "Say hi to your parents for me."

"I don't think anyone's home yet, but I will. Thanks." Wynter climbed out of the SUV and closed the door. Anson scrutinized her as she went. "I'm fine. Really."

"Alright. Later." Anson waited for Wynter to unlock her front door and step inside. He reversed and followed the ring road out of the trailer park, a dusty cloud clinging to his bumper.

The trailer was empty and stifling. Wynter's mother Madeline hadn't yet returned home from her shift as a cashier at the FoodXpress and her father Nolan commuted to the Halston Public Library where he worked as a librarian. He wouldn't be home for at least an hour. It was a perfect time to catch a nap.

Wynter opened the small windows in both bedrooms, the living room, and the kitchen to get a cross-breeze going. However, the weak breeze was warm too. It would have to do. She locked the front door and headed to her bedroom.

Wynter pulled off her work clothes, threw on a tank top and shorts, and flopped onto her bed. Catching some sleep before dinner would be a good idea. Usually sleep came easily to her, but after today she wondered if it would ever be easy again.

○

WYNTER WANTED TO live in a larger trailer someday, or even in a real house. Nine-hundred thirty square feet seemed like a lot at first, but when the trailer measured sixteen feet on one side, everything inside was squeezed together, especially for three people. Privacy was in short supply.

Madeline and Nolan's bedroom terminated one end of the trailer, with the kitchen on the other. In the middle sat the shared bathroom, Wynter's bedroom, and the living room, connected with an "open plan" hallway. Although their respective bedrooms were small, they were comfortable and did not share any common walls.

But the walls were *thin*.

Occasionally, on the nights when she couldn't fall asleep fast enough, Wynter had the pleasure of listening to her parents shake the trailer. She knew it was a normal thing, but not *her* normal. The sounds had inspired images in her head she would not soon forget, if ever.

Her bed was pushed into the corner of the room, leaving access to the small open window. Her mother had wanted to replace the threadbare curtains of her childhood, but Wynter had refused. She wasn't ready to let them go.

Against the adjacent wall to the window sat a small corner desk. Keepsakes and books, more nonfiction than fiction, many on the subject of lucid dreaming and photography, lined the two shelves above.

A narrow half-length mirror hung on the wall between the bedroom door and a small closet just big enough to be functional.

Wynter hung some of her clothes there but used most of the space to store her slowly growing collection of photography equipment.

Sandwiched between the closet and her bed sat a small dresser that doubled as a bedside table and held a reading lamp and a cheap clock radio. The wall above the head of Wynter's bed was her shrine. It featured a large corkboard with a poster of the Sheyenne National Grassland, a map of North Dakota, and dozens of photographs. She had used pins to mark the map with her favorite locations to take photos.

The room was cramped with very little floor space, but it was her *own* space. That made up for a lot.

Despite her mounting exhaustion, Wynter ran her fingertips over the spines of her small selection of books and pulled out her favorite, *Eyes Wide Dreaming* by Dr. A. X. Gardner. She flicked on her reading lamp and opened the book.

Her plan was to reread the section on dreams crossing over into reality, but her body had other plans. She set the open book on her chest and closed her eyes.

That was all it took. Within the sanctuary of her bedroom Wynter's weary mind succumbed to sleep. And as her sleep state deepened, the summer sun headed for the horizon, tracking a stretched yellow square of light across the remaining books on her shelf.

○

WYNTER FACED A wide expanse of grass and trees, lush and green, stretching as far as her eyes could see. The gentle wind caressed her hair and left it warm and sweet like spun sugar.

She stood in the middle of a road. A white sundress, so light on her skin it felt as if she was naked, billowed around her. The painted yellow center line passed between her legs, the asphalt beneath it crumbling into dirt until overtaken by vegetation.

"What is this place?" Wynter thought, but instead heard her own voice as if she had spoken.

A sound rose up behind her. She turned to see the boy, the one with the blond curls and black hoodie. He, too, walked barefoot.

Wynter was at the Main Street Overpass again, except it wasn't. The overpass and the highway beneath had somehow been transported to the middle of the grasslands. The traffic had come with it but made no sound.

The boy stopped and pulled back his hoodie. Tousled by the wind, his hair danced across his forehead.

Wynter took tentative steps toward him. "Who are you?"

The boy gazed at her with his clear blue eyes and said nothing.

"What's your name?" Wynter took another few steps.

The boy turned to look at the never-ending stream of traffic below. He grabbed the railing and began to climb. In three steps his feet reached the top. He turned his stance to face her.

"Not again." Wynter's feet gripped the asphalt as she propelled herself toward the boy. Her dress floated on the wind like a cape. "Stop! Don't jump!"

She could feel his eyes on her, feel his urgency, despite their distance. Wynter hiked up the hem of her dress and ran, bridging the gap between them as fast as she could manage.

The warm air turned hot in her throat and she could now hear the traffic noise below. Just a few more feet and she'd be able to pull this mysterious boy to safety.

The boy's body arced toward the highway below, slowly at first, until gravity took hold. This time he reached forward with one hand.

"He wants to be saved." Wynter was close enough to detect a hint of a smile on his face. She maintained her speed even though the asphalt burned her feet. But the distance between them was too great.

Wynter stretched forward with her hand. An eighteen-wheeler

from nowhere barreled down Main Street across the overpass, its horn shattering her thoughts.

The boy fell out of sight below the overpass. Wynter had no chance to witness the aftermath. The eighteen-wheeler was already upon her.

C

WYNTER AWOKE WITH A JOLT. Her mom sat next to her on the edge of the bed, stroking her hair with a cool, comforting hand.

"There you are, honey," Madeline said. "You were crying out. Hope I didn't scare you."

Wynter let out a breath of relief. "No, Mom." She reached out and gently squeezed Madeline's hand. "Thanks."

"Must have been some dream." Madeline picked *Eyes Wide Dreaming* up off the floor.

"It was."

"I guess books like this don't help much." Madeline held the book on her lap.

"Actually, they do help. Sometimes." Wynter sat up and swung her legs off the bed. "What was I saying? Just before you woke me?"

"I don't know for sure." Madeline paused to think. "Mostly gobbledygook. But there was one part where you said 'wants to be saved' or something close to that. Do you remember anything?"

Wynter shook her head and lied. "No." But she *had* remembered, every part of the dream, every detail.

Her dad knocked on the door and poked his head into the room. His eyes registered the book on Madeline's lap but did not dwell on it long. "Everything okay?"

Madeline glanced at Wynter, then back at Nolan and nodded. "Right as rain." Madeline faced Wynter again. "It's almost eight o'clock. You must be starved."

"We fixed you a plate," Nolan said. "Rotisserie chicken from the deli, baked potato, and corn on the cob."

Wynter's stomach growled as if on cue.

"Plus freshly baked sugar cookies for dessert." Madeline smiled and placed *Eyes Wide Dreaming* on the bed. "Come on, Wynnie."

The three of them moved to the kitchen. Nolan transferred a plate of food from the fridge to the microwave and reheated it. Piles of sugar cookies cooled on racks beside the oven.

"I guess using the oven on a hot day like today wasn't the greatest idea." Madeline picked up a cookie, took a bite and offered the rest to Wynter. "What can I say. I had a craving."

Wynter sat at the kitchen table and popped the cookie into her mouth. "Mom, your sugar cookies are the best."

Madeline waved her off. "Help me ice them later? After they've cooled?"

Wynter nodded.

The microwave beeped its completion and Nolan carried the plate of food to the table.

"Thanks, Dad." Without another word, Wynter dug in. She loved the rotisserie chicken from FoodXpress.

Madeline and Nolan watched their daughter eat. Nolan, who was part Standing Rock Sioux due to his grandmother marrying outside of her tribe, placed his lanky arm around Madeline's shoulder. She took his hand and kissed it.

Wynter noticed their gesture and smiled.

Nolan stood six-two, thin but strong, his face narrow and angular as if it had been carved from sandstone. He wore his long black hair tied back in a ponytail.

Madeline rocked a fuller figure and stood a few inches shorter than Nolan. Her curves complemented his angles. Her laughter was infectious, and it wouldn't take her long to convert a crowd of strangers into friends. She preferred to keep her black hair natural and short. "If God had wanted me to have straight hair, I would've been born with it," Madeline would say.

Wynter was struck by how perfect her parents looked together. "How did you guys, like, know you were meant for each other?"

Madeline looked at Nolan. "You take this one."

Nolan strolled to the kitchen table and took a seat. "As you know, your mother and I met at Woodstock. That's a story in itself, half a million people of all colors and races, coming together to celebrate peace, friendship, and music."

"Don't forget the love." Madeline smiled and took a seat next to Nolan. "So much love."

"I had been at the festival for a day already, enjoying the music and people. It was the second day, Saturday, maybe around dinner time?" Nolan paused to think. "It was evening, close to sunset. Canned Heat had just gone on stage singing 'I'm Her Man.' " Nolan smiled sweetly at Madeline and kissed her forehead. "I saw your mom standing in the crowd and we just connected. I'm looking at her and she's looking at me and it's like the people all around us just faded away. I knew right then that your mom was the one. We spent the rest of the festival together." Nolan's eyes misted up. "I remember it like it was yesterday."

Madeline reached for Nolan's hand and squeezed it. "A week later we were married and you, our red-headed wonder, arrived nine months later."

"And that was a shock," Nolan said. "Thankfully the doctor told us a red-headed child was genetically possible from a mixed-race couple, but the odds were extremely rare."

"You are indeed one of a kind." Madeline smiled.

Wynter finished up her meal. "So you just knew? Just like that?"

Nolan nodded. "Pretty much."

Wynter alternated her gaze between her two parents. "You do realize how romantic that story is, right?"

"Our story, and the music, is the romantic part." Nolan looked at Madeline and started to snicker. "Remember the biffies?"

"Lord, do I." Madeline's body shook with laughter. "Some

genius thought six hundred portable toilets would be enough for all those people. It was nasty."

"Imagine a million shits over three days. The Port-O-San guy had his work cut out for him."

"Port-O-San! That's right. Pew!" Madeline waved her hand in front of her nose. Nolan headed to the living room, kissing her cheek as he went by.

"Okay, stop." Wynter held up her hands and shook her head back and forth. "Too much information."

Nolan parked himself on the living room sofa and turned on the television. Muted sounds of sitcom laughter rose from the set.

Madeline calmed her laughter. "You're right. That trip down memory lane spun out of control rather quickly, don't you think?"

Wynter answered her with a stare.

Madeline tried to match her seriousness, but the odd giggle still slipped out.

"*Family Ties* is starting," Nolan said.

Madeline looked at Wynter. "*Family Ties* or icing sugar cookies?"

Wynter grinned and swept her hair away from her eyes. "Sorry, Alex P. Keaton. I choose cookies. No contest. Besides I haven't had dessert yet."

"That's right." Madeline began collecting ingredients to make royal icing. "Best we get cracking."

As Wynter helped Madeline ice sugar cookies, her mind drifted, wondering when and where she'd meet "the one." And if he'd be blond with blue eyes.

○

NOLAN FINISHED BRUSHING his teeth and slipped into bed. Madeline had the covers pulled up to her chin even though the summer heat still hung heavy in the trailer.

Their bedroom was a little larger than Wynter's, able to accommodate a queen-sized bed. A closet ran the length of the room, divided by two separate doors. Madeline had planned to use each side to separate her clothes from Nolan's but discovered her collection of clothes vastly outnumbered his. But as long as Nolan had some hanger space, he was content with the dresser beside the bed.

Opposite the closet, under the only window in the room, ran one short long bookcase. It held all their favorites. Nolan read quickly and would bring new books home every few days, exchanging them with ones he had finished. Near the foot of the bed was a second entrance into the bathroom. With a teenager in the trailer too, privacy was a precious commodity.

He picked up *The Bourne Supremacy* by Robert Ludlum and opened it to where he'd left off.

Madeline looked at him and sighed. "I've been thinking."

Nolan closed his book. He knew that reading would not be on the agenda tonight. His gut churned. He had a feeling he knew where this was going. "This is about that book, isn't it?"

Madeline returned her gaze to the ceiling.

"Maddie. It's just a book."

Madeline propped herself up on her elbow to face him. "Aren't you worried? You of all people should know about the dangers of certain books."

He looked at her. "No, I'm not worried. It's a book about dreaming, not fascism."

"You don't think those books are harmful, putting thoughts in her head?"

"Any book can make you think. But dreams aren't real. If they were, I'd be in prison for sure." Nolan chuckled.

"You didn't see her, when I went into her room." Madeline's serious eyes held him. "It was like she was struggling or fighting against something. And she was talking."

"What did she say?"

Madeline rubbed her temple with her free hand. "It didn't make sense."

"People have nightmares. It happens."

Madeline slumped back into her pillow.

"Look, Maddie. I'm not trying to shut you down," Nolan said. "I just think this looks exactly like what it is. A nightmare." It was his turn to face her. "Do you remember when we went to see *A Nightmare on Elm Street* in Halston a couple years ago? Did you have bad dreams? Because I sure did."

"But that's different."

Nolan looked toward the bedroom door and lowered his voice. "It's not. Even though that movie gave me bad dreams, the dreams weren't real."

"The movie was fictional. The books she's reading are not."

"I'd call them creative nonfiction," Nolan said. "I know there are many people, credible people, who claim to be able to control their dreams. But there's little definitive proof that it's actually possible. It's anecdotal. You have to take them at their word."

"What about your grandmother? You've heard the stories."

Nolan laid his head back on his pillow. "That's all they are. Stories. No one can verify what she was able to do."

The two of them lay in silence for a moment.

"I'm still worried," Madeline said finally.

Nolan rolled over and kissed her. "Okay. We'll keep an eye on her." He gently pushed Madeline's hair away from her face and gave her his lop-sided smile that she loved so much. "Could I interest the lady in a mattress dance?"

Madeline laughed and pulled him on top of her. "Is there a money-back guarantee?"

"There is…" Nolan laid kisses across her neck. "But you're not going to need it tonight." He disappeared under the covers.

AFTER FINISHING ICING sugar cookies, Wynter had joined her parents for an episode of *Knots Landing*, a show that had become a Thursday night family tradition since she had turned fifteen. Homework had to be completed first, but it was summer now, no school, the best time of the year. CBS ran reruns of *Knots Landing* during the summer and that meant Wynter could watch episodes she had never seen before. After she had dozed off for the third time, Madeline suggested she go to bed early. Wynter needed no convincing.

Sleep found her quickly. It always had but tonight was quicker than most. The raucous vibrations from her parent's bedroom currently moving through the trailer did not wake her. Instead, her eyes ping-ponged beneath her eyelids like she was watching a tennis match on fast forward. *Eyes Wide Dreaming* described the action as rapid eye movement, or REM, a signal to the waking world that she was dreaming.

Wynter found herself back on the sidewalk of the Main Street Overpass, her white sundress hanging limp at her sides. Facing her, just out of reach, stood the blond boy in the black hoodie, his blue eyes probing hers.

"God, those eyes." Again, her thoughts vocalized.

She took a step toward him but the distance between them did not change. "Who are you?"

The blond boy opened his mouth as if to speak, then closed it again.

Wynter bolted toward the boy, but whatever force that was keeping them apart adjusted just as fast. She broke into a sprint. Nothing moved except her feet, sliding on invisible ice. Still, she continued to sprint, hot breath in and out, her legs working at a furious pace.

The boy smiled... and nodded? Did he just nod? Wynter was sure that he had. He boosted himself onto the railing of the overpass.

"Don't jump. Please." The distance between them began to decrease. Wynter was sure of it. "Please stay."

She couldn't maintain her pace forever, but every moment brought her closer to this mysterious boy. She could catch him if she kept going.

He rocked back and forth on the rounded railing. It was then that the world shifted into slow motion, everything except Wynter's feet.

She reached for the boy, so close her leading fingertips brushed against his. A spark of electricity arced between their fingers and she could sense his body heat. But the boy careened backward off the overpass toward the traffic below.

"NO!" Wynter stretched and grasped, again too late. She watched in horror as the boy fell, away from her and toward the highway. He didn't appear concerned despite plummeting to his death.

She gazed at the oncoming traffic. An eighteen-wheeler sped toward the boy below. And she would witness the whole thing.

"No." She turned, squatted with her back against the railing, and closed her eyes. "NO!" Her yell echoed. When she opened her eyes, darkness surrounded her. It took a moment to realize she was back in her room.

She reached up and turned on her bedside lamp, its orange light revealing a drawstring in her hand.

*From the blond boy's hoodie.*

It had to be. She didn't own anything remotely similar to a black hoodie. There was no other explanation.

*I brought it out of my dream?*

Wynter examined the cotton cord, rolling the frayed ends between her fingers. She held it to her nose. It smelled clean and fresh, like a summer day.

She rolled onto her back. "This is impossible," she whispered to the room. But there it was, the drawstring black as night, coiled in her hand.

Wynter tilted her bedside lamp to the side. The plastic base that had been painted to resemble brass was hollow underneath. Objects in plain sight made the best hiding spots and this was one of her favorites. A year ago, she had discovered the cover on the bottom of the lamp was removable. She had used it to hide a joint that she planned on smoking with Quinn. The concealment was successful but instead of getting high, they had coughed themselves red in the face.

A small four ounce metal flask slid out of the lamp's base.

"Forgot about you." Wynter glanced around the room as if expecting to see someone watching her. She unscrewed the cap, sniffed the spout, and took a sip. The heat of Southern Comfort trickled down her throat. After a sputtering cough, she took one more pull from the flask and twisted the cap back on. Even though the alcohol burned going down, it did give her a sense of relaxation.

She coiled the drawstring around the fingers of her right hand and held it under her nose. The fresh scent made her nose tingle. Wynter laid the flask on its side, placed the coiled drawstring on top, and slid both back into the lamp's base.

The Southern Comfort radiated heat from within her, but she didn't feel like sleeping. In the lamp's low light, she scanned her room, over her desk and the shelves above. Her eyes settled on the spine of *Eyes Wide Dreaming*.

Wynter drew back the thin covers from the bed and padded over to face the books on her shelves. She had read every single one.

*Which one would put me to sleep quickest?*

She pulled out a few books, one by one: *Great Photography Made Simple, An Illustrated History of the Sheyenne National Grasslands, Lucid Dreaming: A Case Study*. None looked interesting enough to read at four in the morning.

Wynter had a brainstorm. Music. She shelved the books and pulled out the top drawer of her desk. The odor of pens, wooden pencils, and rubber erasers floated to her nose. Tucked into the corner of the drawer, right where it was supposed to be, sat her beloved red Sony Walkman WM-75 that her parents had bought her for her fourteenth birthday. The portable cassette player was like magic to her. With auto-reverse turned on, never-ending music helped transport her to places beyond the confines of Newhaven. She hated to imagine how many double-A batteries she had gone through since.

Wynter grabbed the Walkman, the headphones next to it, and crawled back into bed. With headphones unfolded and snugged up against her ears, she pressed play. "That Was Yesterday" by Foreigner began mid song. She closed her eyes and imagined Lou Gramm serenading her from the corner of her room. Her celebrity crush had started as soon as she saw him sing in the music video for "Waiting for a Girl Like You." Her thumb found the volume control by touch and she turned the music up.

The next song to play, "I Want to Know What Love Is," was one of her favorites. She had played the entire *Agent Provocateur* album countless times and was amazed that the tape hadn't worn out and snapped yet.

Music carried Wynter to sleep, leaving yesterday behind. And if that was yesterday, what would today bring?

# Take On Me

Wynter woke to an empty trailer. The clock radio on her dresser read 8:08 AM. She noticed that her Walkman and headphones were set beside the base of the reading lamp, the headphone's cable in a careful coil. Nolan must have moved it there. Habitually organized cables were one of his calling cards.

The black spiral of headphone wire reminded Wynter of the drawstring she had pulled out of her dream the previous night. She reached for the lamp, then stopped and cocked an ear.

"Mom?" She waited a moment. "Dad?"

Silence answered back. Satisfied that the trailer was empty, Wynter flipped open the bottom of the reading lamp. The silver flask slid out but there was no drawstring. She took a closer look but there were only wires leading to the lightbulb inside.

*Was I dreaming it all?*

Wynter looked behind the dresser. Nothing but dust and derelict spider webs. She dropped to the floor and peered under the dresser and bed. Nothing.

She couldn't have dreamed it. Wynter grabbed the Walkman, plugged in the headphones, and pressed play. "Stranger in My Own House" sounded in her ears. Side two of *Agent Provocateur*. She had started on *side one* before she had fallen asleep again.

Wynter stripped off her clothes and hopped into the shower,

her mind abuzz. Either Nolan found the drawstring and did something with it, or it had never existed. But its scent still left an echo in her nose. It *had* to have existed. Or maybe she was hallucinating.

After drying off and pulling on her work clothes, she came to one conclusion. There was no explanation. And she couldn't wait to tell Quinn.

Wynter looked at her watch. Twenty minutes to nine. She had just enough time to grab some breakfast and meet Quinn before the plaza opened at nine-thirty. She grabbed her purse, locked the trailer door, and was off like a flash.

Finn's Gas N Go wasn't only the town's number one choice for gas. Local teens and tweens had chosen Finn's as their local candy and junk food stop, Wynter included. The small business had its finger on the pulse of everything young people craved.

Wynter could see Finn's sign, with its stylized handwritten neon letters, burning in the distance even before reaching the Main Street Overpass. She focused on Finn's as she hustled across the highway, content to leave the overpass behind for at least eight hours. She had seen enough of it over the past day to last a week.

She was close enough to see the other reason she'd chosen Finn's: Cash worked the register. Wynter gave her still damp hair a toss before strolling toward the store.

A car's horn caught her by surprise. She turned to see Anson pulling his police SUV into one of the two gas bays.

Through his open passenger window, he called out, "Feeling better?"

Wynter stopped and nodded. "Just getting some breakfast."

Anson raised a brow. "No offense to Finn, but you'd get a better meal at Lucy's."

"Running late." Wynter waved him off and turned to see that Cash had been watching her interaction with Anson the whole time.

*Oh God. Adults can be so inconvenient.*

She straightened her top and strolled into the store. Cash leaned against the back wall behind the counter, his arms crossed against his chest. On the counter was a can of ice-cold Coke and a Hostess Fruit Pie. Blueberry. Her favorite.

"The usual?" He grinned.

Wynter pushed aside her nerves as best she could and smiled back. "Am I *that* predictable?"

"As far as gas station fast food goes, yes."

Finn O'Connor shuffled into the store from a back door, grumbling something under his breath. His greasy coveralls did little to conceal his stocky stature. Beside the door hung a baseball bat he lovingly called *Ciara*. "For the bastards that try to cross me," he had said.

Finn grabbed a dirty and stained coffee mug from under the counter and walked back to the coffee machine. He glanced back at the food on the counter. "That stuff'll kill you."

"People say the same thing about coffee." Wynter popped the top of her Coke and took a sip.

"Kids." Finn huffed and wandered back into the garage.

"I should make T-shirts of Finn's one-liners." Cash tapped the keys to the register. "I'd probably make a killing."

"Yeah, probably." Wynter paid for her items and Cash handed her some change. She tried to look at him but couldn't carry the weight of his gaze.

Cash took out a pack of Wrigley's Big Red gum, slid out a stick, and unwrapped the foil.

Wynter looked at her watch and turned for the door. "I'm going to be late, so..."

"Sure. Later, Wynter." Cash placed the stick of gum in his mouth. "Hey, wait."

Wynter paused at the door, wanting to stay but not wanting to be late. Quinn would not be denied her gab time.

"Doing anything tonight?"

"Uh, no. Why?" Wynter's stomach fluttered.

"No reason."

An awkward silence fell between them.

"Okay. Well…" Wynter pushed open the door. "Got to go. See you." She passed Anson on her way out.

Cash gnawed his gum. "See you," he called back but she was already out of earshot.

Anson observed Wynter's hurried exit as he entered the store. He made a beeline to the coffee machine, filled his thermal travel mug, and stepped to the counter.

Cash rang in the gas charge on the till, his eyes still on Wynter in the distance.

Anson dug out his police department credit card and handed it to Cash. "You should ask her out."

"What?" Cash processed the credit card and handed it back.

Anson smiled. "Fortune favors the bold, my young friend." He stepped out of the store and back to his SUV.

○

As Wynter strode toward Stedford Plaza, she replayed her conversation with Cash in her head, trying to imagine how it could have gone better. She couldn't do it. Every version sucked.

Her watch read just after nine when she pulled open the doors to the plaza. Quinn would be waiting in the small but adequate food court.

Tables and chairs filled the common area of the court, with the FreshWhip stand like a refreshment island all on its own in the center. Quinn didn't mind it. She liked being in full view.

"It's better for business." That was her mantra. "Exposure from all sides."

Wynter had thought it was creepy. "What about all the pervs that watch you, then go to the bathrooms and jack off?"

"I got no problem with them as long as they wash their hands before buying a drink," Quinn had said. "Besides, everyone knows everyone in Newhaven."

That reason wasn't good enough for Wynter. Just the thought of Vinny watching her at work gave her the willies. She'd never let it happen. She'd quit first.

Around the exterior of the seating area were four other fast food outlets. Despite Newhaven's small population, all businesses enjoyed brisk trade all year round. Great American Donut served a variety of donuts and pastries, made fresh daily. Pepperia specialized in pizzas that celebrated a fusion of Italian and Mexican flavors. Hot Twists had mastered the Bavarian-style pretzel, salty and guaranteed freshly baked. The Cast Iron Skillet skewed to an older customer, serving more substantial breakfast and lunch entrées.

Wynter spotted Quinn before Quinn spotted her. She was wiping down the FreshWhip countertop. "Sorry I'm late. I... I slept in."

Quinn gave Wynter a sideways glance and paused her prep work. "What's wrong, Bug?" She stepped out from behind the counter and led Wynter to a nearby table. They both sat. "Something's wrong. Tell me."

Quinn had an uncanny ability to read people. And when someone needed help, she dropped everything. That was one of the positive qualities of her impulsive nature.

Wynter began. "Have you ever had the same dream, over and over."

"A few times."

"Well, I keep seeing this boy—"

"Oh." Quinn raised her brows. "It's one of *those* dreams?"

"No. It's not. I wish it was." Wynter took a breath. "This boy keeps jumping from the overpass and I can't save him. I'm never fast enough."

"Do you recognize him?"

Wynter shook her head. "I've never seen him before, but I *feel* like I have. It's weird. But it gets weirder." She took a sip from her Coke. "Remember yesterday when you saw me stumble on the overpass?"

"And you had that headache."

"Yeah. Well just before you arrived, that boy, the same one in my dreams, jumped off the overpass for real."

Quinn gave Wynter a sideways glance. "Wait. For real? What do you mean? There wasn't—"

"I mean I wasn't asleep." Wynter locked gazes with Quinn. "He was there but he jumped before I could reach him."

"You know that's impossible, right? There would have been cars crashing all over the highway."

"I know it doesn't make any sense but that's what I saw. He was there and then he wasn't."

Quinn squeezed Wynter's hand. "You're scaring me, Bug."

Wynter either didn't hear Quinn's concern or had chosen to ignore it. She scanned the food court, leaned in, and lowered her voice. "Something else happened last night."

Quinn was all ears, still concerned but equally captivated.

"I dreamed of him again. We touched fingers. And..." Wynter drifted like she had lost her train of thought.

"And? Don't leave me hanging, girl."

She settled her eyes back on Quinn. "I had the drawstring to his hoodie in my hand. When I woke up."

Quinn blinked. "What?"

"His drawstring from the dream. It was in my hand."

Quinn slumped back in her chair. She wasn't buying it.

"It was as real as, like, you and me." Wynter held her gaze. "I swear."

"If I could make *my* dreams real, me and Rob Lowe would be married and living happily ever after in the Hollywood Hills."

Wynter sighed. "You don't believe me."

"Come on, Bug. I mean I want to believe you, but—"

"I know. It sounds crazy."

A silent moment passed between them.

"Show me," Quinn said. "The drawstring. Show me."

Wynter felt a headache coming on and closed her eyes. "It wasn't there when I woke up. I think my dad might have taken it but I'm not sure." She looked at her watch. Nine-fifteen. "Look. I got to go set up the store." She stood and ran towards the plaza's main concourse.

"Wynter. Wait!"

Quinn rarely addressed her by name unless it was important. Wynter wiped a tear away with a quick twist of her wrist and faced her.

"Aren't you forgetting something?" She held Wynter's Coke and unopened fruit pie. She smiled and walked it over. "I'm sorry." She stepped up and hugged her, careful not to spill. "If you say it happened, it happened. I believe you."

Wynter let go a breath of relief as she took the soda and pie. "Thanks."

"See you at lunch?"

Wynter nodded.

"You know, we need to cut loose tonight." Quinn smiled. "Dream boys are good and all, but real boys have their advantages too." She flashed her brows. "Starlite tonight? What do you say?"

"Sure."

The two girls parted. Wynter hurried down the concourse and around the corner to Shooters. She unlocked the security gate and slipped inside.

Quinn had worked her magic, even though she didn't know it. For the first time in a while, Wynter's thoughts were on something other than the mystery dream boy.

And Wynter had plans. She smiled to herself and got to work setting up the store for the day.

Wynter faced the mirror in her bedroom. She wore a long white T-shirt, the hem concealing a pair of denim shorts underneath. Her rainbow knee-highs which she reserved only for rollerskating were pulled to the top of her calves.

She glanced at the clock radio on the dresser. Quinn would be picking her up any minute and she hated the way she looked. Wynter dropped to her knees and began digging through her dresser.

"Knock knock." Madeline stood outside her bedroom door. "May I come in?" When there was no immediate answer, she knocked softly and opened the bedroom door a crack. "Wynnie?"

Wynter stomped to the door and flung it open. "What?"

"Oh! You look adorable."

"Stop it. I do *not*." Wynter ran back to her dresser, the floor around it strewn with clothes. "Why don't I have anything nice?"

Madeline raised a brow. "We can have that discussion some other time. Right now we—"

"Look at me." Wynter glanced at herself in the mirror with disgust. "I look like a pillow with legs."

The familiar sound of Quinn's Volkswagen rumbled to a stop outside.

"Shit, she's here." Wynter looked to her mom, her eyes pleading.

"It's just Quinn. She isn't going to care."

"It's *not* just Quinn."

Madeline suddenly understood. "It's everyone else."

Wynter nodded. "I haven't gone skating in a while."

Madeline drew her into a hug. "Oh, honey."

A knock sounded at the trailer door. Wynter could hear Nolan and Quinn's voices but not their words.

"Everything will be okay." Madeline let go of Wynter, kissed her head, and rubbed her shoulders in an attempt to reassure her.

Quinn caught Madeline's gesture. "Hi, Mrs. LaCroix." She

poked her head into Wynter's bedroom. "Hey, Bug. Ready to get your skate on?"

"I'll make myself scarce." Madeline closed the bedroom door.

Wynter sat on the edge of her bed beside her rollerskates. "I look like a frump. I mean, look at you."

Quinn's face flushed pink. She wore Levi denim shorts with a matching cropped denim jacket and a snug red T-shirt underneath. Red Nike knee-high socks and black Vans covered her feet. A brand girl through and through.

"You're hot. You just need a reminder." Quinn smiled. "Let's have a look." Wynter stood and Quinn spun her around. "You're eighty percent there."

Wynter gave her a sideways look of doubt.

"Seriously. Would I lie to you?"

Madeline knocked on the door and stepped halfway in. "This might help." She held a ceramic bowl full of fashion accessories.

"Thanks, Mrs. LaCroix."

Madeline set the bowl on the bed and beat a hasty retreat, closing the door behind her.

Quinn began sorting through the pile. "Your mom's got good taste, but this might be tricky. Try this." She held up a thin red belt and continued digging.

Wynter pulled the belt around her waist and cinched it up.

"Looser. You don't want it to cut you in half." Quinn pulled out a black plastic T-shirt clip and set it aside.

"How's this?"

Quinn stood back, eyed the belt, and went back to the bowl. "Take a look. What do you think?"

Wynter eyed herself in the mirror. "I don't think it works."

"You're right. Take it off and try this next." Quinn handed her the T-shirt clip. "Wait. I forgot to ask you the most important question."

Wynter threw the belt on the bed. "And that is?"

"How much ass do you want to show?" Quinn raised the hem

of Wynter's T-shirt. "Those jean shorts are working for you. How much of it do you want people to see?"

"Um, all of it?"

"Not necessarily." Quinn gathered the front hem of Wynter's T-shirt and held it over Wynter's navel. "This accentuates the front, leaving the behind to imagination." She gathered the sides and drew them together. "This exposes your heinie in all its glory."

Wynter giggled. She could see the possibilities.

Quinn gathered the T-shirt to the side. "You could go for half-and-half. What do you think?"

Wynter took the T-shirt hem and tried out the variations in front of the mirror. "I think exposure from all sides."

They looked at each other. "Better for business," they said in unison and broke into laughter.

Quinn pinched Wynter's T-shirt hem at the sides and pulled them together in the center. She gave the fabric a twist and looped it into a tight knot, exposing a small diamond of brown skin.

She grinned slyly. "Such a *knotty* girl."

Wynter blushed. "You think so?"

"You're hot, Bug. Don't ever forget it." Quinn glanced at the accessories on the bed. "Turned out all you needed was a little *naughti*ness."

"Ha ha." Wynter placed her arms around Quinn's neck and rested her forehead on hers. "All I needed was some of your fashion sense."

"What are friends for?" Quinn looked toward the bedroom door. "Shall we?"

"Yeah."

"Walk or ride?"

Wynter gave Quinn a knowing smile, her anxiety and frustration of earlier long forgotten.

"Blue Belle awaits."

○

QUINN REVVED BLUE BELLE'S engine, let the clutch out, and left
Wynter's trailer park behind. She turned down Jones Avenue.
Starlite SuperSkate was minutes away. KROK 92.9 FM blasted
"Crush on You" by The Jets.

She glanced at Wynter, content in the passenger seat with a
small purse and rollerskates on her lap. Madeline had thrown her
a black scrunchy as they were leaving, to "keep her hair out of
her face." Quinn wasn't a scrunchy girl, she didn't have the hair
for it, but it looked great in Wynter's fiery locks.

"Bug?"

"Yeah?"

"Don't get mad, okay?" Quinn spoke carefully and kept her
eyes on the road ahead.

"What?" Wynter's smile faltered. "What did you do?"

"I was getting gas at Finn's earlier and I might've mentioned
to Cash that we were going rollerskating."

"*Might* have?"

"Okay. I did mention it." Quinn looked at her best friend. "Are
you mad?"

Wynter's lips pursed in thought then curled into a smile.
"Thanks to you, I don't look like a giant marshmallow."

"I take it that's a 'no.' "

"Yes."

Both girls laughed. Quinn slowed for a four-way stop. The
Starlight SuperSkate's neon sign flashed in the distance.

"You know what that means." Wynter's eyes widened. "Jake
will be there too. They're joined at the hip, kind of like us."

"But Jake's a nerd."

"He's sweet. I've seen the way he looks at you."

Quinn could feel the intensity of Wynter's gaze without looking at her. "Great. A *lovesick* nerd."

"Admit it," Wynter said. "You like him."

Quinn drove Blue Belle into the parking lot of Starlite SuperSkate. "We're here."

"You like Jake. Say it."

"The lot's half full already. The rink's going to be packed."

"*Say* it."

Quinn found an empty parking space and killed the engine. "*Sexy* Wynter sure is annoying."

"Say—"

"Alright. Enough." Quinn faced Wynter. "Is Jake hot? Moderately. Not Cash-level hot, though. He needs a dose of style. Do I like him? He's nice enough. Do I want to *fuck* him?" She hesitated. "No. Happy now?"

"You had to think about it."

"There's nothing to think about." Quinn grabbed a compact purse and her rollerskates from the back seat. She retrieved a tube of lipstick and refreshed her lips using the mirror in the purse's flap. "Want some?"

Wynter applied the lipstick and returned the tube. "Does it work with my skin color?"

"You're totally kissable." Quinn threw the purse's string strap over her shoulder. "Let's go."

Both girls ran toward the flashing rainbow neon of Starlite's entryway where a dozen other people were already standing in line.

◯

Quinn and Wynter sidled up to the admission window, just across from the Starlite Arcade. A dozen stand-up video games glowed inside the dimly lit alcove and pumped out a dizzying mix of music and sound effects. Zain, who Quinn once described as a landlocked beach bum, worked the cash register and handled rollerskate rentals. In his mid-twenties, he stood six feet tall, with broad shoulders, shoulder-length bleached hair, and eyes that held fun and mystery behind them.

Last year Quinn had been obsessed with Zain, visiting the Starlite two or three times a week. It was part crush, part fact-finding mission. No one knew Zain's last name. He was just Zain. Or Zany Zain. If his last name ever got out, he'd have teenaged girls calling him out of the blue from across McLeod County. The unintended result: Quinn had become a skilled rollerskater.

"Hey, Queenie." That was Zain's nickname for her. He smiled and Wynter saw Quinn crush on him, just a little, hues of pink rising on her cheeks. "It's been a while. You too, Wynter. Nice to see you both back."

Quinn sighed.

"We've missed the place." Wynter went for her purse as Zain punched in their admission fees.

The sound of the register brought Quinn out of her daze. She placed her hand on Wynter's purse. "I got it this time, Bug."

"Thanks." Wynter gazed around the main foyer abuzz with rollerskaters young and old. A small smile curled at the sides of Wynter's lips. It *had* been too long.

Quinn handed Zain a twenty. "Anything new since we were here last?"

"We're serving nachos now." Zain handed back Quinn's change. "We also got a Donkey Kong machine. Finally. Only took five years."

"Jake's going to love that," Wynter said to Quinn.

Zain laughed. "Jake already knows. He knows everything about that game."

"We know," Wynter and Quinn said in unison. The two girls weaved their way into the crowd.

Wynter leaned in close. "*Queenie?* What was that? Anything you want to tell me?"

Quinn shrugged. "We're just friends. Nothing more."

It was the emphatic "nothing more" that got Wynter's gears turning. They talked often about boys, who was hot and who wasn't. Quinn followed the "love the one you're with" mindset. Wynter wanted everything to be just right, which was a big reason why she was still a virgin, but she wasn't one hundred percent sure that Quinn was too. It had been a while since they had talked openly about it. Things may have changed. Independence could get in the way sometimes.

They found a padded bench beside a vacant locker, removed their shoes, and laced up their rollerskates. After throwing in their shoes, Wynter inserted a quarter and secured the locker door, depositing the key in her pocket. She caught a glimpse of her bare skin under her knotted T-shirt and smiled to herself. She did look sexy.

Across the foyer a small kitchen served up tasty and unhealthy food: soda, ice cream, hot dogs, burgers, fries, and now nachos. The carpet and bench upholstery all bore the same colorful frenetic patterns, like glitter and ribbon got together and exploded on everything.

"I forgot how much I love this place." Quinn sat watching the hustle and bustle of people entering and exiting the rink. "If I didn't have the Starlite, I think I'd go crazy."

Bananarama echoed the synth beat of "Venus" through the rink. A rotating mirrored ball hung over the center of the rink and cast a million rainbow-colored stars across the floor and walls.

"Yeah. It doesn't get much better than this." Wynter said.

"But it does." Quinn pointed to the admission window. Cash and Jake stood in line to get in. "Let's hit the rink so we can make an entrance."

Wynter watched Cash talking to Jake, laughing with a bright smile.

"Come on." Quinn tugged gently at the knot on Wynter's T-shirt. "Before they see us."

They maneuvered to the rink entrance and joined the circling crowd. Quinn had lapped Wynter by the time she found her feet and let muscle memory kick in. Soon the two of them were dancing to the beat of the music.

"Stop here." Quinn pulled Wynter to the sideboards, furthest from the rink entrance. "Let's watch for them."

○

THE LINE OF rollerskaters waiting to get in snaked outside and around the corner of the building. Jake craned his neck, scanning the mingling crowd. "Do you see them?"

"Be cool." Cash was on high alert too but made sure to be more discreet. "Quinn said they'd be here."

Cash wore jeans, a pristine white V-neck with a pair of sunglasses hanging from the collar, and a jean jacket with the cuffs rolled midway up his forearms. It was an obvious attempt at *Miami Vice* cool, but it worked.

Jake, on the other hand, was wearing the same thing as yesterday, complete with a few new food stains. He had tried to cover it up with a plaid button-up. He wore a Casio digital watch on his right wrist and as always, his Nintendo baseball cap rode front and center on his head. He looked toward the entrance to Starlite Arcade.

Cash noticed Jake's displaced attention. "We talked about this. No video games tonight."

Jake huffed. "Donkey Kong's seeing great action, right there at the front."

"How many times have you played that game already? You could have been spending that time with girls."

"I'm in no hurry. Nothing compares to gameplay on a stand-up." Jake gave Cash a once-over. "Besides, look at you, *Sonny Crockett*. Got a girlfriend yet?"

"That's kind of why we're here."

"This better not suck," Jake said. "Otherwise, I'm going to go help Mario save Pauline."

Cash and Jake advanced to the admission window where Zain exchanged a handful of bills with two receipts for rollerskate rentals.

"Okay. Let's size up."

They worked their way through the crowd to the rental desk. Jake returned his eyes to the Donkey Kong machine while Cash scanned the circling skaters in the rink.

The clock above the rental desk read nine-thirty.

*Wynter and Quinn should have been here by now.*

Cash had wanted to hang out with Wynter many times before but always chickened out when it came time to ask. He vowed to make tonight count.

○

QUINN POINTED AT the rink entrance. "There they are. You ready?"

Wynter had been awkwardly practicing a simple walk-in-place dance move to the beat of the music in an attempt to ease her anxiety. It wasn't working and her confidence had been waning as time wore on. "I guess."

"Don't worry. You look hot. Haven't you noticed all the guys checking you out?"

Wynter perked up and gave Quinn a sideways look. "Really? Who?"

"All of them!" Quinn grinned and grabbed Wynter's hand. "Come on."

Cash and Jake ambled into the mix of rollerskaters at the

entrance of the rink. Jermaine Stewart's hit "We Don't Have to Take Our Clothes Off" played from the speakers hanging from the arena rafters.

"It's like the deejay is reading our minds." Quinn laughed. "Let's skate up behind them and surprise them."

The two girls held hands and pumped their legs, gaining speed and closing in on Cash and Jake.

"Ready?" Quinn smiled ear to ear. She was in her element. "Three. Two. One." She skated up behind Jake. "Boo!"

"Yikes!" Jake flinched and lost his balance. Cash grabbed his arm, but his own inexperience and instability caused a chain reaction. Both boys hit the smooth maple hardwood and slid to a stop on their butts next to Jake's upturned baseball hat.

"Oh, shit!" Quinn placed a hand to her mouth to hold back a laugh. "Are you guys okay?"

Wynter leaned into Quinn and whispered, "Be nice. You *like* Jake, remember?"

Cash's eyes were glued to Wynter as she spun around to face him. As she held out her hand to help him up, they locked eyes. She felt the heat of his gaze.

Quinn watched Wynter help Cash up, her eyes giving him a once-over as well, then remembered Jake on the floor. She stuck out her hand in an attempt to appear sincere, but her gesture ended up looking like an afterthought.

Jake snugged his baseball cap on and took Quinn's hand. After a couple rolling fumbles, he stood and sunk his hands in his pockets. "Thanks."

"No problem." Quinn stole a glance at Cash, then redirected her gaze to the floor, other skaters, the disco ball, anything but Jake.

"Yeah, he's the handsome one." Jake wobbled on his feet. "And I'm the nerd. But I'll be running the world in twenty years. You'll see."

"Oh-kay," Quinn whispered to herself.

"Thanks, Wynter." Cash brushed himself off and steadied himself on the rink's sideboard. "As you can see, I don't skate much." His eyes flicked across her outfit. "You look super nice."

Wynter's cheeks blushed pink hues. "You—"

"What am I?" Quinn placed her hands on her hips. "Chopped liver?"

"You look nice too, Quinn," Cash said.

"What about me?" Jake alternated his gaze between the three. "How do I look?" He waited for the girls' responses but was met with silence.

Cash hooked his arm around Jake's neck. "Looks like you need help rollerskating." His eyes pleaded at Wynter and Quinn. "Help us?"

Wynter nodded and shared a smile with Quinn. She hooked her arm with Cash's and motioned at Quinn to do the same with Jake.

Quinn widened her eyes in mock protest and grabbed Jake's arm.

The girls flexed their legs, propelling the four of them forward. Cash and Jake kept their feet stationary and rolled along with them.

"Hey, you got to actually *try* to skate," Quinn said.

Cash took a rolling step, then another. Jake did the same. Soon all four of them were rolling along, experience encouraging inexperience.

Jake saw the end of the rink approaching. "How do we turn?"

"Just lean into it, leg over leg." Quinn crossed her leading leg and stepped into the turn.

Jake tried to mimic Quinn's move, but his right toe-brake clipped his left skate and he lost his balance. Cash let go but Jake pulled Quinn down on top of him.

The two of them slid to the sideboards, Quinn sitting askew on Jake's legs.

Quinn narrowed her eyes at him. "You did that on purpose."

"I didn't. I swear."

She examined his reaction and thought she saw a subtle smile.

"But if I had to choose *someone* to fall on me..." Jake offered a small grin.

Quinn popped herself upright with ease and stuck out her hand once again to pull Jake up. "Let's go, hot shot. But no help this time."

The deejay's voice echoed from the speakers. "Okay ladies and gents, girls and boys. Switch directions." The pounding drums and base of "Danger Zone" by Kenny Loggins fired up the crowd as everyone's trajectory flipped. Career skaters weaved around the newcomers.

Wynter and Cash rolled up to meet Quinn and Jake.

"You fell at just the right time." Cash's smile gleamed.

"I feel the need..." Quinn took Wynter's hand and pulled her away from Cash. "The need for speed. I bet you slowpokes can't catch us." The two girls took off like a shot.

Jake blinked at Cash. "She just quoted from *Top Gun*. I think I'm in love."

Cash laughed and tapped his shoulder. "Let's go. They're getting away."

The energetic music fueled their game of cat and mouse as Cash and Jake chased the girls, their confidence building with every lap.

○

AFTER HALF AN HOUR, the four stopped for a snack break. Quinn, Jake, and Cash rolled to a vacant picnic-style table near the concession.

"I want to try the nachos." Wynter looked around the small table. "Sound good?"

Jake gave an enthusiastic thumbs up. After taking their drink orders, Wynter rolled to the counter to order.

An awkward silence passed between the three of them.

"So Quinn, you like *Top Gun?*" Jake took off his baseball cap to smooth out his hair, then returned it to his head.

"It's got Tom Cruise in it," Quinn said. "What's not to like? He's, like, *so* hot."

"Uh, yeah." Jake shot a look of panic at Cash. "I guess." He let his gaze drift to the Starlite Arcade. There was still a crowd surrounding the Donkey Kong machine.

Cash thrummed his fingers on the tabletop to the beat of the music. "You're a good rollerskater. How long have you been... rollerskating?"

Quinn perked up now that Cash was talking to her. "Since I was... eight? But I got really serious last year. How long have you been rollerskating?"

Cash craned his neck to find a clock. "What time is it?"

"Ten-fifteen," Jake deadpanned.

"I've been rollerskating a whole half hour." Cash raised his brows, sincerity crossing his face. "How am I doing?"

"Not bad for half an hour." Quinn sighed and laid her forehead on the tabletop. "But this conversation sucks hard. Save me, Wynter," she whispered to herself.

"Hold up, guys." Jake motioned to the entrance. "Here comes trouble."

Standing at Starlite's main doors stood Jezebel, Roxy, and Monty, three bad seeds arm in arm.

○

Jezebel and Roxy had enjoyed a reign of terror over those their age and younger ever since Jezebel had moved to Newhaven five years ago. Like Wynter and Quinn, Jezebel and Roxy were inseparable, but the nature of their connection was quite different. Jezebel led the way and Roxy followed her every move like a lost puppy. Both were dressed to skate, wearing gold shorts with blue hosiery underneath, red halter tops exposing their midriffs, and cropped black leather jackets. Their rollerskates hung from their shoulders.

Apart from Roxy being shorter than Jezebel by six inches, they expressed their individuality through their hair. Jezebel crimped her long brown tresses to the extreme, giving her a prickly, electrified look. In contrast, Roxy curled back her short bangs and side layers, framing blond shoulder-length locks parted down the middle. Hair spray kept everything firmly in place.

Next to Jezebel and Roxy stood Monty, ten years their senior. He didn't care much for fashion, with the exception of a black, well-oiled leather jacket. Worn denim and a faded Motörhead T-shirt suited him most days. He wore mirrored sunglasses twenty-four hours a day no matter where he was.

Monty loved money and he wasn't here to skate. Weed, coke, heroin, speed, quaaludes, valium, whatever you needed, Monty could get it. He was well connected. Monty wasn't his real name either. He had given himself the nickname ever since seeing Al Pacino play Tony Montana in *Scarface*.

Zain spotted the trio in the line to get in. He pointed at Monty. "Out! You're not welcome here."

Monty pretended not to hear.

Zain closed the admissions window, walked around the rental counter, and approached Monty. "Walk back out or I call the sheriff."

Monty smirked and turned up his hands. "I'm not botherin' anyone." He addressed the people standing nearby. "Am I botherin' you? No. How about you? No. No one's bothered."

Zain pushed Monty backward. "Out. Now."

Monty puffed up his chest and flexed his arms. "Get your fuckin' hands *off* me. Or I'll fuckin' cut 'em off."

Not wanting things to escalate, Zain turned to Jezebel. "Get your goon out of here." He leaned closer and lowered his voice. "No drugs, Jezebel."

"I ain't no fuckin' *goon*."

Jezebel shot Monty a look, then turned to Zain. "Monty leaves, we get in for free."

Zain scowled. "How about I call the sheriff."

Jezebel shot an annoyed look at Roxy. "How about this." She faced Zain once more. "Monty leaves, we get in for free."

For the sake of keeping the peace, Zain relented. "Alright. Get him out of here."

Jezebel motioned at Monty to leave. She got what she wanted and Monty got his free advertising. Word spread through the arena quickly. He would hang outside the Starlite and deal to anyone interested. Some even followed him out.

Zain leaned close to Jezebel and spoke softly. "Sheriff's going to get a call from me anyway, so your goon better not be hanging around."

"Zain, you talk too much. And he's *not* my *goon*." Jezebel pushed past him into the main foyer, Roxy close at her heels. She spotted Wynter grabbing napkins and straws to go with a tray of nachos and four drinks. Jezebel turned to Roxy but kept her eyes on Wynter. "Look who's here."

Roxy narrowed her eyes and smirked. "Whiner."

"Here's what I want you to do." Jezebel cupped her hand and whispered into Roxy's ear as they made a beeline for Wynter.

○

WYNTER PLACED A wad of napkins and four straws on the tray next to the plate of nachos. The warm scent of melted cheese sauce, sliced jalapenos, and corn chips floated to her nose. She lifted the tray and rolled back to her friends at the table.

She cast her mind back to earlier in the evening, holding hands with Cash and racing around the rink. It had been wonderful. As a smile crossed her lips, she noticed Quinn in her periphery. She was waving her hands and pointing.

Wynter furrowed her brow in an attempt to figure out what she was going on about. "What? What are you—"

Quinn gripped the tabletop. "Behind—"

A heated argument rose up from within a nearby crowd of rollerskaters.

"Fuck you!" Roxy moved backward through the crowd, retreating from Jezebel.

"Too late." Jezebel pushed Roxy backward hard, sending her crashing into the back of Wynter.

Her tray flew forward, hit the carpet, and exploded in a mixture of soda, melted cheese, and shattered corn chips. Wynter lost her balance, her feet rolling out from underneath her, and landed face first on the mess of food.

Quinn stood up from her chair. "Bug!"

Cash craned his neck to see around Quinn.

"What's going..." Jake turned his head, taking in the aftermath. "Oh shit."

Roxy picked herself up and dusted herself off, none the worse for wear. She cast a look at Jezebel, a sly grin on her face. Jezebel nodded back with smug acknowledgment.

"Oh my God, are you okay?" Jezebel shifted her eyes from Roxy to Wynter, feigning concern. "It was an accident. I'm *so* sorry."

Quinn caught the exchange. "Those *bitches*. They did it on purpose." She rolled toward Wynter who lay sprawled on the carpet, a small crowd forming around her. Cash and Jake followed.

Jezebel knelt down beside Wynter and spoke in a whisper. "Enjoy your nachos, *Whiner.*" She gave Wynter an extra push into her spilled food.

Quinn fell to her knees beside Wynter and glared at Jezebel. "Get the fuck away from her."

Jezebel raised her hands and backed away, her lips in a subtle smirk. "Hey, it was an accident. I swear."

"Like hell it was." Quinn placed her arm around Wynter in an attempt to shield her from the collecting spectators. "Bug, you okay?"

Wynter tried to kneel but there were two angry rug burns on her knees. She fell backward onto her butt. Her T-shirt had become unknotted and it was covered with melted cheese and soda. She hid her face behind her arms and began to sob.

Cash exchanged a confused look with Jake. "Did you see what happened?"

Jake shrugged. "No. I was facing the wrong way."

Cash lowered himself, maintaining balance on his skates, and placed a gentle hand on Wynter's back.

Quinn spun around to face him, eyes on fire like a mother bear protecting her cub. "No offense, but you need to back off. Right now."

Cash nodded and did as asked.

"Okay, everyone. Clear out." Zain dispersed the crowd. He kneeled down to Quinn's eye level. "How're we doing?"

"It was Jezebel and Roxy." Quinn's eyes blazed with rage.

"Of course it was." Zain glanced over his shoulder to where Jezebel and Roxy were lacing up their rollerskates without a care in the world. "I should ban them."

"Yeah, you should." Quinn leaned in close. "Bug? You think you can stand?"

Wynter nodded.

"I'm going to help her to the bathroom and get her cleaned up."

Quinn supported Wynter as she stood up, her legs still wobbly from shock. Her arm snugged around Wynter's waist as they rolled with slow strides across the foyer and around the corner of the arcade to the bathrooms.

Zain stood and stared at Jezebel and Roxy. Cash and Jake rolled next to him.

"Take a picture," Jezebel said. "It'll last longer." Both girls laughed.

"I already did." Zain crossed his arms. "Everyone here is on video."

Jezebel and Roxy glanced at each other, their smiles suddenly gone. "It was an accident," Jezebel said. "It could have happened to anyone."

Jake raised a brow. "What kind of cameras are you running?"

Cash poked him. "Jake, this isn't the time."

Jake shrugged. "I was just curious."

Jezebel sent a condescending wave. "Later, *boys*." She rolled to the rink. Roxy blew a kiss and followed.

"The Heat Is On" by Glenn Frey piped through the arena speakers.

Jake glanced at Cash. "I could burn Roxy's house down."

"What? Are you serious?"

"It'd be easy. She lives just down the street from me, remember?"

"No." Cash watched Jezebel and Roxy make the rounds in the rink, a half dozen guys following and skating circles around them. They waved at him as they passed by. "We're smarter than that, Jake."

"Want to hit the arcade?"

"We'd have to return our rollerskates."

Jake raised a brow. "You think Wynter's going to want to skate after this?"

"You got a point. Let's go."

The two of them headed to the rental desk to return their skates and get their shoes back.

Cash looked back at the corridor that led to the bathrooms, watching for Wynter with concerned eyes.

◯

QUINN HELPED WYNTER to the counter in the women's bathroom. She stepped to the three stalls and pushed the doors open one at a time. They were all empty.

"Bug? Can you scoot up onto the counter?" Quinn noticed pooled water on the countertop. "Wait." She pulled out a stack of paper towels and used a couple to wipe away the water. "Okay. Now you're good."

Wynter lifted herself up and slid back on the counter. Her hair hung shrouding her face. What had been red springy curls when the evening began were now limp, soaked with soda and stuck together with clumps of cheese sauce. Tear tracks had dried on her cheeks.

Quinn hunched down to look Wynter in the eyes. "Let's get you cleaned up." She grabbed more paper towels, soaked them under cool water, and rung them out. "Okay, this might sting a bit." Quinn placed the paper towel on Wynter's knees. "How's that?"

Wynter nodded. "Feels good."

"Hold them there." She took a paper towel and ran it around the sodden strands of Wynter's hair. It absorbed the soda but spread the cheese sauce around more. "Maybe Cash has a comb." Quinn turned to go but Wynter stopped her.

"I don't want him to see me like this."

"He won't see you." Quinn saw fresh tears well in Wynter's eyes. "Okay, a hot shower when you get home will have to do." She folded a fresh paper towel and placed her free hand underneath Wynter's T-shirt. "I'm not trying to feel you up, I swear." Quinn winked.

Wynter laughed and wiped her tears away. "I'm not worried."

Quinn wiped the front of the T-shirt with the folded towel, using her other hand behind the fabric for support. It wasn't working.

"I don't know what's in this stuff, but it's like glue."

"Don't bother," Wynter said. "It's going in the trash when I get home. At least my socks and shorts are okay."

Quinn's jaw tightened as she took a step back. "Jezebel's a fucking bitch. She should pay for this."

Wynter shook her head slowly. "She's not worth it. Neither is Roxy." She drew in a shaky breath. "I think I just want to go home."

"Okay." Quinn slid off her cropped denim jacket and handed it to Wynter. "For the ride home." She slung her purse back over her shoulder.

Wynter crumpled the towels from her knees and threw them in the garbage bin. She hopped off the countertop, put on Quinn's denim jacket, and turned to the mirror. "Now I know how Cinderella felt when the clock struck midnight."

"Let's go get our shoes."

Wynter hesitated. "What about Cash?"

"Don't worry about him. He'll be fine."

"But I smell gross."

Quinn sniffed, then whispered into Wynter's ear, "Guys love nachos. You'll be irresistible." She pulled open the bathroom door, letting in the cacophony of music, video game sounds, and chattering voices.

○

QUINN AND WYNTER swapped their rollerskates for their shoes. Between lace twists, Quinn kept her eyes on the rink, narrowing in on Jezebel and Roxy with every pass.

"You'll get yours, *bitch*," she said in a low whisper.

Zain strolled up and squatted. "Hey. Glad I caught you two before you left." He sighed. "Look, I'm so sorry about what happened earlier."

"Thanks," Wynter said.

"You going to ban those assholes?" Quinn held Zain's gaze.

"I'll review the video. If it was planned, then yeah. I'll ban them."

Quinn shook her head. "They're too smart for that."

"Maybe so." Zain presented a voucher to Wynter. "I comped your food. Redeemable any time, hopefully sooner rather than later."

Wynter's eyes bugged out. She showed the fifty dollar voucher to Quinn, then made a move to return it. "Zain, this is way more than I paid."

Zain stopped her. "Don't worry about it. Just come back. When you're ready of course."

Wynter offered a small nod and a smile. "Thanks."

All three stood.

"I hope you find what you need on your video tapes." Quinn hooked a thumb at Wynter. "I got to get Cinderella home before she turns into a pumpkin."

Wynter laughed. "I don't think that's how the story goes."

"Well, something turns into a pumpkin and you're, like, already turning orange, so..."

The two girls headed for Starlite's exit.

"Wynter?" Cash stood at the entrance to Starlite Arcade. "You okay?"

"Yeah, but I'm going home." Wynter assessed herself. "I'm kind of a mess. Sorry."

Cash took a step, hesitated, then bridged the space between them to give Wynter a firm quick hug. He released her before she could reciprocate. "Talk to you later."

Wynter nodded and followed Quinn out the door. It was

almost eleven o'clock and the cool summer air mingled with the warmth of the asphalt under their feet.

They hopped into Blue Belle and were soon on their way toward Sven Dwarfs. A commercial finished up on KROK, followed by "Time After Time" by Cyndi Lauper.

Wynter closed her eyes. "I love this song."

Quinn glanced at her best friend, a survivor of humiliation from Newhaven's worst bully.

*Wynter, you're a warrior but don't know it yet.*

Blue Belle rolled up to pad #7. Quinn killed the engine but let the song finish.

"Thanks." Wynter opened her eyes, her lashes misty. "For everything." She leaned across the gap between seats and hugged her.

"No prob, Bug. Now go have a hot shower."

Wynter kissed Quinn's cheek and stepped out of the VW. "Oh. Your jacket."

"Don't worry about it. I'll get it later."

Wynter nodded and walked to the trailer's front door.

Quinn started Blue Belle's engine. A bluish-gray cloud of smoke burst out of the tailpipe. She stuck her head out the driver's side window. "Call me later."

"I will." Wynter unlocked the door and opened it a crack. She waved at Quinn as she backed out. Quinn waved back and sped off. Wynter stepped inside and closed the door.

Madeline and Nolan sat snuggled on the sofa watching an episode of *Moonlighting*. Madeline shot a look of confusion mixed with mild concern at Nolan. "You're home early. We weren't expecting you for at least another hour."

Wynter walked briskly past her parents. It was obvious that something was up.

"Wynnie? Hon?" Madeline furrowed her brow when there was no answer. She got up to follow her.

"Maddie." Nolan spoke softly. "Go easy."

She nodded and stepped to Wynter's bedroom door, her slippers slapping at the heels of her bare feet. Madeline knocked. "Wynnie? You okay, honey?"

The door opened. Wynter stood with her damp, sticky hair and cheese-encrusted T-shirt on full display.

"Oh, Wynter. What happened?"

"Things didn't go as planned." Wynter's lips trembled as she fought back tears. "I'm going to have a shower and go to bed."

Madeline took Wynter in her arms and hugged her.

"Mom, you're going to get it all over..."

"Shh." Madeline rocked gently side to side, rubbing Wynter's back and letting the silence of the moment do its work. "You leave your clothes for me. I'll get them soaking."

Madeline stood back and held Wynter's shoulders. "Whatever happened tonight, it's over. Tomorrow's another day." She gave Wynter another quick hug and kiss.

"Thanks, Mom." Wynter closed the door and stripped out of her soiled clothes. The smell of corn chips and sour cheese rose from the pile. She grabbed her robe and walked to the adjacent bathroom and started the shower. The inescapable odor of nachos followed her. Wynter gazed at herself in the mirror and cried until the steam clouded her view. She stepped into the shower and pulled the curtains closed. The warm water cascaded over her, washing away the remnants of Jezebel's cruelty.

Wynter tried to picture Cash's face in her mind but couldn't complete the image beyond his blond hair and blue eyes. "Time After Time" floated back into her mind and she began to recite portions of the lyrics.

She stepped from the shower clean, refreshed, but exhausted. Wynter hastily dried her hair, pulled her robe back on, and returned to her room, closing the door behind her. Beside the lamp on her dresser was a cup of hot chocolate and a few sugar cookies.

*Perfect. Thanks, Mom.*

The hot chocolate, now pleasantly warm, went down fast and

easy, as did the cookies. She turned out the light, laid her damp hair on her pillow, and was asleep in seconds.

○

CASH STOOD AT the entrance to the Starlite Arcade, pretending to be interested in Jake's game of Donkey Kong. Jake had amassed a small group of spectators, some placing their quarters on the bezel for a chance to play next. He glanced at the clock above the rental desk: quarter past eleven. The players in the arcade were thinning out but the rink was still packed. Heart belted out "These Dreams." After everything that had happened to Wynter, it was just too much.

"Hey man, I'm going to split."

Jake sent Cash a quick glance before focusing back on his game. "Just a bit longer? I've almost beaten my record."

"Nah. I'll call you."

Jake looked at the quarters lined up on Donkey Kong's bezel, then back at Cash leaving the building. He turned to the small gathering around him as a barrel hit Mario and knocked him off the scaffolding. "Who's next? I got another life. Take over my game." He ran after Cash, leaving the crowd to argue about who would take over the controls.

"Hey." Jake jogged up beside Cash. "Want to crash at my place? Watch some satellite TV? My parents are probably asleep."

"Tempting," Cash said. "But I got to work in the morning. Finn let me leave early tonight in exchange for coming in early tomorrow."

"Bummer."

Cash shrugged. "It's not that bad. Plus, I've been saving up for a car. And for college."

"Yeah, I guess I should think about that. But it's hard to when there's another year of school left."

"Get on it before it's too late."

An all too familiar rumbling echoed from down the street. Cash and Jake glanced behind them to see the headlights of a black 1970 Barracuda approaching.

Jake exchanged a look with Cash. "Shit."

"Stay cool."

The Barracuda slowed to their walking pace and Jezebel stuck her head out the driver's side window. "Hey, boys. Want to play?"

"Keep walking." Cash spoke quietly from the side of his mouth.

"You deaf as well as dumb?"

"Get lost, Jizz-ebel."

"Jizz? Oh, that's original." Jezebel turned to Roxy. "We got a comedian." She revved the Barracuda, causing the front of the car to rise and dip, and pulled onto the sidewalk. "What would you know about it anyway? You sucking each other off?"

Cash placed his fists on the roof of the car. "What you did to Wynter, that was fucked up, you psycho."

Jezebel's smile exuded pure evil. "It was an accident. Everyone knows it."

"Not according to Zain's security video."

Jezebel's eyes flickered uncertainly, but just for a moment. "You're lying."

"I know what I saw. It's called assault."

Jezebel's jaw tightened and her smile morphed to a scowl. "Get your fucking hands off my car." She threw the Barracuda into reverse.

Cash stepped back, the tires narrowly missing his feet. "Looks like someone's running scared."

Jezebel raised her left middle finger out the window. "Fuck you, virgin." She floored the gas and laid a strip of smoking rubber on the street.

Roxy leaned out the passenger window looking backward and flipped them off using both hands. "Yeah, fuck you!"

The Barracuda sped down the road until its brake lights flared red, tires squealing. The car made a U-turn and accelerated.

"You've seen the... oh shit." Jake's eyes widened. "Is she going to try and run us down?"

The Barracuda's bright headlights burned into their eyes, making Cash and Jake squint.

"Yeah, I think so." Cash watched the car's approach, analyzing its speed. "When I say so, break left."

"Oh shit." Jake rocked back and forth on his feet. "Oh shit oh shit oh shit."

The Barracuda barreled up onto the sidewalk about five hundred feet away. Cash stood his ground, but Jake was losing his nerve.

"Come on, Cash. Don't be crazy."

Four hundred feet away.

"Wait."

Now two hundred feet away, Cash could see Jezebel's white toothy grin through the windshield.

"Now!" Cash stepped left, grabbed Jake, and pulled him along. "Jump." The two of them flew into the bushes next to the sidewalk.

Jezebel tried to steer into them, but her speed was too great. There was no time.

Roxy leaned out the window. "MOTHERFUCKERS!"

The Barracuda narrowly missed Cash and Jake and slid across the grass next to the sidewalk. The car shuddered for an instant before Jezebel regained control. She drifted back onto the road and laid a second strip of rubber, this time disappearing into the distance for good.

"Ho-ly shit." Jake wiped sweat from his brow.

"What a couple of assholes." The smell of burned rubber drifted past them, burning their noses with its acrid smell.

Jake took long, heavy breaths. "You've seen the surveillance video?"

"Nah. But looks like ol' Jizz-ball believed I did." Cash surveyed the road. "Maybe you should burn *Jezebel's* house down."

"I could make it look like an accident."

"I'm kidding." Cash raised a brow at Jake. "You're kidding too, right?"

"Yeah." Jake grinned as he caught his breath. "I'm kidding."

Cash narrowed his eyes at him. "Somehow, I'm not convinced."

"I'm kidding," Jake said. "For real."

The two teenagers continued walking.

"So you're *in love* with Quinn, huh?"

"What? No." Jake gave Cash a playful shove. "That was a joke."

Cash laughed. "Well, the sparks sure were flying."

Jake cast his mind back. "She's easy on the eyes, though."

"I knew it," Cash said. "Finally there's something more important than video games in your life."

"Hey, man. Whoa. It's not like I'm going to marry her or something."

Cash looked back at the Starlite SuperSkate in the distance, its neon sign flashing its glow into the night. "Hey, on second thought I think I'll crash at your place for a while. Your parents have any beer?"

"I can arrange that. Plus Skinemax, if we're lucky."

The two friends high-fived each other and headed north, toward the Main Street Overpass and Interstate 94, the highway that never slept.

○

WYNTER LEANED AGAINST the railing of the Main Street Overpass. The warm wind of a July afternoon teased her hair and caressed her bare legs. She reached up and ran her fingers through it and found the dampness gone. Her white sundress, light and soft as silk, moved effortlessly over her skin. Below, bumper-to-bumper traffic moved east and west along the paired double lanes of Interstate 94.

Instead of vehicles inching forward like in any other traffic jam, they moved at full speed. If there had been an accident, the fallout would have been horrific. But there was something else odd.

*No noise.*

No revving of engines, no horns honking, or drivers yelling out of frustration.

Wynter closed her eyes and drew in an energizing breath, despite the frenzy of traffic below her. She formed a picture of the highway in her mind, the way it should have looked, with vehicles separated by cushions of empty space.

She opened her eyes to a much different highway, one that matched her vision. Calm. Relaxed. It was then that Wynter felt his body heat next to her.

The blond blue-eyed boy stood with his back to the overpass railing, his black hoodie missing the drawstring. He gazed at her like she was the only thing that existed in his world. Maybe that was true.

Wynter reached out with a tentative hand. He mirrored her until their hands met, their fingers instinctively interlocking. She took one step closer and the boy did the same. And another step. If there was music, she could have been slow dancing with this mystery boy, close enough to count his eyelashes.

"If I fall?" the boy said.

Wynter's eyes widened with surprise. "I'll catch you. I've been trying all this time." Her words came to her lips without thought, unlocked, as if his question was the key.

The overpass railing faded, leaving no barrier between life and death. The two of them began to tilt into the void over the highway.

"NO." Wynter kept her hand clasped with his and arched her

back against gravity. Her bare feet slid on the concrete sidewalk, but the pull was too great.

*Do I let go?*

The boy careened further, his eyes never leaving Wynter's. A moment of clarity made the decision for her.

*Maybe death isn't down there, but up here.*

Wynter reversed herself and flung her body toward his, wrapping her free arm around his broad, sun-warmed shoulders. The world tipped, turning upside-down, as they plunged toward the rushing traffic below.

# Magic

Wynter and the boy landed with a thud next to her bed, her on top with legs straddling his hips. As exciting and unexpected as it was to be on the floor of her bedroom with a boy, she wasn't ready to be in a compromising position like this so quickly. Wynter scrambled back to the side of her bed and flipped on the bedside lamp. Her red hair hid half of her face.

The boy scooted back partially into the closet but didn't share her look of surprise. Instead, his eyes filled with curiosity.

They sat, staring at each other. Breathless. Wordless.

She heard noises from her parents' room, soon followed by the inevitable knock on her door.

"Wynnie?" It was Madeline, concern present in her voice. "You okay in there?"

Wynter raised her index finger to her lips, signaling the boy to be quiet.

*Could he even understand?*

"Yeah, I'm fine." Wynter scanned her bedroom in a panic, stopping on her bookcase. "I just dropped a book on the floor."

Silence from behind the door. Madeline's bullshit detector was active. Wynter waited, her eyes locked on the boy's.

"Okay, Honey," Madeline finally said. "Don't stay up too late."

Wynter waited until she heard her parents' door close and their bedsprings creak, hoping they wouldn't use this opportunity to have midnight sex. She'd die of embarrassment.

Wynter wrapped her arms around her bent legs and rested her chin on her knees. The boy did the same. She lowered her voice. "Who are you?"

The boy removed the hood from his head and furrowed his brow. "Wynter?"

"No. *I'm* Wynter. Wait. How do you know my name?"

"I don't know," the boy said. "I just do."

"What's *your* name?"

The boy shook his head.

"Do you know where you are?"

"In your bedroom," he whispered.

"No, I mean—"

"Newhaven. North Dakota."

Wynter's eyes bugged out and she swallowed hard. "How do you know that?"

The boy furrowed his brow. "I know some things. Basic stuff."

"This is still a dream, isn't it?" Wynter studied him.

"I don't think so," the boy said. "It feels different to me."

*Yeah. It does feel different.*

Wynter pulled hair out of her eyes and guided it behind her ear. "Okay. So you don't know your name?"

The boy shook his head. "I'm not sure I even have a name."

"We got to fix that." Wynter's eyes roamed her bedroom, looking for ideas. Her gaze ended up on the corkboard above the head of her bed and the poster of the Sheyenne National Grassland. Her eye flicked over to the map next to it. The grasslands were located in Ransom County. She smiled. "How about Ransom?"

The boy smiled back. "Ransom. I like it."

"Okay, Ransom," Wynter said. "Convince me that this is real, that it's not a dream."

Ransom let his eyes roam the closet. He picked up Wynter's Pentax K-1000 and unsnapped the leather carrying case.

"Be careful with that."

Ransom smiled. "Is there film in it?"

"There should be."

He advanced the film lever, held the camera to his eye, and focused. Ransom knew his way around a camera. "Smile."

Wynter did and Ransom pressed the shutter release.

*Click.*

Ransom snapped the carrying case closed and set the camera back where he had found it. "If there's a picture of you on here, then this is real, right?"

"I don't know." Wynter's eyes narrowed. "I've been dreaming of you for days. I need more evidence." She thought for a moment, her eyes settling on the plate on her dresser. A scatter of cookie crumbs remained. "You hungry?"

Ransom licked his lips. "Um, I—"

"Let me guess. You don't know."

Ransom shrugged.

Wynter picked up the plate. "I'll be right back. Stay here and don't move." She eased the bedroom door open and disappeared into the darkness.

She padded to the kitchen and found the Tupperware container holding the sugar cookies. Wynter pulled back the lid. Sweet baked aroma filled her nose. She refilled the plate and replaced the lid. Leaving the kitchen, she passed the phone on the wall. Then it hit her. The idea was so simple.

*Quinn.* She would be the proof.

Setting the plate down, Wynter picked up the phone and dialed. After a few clicks on the line, the handset began to trill in her ear.

Quinn's parents had surprised her on her fifteenth birthday with her own phone on a separate line in her bedroom. It was one of Wynter's dreams to have the same luxury, but that's what it would remain, a dream.

On the fifth ring, a groggy Quinn answered. "Bug?"

Wynter hesitated, then lowered her voice. "How did you know it was me?"

"Who else is going to call me at... one-fucking-thirty in the morning? I got to work tomorrow." Her voice buzzed through the speaker. "Are you okay?"

"Yes. But listen. Can you do me a favor?"

"Yes, I'll kill Jezebel for you."

"No." Wynter squinted at her parent's bedroom door at the end of the trailer. "Listen. This is going to sound weird, but tomorrow, ask me about Ransom."

"Ransom?" Quinn's staticky voice floated in Wynter's ear. "Have you been kidnapped?"

"No. I'm fine. Just remember to ask me."

"About Ransom," they said in unison.

"Yes," Wynter said. "I got to go now."

"Okay, Bug. Ransom. Got it." Quinn hung up.

Wynter placed the handset back on its wall cradle, picked up the plate of cookies, and crept back to her room. Ransom was right where she had left him. After closing the door, she sat cross-legged on the floor and placed the plate between them.

Ransom leaned forward and slid a cookie off the plate. He took a bite. Sugary crumbs cascaded down the front of his hoodie, standing out like stars in the night sky.

"These are good," he said with his mouth full.

"My mom's a good cook." Wynter took a cookie for herself.

It didn't take long for Ransom to wolf down the rest. "Thanks. I usually don't get to eat much."

"Because I didn't feed you in my dreams."

Ransom nodded with a smile. "I guess so, yeah."

"Sorry."

Ransom rocked forward to his knees, pushed the cookie plate out of the way, and crawled across the floor toward her. Wynter drew back but kept her eyes on him.

"I won't hurt you."

*Your eyes are so blue.*

His gaze cut through her as he sat next to her. "I could never hurt you."

*Promise?*

"I promise."

Wynter believed him. He had been in so many of her dreams that he seemed like a good friend already. She relaxed, her body shifting so the two of them sat shoulder to shoulder. "Why were you always jumping from the overpass?"

"I don't know." Ransom studied her face, memorizing it. "Maybe so I could be here, eventually."

"Yeah. I still don't understand how that happened. Are you here forever, or what?"

Ransom shook his head and shrugged.

"You don't know much, do you?"

"I know you saved me." Ransom locked his gaze with hers.

Despite the heat working its way up her neck and cheeks, Wynter yawned. "Sorry. It's definitely not you. I'm just really tired."

Ransom smiled. His teeth and skin were perfect, unblemished. "Then you should sleep."

Wynter sighed and climbed up into her bed, pulling a light sheet over herself. Ransom lay on the floor next to the bed, his hands clasped around the back of his head. She leaned to the edge so she could see him.

"How am I going to explain you to my parents?"

"Why do you have to?"

"What do you mean?"

Ransom motioned at the open bedroom window. "I'll just hop out before they get up."

"But where will you go?"

Ransom shrugged and smiled. "I'll make it up as I go along." He raised his hand to her cheek and caressed it, his finger drawing a line across her lips, never once taking his eyes off hers.

Wynter's brown skin warmed to his touch and every butterfly she had ever felt woke up all at once, fluttering in her stomach. Her emotions fought for control of her words.

"It must not be very comfortable down there."

"It's fine." Ransom set his hand on his chest.

"It's more comfortable on the bed, though."

Ransom sat up. "Are you sure?"

*Oh my God.*

"Yes," Wynter whispered. She slid back from the edge of the bed to make room for him. As her backside bumped against the wall, she realized how small a twin bed really was. Wynter remained under the top sheet while Ransom lay on top on his right side, mirroring her.

They stared at each other for what felt like hours instead of minutes. Ransom reached forward with his left hand, his fingertips searching through her hair.

Wynter took his hand and kissed his palm. His smell was intoxicating. She found she couldn't get enough. Ransom took her hand and ran her index finger across his lips.

"I want to kiss you, Wynter. Is that crazy?"

Wynter shook her head, almost imperceptibly. "No."

Ransom eased toward her until their lips met. One kiss led to two, then three.

Wynter pulled back, her brain ready to short circuit. "I've never done this before. Not like this."

Ransom relaxed and set his head back on one side of the pillow. "We have all the time in the world." He ran a finger along her jawline. "We can just lie here."

"That's perfect." Wynter smiled. Even under the top sheet she could sense the warmth of this mysterious boy's body next to hers. Her initial wariness melted into feelings of comfort and safety, and her thoughts drifted to what her first time might be like. She tried to keep her eyes open, but despite her excitement sleep won out.

When she awoke, Ransom was nowhere to be found. Disappointment mixed with relief fought for space in her head. She was glad she didn't have to explain Ransom to her parents.

Wynter swung her legs out of bed. She padded to the open window and took a cleansing breath. Saturday morning in Newhaven had already begun. She had turned to get dressed when she noticed *Eyes Wide Dreaming* sitting on her desk with a Post-It note sticking out from the side.

She picked it up and flipped to the marked page; the chapter on "Summoning." Her eyes widened as she carefully peeled the sticky note from the page.

Written in neat block letters, the note read: "FIND ME. RANSOM."

*He was real. It was all real.*

Wynter threw on her clothes and headed to the kitchen, suddenly famished. She couldn't wait to tell Quinn.

○

THE SWEET SMOKY smell of bacon hung heavy in the small kitchen. Nolan and Madeline sat at the table, each reading a different section of McLeod County's small daily newspaper. Remnants of their Saturday morning breakfast littered their plates.

"There's some pancakes and bacon on the stove for you." Nolan sipped his coffee without taking his eyes off his newspaper. Pancakes were his specialty. He often bragged that he could make them blindfolded.

"Thanks, Dad. And Mom, for the hot chocolate and cookies last night." Wynter kissed Madeline on the cheek and skipped to the stove. She placed three strips of bacon on a pancake, rolled it up, and took a bite. "Pigs in a blanket, LaCroix-style."

Madeline followed Wynter with her eyes. "You're bright and cheery this morning."

"I got a good sleep."

"Speaking of cookies, know anything about where the rest of them went?"

"The rest? Uh, I had a few last night."

"A few?" Madeline's newspaper drooped. "What's your definition of 'a few'?"

"Four?"

"Well, someone else was hungry last night too. And it wasn't your father."

Nolan glanced at Madeline. "How do you know it wasn't me?"

"Darlin', you're a terrible liar. Besides, I'd smell it on your breath."

Wynter found the Tupperware container on the counter and pried open the lid. Nothing but crumbs remained. She gave her parents a quick side-eyed glance.

*Ransom?*

"I only took four, Mom. I swear." Wynter grabbed her shoes and sat across from Madeline. She held the pancake rollup with her mouth like a cigar as she tied her shoes. Once done, she bit off the sodden end. "I'm going to meet up with Quinn."

Wynter opened the front door and paused. "Dad, thanks for coiling up my headphones the other day."

Nolan nodded. "It's my job, sweetheart."

"Did you happen to see a black drawstring anywhere?"

Nolan scrunched his brows in thought. "Drawstring? Like from a gym bag?"

"From a hoodie. It was Quinn's. I wanted to return it."

"No. I haven't seen anything like that." Nolan returned his attention to his newspaper. "I'll keep an eye out for it."

"Thanks." Wynter stepped out into the Saturday morning sunshine, the air already comfortably warm. The door swung closed.

"Keep an eye out for those cookies too," Madeline called out too late. She turned to Nolan. "Did Wynter seem... *off* to you just now?"

"Off, how?"

"Like not herself." Madeline pushed her chair away from the table and stepped to the front door. She opened it a crack to see Wynter receding in the distance.

"No, but *you're* acting strange."

"When was the last time Wynter sleepwalked?"

Nolan set his paper down. "It's been years. Do you think that's what happened last night?"

Madeline closed the door and cast Nolan a wary look. "I hope not."

○

WYNTER ARRIVED AT the food court in Stedford Plaza just after ten. Quinn and another staff member served a short line of customers at the FreshWhip. Wynter waved and Quinn smiled and sent her a nod.

Wynter found a vacant table nearby and settled into one of the chairs. On most days she found herself content to watch the goings-on in the food court, imagining how she would photograph the people. This morning she could hardly keep still. Her knees vibrated with excitement.

Quinn ran to the table, her Vans squeaking to a stop. "Deb switched breaks with me. I don't have long." She sat opposite Wynter and stared at her intently. "So, what does this mean?"

She dropped a crumpled piece of paper on the table. Scrawled on it in Quinn's groggy handwriting was "Wynter's ransom."

Wynter smiled. "You got my call."

"Uh, yeah. In the middle of the freaking night." Quinn sat back and struggled to get a read on Wynter. "What does it mean?"

"He's real, Quinn."

"Who?"

"The guy in my dreams."

Quinn gave her a sideways look. "Drawstring boy?"

Wynter nodded. "And look at this." She dug the Post-It note with Ransom's message on it from her pocket. "He wants me to find him."

"What do you mean?" Quinn glanced at the note and dismissed it. "If he's real, then he must live here. Maybe he's a customer or something, and—"

"Quinn." Wynter took Quinn's hands in hers. "Ransom came from my *head*. My *dream*. I know how crazy this sounds but I grabbed him before he fell, and the next thing I knew we were on my bedroom floor. You know what this means?"

"Your parents are going to send you to the loony bin?"

"Funny. No." Wynter's eyes blazed. "We can make our own boyfriends."

Quinn crossed her arms and returned her gaze. "So where is this *Ransom*? I want proof."

"I don't know." Wynter deflated. "He was gone when I woke up."

"Probably a good thing. Your parents would have killed him. And you." Quinn ran an aggravated hand through her hair. "Now you got *me* talking like he's real."

"He is." Wynter lowered her voice. "And we made out."

Quinn rolled her eyes in disbelief. "Come on, Bug."

"He's hot." Wynter raised a brow at her.

That shifted Quinn's attention. "Hotter than Cash?"

Wynter nodded. "We have a connection. I haven't felt anything like this before."

"Okay. You need to introduce me. How are you going to do that?"

"It has something to do with lucid dreaming." Wynter paused to think. "Maybe I can find him in a dream again."

"So I get to watch you sleep," Quinn said. "Sounds like a fun Saturday night."

"Please, Quinn? I have to try, right?"

Quinn looked back at the FreshWhip stand. Deb tapped her wrist. "Look, Bug, I got to get back." She stood.

Wynter followed her. "Let's meet tonight at the park. Ten o'clock? Please?"

"Okay," Quinn said. "But you are going to owe me big time."

"You won't regret it."

"I'll be the judge of that." Quinn stepped behind the FreshWhip counter. "See you tonight." She smiled and waved but it didn't feel genuine.

Instead of anticipation and excitement, Wynter left the plaza filled with more questions and doubt. She had to prove what she knew in her heart to be true. Would she be able to find Ransom? Would he look and act the same? Or was she crazy like Quinn thought she was?

Wynter hoped the answers to everything would reveal themselves tonight at Windspeaker Park. Quinn would have no choice but to believe her then.

○

MADELINE SNUGGLED UNDER Nolan's arm, both of them giggling at an episode of *The Golden Girls* on television. Wynter sat next to them on the opposite end of the sofa, immersed in her go-to book, *Eyes Wide Dreaming*. Her right leg vibrated up and down, a subconscious movement she made when anxious. It always happened when she took exams and if she had been paying attention, she would have seen Madeline's aggravation slowly build.

The TV show's cheesy credit music caught Wynter's attention.

It was nine-thirty. Time to go. She closed the book with an unintentional slap, startling Madeline and Nolan.

"Oops. Sorry." Wynter stood and walked to her room. "I'm going to Quinn's for a while," her voice echoed back through the hallway.

Madeline glanced at Nolan, grinned, and raised an eyebrow. "You guys got plans?"

"I don't know. Listen to music?" Wynter popped her head back into the living room, her purse and her camera slung over her shoulder. "Maybe watch something other than sitcoms?" She slipped on her shoes and tied them up.

Madeline smiled warmly at her daughter.

Wynter frowned. "What's that look for?"

"Seeing you all grown up." Madeline sighed. "It's bittersweet sometimes but nothing for you to worry about."

Wynter strolled to the sofa, leaned down and planted a kiss on Madeline's cheek.

"Hey. Forget something?" Nolan tapped his cheek with his index finger and Wynter gave him a peck, too.

"Don't be too late."

"I won't. Later, *lovebirds*." Wynter stepped out of the trailer, closing the door behind her.

Madeline gazed at Nolan. "What are we going to do now?" They both grinned at each other. Nolan found the TV remote, clicked it off, and took her into his arms.

○

WYNTER WADED THROUGH the knee-high grass of the trailer park's recreation field. The grass made her bare legs itch and she thought about going back and changing into long pants. But it was too warm and her parents were probably naked already anyway.

"Wynter!" a voice called out from behind. She turned to see Cash waving and jogging toward her. At any other time she would have been glad to see him. But tonight, meeting Quinn and trying to prove Ransom's existence, it could get awkward.

"Hi Cash."

"Whatcha doing?"

Cash did weird things to her brain. Her words were out of her mouth before she had a chance to lie. "Meeting Quinn at the park."

"Just got off work. Can I come?"

"Well..." Wynter struggled to find a reason to say no.

Cash gave her a sideways look and a shy smile, a combination for which she never had a defense. "Please?"

"Yeah, okay. But I warn you. We're going to be talking about lucid dreaming. It might be boring."

"Not if *you're* there." Cash beamed. He was nothing if not smooth. "What does lucid dreaming mean, exactly?"

Wynter smiled. "It's where you can control your dreams while you sleep. I've been practicing all summer so far."

"But why?"

"Haven't you ever had a dream where it, like, didn't go the way you wanted?" Wynter watched Cash with interest as he considered her question.

"I guess so."

"Lucid dreaming changes all that."

"Cool. That'd be a handy skill to have." Cash watched Wynter's hair sway in the warm breeze as they marched out the trailer park's front gate. "It's Saturday night. We should get some beer."

Wynter looked at him. "How?"

"I've got connections." Cash winked at her. "If you don't mind passing by Finn's on the way to the park."

Wynter knew Quinn was never one to pass up a chance to drink alcohol. Bringing beer would go a long way toward making things better between them.

"You're on," Wynter said.

"Alright." Cash clapped his hands and rubbed them together. "Hey, guess who tried to kill me and Jake last night."

Wynter's eyes darkened. "Does she drive a Barracuda?"

"Yup. She tried to run us down, over by the Starlite." Cash shook his head. "That girl's psycho."

"So's Roxy."

Cash recounted his brush with death as the two of them headed toward the Main Street Overpass and the town beyond.

○

WINDSPEAKER PARK SAT in the heart of north Newhaven, surrounded on three sides by the winding Sheyenne River. It felt like an island, with 3rd Street and one pedestrian bridge connecting it to the rest of the town. Picnic tables were scattered across the park, and a band shell and concession offered occasional entertainment and refreshments during the summer months. Other park amenities included a kiddie playground, tennis courts, and plenty of trees and foliage to keep birdwatchers busy. Walking paths wound their way through the green space, lamps fitted with wind chimes lighting the way. On breezy days, the park made its own music.

The centerpiece of the park, an open area with a large medicine wheel replica, sat embedded in the well-kept lawn. A ring of interlocking concrete bricks encircled a central marker, with interior lines of bricks connecting the ring to the marker. For hundreds of years Indigenous people had used a similar wheel constructed of river stones. The current wheel had been built in 1976 on top of the old stones to preserve their locations and Indigenous significance. The wheel could track the seasons and the hours in a day. Some believed the wheel held magical powers.

A week earlier had been Newhaven's 4th of July celebration

weekend. Fireworks on Friday evening kicked off a two-day festival of music, art, and dance. There was nothing special about July 12th. At ten o'clock at night, the park was dark and deserted, just as it should have been.

Quinn sat on one of the adult swings next to the playground and pushed herself back and forth in lazy arcs. The sun had set almost an hour ago and cast the sky in rich blues and purples, salted with stars.

"Where are you, Bug?" Quinn didn't scare easily, but sitting alone in the park knowing there were only two ways out set her on edge. She could swim if she needed to, but the river was almost 150 feet across at parts. She didn't enjoy swimming at the best of times and the thought of crossing the river at night sent a shiver down her back.

"Quinn!" Wynter's voice called from behind. "Look who I found along the way."

She looked over her shoulder to see Wynter and Cash strolling toward her. Wynter was drinking... a beer?

"I come bearing gifts." Cash pulled a six-pack of beer with one can missing from a brown paper bag. "Want one?"

"Grain Belt?" Quinn squinted at the cans with a dubious eye. "Is it better than Coors?"

Cash shrugged. "Don't know." He pointed at the label. "At least it's 'the friendly beer.' Finn and I have an understanding, so my choice is limited."

"Maybe later." Quinn looked at Wynter gulping her beer. "Since when do you drink beer?"

"I thought it would help me relax." Wynter burped and began to giggle.

Quinn exchanged a look with Cash. They both enjoyed seeing Wynter cut loose a little bit, especially after Jezebel's stunt at the Starlite the previous night.

"You're a cheap drunk," Quinn said. "So maybe it will."

Cash alternated his gaze between Wynter and Quinn. "What do we do now?"

Quinn raised her brows. "She didn't tell you?" She chuckled. "You're in for a treat."

"What do you mean?" Cash looked confused, a logical response.

"Bug can pull things out of her dreams." Quinn looked at her. "Isn't that right?"

Wynter nodded as she swigged her beer.

Cash narrowed his eyes. "Things?"

"People. Wynter says she can pull people out of her dreams," Quinn said. "We're here to witness it."

"And to learn how to do it." Wynter burped again. "Maybe."

Cash pulled a can of beer from the bag and cracked it open. "I think I need a friendly beer."

"Where are we going to do this?" Quinn scanned her immediate surroundings.

"We could try the band shell," Cash said. "In the back of the stage."

Quinn shivered, her apprehension clear even in the fading light. "That place is totally creepy during the day. I'm not going in there at night."

"What about under the slides?" Wynter pointed to the main feature of the kiddie playground: a collection of plastic slides that rose at a common center and slid out in four directions. Under the center was a secluded patch of sand.

Wynter stumbled toward the slide grouping. She stepped to the top, chose a slide, and rode it down laughing.

"It's going to be an interesting night," Quinn muttered to herself as she crouched between two slides. The enclosed space was semi-private but still offered a way to watch their surroundings through the gaps between the slides. She sat cross-legged on one side of the sandy vestibule.

Cash helped Wynter underneath the slide structure. She crawled toward Quinn, then pretended to fall asleep. Cash sat against the opposite side of the small space, his long legs crossed at the heels and his sack of beer at his side.

Quinn nudged Wynter's shoulder. "If you're going to sleep, at least be comfortable. Come here."

Wynter crawled to Quinn and flipped onto her back, her head supported by Quinn's crossed legs. "Grain belt. Grain belt. You ever notice how weird words sound when you say them over and over?"

"Stop talking, Bug." Quinn ran her fingers through Wynter's hair. "I don't want to be here all night."

Wynter sighed and closed her eyes. "Feels nice."

"You know what you need to do?"

Wynter returned a small nod.

Cash watched Quinn and Wynter interact and swigged his beer. "Is this really going to happen? Because it's kind of hard to believe."

"Apparently," Quinn whispered. "Now shhh."

Wynter fell asleep in minutes.

"Jesus," Cash said softly. "I wish I could do that." He finished his beer and tossed the empty can aside.

"You and me both."

A couple minutes of awkward silence passed before Quinn broke the ice.

"She likes you, you know."

Cash smiled. "I know. I like her, too. Have for years. But..." He lowered his gaze to the sand.

"What are you waiting for?" Quinn stared at him across the small space. "She's making up her own imaginary boyfriends now."

The word "boyfriend" caught Cash's attention. "What do you mean?"

"You'll see. Maybe. Unless she's crazy."

Wynter snored quietly in Quinn's lap. Wind chimes within the park lights played their metallic music, carried by the noticeably cooler summer breeze.

"How long is this going to take?"

Quinn shook her head. "I don't know."

Cash closed his eyes. Soon he was asleep as well.

"Typical." Quinn glanced at Cash, then at Wynter. "Everyone at the party passes out except me." She focused on the park's wind chimes and closed her eyes, only for a second or two.

But it was for much longer than that.

○

WYNTER WORE HER white sundress and stood center stage in the band shell, escaping the heat of the midday sun hovering directly overhead. The audience wasn't as lucky, sitting in front of her twenty per row, a dozen rows deep, and bearing the full brunt of the sun's wrath.

She scanned the audience. "Ransom?"

"Get off the stage!" yelled a member of the audience.

Wynter began to sweat. She had to find Ransom and bring him back. She had to prove to Quinn that she wasn't losing her mind.

"Ransom? Where are you?"

"You suck!" a voice called out.

"Go back where you came from!" someone else said.

Wynter shaded her eyes with her hands to get a better view of the audience. Hundreds of Cashs and Quinns stared back at her. Soon the entire crowd of clones were throwing catcalls and insults at her.

She took a panicked step backward and bumped into a warm body with an intoxicating scent.

"Don't turn around." Ransom's voice was unmistakable. "Make them leave."

"How?"

"Get creative." Ransom's breath across her ear sent shivers through her body. "Remember. It's only real if you want it to be."

Sink holes, tsunamis, hurricanes, and other disastrous consequences flipped through Wynter's dreaming mind. But these scenarios didn't feel right. "I don't want to hurt them."

"Then don't." Ransom stood behind her and placed his hands lightly on her shoulders.

Wynter smiled. She placed a hand over her mouth. A wave rippled through the crowd of Quinn and Cash clones. Their mouths disappeared, leaving smooth patches of skin and silence behind.

"It worked. I silenced them."

"Of course it did. This is your dream."

Wynter spun to face Ransom. "Now I want to show them that you're real." She grabbed his hoodie with both hands and pulled him close, planting her lips firmly on his. The warmth of their kiss spread through her body.

The stage of the band shell morphed into a king-sized mattress. Their feet fought to keep them steady on the soft, springy surface. Wynter tilted her body backward, like the trust falls she'd done with Quinn for drama class last year.

Their bodies toppled, linked in a kiss of longing and desire. Wynter landed on the mattress on her back with Ransom on top of her.

The cool feeling of sand on her skin jolted her body awake.

○

QUINN OPENED HER eyes to Wynter talking in her sleep, her hands twitching randomly. Across from her, Cash slept, his chest rising and falling with a calm, steady rhythm.

"Cash," she whispered.

He didn't respond. Quinn surveyed her surroundings. Everything looked the same, maybe a little darker. She couldn't have been asleep for long.

Quinn picked up a small pebble and threw it at Cash. The small stone bounced off his forehead, waking him at once. She stifled a laugh.

"Ow. What happened?" Cash looked around, groggy.

"She's been talking in her sleep."

"Saying what, exactly?"

"Mostly nonsense." Quinn picked up Wynter's wrist. Her watch was difficult to read in the dark, but she was sure it was after midnight. "We've been asleep almost two hours."

"Shit, really?" Cash yawned. "Time flies when you're having fun, or so I'm told."

Wynter twitched. "Ran-som." The words floated from her mouth, barely audible.

Cash leaned forward and frowned. "What'd she say?"

"Ransom," Quinn said. "It's the name of the boy in her dream."

"Ransom?"

"Ran…" Wynter trailed off, her lips moving like she wanted to say something more but couldn't.

Cash leaned forward to get a better look at Wynter. "This is really—" The air in the small space cracked, as if a large balloon had just popped, buffeting Cash and pushing him back.

Wynter's whole body twitched and all at once there were four people under the kiddie slides in Windspeaker Park.

"Holy fuck!" Cash tried to propel himself backward in the sand. "Who's that?"

Quinn saw the boy, too. A blond boy in a black hoodie, white T-shirt, and jeans lying on top of Wynter, his lips locked with hers. Mixed with astonishment, a flash of unanticipated jealousy ripped through her.

Cash moved to the side to get a better look. "What's he… is

he kissing her?" He scrambled to his knees and pushed the boy. "Get off her, man."

Quinn raised her hand to Cash. "Wait."

Wynter opened her eyes and gazed up at Quinn's upside-down face. Then she looked past Quinn's hand to Cash. Her face went beet-red in embarrassment, a fact hidden in the darkness. She placed her hands on Ransom's chest and pushed him back.

"That was nice. What's wrong?" Ransom remained focused on Wynter.

"We're not dreaming anymore." Wynter raised herself onto her elbows, then into a sitting position next to Quinn.

Ransom kneeled and sat on his feet. His blue, almost iridescent eyes shifted between Wynter, Cash, and Quinn.

Cash stared back at this strange boy, his jaws clenching in angry angles.

Wynter took Ransom's hand, fingers intertwined. Cash flinched, as if the gesture had hurt. "Ransom, these are my friends, Quinn and Cash."

Quinn looked at Cash. "I think I need that beer now."

Cash reached for the paper bag, extracted a beer, and tossed it to her. Ransom watched her crack the seal and take a sip. Cash swallowed hard, pulled out a second beer, and offered it to Ransom.

"Thanks." Ransom opened the beer, guzzled it, and dropped the empty beside him.

"Wait, what the fuck?" Cash shook his head in disbelief. "Am *I* dreaming now? How is this even happening?"

Quinn gazed at Wynter. "I'm sorry I didn't believe you, Bug."

"But you believe me now, right?"

Quinn shifted her eyes to Ransom, taking in his perfect face, free of any trace of acne, framed by blond curls. He returned a warm gaze. She could only imagine what he looked like under his clothes. "How can I not?"

Wynter took out her camera, advanced the film, and handed it to Quinn. "Take a picture. For proof."

"It's going to be all black," Cash said. "Not enough light."

"Bite your tongue." Quinn drank from her beer. "You're talking to Miss Pentax 1986."

"It'll be fine," Wynter said. "Got 1600 ISO loaded. And my fifty mil is fast."

Cash shrugged and crossed his arms against his chest.

Quinn took the camera, pointed it at Wynter and Ransom, and took a picture.

"You didn't focus. Set your beer down, you drunk, and take it again. But, like, focus first."

Quinn sandwiched her beer between her legs, snapped a second photo and handed the camera back to Wynter. She raised the beer to her mouth and finished it.

"Cash?" Ransom looked at him with wary eyes. "Can you toss me another beer?"

Cash gritted his teeth and hesitated. He pulled the beer out of the bag. Two cans hung from the plastic rings. He pulled one off and handed it to Ransom but pulled it back. "Wait. Where do you live? I mean it's got to be close."

Ransom looked at Wynter, then back at Cash. "I live in her head."

"Right." Cash scoffed. "And how does *that* work?"

"I don't know. Only Wynter knows for sure."

"I've been able to control my dreams for a while. But pulling things out is new." Wynter glanced at Cash but couldn't hold his gaze. "All I know is I was tired of being alone."

"So is Ransom your *boyfriend* now?" Hints of jealousy rose in Cash's voice.

"I guess for now, he is. Yeah," Wynter said.

"But he's *not real.*"

"He's real *enough.*" Wynter's eyes blazed.

Cash had always found Wynter's determination attractive, but not now. He focused on the beer in his hand. His eyes flicked at Quinn and she returned a look that said, "I told you so."

Ransom reached forward again. "Beer? Please?"

Cash slapped the can in Ransom's hand. "When do you go back into her head?"

"I'm not sure." Ransom opened the beer and took a long pull. "I'm a dream come to life. I guess it has something to do with sleep."

"So if you sleep, or Wynter sleeps, you disappear?" Cash had balled his hands into fists without realizing it.

Ransom shrugged. "Something like that."

"That would explain a lot." Wynter exchanged a look with Quinn.

"The drawstring?" Quinn asked.

Wynter nodded. "My dad didn't know anything about it."

"How about if I beat the shit out of you?" Cash vibrated, his jealousy replaced with anger. He grabbed Ransom's hoodie at the collar and threw him down to the sand. "You think you might disappear then?" He landed a clumsy punch across Ransom's face, splitting his lip.

"Get off him!" Wynter pulled Ransom back toward her. "Asshole."

Quinn held Cash's shoulders. "Let it go," she whispered in his ear. "Not the time." He struggled against her grasp. "Cash!" Quinn's hard stare broke through his fury.

Wynter sat cradling Ransom in her arms and spoke to him in consoling whispers. He wiped a trail of blood from his face and smeared it on his hoodie.

Remorse flooded Cash. He slumped against the opposite side of the alcove, his fists replaced with open hands of apology. He forced himself to look at Wynter, acknowledging the anger in her eyes. "I'm sorry."

"You should be." Wynter paid Cash barely any attention, instead choosing to focus on Ransom.

Cash dropped the remaining can of beer on the sand. "I think I better go." He stood to leave, pausing first to look back at Ransom. "I really am sorry." He squeezed between the plastic slides and disappeared into the night.

Quinn lay on her side and propped her head up on her arm. "Well that went well." She picked up the can of beer and reached toward Ransom. "This might help with your lip."

"Thanks." Ransom took the can and placed it next to his split lip for a moment, then reconsidered. "On second thought..." He cracked the seal, guzzled the contents, and let loose a belch. "Better in than out."

Quinn rolled her eyes. "Even dream boys are pigs."

Wynter yawned and counted on her fingers. "You've drunk more than all of us, but why does it feel like I'm the one who's shitfaced?"

"If he's part of you, then maybe you feel it too?" Quinn raised a brow.

Ransom smiled. "I'd buy that."

Wynter waved her hands. "Too complicated." She looked at Quinn, her eyelids half open. "Want to learn how to do this?"

"You mean make my *own* hot guys for... fun and profit?" Quinn winked, her lips curling slyly. "Fuck, yeah." The two girls slapped hands.

Ransom glanced at the gap between the slides where Cash had squeezed through. "I'm not mad at him. He's known you longer. He was protecting you."

"Cash is a good guy," Quinn said. "You just caught him off guard."

"I'd have done the same thing." Ransom looked over his shoulder at Wynter, who was slumped to one side asleep again. "Looks like it's just you and me."

Real or not, Ransom was Wynter's new boyfriend. But despite that, Quinn could not deny her flirtatious nature. She gave Ransom her best seductive look. "Don't get any ideas." They stared at each other across the darkness, Ransom returning a look of his own, until the heat between them became too much.

"Oh my God," Quinn whispered as she forced herself to look away. She closed her eyes and inhaled several calming breaths. "What are you—"

Quinn looked up to find Wynter asleep next to her. Ransom had vanished. A brief sweet and pungent whiff of ozone hung in the air before dissipating in the night's cool eddies.

Quinn nudged Wynter with her foot. "As much as I'd like to let you sleep it off, I'd rather be home in my own bed."

Wynter snorted, shifted her position, and remained asleep.

Quinn kneeled and placed her lips next to Wynter's ear. "Bug. Bug-bug. Bugaboo." She blew across Wynter's earlobe and cheek.

Wynter continued to snore softly.

"BUG!" Quinn shook Wynter's shoulder, annoyed and long past caring about the volume of her voice. "Come on. Up and at 'em." She grabbed one of Wynter's hands and dragged her out from under the slides.

"Wait." Wynter formed groggy words. "What's going on? What are you doing?"

"I'm taking you home."

"Stop." Wynter yanked her hand back. "I can walk." She stood on wobbly legs and steadied herself on the side of a plastic slide. "Where's Ransom?"

"I guess he's back in your head." Quinn placed her arm around Wynter and joined one of the lighted paths curving through the park. "He disappeared a bit after you fell asleep."

"Did you see him vanish?"

Guilt flooded Quinn, making her feel hot and self-conscious. But her lie came easy. "No. I turned my head for a second and he was gone."

"Wait. Where's my camera?" Wynter stumbled back to the slides, returning a moment later with her SLR slung over her shoulder. "Do you think he'll show up on film?"

"Only one way to find out," Quinn said. "By the way, can I crash at your place?"

"Of course, if you don't mind slumming it." Wynter laughed and hooked her arm around Quinn's neck.

"A roof and a bed is all I need."

"We'll have to share."

"Ransom, too?"

Wynter gave Quinn a playful push.

They both laughed but Quinn was only half joking.

# Talking In Your Sleep

THE SUMMER AIR still held a chill in the middle of the night and the walk home had helped Wynter sober up. She unlocked the front door to the trailer and eased it open. Both girls slipped off their shoes and tiptoed to Wynter's room.

"I need to pee," Quinn said. "What if I wake your parents?"

"I'll go with you."

Quinn recoiled. "I love you, Bug, but I won't do that."

Wynter put her hand over her mouth to stifle a laugh. "Not at the same time! Ew. I mean I'll be in the bathroom with you, in case they say something."

"Oh. Okay," Quinn said. "I feel slightly better now."

"And I won't watch."

"Nothing to see anyway."

Wynter took Quinn's hand. "Ready?"

Quinn nodded.

Both girls crept into the bathroom and closed the door behind them. Quinn unbuttoned her jeans and looked at Wynter, twirling her finger and mouthing "Turn around."

Wynter faced the bathroom door. Seconds turned to minutes. "What's taking so long?"

"You ever tried peeing with someone standing right next to you?"

"I could turn on the water."

"Don't bother." Quinn closed her eyes and released a calming breath. Tinkling echoed from within the toilet bowl.

"Don't flush," Wynter whispered. "Or wash your hands."

"Gross. Why?" Quinn wiped, pulled up her pants, and buttoned up.

"I need to go now, too."

Wynter and Quinn switched places. Silence surrounded them again.

"See?" Quinn said softly. "Not as easy as it looks."

After Wynter finished, they both ran their hands through a trickle of water and tiptoed back to Wynter's room. With the bedroom door closed, they felt secure again.

"You didn't flush," Quinn said.

"Too risky." Wynter turned on the bedside lamp, pulled back the top sheet on the bed, and laid on her back closest to the wall. Quinn lay down next to her, sharing her pillow.

They stared at the ceiling for a moment. "So you have a boyfriend now," Quinn said.

Wynter smiled. "Yeah. And he's hot."

Quinn rolled onto her side and propped her head up on her hand. "Cash sure got jealous."

"I know. But he's known me practically my whole life and hasn't made a move."

"But you've never made a move either."

Wynter shrugged her shoulders. "I know. But Ransom is what I needed... at least for now."

Quinn's eyes roamed the room, settling back on Wynter. "He drank three beers, Bug."

Wynter looked at her. "Yeah? So?"

"Where did the beers go?"

Wynter shrugged. "With him when he disappeared, I guess."

"Don't you find that amazing?"

"It's all amazing." Wynter's lips curved at the corners, as images of the evening flashed through her mind.

"Have you guys, you know, done it yet?"

Wynter blushed. "Not yet."

"I think we need a weekend alone," Quinn whispered. "Just me and you... and Ransom too of course." She ran her tongue along the edge of her teeth. "Call it research. What do you say?"

Wynter smiled. "Most definitely."

◯

MADELINE AND NOLAN woke up to waffles, bacon, and coffee, hot and waiting on the breakfast table, as well as the mess that came with a teenaged breakfast extravaganza.

Wynter and Quinn sat at the table chattering excitedly, their breakfast finished.

"Wow." Madeline took a seat. "To what do we owe this spread?"

"No reason," Wynter said. "We just wanted to make you breakfast." She exchanged a look with Quinn and both girls giggled.

Madeline raised a brow at Nolan as she lifted a waffle onto her plate.

"You two got in late last night." Nolan speared a waffle with his fork and snatched some bacon.

"Sorry." Wynter looked at Quinn and snickered. "We tried to be quiet." She poured coffee into the two mugs next to her parents' plates.

Madeline spread butter on her waffle and smothered it with syrup. "Your parents know where you are?"

Quinn nodded. "I called them when I got up."

Nolan carved a bite of waffle and placed it in his mouth. "Not bad, grasshopper."

"Yes. Very tasty."

"Thanks."

Wynter and Quinn sat and watched Madeline and Nolan eat.

Nolan crunched his bacon. "I'm getting a strange feeling, Maddie. Like someone wants to ask us something."

"I'm getting that feeling too." Madeline looked at Wynter and Quinn. "Well?"

"Um, I was wondering if I could go to Quinn's cabin next weekend." Wynter glanced at Quinn ever so briefly. "It'll be just the two of us."

"Yeah, Friday and Saturday night," Quinn added.

Nolan chuckled. "Special breakfasts usually come with an ask."

Madeline stirred sugar into her coffee and took a sip. "Have you cleared it with your parents?"

"Not yet, but they'll be cool with it, Mrs. LaCroix," Quinn said. "I'm certain of it."

Madeline turned to Nolan. "What do you think, hon?"

Nolan sat back in his chair and clasped his fingers behind his head. "I don't know. I guess if they're cool with it, I'm cool with it."

Wynter and Quinn shifted their gaze to Madeline. She always held the veto power.

Madeline smiled and shrugged. "Sure, why not. But under one condition."

Wynter and Quinn froze, not knowing what to expect.

"You need to clean up that mess." Madeline hooked a thumb at the kitchen, with dirty bowls, utensils, and a waffle iron that looked like it had been dipped in batter.

Wynter threw her arms around Madeline's neck and kissed her cheek. "Thank you, Mom. And Dad."

"Standard rules apply." Madeline's eyes meant business. "If you drink, don't drive. Make smart choices and check in with us every once in a while."

"Yes, of course." Wynter hugged Nolan.

"Thanks, Mr. and Mrs. LaCroix." Quinn smiled, then joined Wynter at the kitchen sink.

Wynter leaned into Quinn's ear. "This getaway is going to be so fun," she whispered.

"I know," Quinn whispered back.

As Madeline and Nolan finished their breakfast, Wynter and Quinn threw themselves into cleanup mode. Both imagined what would happen next weekend. If they were to compare their innermost private thoughts, they would have discovered very different versions.

○

MOST DAYS WYNTER'S shifts at Shooters flew by, but the week leading up to Quinn's cabin trip felt like a month. Working there had its benefits. Wynter had access to equipment she'd never be able to afford, and she genuinely enjoyed talking to people about photography. But this week the anticipation made the time drag until Friday finally arrived. Shortly after five-thirty, Quinn strolled into Shooters, still dressed in her FreshWhip uniform.

"Hey Bug. Ready to go?" She rocked on the balls of her feet.

"Shit, yeah." Wynter ran into the stockroom to get her things.

Daytona pushed through the stockroom door as Wynter passed, her face flushed with a light sheen of sweat. She ran her hands across her forehead and hair, and pulled down the hem of her T-shirt. "Hi, Quinn."

Quinn offered a small wave. "Hi. How's business over here?"

"The usual."

Hunter emerged from the back room and laid a kiss on Daytona's neck. "More like the *unusual!*" He did something unseen with his hand that caused Daytona to jump.

"Stop it, you *pig.*" She smirked and gave him a slap.

"The big weekend's here, huh?" Hunter leaned on the display

case next to Daytona and grinned. "Wynter's been talking about it all week."

"What's she been saying?"

Daytona grabbed her purse from behind the display case. "Oh, like it's going to be the 'best weekend of her entire life.' " She air quoted her words as she pulled out a pocket mirror and checked her makeup.

"*Lez-be* friends." Hunter guffawed.

"Shut up." Daytona slapped him again.

"Then give my mouth something else to do." Hunter laughed and began checking expiry dates on film stock.

Quinn rolled her eyes. Under her breath she said, "Bug, where are—"

Wynter popped out from the stockroom doors, a big duffel bag slung over her shoulder. "Okay, let's go." She turned to Daytona and Hunter. "Later, guys."

"Makin' plans." Hunter gave her a thumbs up. "Lookin' good."

"Thanks," Wynter called back as the two of them strolled toward the exit of the plaza.

"I thought you had gotten lost back there." Quinn pushed open the doors. The summer heat knocked back their hair as they made a line to Blue Belle. The little 1976 VW Beetle stood out like a fly on a wedding cake.

"I wanted to make sure I had everything."

"And?"

"I got everything." Wynter smiled from ear to ear.

Quinn unlocked Blue Belle and hopped in. "Holy crap!" She unlocked the passenger door for Wynter then reached into the rear seats. "Watch it. The seats are freaking hot." She grabbed two towels and gave one to Wynter. "We can sit on these."

Wynter dropped her duffel bag on the back seat and sat on the folded towel.

Quinn did the same. "Ready?" Her eyes gleamed as she inserted the key into the ignition slot.

"Go girl!" Wynter rolled down her window.

With a quick twist of Quinn's wrist, Blue Belle's engine cranked up, blasting a cloud of exhaust behind them. She backed out of their parking spot and navigated to Main Street and the on-ramp to Interstate 94.

Prince crooned "Little Red Corvette" from the Beetle's speakers. "Turn it up. I love this song," Quinn said as she rolled down her window.

Wynter twisted the volume knob on the radio and joined Quinn singing about finding love that lasts.

Quinn merged Blue Belle onto the highway traveling west. "You think you can sleep? You know, get this party started early?" She grinned.

"I don't know. I'm pretty excited, but I'll try." Wynter eased her seat back and closed her eyes. But the engine noise and the music on the radio, combined with her anticipation, kept her awake. "It's too noisy."

"Okay. Switch to plan B."

Wynter twisted to get at her duffel bag and pulled out *Eyes Wide Dreaming* before resetting her seat. "What would that be?"

"Whoppers to the max. With fries, drinks, everything." Quinn gave Wynter a quick glance. "You know, a full tummy brings the sleepies."

Wynter flipped through the book's pages. "I don't want to sleep the weekend away."

"No," Quinn said. "Only long enough to invite our special guest."

Wynter fell silent for a moment. "Do you think that's lying? We told our parents that it would only be us."

"Technically it still is," Quinn said. "You, me, and your dream-boy. Besides, you think they would have said 'yes' if you had told them you wanted to get away so you could lose your virginity?"

Wynter blushed. "When you say it that way, no. But still, it feels weird."

"I think you might change your mind once you're in Ransom's arms."

The two girls grinned at each other and burst out laughing. Twenty minutes later, including a stop at Burger King, Quinn rolled into the driveway of her parents' cabin on Lake Gilberg.

○

THE BENOIT CABIN sat on a ten-acre parcel of land on the southeastern shore of Lake Gilberg, nestled among groupings of ash, elm, and boxelder maples. A dock and a small boat house lined the shore, with a welcoming expanse of overgrown grass leading up to the cabin's deck.

Quinn and Wynter lugged their bags and fast food to the porch. Quinn unlocked the front door to the cabin and nudged it open with her foot and dropped her bag. Hints of must, wood smoke, and cedar washed past them.

Wynter let her gaze wander. "I forgot how beautiful this place is. Why aren't you here all the time?"

"I'd spend all my money on gas," Quinn said. "Besides, I want to be in the heart of the action."

"Hate to break it to you but Newhaven isn't the heart of anything..." Wynter paused and glanced at Quinn.

"Except the Starlite," they said in unison, both laughing.

The cabin featured an open design living area, with the kitchen, dining room, living room, and bathroom all connected on the main floor. A sliding door beside the dining room table led to the deck overlooking the lake.

In the living room, next to the fireplace, entertainment center, sectional sofa, and matching coffee table, a spiral staircase constructed of modern wrought iron rose to loft bedrooms and a shared bathroom.

Quinn deposited the Burger King bags on the dining room

table, unlatched the sliding doors to the deck, and pulled them open. The summer air, warm and fresh, filled the cabin. She unpacked the bags: four Whoppers, two large fries, and two large Pepsis.

"Hope you're hungry."

"Four Whoppers?" Wynter whistled and placed her book on the table.

"Two for each of us." Quinn looked over the rims of her glasses. "I ain't messing around. Shall we?"

Wynter pulled out a chair next to Quinn. "Thanks for getting this."

"Buy me breakfast at Lucy's and we'll call it even."

The girls dug into their meals.

"So I've been reading," Wynter said between mouthfuls. "Our actual dreams begin about ninety minutes after we fall asleep."

"No wonder it took so long at the park last week," Quinn said. "Can you make it happen faster?"

"It says that extreme relaxation in a dark environment helps."

"I could call Monty. I got his number." Quinn dug into her purse.

Wynter nearly choked on a sip of Pepsi. "Are you crazy? That guy is nuts."

"You're right. Never mind."

"Would *you* trust him?"

"Fuck, no. Bad idea." Quinn clicked her tongue in thought. "I think I've got something that will help." She got up from the table and filled a kettle, setting it to boil on the gas stove. She found a mug in the cupboard and set it on the counter.

"What are you doing?" Wynter munched on her fries.

"Chamomile tea," Quinn said. "Supposed to help with sleep. My mom swears by it."

A few minutes later, Quinn presented a cup filled with brackish fluid to Wynter.

"That's chamomile?" Wynter eyed the cup dubiously.

"Yep. Triple strength."

Wynter took a sip, grimaced, and set the cup down. "Tastes like I just mowed the lawn with my teeth."

Quinn took a sip and shuddered at the strong flavor. "Oh my God, it does." She looked at Wynter expectantly. "Think you'll be able to choke it down?"

"Yeah, maybe." Wynter took a bite of her Whopper and a big sip of tea, chewed, and swallowed. "Better, by *that* much." Her thumb and index finger almost touched.

Somehow, Wynter managed to finish her first Whopper, all of her fries, and the tea. But then she hit a wall. She pushed the rest of her food away. "I'm done. For now, anyway." She looked at her watch. The hands read just past six-thirty.

"Let's get you to bed so we can get this party started." Quinn led Wynter up the spiral staircase to one of the bedrooms. "I'll go get your bag."

Wynter scanned the room. It was sparsely furnished and decorated, with a bed, a small reading lamp on a bedside table, and a dresser in front of a closed window. It wasn't much different than what she was used to at the trailer, maybe a bit smaller. But the walls met the ceiling in sharp angles, causing the light and shadow to stretch in unsettling ways.

*I've been here before. It's just a room. Quinn's home away from home.*

But even Wynter's thoughts couldn't calm her sense of unease. She laid down on the bed and closed her eyes. Sleep beckoned her. Sleep would help and it wouldn't take long.

Quinn entered the room with Wynter's duffel bag and a large fluffy quilt.

Wynter cracked open her eyes.

"Introducing the 'coma-quilt.'" She laid the quilt over Wynter, tucked her in, and pulled the blinds down on the window.

"I feel like a kid being put to bed early for being bad."

"Well, you're no kid." Quinn stood and ran her hands down

her body, emphasizing her own curves. "But you and I got the *goods* and I have a feeling you'll be *bad* later." She stood at the doorframe. "I'll be just downstairs waiting."

Quinn left, closing the bedroom door behind her.

Wynter closed her eyes again. The warmth under the quilt, her full stomach, and the chamomile worked together and lulled her to sleep, the angry shadows a footnote. Soon she would see Ransom again.

○

THE WARMTH UNDER the quilt became too much. Wynter opened her eyes and moved her arms out from under the covers. The room was different, boxier like at home, but the strange shadows still danced on the wall.

"Ransom?" Wynter pulled the covers off and sat up on the bed. She walked to the window and raised the blinds. Framed in the glass panes was the unmown central field back at the trailer park as if she was standing on her front steps. She could see Cash's trailer in the distance and someone standing next to it.

She furrowed her brow and pried open the window. "Ransom?" Wynter turned to see the quilt standing up on its own near the side of the bed, draped on a central support like a patchwork ghost. She gasped and stepped back, knocking the dresser with her feet.

*No. Someone's underneath.*

Swallowing her fear, Wynter followed the quilt's folds and checkered patterns to the floor. Two white-socked feet poked out from under the hem. "Ransom? Is that you?"

"You're going to have to come under here and find out." His voice sounded exactly as she had remembered from the park the previous week.

Wynter tiptoed to the bed and sat down next to the quilted

apparition. She raised the edge of the quilt until she could see Ransom's face, smiling back at her.

"Come in," he said. "It's nice under here."

Wynter pulled the quilt over her head and shifted her body close to Ransom. "You scared me half to death, you know."

"Your dreams are just a reflection of your current state of being."

"You sound like my book."

Ransom grinned his perfect teeth. "This is your dream. Makes sense that I'd have to exist within it." He slid a warm arm around her waist and pulled her close. He snapped the fingers on his free hand and a flame ignited on his thumb, illuminating the secret cave under the quilt like a magic Zippo.

Their eyes locked and they kissed.

Wynter looked at his thumb, the fire burning bright. "Doesn't that hurt?"

"No. Try it."

Wynter snapped her fingers and a flame burst out of her thumb too, the cool fire licking at her thumb tip. The patterns on the underside of the quilt danced before their eyes. She kissed Ransom again, this time long and sweet. "Want to come to my world for a while?"

"Absolutely."

Wynter grabbed Ransom's hand in hers, stood, and flung the quilt off their heads to the floor. The strange angles were back, holding the walls and ceiling together like a shadowy web.

Quinn stood framed in the bedroom door, her eyes wide and jaw agape.

○

QUINN PLUGGED HEADPHONES into the receiver of the entertainment unit and tuned it to KROK. "You Dropped A

Bomb On Me" by The Gap Band filtered through the headphone's speakers as she placed them on her head. She picked up *Eyes Wide Dreaming,* flopped onto the sectional, and turned the book over in her hands. The hardcover's edges had been worn smooth from repeated readings and many of the pages were dog-eared. Some had their corners intentionally turned down.

*The important pages.*

Quinn began reading, trying to educate herself about lucid dreaming and how she could conjure a boy toy of her own. It came so easy to Wynter. At least it appeared that way. But it would take work and she knew it.

Despite the music, the reading made her eyes heavy and reminded her too much of homework and book reports of years past. After reading the same paragraph three times in a row, she closed the book and set it on the coffee table.

A *snap* echoed down from the loft bedroom.

*Wynter's room.*

It was loud enough that she heard it over the music broadcasting through her headphones. She pulled them off, turned off the receiver, and cocked her head to one side.

The cabin fell silent.

"Bug?" Quinn stood and listened.

Then a *thud.*

Like a shot, Quinn raced to the spiral staircase and clambered up to the loft. She stepped gingerly on the balls of her feet until she reached Wynter's door.

She placed her ear to the door, held her breath, and listened. Quinn thought she heard a voice—no, *two* voices—behind the door.

"Bug? You awake?" The voices she had heard just a moment ago had stopped.

Quinn brought her hand close to the doorknob to Wynter's room and saw that her fingers were trembling.

*Get a grip, Quinn. It's just a door.*

She wrapped her hand around the knob and twisted it, unlatching the door. Quinn gave the door a push and let it swing wide open.

On the bed sat a shrouded figure. Quinn froze.

*A ghost.*

Except she knew it was just Wynter under the "coma-quilt." She could see Wynter's feet, flat on the floor, but the lack of movement bothered her the most. The quilt hung limp and motionless.

"Bug?" Quinn's voice came out in a raspy whisper.

The form under the quilt—*Wynter?*—stood and cast the quilt aside, revealing Wynter *and* Ransom, arms around each other's waists. Quinn's eyes bugged out.

Ransom was dressed in the same clothes as he had worn at Windspeaker Park: white socks, jeans, black hoodie over a white crewneck T-shirt.

"Hey, Quinn," Ransom said. "What's wrong? You see a ghost?"

Quinn answered his question with a stare of amazement.

"I did it." Wynter smiled ear to ear and pointed to her watch. "And in less than ninety minutes. So let's get this party started." The two of them walked past Quinn in the doorway.

Ransom placed his hand under Quinn's jaw and raised it gently, closing her mouth. "Don't want you to catch any flies."

Quinn followed the two with her eyes as they navigated the spiral staircase to the lower level of the cabin. "I need to learn how to do that," she whispered to herself as she followed them down.

○

"ONE DOWN, ONE TO GO." Ransom licked his fingers and dug into the last Whopper. A blob of mayonnaise and ketchup clung to the corner of his mouth.

Quinn and Wynter sat facing him from the opposite side of the dining room table. They exchanged a quick glance. Ransom noticed.

"What?" Ransom spoke with his mouth full.

"He's checking all the 'oblivious guy' boxes," Quinn whispered to Wynter.

Ransom swallowed his mouthful. "You think I'm oblivious?"

Quinn did a double-take. "Wait, how did you—"

"I hear what Wynter hears," Ransom said. "Well, not exactly. It's more like I know what she hears, kind of. I'm from her head, remember." He took another bite of burger.

Quinn crossed her arms. "Okay, let's do a test. I'll take Wynter into the other room and ask her a question." She looked at Wynter. "Come on."

The two girls disappeared into the living room for a moment, then returned, giggling at him.

Ransom smiled back. "You both know my hair isn't blue. My eyes are."

Quinn's jaw dropped. "Holy shit."

"No more secrets, huh?" said Wynter.

"Can you read her thoughts?"

Ransom shook his head at Quinn. "No more than you can. But I do know what she knows. Like general knowledge and stuff. More or less."

Quinn rubbed her temples. "This is crazy."

"And these burgers are crazy good," Ransom said. "This is the first time I've eaten anything since those sugar cookies before."

Wynter smirked at him. "I knew that was you. I got in shit because of that." She looked at Quinn. "He ate all my mom's sugar cookies. Made it look like I did it."

"Sorry about that. Couldn't resist." Ransom burped and wiped his mouth with a napkin.

Quinn raised a brow at Wynter. "So if you share Wynter's

head, you'd know what her mom's sugar cookies tasted like already."

"I wanted to experience them again for myself," Ransom said. "It's like looking at a photo of New York and actually being there. I don't know how long I'll be around, so I want the raw experiences as soon as possible."

Quinn nodded. "Makes sense."

The three of them stared at each other before Wynter broke the silence. "Can we start the party now?"

"What kind of party do you want? Dance? Movie?" Quinn looked at Ransom. He shrugged his answer back at her. Wynter yawned.

"You tired already? It's barely eight o'clock."

"I know. Maybe I'm feeling all the food Ransom ate," Wynter said. "I mean we are connected." She collected the Burger King bag and wrappers, crumpled them into a ball, and threw it into the garbage under the sink.

"Are you feeling sleepy, Ransom?"

"Maybe a bit," he said. "But I'm thirsty too."

"I've got an idea," Quinn said. "You haven't seen *The Terminator* yet, right? The one with Schwarzenegger?"

"No. Is it good?"

"Hell yeah, but let's make it interesting. Come on." Quinn skipped to the entertainment center and pulled open a storage compartment. "You find the movie. I'll be right back."

Wynter kneeled by the sofa and rooted through the movies in the compartment. Ransom sat on the sofa next to her and placed his hand on her back. She found *The Terminator* right away but dug through more videos to prolong the moment.

Quinn strolled back to the living room with a plastic bag containing a two liter bottle of Coke, a bottle of rum, three tumblers and three shot glasses. She set it all down on the coffee table and removed the shot glasses.

"What's all that?"

"You'll see." Quinn grinned. "Find the movie yet?"

Wynter sat on her heels and placed *The Terminator* next to the shot glasses. She cast a wary eye at Quinn. "You sure about this?"

Quinn leaned in between Wynter and Ransom and whispered in Wynter's ear. "Trust me, Bug. It's not so much the movie but what you do *during* the movie. It's pretty intense so you might need someone to hold on to."

Quinn turned her head and smiled at Ransom, then took a seat next to the two of them. "The rules are simple. Everyone gets a rum and Coke. But every time we see the world from the Terminator's point of view, we drink a shot. If you don't want to, that's okay. It's just more fun if everyone plays. Ready?"

"Okay." Wynter leaned into the sofa's backrest. Ransom gave Quinn a thumbs up and a grin.

"Great." Quinn mixed up three rum and Cokes and handed one each to Wynter and Ransom. She poured rum into the shot glasses, grinning. "Just getting prepared."

Quinn grabbed the video cassette and hopped to the entertainment center. She pressed some buttons on the remote control, inserted the movie into the VCR, and pressed play. She ran to the kitchen and turned off the lights. Being the only light source now, the television cast an eerie blue glow across the living room.

After Arnold Schwarzenegger and Michael Biehn strutted their naked butts across the screen during the first few minutes of the movie, Quinn turned to Wynter and Ransom. "What do you think so far?"

"Handsome dudes." Ransom sipped his rum and Coke. "But the big guy might be a little too big."

Quinn giggled. Wynter joined in, then turned serious as gunfire echoed from the TV. "Is there a lot of killing in this movie?"

"It *is* about a terminator from the future," Quinn said. "So, yeah. There is."

"Maybe we could watch something different after this?"

Wynter grinned and narrowed her eyes at Quinn. "Something more *romantic?*"

"You mean porn?"

Wynter recoiled. "Porn's romantic? I saw some strange titles in there."

"It depends," Quinn said. "I'll pick a good one. What do you think, Ransom? Want to watch some porn later?"

Ransom beamed. "I'm up for anything."

The three of them nursed their drinks until the pivotal scene when the dance floor at TechNoir erupts in gunfire.

"This is one of my favorite lines coming up." Quinn sat up, then spoke in sync with the movie. " 'Come with me if you want to live.' Oh my God, Michael Biehn is so hot." The central characters fled, the Terminator in hot pursuit.

"There it is." Quinn whooped. The TV screen turned red with computer code and analytics flashing across it. "The first Terminator POV. Drink up, ladies and gents." She passed shots to Wynter and Ransom and raised her own. "Down the hatch."

Quinn downed her shot in one gulp as did Ransom. Wynter choked on hers, sputtering half of it onto her shirt.

"Ugh. That's nasty."

"Don't worry," Quinn said. "The next one will go down easier."

"For my first actual movie experience, this is a great choice." Ransom held up his tumbler and reached to clink glasses with Quinn. He took a sip and set the glass down. Wynter snuggled closer and Ransom put his arm around her.

Quinn traced Ransom's arm with her eyes before pouring three more shots of rum. He paid no notice, instead entranced by the movie.

It was half an hour later when the Terminator's angry red point of view showed up again. All three downed their shots. Wynter looked a little green, even in the flickering glow of the TV.

"You okay, Bug?"

"Feeling a little dizzy." Wynter blinked slowly.

"How about you, Ransom?"

He looked at Quinn, his bloodshot eyes clashing with his wide smile, the poster-boy for *Horny & Wasted Magazine*. "Doing great."

Quinn knew it was an act. She pulled a throw pillow to her face to hide her smile and slid down on the sofa cushions, her feet propped on the coffee table.

Tonight was getting good. There was no telling where things might lead.

C

CASH STROLLED UP to Jake's house in the northern section of Newhaven. The two-story Cape Code-style home, light gray with white trim, complete with two dormer windows and an attached double-wide garage, sat atop the slightly inclined Mortimer Avenue.

Having lived his entire life in a trailer park, Cash had always felt a little out of place among the "northies." But his dad's voice rang out in his head, loud and clear. "Fake it till you make it. Never let them see you sweat." Part cliché, part deodorant commercial, it did have a good message. He'd make it one of these days, and if he was lucky, Wynter would be at his side.

Not quite eight o'clock yet, the clear summer sky offered warming light as the sun headed to the horizon. The air carried the scent of freshly mown grass with hints of motor oil. Simple and pleasant.

He stepped to the house's grand entrance, took a fortifying breath, and rang the doorbell. Almost at once he could hear thumping and thudding as Jake made his way down the stairs.

"I got it!" Jake yelled from behind the door. The latch rattled and swung open. "Hey dude, come on in."

Cash knew the drill. He slipped off his shoes and placed them on a mat beside the door.

Jake's father sat in a recliner in the living room, a newspaper spread out in front of him. He crimped the top down and gave a nod. "Nice to see you again, Cash."

"Come on." Jake was already half-way up the stairs. "I've got something to show you."

Cash paused at the entrance to the living room. "Thanks for having me over, Mr. Peterson." Jake tugged at his coat sleeve. "I'm going to head up, so..."

Mr. Peterson raised a brow. Cash detected a small smile on the man's face before the shield of newspaper raised again.

Jake led the way up the stairs and disappeared into the last room of the adjoining hallway. Cash passed a closed door, a placard with the name "Chloe" hanging on it surrounded with delicate paper flowers. He imagined the interior of the room to be just as light and delicate.

Cash entered Jake's room, which looked like a pawn shop and an electronics store had collided head on. Jake claimed it appeared disorganized only to the casual observer. The dormer window let in ample natural light during the day, but Jake had turned on the bedroom's overhead light to help illuminate the entire room.

"How's your sister doing?"

"Oh, you mean the golden child?"

Cash shrugged.

"Chloe's doing fine. She finished her first year at RISD and chose to stay in Providence and work over the summer." Jake huffed and closed the door. "I'm going to invent my own career. I hope my parents invest in me the same way."

He pulled out a molded plastic case with "JVC VideoMovie" in bold white lettering on the side. Jake laid it on the bed, flipped the latches and opened it. "Look at this baby."

Nestled inside the case in form-fitting sections sat a small video camera and all its accessories.

"Remember the video camera Marty McFly used in *Back to the Future?* That was the GR-C1." Jake's eyes were wide with excitement, his sister and parents temporarily forgotten. "Well, this baby is next generation. The GR-C7. It just came out."

"Wow." Cash admired the camcorder's sleek lines. "I like that it's red. Really stands out."

"Aren't you going to ask me how much it was?"

"I wasn't, actually," Cash said. "But how much?"

"If I told you, I'd have to kill you." Jake laughed. "It wasn't cheap." He lifted the camcorder out of its case, slipped it onto his right hand, and turned on the power. He aimed the camcorder's lens at Cash. "And, action!"

"Nope." Cash blocked the lens with his hand. "Are you recording?"

"No tape loaded." Jake panned around his room, then stepped to the window. "The zoom's pretty good too." The lens whirred and spun. "I can see Roxy's house from here."

"Let me see."

Jake handed the camcorder to Cash. "If you drop it, I'm dead meat."

Cash looked annoyed. "I won't drop it. This isn't rocket science." He palmed the camcorder and placed the viewfinder to his eye. "How do you zoom?"

"There's a rocker at your fingers or use the lever on the lens."

Cash pointed the camcorder out the window toward the street and houses below. "Jake, this is so damn cool." He panned left and right, taking in the details of the street through the miniature TV screen in the viewfinder.

A car's engine noise reverberated along the street and made the window rattle. Cash looked up from the camcorder, isolated the source of the sound, and returned his eye to the viewfinder.

*A black Barracuda.*

He followed the car until it stopped at a driveway across the street, two houses down. Cash zoomed in all the way, the viewfinder's image expanding before his eye. "Bullseye. Guess who just pulled up?"

"Who?" Jake continued to flip through the camcorder's manual without looking up.

"If I had a rocket launcher..."

"What?" Jake dropped the manual. "Let me see."

Cash braced himself against the window frame. "I knew Roxy lived close to you, but I didn't realize it was *this* close."

Jake peeked out the window to confirm what Cash was looking at. "Shit, dude. Step back." He ran to the bedroom door and killed the overhead lights. "You were backlit. She could have seen you."

"Relax." Cash handed the camcorder back to Jake. "She didn't."

Jake pressed his back against the wall and inched the camcorder's lens just above the lower window frame. "Don't underestimate her." He looked through the viewfinder to see Roxy run out of her driveway and hop into the passenger seat. The Barracuda peeled out leaving a blue cloud of smoke behind. "She's smarter than she looks."

"Who?"

Jake turned back to Cash, confused, then his eyes cleared. "Both of them. But especially Jezebel."

"Jizz-ball." Cash laughed.

"Whatever. I don't want to talk about her anymore." He turned off the camcorder and set it back in its case and closed it. He sat on the hardwood floor and used the foot of his bed as a backrest.

Cash studied Jake's room and all the technology it represented. "So are you going to become a famous movie director now?"

"I don't know. Maybe. But if I had to decide right now, I'd go into video games." Jake looked at his collection of video game consoles with fondness. "Like actually programming them."

"I guess that's a thing now." Cash sat on the floor opposite Jake, his back against the wall. "Never realized people actually made video games, but of course they do."

"I just have to convince my parents it's a thing with a future. Shouldn't be hard since they love board games. What about you?"

Cash shook his head, resigned. "I'll probably pump gas for the rest of my life. This town has me by the balls."

"Only if you let it." Jake looked Cash square in the eye. "You're good with people. I'll make the games. You sell them. Together we get rich."

"Sounds good." He tried to sound optimistic, but in his heart Cash knew it would never come to pass.

"We could hire your girlfriend to take photos."

Cash waved him off. "Wynter's not my girlfriend."

"Bullshit. You knew who I was talking about." Jake smirked. "Have you asked her out yet?"

"Not directly."

Jake narrowed his eyes and gave Cash a sideways look. "What does that mean?"

"I did hang out at the park with her and Quinn last Saturday, but I sort of invited myself along."

"Dude. You and Wynter... *and* Quinn?" Jake eyed him with surprise. "Why didn't you invite me?"

"Sorry. It was a spur of the moment thing," Cash said. "I ran into her after my shift."

"Don't worry about it. I was at the Starlite."

"Donkey Kong?"

Jake smiled and nodded. "You know me too well."

"Could you find a girlfriend there?"

"Maybe. They've got Ms. Pac-Man at the Starlite. Girls love that game, but I suck at it."

"Practice makes perfect."

"Whatever." Jake rested his arms on his raised knees. "Back to you and two hot girls at the park. On a Saturday night."

"With a six-pack of Grain Belt."

"And beer? Fuck. What base did you get to?"

"It's not like that. I struck out."

Jake stared at him, incredulous. "What happened?"

Cash tugged at a frayed hole on his socks. "Wynter brought this guy with her. He came out of nowhere."

"Wait. What?" Jake did a double take.

"I'm serious," Cash said. "I literally blinked and this guy was on top of her. They were making out, definitely first base, maybe second. I don't know. He stopped when he realized we were watching him. She called him Ransom. But here's the weirdest part."

"There's more?" Jake ran a hand through his unkempt hair.

"This guy is apparently from Wynter's dreams."

Jake slumped back against his bed and stared at Cash. "No. You're fucking with me."

"I'm not." Cash met Jake's confused gaze. "I swear."

The bedroom fell silent as Jake tried to process Cash's words. "Don't make me regret asking this, but... what happened next?"

"I got into a fight with the guy and I left."

"Dude!" Jake buried his face in his hands. "Shit, I hate cliffhanger endings!"

Cash laughed. "Sorry."

"Have you talked with her about it?"

Cash shook his head. "She normally buys breakfast at Finn's before her shift at the plaza, but not last week. I didn't see her at all."

"You should call her."

"I know. I will."

Jake jumped up and grabbed the cordless phone from its cradle by his bed. "Call her now." He handed the phone to Cash.

Cash stared at the numbers on the handset, his hand trembling with anxiety. He knew Jake wouldn't let up until he called her.

*What's the worst that could happen?*

Cash stood, dialed, and began to pace the room. The line trilled in his ear. "It's ringing."

Jake stepped close but Cash waved him off.

"It's just ringing. Listen." Cash placed the handset's speaker to Jake's ear.

"Someone picked up," Jake whispered and pushed the phone away.

"Uh, hello?" Cash waited. "Hi Mrs. LaCroix. Is Wynter home? Oh, this is Cash, by the way." He silently chastised himself for his poor delivery and listened. "Okay. I'll try again later. Sorry for bothering you. Bye." He ended the call and handed the phone back to Jake.

He returned the phone to its charging cradle. "Well?"

"She's up at Quinn's cabin. Back on Sunday."

"Probably with her imaginary boyfriend." Jake's words were out before he could stop them. "Sorry, dude. I... I didn't mean—"

"Forget about it. It *is* as crazy as it sounds." Cash jammed his hands into his pockets. "Want to hit the Starlite? Play some Donkey Kong?"

"You're on." Jake grinned. "Maybe some Ms. Pac-Man too. You can be my wing man."

Cash followed Jake out of his bedroom, but even with their new plans set in motion, he couldn't get the image of Wynter and Ransom out of his head.

C

"Bug! Wake up." Quinn's voice filtered through the glistening metal endoskeleton that had surrounded Wynter's troubled sleep. The movie had left a mark. Even in the dim light of the cabin's living room, she could feel a dull pounding build behind her eyes as she cracked her eyelids open.

"He's gone." Quinn sat on the edge of the sofa next to Wynter. The TV flickered with a late-night infomercial for the ThighMaster.

"What?"

"Ransom disappeared. I looked away for a second and he was

gone. I don't know who fell asleep first, you or him, but just like that." Quinn snapped her fingers. "He was gone."

"When did it happen?"

"Like, five minutes ago."

Wynter rubbed her temples. "I was just dozing."

The gears in Quinn's brain began to turn. She accentuated her thoughts by counting on her fingers. "Last week at the park, you fell asleep first. Tonight, Ransom was first. So for Ransom to stick around longer, both of you need to stay awake." She looked at Wynter. "What do you think?"

Wynter rolled the theory around in her head. "It sounds right. But we might need to test it a few more times to make sure."

"Okay." Quinn looked at the TV. "What do you want to do now? Watch a porno?"

Wynter groaned.

"Forget that. How about *Sixteen Candles* or... wait. What about *Dreamscape*? Have you seen that? We might get some ideas."

"Sorry to be a buzzkill, but I'd really like some Tylenol." Wynter's hair shrouded her face. "And some real sleep. Start fresh tomorrow."

Quinn smiled and nodded but Wynter could see her disappointment underneath. "Sure. I'll be right back." She disappeared into the bathroom off the kitchen and returned a moment later with two white pills and a glass of water.

Wynter popped the pills onto her tongue and washed their bitter taste down with a gulp of water. "Thanks. Tomorrow will be better, I promise."

Quinn shut down the entertainment center and followed Wynter up the spiral staircase, stopping at Wynter's bedroom door. "Can I sleep in your room?"

"Like the slumber parties we used to have." Wynter smiled. "Absolutely."

"Cool."

"Or you could—" Quinn had run to her room to grab her

mattress before Wynter could suggest sleeping in the same bed like they had a week ago. It had felt comfortable and safe, without the sexual tension she felt with Ransom. It was what Wynter needed right now, just two friends sharing the same space.

Quinn slid a twin mattress out of her room and flopped it onto the floor next to Wynter's bed. "There. I'll get some extra pillows and blankets."

Wynter thought her headache was easing a bit, but the sooner she was in bed the better. She smiled at the sleeping arrangement. A mattress for Quinn in the same room would work out fine. They'd be like sisters.

She dug out her pajamas and toiletries and headed to the bathroom, passing Quinn with an armful of pillows and blankets on the way.

"You want some popcorn?"

"Sure," Wynter said, not wanting to disappoint Quinn again. "Do you have the butter kind?"

Quinn was already descending the stairs to the main floor. "Yup."

Wynter stepped into the bathroom and closed the door. As bathrooms go, it was basic, with a sink, toilet, towel rack, and a stand-up shower. It reminded her of home. She undressed and pulled on her pajamas. She took out her toothbrush but the smell of buttered popcorn filtering under the door convinced her to put it back. Her stomach growled.

She pulled open the door. "Damn that smells good."

"Tastes even better." Quinn's voice called back from the bedroom.

Wynter returned with her clothes, leaving her toiletries next to the sink. Quinn had filled two Tupperware bowls with hot popcorn and had the rest of the two liter bottle of Coke from earlier. Two clean tumblers sat on the dresser.

"Don't worry. No rum this time."

Wynter planted herself next to Quinn on her mattress and took one of the bowls. "Thanks." She stuffed a handful of popcorn into her mouth and relaxation washed over her. "This is exactly what I needed." She looked at Quinn. "If you're willing to drive, I'll take you to Lucy's for breakfast tomorrow. Okay?"

"You're on."

The two girls slapped hands and continued munching on their popcorn.

"Do you ever wonder why Ransom appeared in your life?"

"Not really," Wynter said. "Why?"

"Maybe he's here for a reason."

"Yeah, to be my boyfriend." Wynter glanced at Quinn. "Ransom will do anything for me."

"It's just that I always thought you'd end up with Cash."

"He does make my knees trembly and skating with him at the Starlite was fun." Wynter shrugged. "But he hasn't asked me out yet."

"Maybe he's shy."

"I don't know. I'm just happy to be living a fantasy for a while."

Quinn ran her fingers through her popcorn, then licked her fingers. "It's going to be weird when we go back to school."

"I haven't even thought past next week, let alone September." Wynter raised her chin high and sighed. "I'm just going to enjoy my summer." She laid her head on Quinn's shoulder. "Tell me about *Top Gun*."

Quinn was the movie queen. She saw more movies than Wynter could keep track of. For some movies they went together, but most of them were a family affair. Quinn had an amazing ability to remember the plots and describe them in detail. It was her secret superpower. *Top Gun* was no exception, particularly because of all the "beefcake," action, and romance.

The two of them ate popcorn and finished the Coke as Quinn recounted the movie until neither of them could keep their eyes open.

○

Wynter found Ransom lying in the long grass in front of the cabin wearing his usual hoodie, white T-shirt, and jeans. The sun warmed her shoulders but hadn't quite reached the moist roots of the grass. Her feet glistened with dew. She laid down beside Ransom, her white sundress billowing, and snaked her arms around his waist.

"I've been looking for you, like, forever," she whispered into his perfect ear.

Ransom stirred. "Wynter?"

"Who else?"

He rolled to face her. "It's weird to sleep in your dreams. I'm usually awake."

"When you're in my world, the rules are different," Wynter said. "Rum really does have an effect."

"When you're in my world, there are no rules." He smiled and kissed her.

"Maybe, but your world's inside mine."

"Okay," Ransom said. "There are no rules in *our* world."

Wynter laid a hand on his temple. "How's your head?"

Ransom tilted his head in thought. "My head's fine. Clear as a bell."

"You're lucky."

"Yes, I am." He leaned in for another kiss, this time longer and hotter.

Wynter eased away and took a breath. If she wore glasses like Quinn, the lenses might have fogged up. "Horny, too, I see."

Ransom shrugged. "Guilty as charged."

"I think I had my first hangover last night. I still feel it just a little."

Concern spread across Ransom's face. "Is there anything I can do?"

"How about breakfast? Me and Quinn are going to Lucy's. It'd be a new experience."

"I don't have to be asked twice." Ransom held Wynter's hand. She smiled and kissed him. "Let's go."

○

WYNTER OPENED HER eyes to find Quinn sitting cross-legged at the side of the bed, nose to nose with her, dressed and ready to go.

"I'm starving." Quinn clacked her teeth behind a grin.

Wynter yawned. "So am I."

"Me, too." Ransom poked his head over Wynter's shoulder. "Breakfast at Lucy's?"

Quinn rocked backward, supporting her body with her hands. "Wait. How does he…" She alternated her gaze between Ransom and Wynter.

"I told him," Wynter said.

"Of course you did."

"That was okay, right?"

Quinn laughed until she felt the power of Ransom's smile and blue-eyed stare. She swallowed hard and returned her eyes to Wynter. "Of course, silly. What are you waiting for?"

Wynter leaped from the bed and sent the covers flying. She grabbed her clothes and shuffled to the bathroom. "I'll get dressed. Then we can go."

Ransom sat up and swung his legs off the bed. He wore the same shoes as Wynter. "Lucky I'm already dressed."

"Is it?" A sly smile crept across Quinn's lips and she narrowed her eyes. She arched her back, pretending to stretch.

Ransom raised a brow at her display.

She stood, bounced to the door, and called down the hall so Wynter would hear. "I'll be in Blue Belle waiting." Ransom followed Quinn with his eyes as she disappeared down the staircase.

Wynter popped out of the bathroom dressed, with her pajamas balled up under her arm. "I'm right behind you." As she reached her bedroom, she dodged Ransom waiting for her and threw her pajamas on the bed. She stood on tiptoes and kissed Ransom's nose. "Let's go." She held out her hand and he took it.

Quinn had Blue Belle's engine purring when they stepped out of the cabin. "Lock the door," she called back.

Wynter fiddled with the turn button on the doorknob until it locked and closed the front door behind her. Ransom followed her to the passenger side of the car.

"I'll get in the back." Ransom tilted the backrest forward and climbed onto the rear bench seat.

Quinn shot a quick glance at Ransom through the rear view mirror, then looked at Wynter. "You're probably going to have... the Belgian waffles with strawberries and whipped cream, right?"

Wynter smirked back. "Not sure, but the odds are good." She looked back at Ransom. "You're going to love Lucy's."

Quinn twisted in her seat to face Ransom. "Promise me you won't eat everything on the menu."

Ransom shifted his eyes back and forth between the two girls. "Okay. I promise."

Quinn backed Blue Belle out of the driveway and followed the road back to the interstate.

Halfway between Lake Gilberg and Newhaven, Lucy's Burger Stop had served travelers of I94 since 1963. The restaurant was a particular favorite with long-haul truckers due to the ample parking lot designed for eighteen-wheelers. Extra stalls close to the restaurant were provided for regular vehicles.

Lucy's offered burgers twenty-four hours a day, seven days a week, but also varied the menu depending on the time of day. Breakfast was one of their specialties.

Quinn found a parking spot close to the entrance. The three of them hopped out of the VW and headed inside, the entrance door jingling. Quinn waved at one of the waitresses and she gestured them in.

"Sit anywhere, Quinn," the waitress called out.

"Is that Lucy?" Ransom asked.

"No, that's Rhonda." Quinn navigated through the restaurant looking for an empty booth. "She's been here, like, forever. She's awesome."

Lucy's must have had a deal with Coca-Cola because branded memorabilia going back decades, before the diner existed, filled every nook and cranny. From gas pumps turned into gum ball machines, to toys, figurines, planter boxes, and curtains, every seat offered a view of something with the Coca-Cola logo on it.

The restaurant provided a row of counter seating for those eating alone and booths for groups of up to six, if you didn't mind getting a little friendly. The three teens slid into one of the last remaining booths, the red vinyl bench seats with white trim worn smooth from twenty-three years of backsides. Quinn sat on one side of the booth's Formica table top, Wynter and Ransom facing her. They all flipped their coffee mugs over.

A young server approached the table with a glass decanter half filled with coffee and filled their cups. "Your server will be right with you," she said before flitting to another table.

Rhonda approached their booth holding three menus. "Quinn. And…" She thought for a moment. "Wynter?" She gave Ransom a once over. "You, I've never seen before."

"My name's Ransom." He held out his hand.

Rhonda sent the girls a side look. "A gentleman, too." She took Ransom's hand and they shared a quick, firm handshake.

"Nice to meet you, Rhonda," Ransom said.

"Likewise." Rhonda handed out the menus. "I'll be back in a bit to take your orders."

"Remember, you promised not to order everything," Quinn said. "We still have to pay for it all."

Wynter reached across the table and placed her hand on Quinn's. "It's my treat, remember?"

Ransom leaned in and lowered his voice. "What's the worst thing on the menu?"

Wynter and Quinn looked at each other and giggled. "Liver and onions," they said in unison.

"Hands down, the worst," Quinn added as she picked up her menu.

"Okay. I'll order everything *except* that." Ransom eyed both girls playfully.

Wynter shoved his shoulder. "You'll order one meal because that's all I can afford."

"I'm joking." Ransom picked up the menu and scanned its offerings. "What's good?"

"First, what are you having, Bug?"

"Belgian waffles with strawberries, whipped cream, *and* bacon."

"I knew it." Quinn set her menu down. "I'm having French toast with a side of hashbrowns." She looked at Ransom. "Pick something different so we can all share if we want to."

Quinn watched Wynter lean in to Ransom as she pointed at his menu.

"The big breakfasts are always good," Wynter said. "So are the bennies and the omelets. You really can't go wrong."

"I'm super hungry, so I'm going to get the 'New-Heaven Big Bite.' "

Rhonda reappeared as if by magic. "Looks like you're ready to order." All three relayed their choices as she scribbled them down on her order pad. "It'll be about fifteen minutes."

"She And I" sung by Alabama floated from speakers in the

shape of Coca-Cola soda cans strategically placed throughout the diner.

The entrance door jingled and Anson stepped in. One hand held a Great American Donut branded thermos. Rhonda waved at him. He tipped his wide-brimmed campaign hat at her before taking it off and placed his thermos on the counter.

Anson scanned the diner. It didn't take him long to spot Wynter and Quinn. He strolled over to their booth. "You're a little far from home on a Saturday morning."

"We're staying at my parents' cabin for the weekend." Quinn's eyes lingered a little too long on Anson. She mock-fanned herself, mouthing the words "so hot."

"Now, you..." Anson pointed at Ransom. "We haven't met."

Ransom jutted out his hand. "My name's Ransom, sir. I'm just visiting for the summer."

"Ransom." Anson raised a brow. "That's a unique name."

"Everyone says so. I like it."

Wynter and Quinn exchanged a nervous glance.

"Well, you lucked out with these two," Anson said. "I can't think of anyone better than Quinn and Wynter to give you a tour of Newhaven."

Rhonda returned with Anson's thermos. "Filled with the good stuff."

"Thanks, Ronnie." Anson eyed the counter. A customer stood to leave, freeing up a seat. "I think I'll stay for a slice of pie. What's good today?"

"Fresh chokecherry."

"Sold." Anson turned back to the booth. "Welcome to Newhaven, Ransom. I'm sure the girls have lots to show you." He strolled toward the free seat at the counter.

Quinn choked on her coffee, sputtering into her napkin. She slid off her bench seat. "I need to go to the bathroom." She motioned to Wynter to join her.

"Me too. I'll be right back." Wynter scooted off the bench, then hesitated with a look of uncertainty. "Are you…"

"This might not be my regular world, but I know what you know." Ransom blew on his coffee and took a sip, watching Wynter and Quinn disappear into the women's restroom.

Ransom surveyed the room. It held so much detail, nothing like the dream worlds he was used to inhabiting. They were often so limited, like being on a movie set where the world ended at the exterior walls. He would only see what was needed in the context of the dream. But reality was vast and seemed to go on forever. He could get used to this.

The entrance door jingled, bringing Ransom out of his thoughts. Two teenaged girls about his age, one brunette, one blond, stood at the nexus of the diner. He felt he knew them – or Wynter knew them—but their names were fuzzy.

Anson glanced behind him from his seat at the counter. He straightened his posture upon seeing the girls. They looked at him and moved on, uninterested. His eyes flicked to Ransom ever so briefly before returning to his pie.

The girls strolled through the diner looking for a free booth and spotted Ransom. Without asking they slid onto the bench seat across from him.

"Hey handsome," the brunette said. "You lost?"

Ransom shook his head slowly and sipped his coffee, watching them both. The one with crimped brunette hair locked her gaze with his. He could feel attraction between them, just as intense as anything he had felt with Wynter, but it was different. There was an undercurrent of discomfort that he didn't like.

"You don't talk much."

Ransom sat quietly. He flicked his eyes toward Anson for just a second and saw that he was monitoring them from the row of counter seats. The brunette caught his move.

"Officer Jacobs is a pussy," she said. "He won't do jack. Especially here."

Then, like a magic eight ball revealing its secret answers, their names bubbled up in his head.

*Jezebel and Roxy.*

And they were bad news.

○

THE COCA-COLA campaign continued in the bathroom. The stall doors were painted to look like old Coca-Cola vending machines, which Wynter thought was a poor choice considering toilets sat behind them. Frosted glass Coke bottle shades hung from the lights, and the red porcelain sinks featured Coke's iconic white wavy line.

Wynter stood at the sink washing her hands. She half expected Coke to flow from the taps instead of water. Quinn touched up her lipstick.

"Why are you doing that?" Wynter dried her hands. "You're just going to end up eating it."

"Do I need to spell it out for you?" Quinn looked at her through the mirror. "*Anson.*"

"Now that's a dream."

"Let me live the fantasy. Maybe I should make myself my *own* Anson." Quinn pressed her lips together, puckered, then smiled. "So, have you gone all the way with Ransom yet?"

"No." Even though she was talking to Quinn, her best friend, she could still feel the heat of embarrassment rise in her cheeks.

"Not even in your dreams?"

Wynter shook her head, feeling more self-conscious with every passing second.

"What are you waiting for? This ability of yours might disappear as quickly as it came."

"I'm just not ready."

Quinn touched up some lipstick at the corner of her mouth.

"I've been thinking about you and Ransom and how the whole sex stuff would work."

Wynter shushed Quinn with an index finger held to her lips, tiptoed to the first stall, and knocked. The door rocked open slightly. She did the same to the other two stalls and was met with silence.

"Sorry," she said. "I didn't want anyone to overhear us. You were saying? About the sex stuff?"

Quinn was more experienced in the ways of dating and boys even though they had gone through the same sex education classes in high school. With her real world experience, she had become Wynter's living encyclopedia.

"We know Ransom disappears. So, like, would his cum disappear too, assuming he cums? Would that make him sterile?"

Wynter glanced at a small pool of translucent liquid soap that had collected on the counter and shuddered. "Whatever he eats disappears, so that must mean what he leaves behind disappears too. Remember his drawstring."

"Right. I forgot about that. But we have to be sure." Quinn placed her hands on Wynter's shoulders. "You know what this means, don't you?"

"What?"

"We have to test this." Quinn held her gaze.

"How?" Wynter knew what the answer was going to be but asked anyway.

"You have to give him a hand job."

Wynter swallowed hard against the gorge rising in her throat.

Quinn could sense her trepidation. "I don't mean a blow job, not unless you want to."

Wynter shook her head, her face a shade paler. "Not there yet."

Quinn wrapped her arms around her in a quick tight hug. "Oh Bug, it's just your hand, his thing, and some K-Y. I can show you how later if you want."

"Show me...?" Wynter's eyes went wide.

"No, I don't mean on Ransom." Quinn stepped back and laughed. "I'd use a banana or a carrot or something." She scanned Wynter's face. "You look like you're going to throw up."

"It's that obvious?"

Quinn sighed. "You don't have to do this. We can figure out another way. But think of the possibilities. If his cum disappears, you can't get pregnant."

"And if it *doesn't* disappear, then what?" Wynter scrunched her brows as her thoughts ran wild. "Ransom came from *my* head, so I'd get *myself* pregnant?"

"You could actually go fuck yourself!" Quinn snickered. "But getting knocked up can't be possible."

"Ransom shouldn't be possible, but he's physically out there." Wynter pointed to the bathroom door.

"Real but imaginary," Quinn said. "A paradox. Do you think it's possible to have a real imaginary baby?"

Wynter shook her head. "I have no idea, but I'm going a little crazy thinking about it."

The two girls stared at each other for a moment. A customer pushed open the bathroom door and entered a stall.

"You think our food's ready?"

"Probably. It feels like we've been in here for hours." Quinn puckered at the mirror and gave her lips one last inspection before pushing open the door. "What the fuck?"

Wynter spotted Jezebel and Roxy sitting across from Ransom and her stomach dropped. "Oh, shit." She summoned her courage and followed Quinn across the red, white, and black tiled floor, directly toward their booth.

○

RHONDA STEPPED UP to Ransom's booth and did a double take at Jezebel and Roxy. "Am I missing something?"

"Nope." Ransom pointed at the girls. "They were just leaving."

"Says who?" Jezebel snarled. "I haven't had breakfast yet. And I see three plates."

"They're ours." Quinn stepped up behind Rhonda. "You can set the plates down." She leaned into the table and lowered her voice. "And you two can get the *fuck* out of here."

"Or what?" Jezebel matched Quinn's steely stare with one of her own.

"Or things get messy."

"Or I kick out the whole lot of you." Rhonda glanced up the row of counter seats and motioned at Anson, who was already watching the developing scene. He wiped his mouth with a napkin and slid off the stool. She set the plates down on the table and backed away.

"You're not invited." Wynter slid onto the bench seat beside Ransom. She pulled his face to hers and landed a slow kiss, then hooked her arm around his neck, a satisfied smirk on her face. "You deaf *and* dumb? What part of 'you're not invited' don't you understand?"

"How are things going over here?" Anson stepped up to the booth next to Quinn. "Jezebel. Roxy. How about you find somewhere else to sit."

Jezebel spoke out of the side of her mouth but dead-eyed Wynter. "Let's move, Roxy. Something here *stinks*." She slid off the bench seat followed by Roxy.

The diner's ambiance had fallen into a hush, as if placed on pause. Quinn and Anson stepped back to give the intruders space to leave.

Jezebel spun around and leaned on the table toward Wynter. "I always get what I want, *bitch*." She jammed her hand into the strawberry waffles, grabbed a handful, and took a bite, dropping the rest in a mangled mess on Wynter's plate.

Licking whipped cream and strawberry juice off her fingers suggestively, Jezebel faced Anson and wiped the rest of her hand on his shirt. "You're a gutless turd." She let her eyes roam the length of his body, hovering on the revolver strapped to his hip. She flipped his tie with her hand and walked to the entrance of the diner.

"She's right, you know." Roxy giggled and followed her leader outside. "Gutless," she said in a sing-song voice.

"I thought she couldn't talk," Ransom said.

Quinn reclaimed her seat across from Ransom and Wynter. "Roxy can talk. She just doesn't have many words floating around in that empty head of hers." She looked at Anson. "Why do you let her walk all over you?"

"That's not a battle worth fighting." Anson surveyed the diner as the ambiance returned to normal. "I'd rather everyone here have a good and safe experience."

"I'd rather you kicked her ass." Quinn pulled her French toast across the table and dug in.

Wynter grimaced at the mess on her plate and pushed it away. It looked like fresh road kill.

Ransom leaned in to her. "I guess ordering the Big Bite was a smart move. We can share." He began cutting up the bacon and potatoes into smaller pieces.

"I'll leave you three to your breakfast." Anson strolled toward the diner entrance. Before leaving he caught Rhonda leaving the kitchen with a plate of strawberry waffles. He looked at the plate and smiled. "You're a class act, Rhonda. And the pie was..." He kissed his fingertips. "Perfect." He pulled a ten dollar bill from his wallet and handed it to her. "Not negotiable today."

"Thanks. I appreciate it."

"What goes around." Anson placed his hat on his head and exited into the morning sunshine, his thermos handle looped through one finger.

Rhonda approached Wynter with a new plate of strawberry waffles and swapped it for the mess that Jezebel had created.

Wynter's eyes brightened. "Aw, thanks, Rhonda! You didn't need to do that."

"Happy to do it, Wynter, darling. We take care of our customers." Rhonda looked to the front entrance. Jezebel and Roxy were nowhere in sight. "We might have to ban those two. This wasn't the first time they've caused trouble." She returned her eyes to the table. "Enjoy your breakfast." Rhonda placed the bill on the table and hustled off to help another customer.

Wynter grabbed the bill and pulled it next to her plate, then dug into her waffles.

Quinn spoke between bites of French toast. "So where did those balls come from?"

"What balls?"

"I think she means the 'deaf and dumb' comment earlier." Ransom looked to Quinn for her reaction. "Am I right?"

Quinn nodded. "That's something I would have done."

Wynter shrugged. "I was with you guys. I guess I felt safe."

"We need more of that 'take the bull by the horns' attitude from you, Bug." Quinn sipped her coffee. "I liked it."

"I'll work on it." Wynter cast her eyes down to her plate and smiled subtly to herself.

Ransom speared a piece of sausage with his fork. "So, what are we going to do today? Any interesting *jobs* planned?"

"Jobs?" Quinn sent a confused look at Ransom, then to Wynter. "What do you mean job—?" She coughed and her eyes went wide. "Oh my God." She hid her face with her hand.

Both girls blushed.

"What?" Ransom raised a brow. "Was it something I said?"

"Let's just eat." Quinn finished her French toast and washed it down with coffee. She looked at Wynter, then at Ransom. "Maybe the Big Bite isn't big enough."

Ransom mopped up his eggs with his potato hashbrowns. "I could eat more. What did you have in mind?"

"How about a Bennie Big Stack." Quinn winked at Wynter.

"It's two servings of Eggs Benedict stacked on top of each other. With more hash browns."

"Sounds great." Ransom looked up and licked his lips.

Quinn caught Rhonda's attention and ordered Ransom's second breakfast.

"This one is on me," Quinn said.

When the food arrived, Wynter and Quinn watched Ransom eat.

"Where does it all go?" Wynter propped up her head with her hand, her eyes blinking heavily.

"Somewhere good I hope." Quinn smiled almost imperceptibly.

○

AFTER BREAKFAST ALL three returned outside to Blue Belle. Quinn backed out of the parking lot and merged back onto the Interstate, heading west toward the cabin. "I think we're all going to need a nap after that feast."

There were no complaints from Wynter in the passenger seat or Ransom in the back. His eyes looked heavier in the rear view mirror and Quinn hoped it wasn't a distortion.

The Volkswagen was on the highway no more than a minute when a black Barracuda roared up behind, tailgating within inches of the back bumper.

"Guess who's back." Through the rear view mirror, Quinn saw Jezebel and Roxy staring back at her. Jezebel looked furious.

Wynter and Ransom turned in their seats to look. Roxy laughed and raised both her middle fingers at them.

Quinn's mind began to work. She had to ditch them but Blue Belle was no match for Jezebel's Barracuda and its V8 engine. That black bitch could outmaneuver and outrun her little VW.

And if Jezebel found the cabin it would bring the weekend to screeching halt.

The sign alerting drivers to Exit 183 to Lake Gilberg shot past the right side of the car. If Quinn missed the turnoff the next exit was at least an hour away.

"Hey guys. Hold on." Quinn gripped the steering wheel with white knuckles. "It's going to, like, get a little freaky."

"What are you going to do?" Wynter alternated her worried gaze between Quinn and the hulking black machine in the back window.

Quinn shut out all distractions, narrowed her eyes, and focused on the road ahead. She hit the brakes for a moment, tapping the Barracuda's front bumper, then floored the gas. The little Volkswagen's back end dipped as its engine strained and pulled ahead of the Barracuda. But the gain was short-lived.

"They've switched lanes, Quinn." Ransom followed the Barracuda out the VW's driver-side windows.

"Shut up! I know." Quinn managed a quick glance out her window to see Roxy screaming at her.

"We're going to fuck you up, bitch!" Roxy sat back and laughed. Jezebel's face was just as determined and hard as Quinn's.

"That's our exit!" Wynter pointed straight ahead. "We're going to miss it."

"Quiet!" Quinn looked ahead. Exit 183 was closing fast, maybe 400 feet away. It was now or never. "And hold on."

Quinn counted for two seconds before pulling the steering wheel hard right. The Volkswagen lurched right across a strip of grassy median and onto the exit ramp, missing the exit sign by inches.

Jezebel had no chance to follow. The Barracuda shot down the highway with no opportunity to turn around. Quinn laid into her horn and laughed like a maniac. "Take that, motherfuckers!"

She looked at Wynter, at her hand clutching the door handle with all her strength.

"Sorry, Bug."

"I thought I was going to die." Wynter took heavy breaths to try and calm herself. "Seriously."

"I had no choice." Quinn turned onto a backroad shrouded by trees. "I had to lose them."

"Now I really need to lie down."

"Sure thing," Quinn said. "We're in the clear and the cabin is about ten minutes away." She cast a glance in the rear view mirror. "How're you doing back there?"

Ransom locked his gaze with Quinn's and gave her a thumbs up. He looked tired.

A shiver ran up Quinn's back. She navigated through back roads and beside farm fields, all the while replaying her bathroom conversation with Wynter. The future was unwritten, but she hoped to guide it a little.

○

THE BARRACUDA'S SIGNATURE engine noise had burned itself into Cash's brain. His brush with death outside the Starlite a week ago had made sure of that.

When Cash heard the tell-tale rumble through the store's open door, he knew two things for sure: Jezebel was back, and she would raise shit. Lucky for him, the station was presently free of customers.

As expected, the black Barracuda rolled up next to pump number one, Jezebel driving with Roxy riding shotgun.

Finn's Gas N Go operated self-serve pumps. "I ain't nobody's servant," Finn had said. The pumps were controlled from within the store and once a customer had prepaid for their gas, Cash would turn the pump on, allowing them to fill up.

When Jezebel remained in the car, Cash knew something was up. She revved the engine then laid into the horn long enough to rouse Finn from the back of the garage.

"What in the hell is going on out here?" Finn recognized the Barracuda too. "Shite. What's wrong with those gals? Take care of it or I'll take *Ciara* to her."

Cash glanced at the bat hanging beside the back door to the garage. In all his time working at Finn's, he had never seen Finn use the bat on anything. He didn't want to start now. "Yes, sir," he said and walked out of the store.

Cash leaned against pump number one, careful not to get too close to Jezebel's open window. "What do you want?"

Jezebel took her hand off the horn and rested her arm out the window. "Where's your girlfriend?"

"What girlfriend?"

"*Whiner.*" Jezebel sneered. "The red-headed bitch who likes to *wear* nachos instead of *eat* them."

Roxy yukked at the insult.

Cash felt his temper rise but he had to keep his cool, especially at work. "She's just a friend."

"Wait. Maybe you're right. I saw her locking lips with some hot guy at Lucy's this morning." She turned to Roxy. "Cash has turned to trash."

Cash grew impatient. "What do you want?"

Jezebel let her eyes wander down his body. "You tell your *ex*-girlfriend that I'm coming for her. Her new boyfriend too."

"Fuck you."

Jezebel spoke through clenched teeth. "Have it your way." She floored the gas and laid a strip of rubber past the pumps all the way to the street.

Cash choked on the bitter smoke as he waved it away from his face. He would taste burnt rubber for the rest of the day.

Finn waddled out of the back of the garage grumbling under his breath. "Without that 'Cuda, those gals would be nothing.

Damn fine vehicle, though. Don't make V8s like that anymore." He tapped Cash on the shoulder with a firm greasy hand. "Nice work, son."

"Thanks, Mr. O'Connor." But Cash didn't believe it. He knew Jezebel and Roxy were dangerous with or without the car. As the smoke cleared, he wondered just how far they would go.

# Queen Of Hearts

Quinn rolled Blue Belle into the cabin's driveway and cut the engine. She rested her forehead against the top of the steering wheel, her left hand still gripped to the curved black plastic as if it had been super-glued there. She looked at Wynter. "Your idea of a mid-morning nap sounds really good."

"Yeah, I thought so."

"What about you, Ransom?"

Both girls twisted in their seats to see the unblemished boy in the back. Ransom's eyes were closed and his body looked relaxed and unmoving against the side of the VW.

"Is he asleep?" Wynter whispered at Quinn.

She shrugged, wide-eyed, then mouthed "tickle him."

Wynter scrunched her brows and shook her head.

Quinn pulled her close and placed her lips close to Wynter's ear. "Tickle him."

Wynter gazed at Ransom's lanky body and leaned out past her seat. She reached forward to run her fingers across Ransom's abdomen when he broke the silence.

"I'm not asleep." He cracked one eye open and smiled at them.

"He knew I was going to tickle him."

"Yes, I did." Ransom sat up and stretched. "Are we going inside any time soon?"

"Of course. And now we don't have to carry you." Quinn rolled her eyes and slipped out of the car. "I wasn't looking forward to that." She shut the door behind her.

Wynter stepped out of the car and folded the seat forward. Ransom twisted himself out, kissing her on the neck as he passed. She took his hand and they both strolled up to the front of the cabin.

Quinn unlocked the door and led the three of them inside. "Holy crap, what a ride."

Wynter flopped onto one half of the sectional. "I'm still vibrating."

Ransom looked down at her. "Is there room for me?"

Quinn hung her purse on the barstools by the kitchen counter. Wynter felt her eyes on her and cast her a glance.

"Don't mind me," Quinn said. "I might join you." She quickly added, "On the other part of the sofa, I mean. Or I can go upstairs if you guys want to be alone."

"It's fine, Quinn." Wynter gazed at Ransom. "We're just going to snuggle."

Ransom took the invitation and laid on his back. Wynter positioned herself between him and the sofa back and tucked her shoulder under his. She closed her eyes and let his body heat soak into her.

*What a way to begin a Saturday morning.*

Wynter's thoughts melted away as sleep took hold of her. Ransom followed soon after.

Quinn watched the two of them, their chests rising and falling gently, content even after the harrowing run-in with Jezebel on the highway. She looked at the clock above the fireplace, noted the time, and began flipping through the pages of *Eyes Wide Dreaming*. Ideas swirled in her head.

Sleep pulled at Quinn's eyelids. Instead of giving in, she padded to the kitchen, filled a kettle, and set it to boil. She placed three scoops of instant coffee in a cup.

She caught the kettle before it started its whistle and poured the boiling water into her cup. The resulting coffee tasted too strong to drink black. She added several spoons of sugar to make it palatable and carried the coffee back to the living room.

Quinn nearly dropped her mug when she saw Ransom was gone. She hustled to the coffee table, set her mug down, and sat next to Wynter. The cushions were still warm where Ransom had been lying.

She shook Wynter's shoulders gently. "Bug, wake up." She continued rocking her until Wynter's eyelids fluttered open.

"What? What is it?" Wynter looked around, panicked. "Where's Ransom?"

"It's okay. He's back in your head."

"Shit, Quinn. I was enjoying myself."

"I know, but I woke you for a reason."

Wynter sat up and crossed her arms. "It better be good."

"Okay, remember when I made you the chamomile tea? And it helped you get to sleep faster? Or at least it seemed to help?"

Wynter nodded. She looked at Quinn's coffee. "Are you going to drink that?"

"Wait." Quinn ran back to the kitchen, grabbed another mug and the kettle, and returned to the sofa. She split the coffee between the two mugs and topped up each of them with hot water.

Wynter grimaced.

"Trust me," Quinn said. "It was way too strong to begin with." She handed a mug to Wynter. "So anyway, it's a pain in the ass to brew chamomile tea all the time."

"Plus it tastes gross, especially when it's triple strength."

"What if it came in a pill?" Quinn's eyes gleamed. "Then you could just pop a few when you wanted to fall asleep fast."

"I wouldn't have to taste it either." Wynter smiled, then her smile faltered.

Quinn could tell that they were on the same wavelength. Their brains were in sync.

"But making a pill sounds complicated." Wynter sipped her coffee. "What if they were like gummy bears?"

Quinn snapped her fingers. "Finger Jell-O. You just add more gelatin and less water."

"And instead of water, it's concentrated chamomile... wait!" Wynter's eyes went wide. She set her mug down and reached for *Eyes Wide Dreaming*. "They talk about natural sleep aids in here." She found the pages quickly and scanned to the relevant section. "It says 'chamomile, valerian, hops, passionflower, lavender, and ginseng all promote relaxation and sleep.' Apparently, valerian root is often called 'nature's Valium.' " She looked up at Quinn. "What if we made a super brew with all this stuff and made—"

"Made finger Jell-O out of it," they said in unison.

A wide grin spread across Quinn's face. "See? I had a good reason for waking you up. Should we get started?"

Wynter nodded and joined Quinn to rip through the pantry and cupboards. Other than chamomile tea, two packages of flavorless gelatin, and a box of lime Jell-O, they came up empty.

"There's a health food store not too far from here," Quinn said. "I'm sure they'll have everything we need."

Ten minutes later they found themselves roaming the aisles of Gilberg Market. Rows of fresh produce in every color of the rainbow surrounded them.

Quinn stopped by the cucumbers. "You think you'll need one of these for later?"

Wynter gave her a side-eye. "For...?"

Quinn picked up a large cucumber, held it vertically in one hand, and began stroking it slowly with the other.

Wynter looked around for other shoppers or staff. "Stop."

Quinn pointed the end of the cucumber at her open mouth. Already mortified, Wynter grabbed the vegetable and put it back with the others. She looked at Quinn, eyes wide and cheeks flushed. They both started to giggle.

"Have you ever done that before," Wynter whispered. "Like for real?"

"I'll never tell." Quinn smirked. "Let's just say I read a lot of *Cosmo*."

Apart from getting temporarily sidetracked in the Sexual Health aisle, they found all of their special ingredients with the exception of hops in the sleep supplements section.

"If you really want the hops, you could wash everything down with beer," Quinn said.

"I'd rather stay away from alcohol for a while."

Once back at the cabin, Quinn dumped their supplies on the kitchen counter. Plastic containers rolled every which way, including a tube of K-Y Jelly. "Just thinking ahead." She grinned. "Now what?"

Wynter looked at the book. "We mix it up in a pot with some water and boil it."

"You mean make a pot of tea out of it?"

"I guess." Wynter picked up a package of gelatin and read the directions. "Then we add it to the gelatin and let it cool."

"Let's get going." Quinn pulled out a large pot. "If we're lucky you can try it out tonight."

Wynter set the book down, her eyes uncertain.

"You know. We have *research* to do." Quinn air-quoted the word. "Well, you do anyway."

"Right."

"Don't worry about it," Quinn said. "With the right person, it's fun."

"If you say so." Wynter twisted off the cap to the valerian root supplement. She removed a capsule and pulled it apart over the pot. A powdery substance fluttered to the bottom. "Only a hundred-nineteen to go."

Quinn joined her. The extraction went quicker than expected

and soon they had a pile of various supplements lining the bottom of the pot. She added water and set the mixture on the stove on medium heat.

Once boiling, they added the gelatin packages, the lime Jell-O, and let it all dissolve. The green color of the Jell-O mixed with the brown of the supplements changed the whole concoction to a dark blackish brown.

Wynter plugged her nose. "It smells terrible."

"Probably tastes even worse, but as long as it works." Quinn found a baking pan under the stove and set it on the counter. "You're probably not going to chew it anyway."

Wynter poured the mixture into the pan and together they carried the pan to the fridge and slid it inside.

"You think it's going to work?"

"How can it not?" Quinn eyed the tube of K-Y Jelly. "I think there's some carrots in the fridge. Want to practice your technique?"

"I think I'll be fine. It's not rocket science."

"More like rock-hard science." Quinn laughed. "Want to watch a movie? You pick. I'll make popcorn."

"Sure." Wynter dug through the movies in the entertainment center and pulled out *Dreamscape*. "Perfect," she said to herself.

Wynter and Quinn spent the afternoon watching a double feature and eating popcorn. But while Quinn drooled over Tom Cruise in *Risky Business,* Wynter found her thoughts on the experiment in the fridge and wondered whether it would work or not. And if it worked, what would happen after that?

○

THE CREDITS ROLLED on *Risky Business.* Quinn sprawled out on the sofa, her head hanging upside-down off the cushion and her legs dangling over the backrest. She gazed at Wynter and swooned. "Tom Cruise is just the dreamiest."

"He's okay, but what about Christopher Atkins. So hot. Remember *The Blue Lagoon?*" Wynter sighed.

"I know you like blonds." Quinn stretched her legs up and wiggled her toes. "Should we check the gummies now or—"

"Now!" Wynter leaped over the back of the sofa, intent on beating Quinn to the refrigerator, but her sock feet were no match for the traction of Quinn's bare soles.

Quinn yanked open the refrigerator door and Wynter lifted out the pan. It looked like a sheet of black licorice.

"I hope it tastes better than it looks."

Wynter set the pan on the counter and pressed the concoction with her index finger. It sprung back like rubber, her indentation disappearing. "It's lime, so it's already grodie."

Quinn grabbed a plastic flipper and tried to pry the gelatin out. "It's stuck pretty good."

"Let's cut it into cubes first." Wynter found a knife and scored the gel along the pan's length and width in parallel cuts. With the pieces smaller, little semi-translucent cubes popped out when Quinn ran the lifter along the base of the pan.

"They look like little dice, like in Vegas, but without the dots." Quinn picked one up, took a nibble, and grimaced. "Bug. It's gross."

Wynter tweezed a cube with her fingers and smelled it. The odor reminded her of grass clippings mixed with dirt. She could still detect traces of lime Jell-O, but everything else overpowered it. She bit a piece off, rolled it around in her mouth, then spit it out. "Yeah. That's gross. But I don't have to chew it. I can swallow them whole. They get pretty slippery." She looked up at Quinn. "How many should I eat?"

Quinn shrugged. "I have no idea."

"You count how many little cubes we have." Wynter collected the empty supplement bottles and wrote down the quantities that were in each one. After a little math, she decided that six should be enough to eat at one time.

"We should eat dinner first," Quinn said. "How about pizza? Totino's?"

"Okay, but Ransom's going to be pissed that he didn't get to eat any of it."

"We don't have to eat it all." Quinn pulled a boxed pizza from the freezer and set the oven to preheat. "Besides, he's never going to starve."

Wynter vibrated, raising herself up and down on the balls of her feet. "How long is it going to take?"

"I don't know. Half an hour?" Quinn looked at her. "Excited to see Ransom?"

"Is it that obvious?"

"Patience, grasshopper."

Wynter rolled her eyes. "Oh God, now you're saying it. My dad says that, like, all the time."

"Come on." Quinn walked to the living room. "Read to me. From your book."

If there was anything that could distract Wynter, it was *Eyes Wide Dreaming* and Quinn knew it. Wynter planted herself next to her on the sofa.

"What do you want me to read?"

"I don't know." Quinn stretched out on one half of the sectional. "Pick something interesting."

She opened the book to the chapter on summoning. "Remember that Post-It note I showed you the first time I told you about Ransom?"

Quinn nodded.

"He bookmarked this chapter with that Post-It note." Wynter began to read.

◯

QUINN AND WYNTER were so immersed in the book that they nearly forgot about the pizza in the oven. It was only the smell of well-done crust that brought them out of their focus.

They rescued the pizza and ate most of it, leaving the three most burnt slices for Ransom in case he was hungry.

"Does he know your thoughts when he's in your head?" Quinn had asked.

"I don't think so, but I don't know for sure." It had been a worry of Wynter's since the first time Ransom had crossed over.

Now Quinn and Wynter sat facing each other at the kitchen table. A pile of small dark brown gelatin cubes sat on a plate between them.

Wynter had lined up six of the cubes on the table. She picked one up and squished it between her fingers. The cube bulged at its center as her fingers flattened it, then regained its shape as she relieved pressure. "We got to find a name for these."

"If they work." Quinn picked a cube off the pile and smelled it. "It's not working for me."

"Maybe if it was cherry."

"Doubt it."

Wynter looked up in thought. "What about 'winks,' but with an 'x' instead of 'ks'?"

"Yeah, maybe. Or 'sleepies.' "

"Doesn't that already exist?"

"So? It's spelled different and it's not like we're going to sell it," Quinn said. "Anyway, are you going to do this or what?"

Wynter collected the six cubes, crammed them all into her mouth, and swallowed.

"Whoa. You don't mess around."

"They're super easy to swallow whole, but they taste like ass."

Quinn looked at the clock on the cooking range. "How long do you think it will take?"

"Hopefully less than an hour. Technically that shouldn't be possible, but maybe the *winx* will help."

"You mean *sleepies*."

"Agree to disagree. Where should I lie down?"

"The sofa. I got to keep my eye on you." Quinn bounded up the spiral staircase and disappeared into Wynter's bedroom. "Get comfy. I'll be right back."

Wynter nestled into the backrest of the sectional. Quinn stepped down the stairs with something draped over her shoulders. She looked like royalty.

"A nap wouldn't be complete without the coma-quilt." She flung it over Wynter. "Are you feeling anything yet?"

Wynter did not answer. She was already asleep.

Quinn pulled out a set of over-the-ear headphones and plugged its long cord into the entertainment unit. She turned on the receiver and lay down on the other half of the sectional. "Here I Go Again" by Whitesnake played through the headphone's speakers.

"KROK, you know me too well." Quinn closed her eyes and let the rock and roll music help her pass the time.

○

"RANSOM! WHERE ARE YOU?" Wynter stood in the center of the cabin, except it wasn't really there. She held a flashlight in one hand but instead of light, the device cast transparency. She could see through the walls to the outside like she had X-ray vision, and instead of wooden floors, uncut grass crept up her legs. The cabin appeared derelict like it had been left in the wilderness unused for years.

Wynter pointed the flashlight out to the lake. "What the..." A chair from the dining room sat at the end of the dock with a figure perched on it. "Ransom?"

She darted toward the dock, forgetting about the transparency and slammed face first into a wall. Despite appearing transparent, the cabin walls remained very much solid. Wynter rubbed her face and headed toward the front door.

With the special flashlight, she could see Blue Belle sitting outside in the driveway. She rested her hand on the top of the sofa sectional as she passed it. The fabric frayed under her fingertips, dirty and rotted.

Wynter grabbed the front door handle, twisted it, and pushed the door open. Instead of fresh summer air, staleness and decay flooded her nostrils and the uniformly gray sky hovered over the trees.

"Ransom?"

She dropped the flashlight and ran to the dock. As she approached the chair, she noticed that the figure's ankles were tied to the chair's front legs and his arms were bound behind him in a tight knot, all using the same bright red fabric.

It had to be Ransom. The black hoodie, white socks, and jeans, it all checked out. Still, Wynter approached with caution and kept her distance as she circled to the front.

She knelt and looked up at the figure's face, still obscured within the black hoodie. "Ransom?" she whispered.

The figure's head twitched and Wynter caught a glimpse of his blue irises, the ones she remembered, except the whites surrounding them were heavily bloodshot. Stretched across his mouth was a red fabric gag and dirty tear tracks stood out on his cheeks.

"Oh, Ransom." Wynter scooted forward, pulled back his hoodie, and untied the gag. "What happened?" She began working at the knot binding his hands together.

"You left me behind."

"I didn't mean to. Quinn woke me before I could take you with me."

"Do you have any idea what it's like? To be left?"

Wynter had been chosen last on countless teams at school but she shook her head anyway. "No." She let the fabric strands at Ransom's wrists fall away and moved to his ankles.

Ransom looked around from his seated vantage point. "This world, it's *your* creation." He turned to face her, his eyes blazing. "When you go, all this goes with you, leaving nothing behind. Imagine all your senses gone. No sight, sound, touch, smell... so I wait in the darkness."

Wynter finished untying one of Ransom's legs and threw her arms around him. His body stiffened at her embrace. "I'm sorry. I had no idea."

"I don't know how much real time passed, but for me it was an eternity." Ransom rubbed his wrists. "It took long enough to get to you. I don't want to relive that." He paused. "Reality is so much better."

Wynter tugged at the remaining fabric tied around his left ankle and hugged him again, kissing his salty neck. "Sometimes I can't control when I fall asleep or when I wake. That's just the way it is. But Quinn and I created something today I think you'll like." She stood and held out her hand. "Come with me. I'll show you."

Ransom glanced back at the cabin. Quinn stood on the deck, backlit by the sun, wearing a sheer sundress and nothing else. She watched them both, smiled, and waved.

He returned his gaze to Wynter, his eyes wary. He took her hand and they walked to where the dock joined the tall grass. She took his face in her hands and guided it to hers.

"I really am sorry. You believe me?"

Ransom looked at her, then at the deck of the cabin. Quinn was gone. He faced Wynter again and nodded. "I do."

Wynter kissed him and wrapped her arms around him, running her fingers through his curly hair. It was a kiss like no other she had experienced with him before. And it transported them back to reality.

O

WYNTER OPENED HER eyes to Quinn staring at both her and Ransom from across the coffee table, the three remaining slices of pizza on a plate between them.

"Déjà vu, much? Welcome back." Quinn hooked a thumb back at the kitchen. "It's only been thirty-five minutes. I checked." She looked at Ransom. "The pizza's cold but it's yours if you want it. I thought you'd be hungry."

Ransom sat up like he was a dog who had just spotted a squirrel. Quinn half expected him to start panting and drooling. She pushed the plate in his direction and he pulled it the rest of the way across the table. He grabbed a piece and tore into it, casting her a hungry look.

"Thirty-five minutes? That's awesome," Wynter said. "Normally REM sleep doesn't even start for at least ninety minutes."

"And REM sleep is...?" Quinn looked a question at her.

"REM sleep is when we dream. So that's when the lucid action happens. Just call it dream sleep."

"Maybe that sleepy stuff we made really works."

"What stuff?" Ransom said between mouthfuls.

Quinn bounded off the sofa, ran to the kitchen, and returned with the plate full of gelatin cubes.

As Ransom ripped into the last piece of pizza, he eyed the plate of cubes like it was more food for him. He reached for one and Quinn pulled the plate back.

"Nope. Not for you."

"Wait. Why not?" Ransom's words mixed with a mouthful of pizza.

"Those are just for me," Wynter said. "It helps me dream faster so I can get to you faster. If you ate them, you'd drift back into my head. I know you'd rather be real."

Ransom burped and licked his fingers. "I'm much better out of your head."

"We all are." Quinn rummaged through a compartment in the entertainment unit. She returned to the sofa and placed a deck of cards on the coffee table. "I say we play some strip poker."

"I don't know, Quinn," Wynter said. "Isn't there something else we can play?"

Quinn scooted around the coffee table and whispered in Wynter's ear, "Don't you want to see him naked?"

She looked at Quinn and they both giggled.

Ransom raised a brow and alternated his gaze between the two girls. "What?"

Quinn returned to her side of the sofa and eyed them both. "You do know how to play, right?"

"Kind of?" Wynter shrugged. "I've only played the regular kind a couple of times."

"It's the same, except instead of money, you bet something you're wearing."

Wynter nodded but Ransom appeared unsure of himself.

"I'll go over the rules super quick. It's not hard." Quinn slid the deck of cards out and riffle-shuffled them several times. Her fingers worked nimbly and independently as she spoke, her eyes always on Wynter and Ransom.

"We'll be playing five card draw. Everyone decides on something they're wearing to bet. It has to be clothes. Jewelry isn't allowed. I'll deal five cards to each of us." Quinn dealt a five card sample hand face down onto the table. "Without letting anyone see your cards, pick any number of cards to throw away, if you want to that is, and I'll replace them."

She took two cards out and dealt two more. "Then we show our cards. Whoever has the lowest hand must take off the clothing they bet." She flipped over the sample hand. "High card, eight of diamonds. That's the lowest hand you can have. If I had this hand, I would probably lose." Quinn smiled across the coffee table as she collected the cards and began shuffling again. "Make sense?"

Wynter and Ransom looked at each other, shrugged, then both nodded.

"Can we go back to Lucy's after this?" Ransom ran his hand across his stomach.

"You're still hungry?" Wynter pulled the coma-quilt around her.

"Yeah," Ransom said. "Aren't you?"

"No."

"Hopefully, you'll be hungry for something else." Quinn winked at Wynter. "Ready?"

Wynter gave Quinn a thumbs up. "Let's play."

"I'll be dealer." Quinn turned to Ransom. "What are you betting?"

Ransom tapped his chest. "My hoodie."

"Excellent." Quinn looked at Wynter. "Bug?"

Wynter stuck out a foot. "I bet my left sock."

"A hoodie and a sock. You guys are high-rollers. I bet my... shorts." Quinn tugged at her denim belt loops.

Wynter's eyes narrowed. Quinn seemed to want to get naked faster than she did. "Can I change my bet?"

"Go for it," Quinn said. "As long as you decide before I deal."

"Then I bet my shorts as well."

"Okay. Time to deal." Quinn laid down cards face down in a clockwise fashion, starting with Ransom, and set the remaining deck aside. "Now look at your cards and decide how many cards you want to exchange."

Wynter picked up her cards and spread them in her hands. She had a pair of nines. "How are the hands scored?"

Quinn set her cards down and pulled out a Rummoli box from

the entertainment center. She refolded the game sheet inside to highlight the space labeled "Poker Pot."

"This shows all the possible Poker hands and what beats what."

Quinn watched Wynter and Ransom study the chart. "Ransom? How many cards do you want?"

Ransom's eyes flicked between his hand, the chart, and Quinn. He glanced at Wynter and she leaned away, shielding her cards against her chest.

"No peeking!"

"Sorry. I didn't mean to." Ransom picked three cards from his hand and set them on the table.

Quinn dealt Ransom three more cards and tapped on the cards he threw away. "This is the discard pile." Her eyes slid to Wynter's. "Bugaboo?"

Wynter studied the chart to make sure that she wasn't missing anything important. "I'll take two." She placed her two cards in the discard pile and Quinn dealt her two more.

"I'll take two as well." Quinn removed two cards, dealt herself two, and rearranged them in her hand. "Okay. Ready to see who won? Lay down your hands."

"I hope it's me," Ransom said. "I'm getting too hot in this hoodie."

All three spread out their cards on the table and Quinn looked them over.

"You're going to have to stay hot for a little while longer, Ransom, because you win this round with two pair." Quinn examined Wynter's hand. "And... it looks like I'm the loser this round. Bug's got a pair of nines and that beats my pair of sixes."

Quinn stood up and unbuttoned the top of her denim shorts. "No peeking." She waited until Wynter and Ransom had covered their eyes with their hands, then unzipped the front of her shorts and worked them down to the floor.

Wynter sensed vibes between Ransom and Quinn and wanted evidence. She separated her fingers just enough to see Quinn changing and expected her to be wearing something provocative like what she usually saw on MTV. But Quinn's panties were basic white with a random daisy pattern on it. Nothing special.

Quinn sat cross-legged on the sofa, grabbed a throw pillow, and placed it strategically in her lap, concealing her panties from view. "Okay. I'm decent." She leaned out to collect the cards, shuffled, and dealt the next hand.

Ransom got his wish. He lost the hand and took off his hoodie. His arms looked scrawnier than Wynter thought they would.

The rounds continued. Wynter lost her nerve and instead of betting her shorts like Quinn, she bet one sock at a time on every round while she could. The strategy worked for a while.

By the beginning of the tenth round, Wynter had lost both socks and her shorts and Quinn had lost one of her socks. Ransom had his white T-shirt and boxers left.

Quinn dealt their hands and made card substitutions. Ransom lost again with a single pair.

Wynter couldn't help but wonder if he was trying to lose. Being naked in a private cabin with two girls on a hot summer night would be any guy's fantasy.

Ransom pulled off his T-shirt, Quinn and Wynter watching his every move. But the Adonis they had imagined him to be was replaced with a thin body that lacked any muscle definition. He looked like a skeleton covered with skin. Stranger than that was the lack of nipples.

"Holy shit." Quinn's words escaped her mouth before she could stop them.

"What?" Ransom appeared completely content with the way he looked. "Is there something wrong?"

"Um. Dude." Quinn looked to Wynter for support, but she was gawking at Ransom instead. "Where are your nipples?"

Ransom looked down and placed his hands on his chest like he was searching for them by feel. He scrunched his brow. "I don't know. I've never looked. Never needed to."

"That's weird."

Wynter shot a look at Quinn that said, "What the hell?"

Quinn shrugged back.

"One more hand." Ransom grinned and crossed his frail arms over his gaunt body.

"Oh-kay." Quinn shuffled and dealt three piles. They all sorted their cards, made substitutions, and laid down their hands on the table.

"Ransom, you have nothing," Quinn said. "Ten high."

"Oh well. I guess I lose again." He raised an eyebrow and looked at Wynter. "My underwear's coming off. Don't look." He waited for them to cover their eyes just as he had done for them earlier.

Except Quinn and Wynter couldn't help themselves. The fantasy of Wynter's dream boy was imploding before her eyes in real time. They had to watch.

Ransom turned his back to the girls and pulled his boxers down, revealing that he had no butt crack. Quinn and Wynter stared at each other, wide eyed. He faced them and sat down again, his hands cupped over his hairless crotch.

Quinn said what Wynter was thinking. "You don't have any junk, do you?"

Ransom thought for a moment, peeked under his cupped hands, and settled his gaze back on Quinn. "I guess not."

"Oh, my God," Quinn whispered to herself as she charged toward the kitchen. "Bug, can I talk to you for a sec? Bring the sleepies."

"I'll be right back." Wynter dropped the coma-quilt over Ransom's lap. "In case you're cold." She picked up the plate of gelatin cubes and followed Quinn to the kitchen.

Quinn pulled Wynter into the dining room, out of sight of Ransom. They spoke in whispers.

"He looks like the little brother of a Ken doll, but without the muscles." Quinn rolled her eyes. "I can't believe I'm talking about this. What happened?"

Wynter shook her head. "I don't know."

"What have you been doing... or *not* doing in your dreams?"

"The usual," Wynter said. "You know. Kissing, talking, snuggling. That kind of stuff."

"You haven't had dream sex yet?"

"No. I wanted it to be just right."

"But if it's in a dream, can't you make it whatever you want?" Quinn peeked around the dining room wall to see Ransom sitting on the sofa, the coma-quilt draped over his shoulders. "Make it perfect?"

"Yes, but I wanted the first time to be real. As real as it could be, I mean."

"That's not going to happen the way he is now," Quinn whispered. "He's got no... *you know*, cock. It's like he hasn't finished forming. Could you dream him into a bitchin' bod?"

"Maybe. It's worth a shot."

"Well, if you ever want to have sex with him, he needs some jingle jangle. Do you think you'll need some sleepies?"

Wynter grabbed a handful of the gelatin cubes, crammed them into her mouth, and swallowed.

"Holy shit, how many did you take?"

"I don't know. More than six." Wynter looked around the dining room. "I think I should lie down now."

"Come on." Quinn placed her arm around Wynter's waist and led her back to the sofa, whispering in her ear along the way. "Remember. Give him muscles. Give him some junk. Think Christopher Atkins. And while you're at it can you make me a boy toy too."

"*Blue Lagoon,*" Wynter said to herself as intense relaxation set in. Images of crystal clear water and warm sand on her feet flooded her senses.

Wynter had seen the film countless times since its release in

1980. She had bought her own VHS copy from Vinny and had hidden it in the back recesses of her dresser. She would watch it when Madeline and Nolan had to work late.

Ransom looked up at Wynter, concern flashing on his face. "Everything okay? You've been talking about me, right? About my lack of..." He looked down at his cupped hands.

"It's fine. Bug just needs to recharge." Quinn laid Wynter down on her side. "How about you lay next to her. Keep her warm and safe."

Ransom nodded and shifted his position behind Wynter, but kept his eyes on Quinn's bare legs. Wynter sighed and snuggled close into his boney body.

Quinn stepped to the entertainment center and retrieved the headphones. "Sleep tight." She waved with one hand, then snugged the headphones around her ears. Closing her eyes, music from KROK once again filled her ears. Quinn closed her eyes and let the music carry her away.

Ransom shifted his focus from Quinn to Wynter. He guided a lock of her red hair behind her ear and kissed her shoulder lightly. He didn't have a chance to close his eyes before he drifted away in a cloud of ozone.

◯

Wynter cracked her eyes open, pushed herself upright, and brushed warm sand from her cheek. Instead of her usual white sundress, a torn white blouse hung loosely from her shoulders and hid the bra and panties she had been wearing back at the cabin. She worked sand between her toes, mixing the hot crusty top with the cool layers beneath.

The palm trees next to the shelter cast shifting patterns on her back, warming her blouse and her brown skin underneath. Waves of teal water crested, bubbled, and rolled up along the white sand before retreating back to the ocean. Gentle wind and a cloudless azure sky surrounded the cove. It was exactly as she remembered it in the movie.

*And it's all mine.*

Wynter ran to the water's edge, kicking clumps of seaweed and sand into the surf. Even the water at her feet was warm. She strolled partway down the beach before remembering why she was there.

"Ransom?" She surveyed the length of the beach, shielding her eyes with her hands. Not a soul to be seen anywhere.

Wynter headed toward a small outcropping of rock at one end of the beach but as she drew near, she realized it wasn't rock at all.

*The coma-quilt.*

She quickened her stride. The quilt moved as she approached. "Ransom?"

The quilt ruffled and turned, and Ransom's head popped out, his hair teased and kinky with dried salt water and his smile as bright as ever. "I was wondering when you were going to show up."

A necklace of small sun-bleached shells rattled around his neck as he worked the sand into a large mound. "Going to be a sandcastle," he said between breaths. "Want to help?"

Wynter dropped to her knees and began moving mounds of sand, adding to his pile. Her eyes followed his hands working and realized his arms were no longer spindly and underdeveloped but strong and full of toned muscle.

Ransom smiled at her and allowed his eyes to drift to the rips in her blouse. From the right angle he could see more than any boy had ever seen before. She imagined his new strong arms holding her.

And she liked it.

Ransom fell back on his haunches and rested his elbows on his knees, the quilt sliding off his back. Wynter saw his chest, abdomen, and legs were just as developed and refined as his arms. And he had nipples now.

Completing her movie memory, Ransom wore a threadbare loincloth pouch made of the same fabric as her blouse. It looked like there was something underneath, but she had to be sure.

"You want to see, don't you?"

Ransom's voice caught her by surprise and she averted her eyes from his. Even with the sun on her shoulders she could feel the heat of embarrassment spreading up her neck. She nodded.

"It's okay." Ransom shifted onto his knees, hooked his thumbs into the waistband at his hips, and began to pull them down.

"Wait." Wynter kneeled and shifted herself in the sand until she was close enough to feel the warmth of his skin. She placed her hand on his chest and watched her fingertips travel lightly over his skin, down toward the loincloth. Even in her dreams, her nerves took over and made her hand tremble.

She looked up at Ransom. He smiled back, took her hand, and placed it lightly on top of the loincloth. She moved her hand slowly over the fabric. There was no need to guess what was underneath. She could feel it. Her eyes ran a line back down toward his navel.

Ransom took hold of the waistband and pulled his tattered loincloth down. Without much coaxing, the frayed garment dropped to the sand.

"Well?" he said. "Is it all that you imagined?"

Wynter stared at Ransom's penis. This being her first glimpse, she thought it looked to be just the right size. She could hear Quinn in her mind making a Goldilocks joke.

"Yes. I mean... wait." Wynter gazed up at him. "Can you turn around?"

"So you can see my butt?" Ransom laughed and turned slowly in front of her. There it was, two cheeks, round and smooth, looking like what a butt should look like.

Facing her again, Ransom held Wynter's face and pulled it

toward his, kissing her deeply. He fell backward onto the quilt, pulling her with him.

It was difficult for Wynter to know how long they kissed, there on the beach, but she could feel a firmness pressing against her abdomen. She knew it was Ransom—it had to be—but felt too self-conscious to look and make sure. Still, the fact that she was eliciting a physical response from him this way sent her heart soaring. Wynter leaned into him and kissed him harder.

As quick as the wind, Wynter felt the world drift.

"The love birds are back," a familiar voice said.

○

THE LOW SOUNDS of Wynter moaning roused Quinn from her light sleep. She yawned and pulled off her headphones. The clock above the fireplace read a quarter to eleven.

"That can't be right," Quinn whispered to herself as she scrunched her brows. "The weekend's almost over and..."

Wynter stirred and sighed. Quinn watched her sleep, her chest rising and falling, her cheeks appearing a little flushed under the low light of the living room. What she really wanted to do was take Wynter's pulse, but that would wake her up.

Ransom materialized behind Wynter like he had been transported from an episode of *Star Trek*. One moment Wynter was alone and the next he was kissing her neck, his free hand on her T-shirt over her breast.

"Nice work, Bug," Quinn whispered. She was pleased to see his body now had muscles in *all* the right places, some currently harder than others. He opened his eyes and connected with Quinn across the coffee table. She had turned on her bedroom eyes without even thinking about it. Ransom pulled the quilt over his abdomen and sat up.

"The love birds are back." Quinn eyed them slyly.

Wynter peeked back at her, stretched, and slumped back onto the sofa, smiling. "I'm still feeling tired."

"You did eat a lot of zees," Quinn said. "Should I make some coffee?"

"That's a good idea." Wynter gave her a sideways look. "Are we calling them 'zees' now?"

"Maybe." Quinn singled out Ransom. "Looks like someone got an upgrade."

"Yeah. It's pretty sweet, huh?" Ransom flexed a bicep and surveyed his abdominal muscles. "Not sure how this happened." He looked at Wynter. "Did you do this?"

She grinned sheepishly and nodded. "I had to make sure you were *complete*." Wynter yawned and tilted her head toward Quinn. "*Blue Lagoon* style."

"Speaking of *Blue Lagoon,* how about we all go skinny dipping?" Quinn pulled her T-shirt over her knees, making her look like a giant marshmallow. "The moon's up and after a day of sun the water should almost be warm."

Wynter raised a brow. "Almost?"

"Well, let's say lukewarm. Who's in?" Quinn shifted her gaze between the two of them. "We're practically naked already."

"I can barely keep my eyes open." Wynter yawned. "Hate to be a party pooper but I need to go to bed."

Quinn popped her legs out of her shirt and stood. "No decisions until after I make coffee. Okay?" She bounded to the kitchen.

Ransom wrapped the quilt around his shoulders and drew the seams together in front. "You got anything to eat?"

"Maybe," Quinn called back from the kitchen. "You can look in the freezer if you want."

"Can I get you anything?" Ransom looked at Wynter's eyelids hovering half closed and kissed her forehead.

"Surprise me." Wynter sent him a suggestive smile.

"You got it." Ransom strolled to the kitchen, working his newly acquired muscles.

Quinn filled the kettle and set it on the stove to boil. She began measuring instant coffee into mugs when Ransom passed her on his way to the freezer.

Holding the quilt with one hand, he pulled open the freezer with the other and began rummaging around inside. "Hot Pockets or Pizza Rolls? Which would you pick?"

"Coffee's almost up," Quinn called back to the living room as she walked to the freezer. The cold air felt good on her skin, but it did nothing to cool the heat she felt standing next to Ransom. It was now or never.

Quinn made a quick glance over her shoulder, then pushed Ransom against the wall with one hand and planted a kiss squarely on his lips. Her other hand snaked down the front of the quilt, searching his body hidden under the folds of fabric.

She lost herself in passion but somehow forced herself to step back. "Whoa. You're *dangerous*."

Ransom studied her face, confused. "Why did you do that?"

"I'm sorry. I couldn't help myself." Quinn resumed measuring instant coffee as Ransom collected and readjusted the quilt draping his body. "Please don't say anything."

"I won't."

"Wait. Does she know what you know? Like the opposite of—"

"It doesn't work like that."

"Are you sure?"

Ransom nodded, pulled out the box of Hot Pockets, and set it on the counter.

"I'll heat them up." Quinn kept her eyes on the coffee mugs in front of her. "Go back and keep Wynter company."

"Alright." Ransom passed behind her on his way back to the living room.

"Ransom."

He stopped and they faced each other.

"I'm not trying to steal you away from her. Honest." Even

though Quinn knew what she had done was wrong, her eyes remained clear.

Ransom approached her quietly. "I know." He kissed her back.

All of the lust Quinn had managed to keep a lid on almost bubbled over again. The kettle screeched on the stove as their lips parted. Ransom lifted the kettle off the heat, turned off the stove, and walked back to the living room.

"Oh, my God." Quinn ran a finger lightly across her lips, her guilt flooding her mind with shadows. "What am I doing?"

○

QUINN BALANCED THE mugs of coffee and Hot Pockets on a tray and carried them into the living room. Ransom sat behind Wynter, one of his arms curved around her waist. He whispered something in her ear and she smiled. An unfamiliar jolt of jealousy doused Quinn's guilt in an instant, surprising her with how easy it was to justify her kitchen rendezvous.

Quinn set the tray on the coffee table and turned on the television, flipping through the channels to try and distract herself. "Eat up while it's hot."

Wynter grabbed her coffee, blowing on it before sipping. "You're the best, Quinn. Thanks."

*Sure, rub it in.*

Quinn nodded at Wynter before taking her own mug. "No problem." She flipped onto *Night Flight* on USA Network. A strange B movie played, which on any other night would have kept her interest. Tonight, every distraction failed and left her with thoughts of the only thing—or person in this case—that she couldn't have.

Ransom finished one Hot Pocket and started on another.

"Take it easy on those, big guy," Quinn said. "Now that you

have a functional butt, sooner or later you're going to have to deal with all that food."

"How do you know it's functional?" Ransom raised a brow at her and continued eating.

"You mean it's not?" The gears inside Quinn's head began to grind.

"I don't know," he said.

Quinn tore off a corner of one of the remaining pizza pastries and threw it at him. Ransom caught it with one hand and ate it.

"You missed," he said.

Wynter yawned. "This coffee isn't working. Remind me not to eat so many zees next time. I'm going to bed." Her bare feet padded to the spiral staircase and she headed up to the loft.

"Follow her," Quinn whispered at Ransom through gritted teeth.

Ransom grabbed the last Hot Pocket and shuffled toward the stairs, dragging the quilt up the steps.

Quinn stretched and yawned. "I'll be right up, guys." She turned off the TV, collected the mugs, and carried them to the kitchen. Standing in front of the counter, she balled her fists and tried to fight the desire she was feeling.

She left the mugs by the sink and made her way up the stairs. The thought of sleeping in the same room as Ransom raged in her head. She wanted to remain true to Wynter, but at the same time she had tasted the sweetness of Ransom's kiss. Still fresh on her lips, she wanted more.

From the bedroom door, Quinn watched Ransom climb under the covers with Wynter, who was already snoring lightly. Shards of blue moonlight ran across his newly muscular frame.

Quinn imagined how smooth his skin would feel next to hers and that was it. She couldn't take it anymore. She grabbed one end of the mattress and slid it out of the room.

"I think you guys need some privacy."

Ransom nodded and mouthed the words "thank you," then set his head next to Wynter's.

Quinn wrestled the mattress back onto the box spring in the other bedroom. She climbed under the sheets and closed her eyes, but all she could see was Ransom's blue eyes staring back at her.

Her only choice was to replay their kitchen kiss in her mind and imagine different endings. Happier more exciting endings. She slid her hand into her panties and helped herself along. Her fingers and her body moved as one. Then, breathless and sated, she drifted to sleep.

○

THE RISING SUN woke Quinn. She sat up and rubbed the sleep from her eyes. The bedsheets slipped off her shoulders and she discovered she was naked. She stuck her head under the sheets but the T-shirt, panties, and sports bra she had been wearing when she went to bed were nowhere to be found.

It was then that she noticed her bed was on the deck. Outside. In fact, the rest of the cabin was gone too.

"What the…" Quinn grabbed the bedsheet with both fists and brought it up to her face.

"Beautiful view, isn't it?"

Quinn spun around to find Ransom reclining in a chaise lounge, the coma-quilt draped over his body.

"What the hell, Ransom!" Quinn pulled the bedsheet around her body. With the morning sun backlighting her, it did little to hide her nakedness. "You scared me." She looked around again. "What is this?"

"It's a dream," Ransom said. "*Your* dream."

"I thought I couldn't do this."

"Do what? Dream?" Ransom crossed his ankles under the quilt. "Everyone dreams. It's the only place where anything goes and there are no consequences." He gave her a sideways glance and a coy grin. "Sorry for scaring you."

He moved to the bed and sat next to her. "I can't stop thinking about that kiss."

*Oh, my God!*

"Me too." Quinn loosened her grip on the sheets wrapped around her, exposing a bare shoulder. Maybe she could make her dreams work for her for a change. He took the bait and kissed it gently.

"What should we do about that?"

Quinn faced him. Her eyes took him all in. "Pick up where we left off?"

Ransom reached for one of her hands and guided it down the front of the quilt. "I think you were right about *here*."

Quinn let the rest of the sheets go and pushed Ransom back against the bed. The quilt unfurled, all of his naked body on display just the way she had envisioned it.

She eased herself on top of him and they began to kiss.

○

THE BED'S HEADBOARD knocked against the wall, waking Quinn with a start. A faint smell of ozone drifted out the open window.

She rocked backward and sat on her heels. Ransom stared up at her, naked and toned. Beautiful. He raised a brow, waiting for her to speak.

"What the..." Quinn touched her T-shirt, then pulled the collar out and looked down. She still had her panties and sports bra on. "This doesn't make any sense," she whispered. "I thought Wynter—" She tilted her head to listen. "Did we wake her up?"

"I don't know. I—"

"Shh." Quinn concentrated but she heard only sounds of the cabin cooling in the night. She let go a sigh of relief, then let her eyes wander from Ransom's face and across his chest. She began to shake her head. "No. We can't do this. I can't."

Ransom sat up and kissed her, working his way to an ear and down her neck. Quinn let him do it, but her guilt still fought to be heard.

"This isn't a dream anymore," she said. "What we're doing, there's consequences now."

Ransom stood and walked to the bedroom door. "I guess you need to make a choice." He pulled the door open and stepped out onto the loft.

"Wait!" Quinn tried to impart urgency in her whisper but he was already out of earshot. She ran to the door and peered out. Ransom strolled along the loft hallway and stopped in front of Wynter's room, his naked profile accentuated by moonlight from the bedroom window. He looked back at her, his eyes alight with heat, before descending the spiral staircase.

"Oh, *my...*" Quinn licked her lips. Her desire had won out over her guilt. She ducked back into her room and dug through the bottom drawer of her dresser until she pulled out a condom. She tucked it into the waistband of her panties and tiptoed to the spiral staircase.

Passing Wynter's bedroom door, Quinn looked at Wynter sleeping, calm and peaceful. Right then she almost changed her mind, but the sound of the sliding door being unlocked from below pulled her downstairs.

Quinn could see Ransom out on the deck, leaning on the balcony facing the lake. She crossed through the kitchen and dining room with slow careful steps and moved onto the deck. The cedar planks felt cool on the soles of her feet.

"Ransom." Quinn forced her voice to a hush as she pulled the sliding door closed. "What are you doing?"

He turned around and rested his elbows on the railing. "Waiting for you."

The thought of Wynter sleeping soundly upstairs tugged at

Quinn's conscience. But Ransom and his perfect body was right there in front of her. It would be so easy.

Ransom walked toward her. "There's something between us, Quinn. I've felt it since the moment I saw you."

Quinn watched his approach. "I know, but we... we can't."

Now inches away from her, Quinn could feel Ransom's heat in the cool night air. He snaked his hands around her waist, over the condom concealed underneath. "I see you've come prepared." He leaned close and whispered, his hot breath tickling her ear. "I'll never tell."

Quinn couldn't stand it any longer. Her guilt was gone, replaced with a burning need to be with him. She grasped his face and kissed him hard. Gaining momentum, she directed him onto the chaise lounge.

She pulled off her T-shirt and sports bra and dropped them in a heap by the chaise. They resumed the kissing that had started in her dream before it became real.

Quinn's thoughts evaporated, replaced by hot breath and skin on skin. She laid a trail of kisses down Ransom's neck, between his pectorals, and toward his abdomen. His warm skin, his clean, slightly musky scent propelled Quinn over the edge.

Ransom watched her every move and it made her even hotter. She kneeled between his legs and inched her panties off, placing the condom to one side. Quinn shifted to one side and unhooked her panties' waistband off one foot, then the other.

Unencumbered by clothes, she tore open the condom. Her hands trembled, part anticipation and part nerves, as she unrolled the latex sheath over his length.

Quinn straddled his abdomen as Ransom reached toward her. They met in the middle, hugging, kissing, their hands roaming over each other's bodies. She raised her hips and guided him inside her.

Moving as one, their worlds came together.

Afterward, Quinn and Ransom laid in each other's arms for

what felt like hours. Stars salted the clear night sky but hints of orange had begun to creep up from the eastern horizon. There wasn't much night left.

Quinn rolled over, kissed Ransom, and sighed. "It's almost morning."

"So it is."

"I have to get some sleep. But before I do…" Quinn began kissing Ransom's neck and chest. "Think you got it in you?"

"Are you crazy? Of course." Ransom flashed a perfect toothy smile and sat up on the chaise. They looked down and saw that he was ready to go.

Quinn raised a brow. "That was fast."

Ransom shrugged. "What can I say? You have a magical effect on me."

"No, you're just a horny guy." Quinn straddled him and ran her hands over his chest.

Ransom sat up. "Do you have another condom?"

Quinn sent him a sly, sleepy smile. "Nope. Don't think I'll need it." She hoped she wouldn't need it. Sex with a boy was one thing, but with a boy born from dreams was quite another. She needed to know, and she was willing to risk getting pregnant to find out.

"Are you—"

"Shh." Quinn lowered herself onto him, wrapped her legs around his waist, and hooked her ankles together. "This is called 'The Lotus,' " she whispered.

The sun broke the horizon and spilled its color across the sky.

As they moved together, Quinn whispered, "This is also the last time."

"I know." Ransom's words were hot in her ear.

But would it be the last time? Quinn wasn't sure. Not by a long shot.

○

WYNTER WOKE TO a silent cabin. Through the bedroom window she could see blue sky peeking through the trees and although she woke feeling refreshed, an overwhelming sense of worry hung over her.

She picked up the coma-quilt and brought it to her nose. Wynter could still smell Ransom's scent. She wrapped herself up in it and wandered to Quinn's room.

Quinn lay under a top sheet, splayed and prone across the mattress with one arm hanging off the edge. Her daisy-patterned panties, sports bra, and T-shirt sat in a heap by the foot of the bed. Confused, Wynter lifted a corner of the sheet and peeked underneath.

*Yup. Definitely naked.*

Quinn groaned at the disturbance and rolled toward the wall, wrapping herself in the sheet as she went.

"Sorry for waking you."

Quinn peeked out from the sheet, squinting at the bright morning light. "Bug?"

"Looks like the party was here last night," Wynter said.

Quinn sat upright, suddenly wide awake. "What do you mean?"

Wynter motioned at her clothes on the floor.

Quinn pulled the bedsheets around her and peered over the edge of the bed. "Oh. That." She rolled back onto the bed and pulled the sheets over face, then peeked out. "I was too hot last night."

"Weird. I slept really well but I couldn't find Ransom anywhere." Wynter sat on the floor next to the bed. "Normally he's right there, in my dreams." She looked at Quinn, her face full of worry. "What if those sleepy zees did something to me? What if I've lost him forever?"

"You haven't lost him," Quinn said.

"But he's always been there, Quinn. Ever since I pulled him off the bridge he's been there, in my dreams, every night."

"He'll be back."

"When?" Wynter held back her tears. "How do you know?"

"I guess I don't know for sure, but you're both connected. He'll be back." Quinn's eyes clouded over. "I'm going to jump in the shower. Go have some breakfast and I'll meet you in ten."

"Okay." Wynter stood, then leaned over to hug Quinn. "Thanks."

"Any time, Bug."

As Wynter pulled away, she caught a whiff of something familiar, a scent she had grown to love.

*Ransom.*

Wynter smiled and gazed out the bedroom window. "I even smell him around me. Isn't that weird?"

"It's not weird." Quinn pivoted and swung her legs off the edge of the bed. "It just means you'll see him again." She waddled to the bathroom, the bedsheets dragging behind her.

Moments later, Wynter found herself digging through the kitchen pantry and cupboards looking for breakfast food. She found half a box of Cheerios but considered them barely a step above cat food. Besides there was no milk to go with it and she refused to eat them dry.

What Wynter really wanted on this sunny Sunday morning was her dad's famous pancakes with lots of butter and maple syrup. She was about to give up her search when she found a box of strawberry Pop-Tarts.

"It's not blueberry, but it'll have to do," Wynter said to herself. She pulled one of the mylar packets out of the box, broke it open, and placed the pastries on a plate. She crumpled the mylar into a tight ball and tossed it into the garbage.

As she closed the door under the sink, something sparkled in the garbage bin and caught her eye. Wynter took another look to satisfy her curiosity. She could see the Burger King bag, several microwave popcorn bags, and a frozen pizza box. But there, tucked on one side of the garbage bin, was a...

Her stomach dropped and the color drained from her face. She reached into the bin and with tweezed fingers extracted an empty condom wrapper, still moist with lubricant.

○

QUINN STOOD IN front of the bathroom mirror, a towel wrapped around her torso. She ran a smaller towel through her hair. Images of her late-night rendezvous with Ransom flashed in her mind, but each time they were pushed aside by the look of concern she had seen on Wynter's face earlier that morning. She sighed knowing her guilt would outlast any memory of last night.

Quinn stepped out of the bathroom and headed towards her bedroom. "Just getting dressed," she called downstairs. "I'll be down in—"

Wynter sat on her bed, waiting for her. Her cheeks were flushed hot and her eyes blazed.

"Bug?" Quinn felt her knees weaken but she held steady. "What's wrong?"

"Were you ever going to tell me?"

The moisture in Quinn's throat evaporated. "What do you mean..." She trailed off as Wynter held up the empty condom wrapper. "I..."

Quinn fell silent. She couldn't lie. Wynter had gone through the garbage and would know. She couldn't tell the truth either. It was the worst betrayal a friend could ever experience. How could she have been so stupid?

"Say something!"

Quinn could see that Wynter was barely holding herself together. "Bug. I—"

"And here I thought my mind was playing tricks when I smelled him before..." Wynter took a trembly breath. "But that's 'cause I smelled him on *you!*"

Quinn walked to the bed and sat down, noticing Wynter flinch as she did so. She hung her head, her damp hair covering her face in stringy clusters.

Wynter flicked the condom wrapper to the floor and balled her hands to fists. She faced Quinn. "You *fucked* him, didn't you?"

Quinn nodded. Hot tears breached her eyelids and ran salty tracks down to the towel wrapped around her.

"I want you to say it."

Quinn's lips trembled as she tried to form the words. She wanted to say she was sorry, to take it all back. Finally, she said, "Yes. I slept with him."

Wynter charged to the door. "You could've had any guy you wanted, and you chose Ransom. He's MINE." She trembled with fury. "You're such a *bitch!*" Wynter returned to her bedroom and slammed the door.

Sobbing, Quinn picked up her T-shirt and smelled it. Ransom's scent was all over it, which brought more tears. She grabbed her panties and sports bra and stuffed them all into her suitcase. As she did, the spent condom fell to the floor. She picked it up and held it to the light streaming in through the window.

The condom was empty now. It certainly hadn't been that way three hours ago. Quinn had made a point of remembering that detail.

Maybe there was a way she could repair the damage she had done. At least partially. She had to try.

○

Quinn paused outside Wynter's door for what seemed like an eternity. Every time she had gathered the courage to knock, she thought she heard Wynter crying behind the door and it stopped her cold.

She took a deep breath to try and calm her nerves and knocked. Rustling and walking sounds filtered through the door.

The door flew open. Wynter stood in front of her with her duffel bag slung over her shoulder. "Get out of my way."

Quinn stepped aside. "Let me explain."

"Fuck you." Wynter charged to the spiral staircase and descended to the main floor.

"Please, Bug." Quinn leaned over the railing of the loft. "It's not what it looks like."

"It's not?" Wynter marched past the sectional sofa and pulled open the front door of the cabin. "Did you or did you not have sex with Ransom?"

Quinn lowered her voice. "I did." Admitting her mistake out loud didn't help her feel any better. "But I did it for a reason."

"You fucked everything up. And you don't get to call me *Bug* anymore." Wynter slammed the door and trudged past Blue Belle onto the road.

"Shit." Quinn collected her things and ran down the stairs two steps at a time. On the coffee table sat Wynter's book *Eyes Wide Sleeping*. She jammed it into her bag, slipped on her shoes, and stepped out of the cabin.

She unlocked Blue Belle, threw her stuff into the back seat, and hopped behind the steering wheel, but instead of starting the engine, she sat there gripping the wheel with white knuckles.

Quinn screamed and pounded on the top of the steering wheel with her fists. "So stupid," she said, shaking her head.

She inserted her key and started the engine. In a cloud of gray smoke, she backed out of the driveway and sped down the road, her eyes searching for Wynter's signature red hair.

In the time it had taken Quinn to gather her things, Wynter had walked halfway to Gilberg Market. The highway wasn't much further than that. Fury had a way of propelling one great distances, sometimes in the wrong direction.

Quinn cruised up beside Wynter walking defiantly on the road's shoulder. She reached across the car to roll down the passenger window, but her foot slipped off the gas and she stalled the engine. Wynter didn't stop or pay any notice to the familiar car. Quinn finished with the window, restarted the Beetle's engine, and caught up to Wynter.

"Bug!"

Wynter kept her eyes forward and her pace steady. "Don't call me that."

Quinn sighed. "Wynter, this is crazy. Get in the car."

"Screw you."

"It's going to take you hours to walk home." Quinn matched Wynter's walking pace. "Let me drive you home. It's the least I can do."

Wynter stopped and pulled open the car door. She threw her duffel bag in the footwell and buckled herself in. Quinn accelerated down the road, the Gilberg Market visible in the distance.

"Do you want something to eat?" Quinn looked at Wynter. She had her arms crossed and her eyes aimed straight ahead.

Quinn drove past the market and crossed the highway, preparing to merge onto the highway headed east back to Newhaven. She turned on the radio to "I Want to Know What Love Is" by Foreigner playing mid-song.

"Nope." Wynter reached forward and snapped the radio off with a twist of her wrist. "You don't get to ruin anything else for me."

"Okay."

The two girls drove in silence with an invisible wall between them a mile thick. Ten minutes later the sign for Exit 182 flew past. Quinn eased into the off-ramp that led to south Newhaven.

"Bu... Wynter. Please can we talk?"

Wynter remained silent.

"Then please just listen. I know what I did was wrong." Quinn gripped the steering wheel with tight fists and turned onto Jones Avenue. The crippled Sven Dwarfs sign blinked in the distance even though it was day.

"I'm so sorry, Wynter." Quinn's voice cracked. "If I could take it all back I would."

Wynter stole a glance at Quinn and saw tears welling in her eyes. She pulled her duffle bag onto her lap in preparation for arrival.

Quinn drove by the trailer park's entry sign and followed the circular road to pad #7. She rolled to a stop behind Nolan's 1981 Plymouth Reliant and killed Blue Belle's engine.

Wynter had her hand on the door latch ready to go but Quinn grabbed her arm.

Wynter daggered a look back at her. "Let go of me."

"If our friendship meant anything to you, ever, then listen."

Wynter relaxed and Quinn released her arm. "You have one minute."

"Wynter, please believe me when I say I'm sorry. I mean it." Quinn swallowed hard. "I should have told you what I was doing."

"Tell me? Why?" Wynter's eyes narrowed. "Like I'd *let* you fuck my boyfriend." She turned to the door.

"Wait. I didn't do it just for me. I did it for you, too."

"For me? Why? To make sure I'm always a virgin? Is that it?"

"No." Quinn pulled her satchel from the back seat and dug into it. "I want to show you something." She pulled out a Ziploc baggie, the spent condom inside.

"And now you're rubbing it in my face? You're gross." Wynter moved to the door again.

"Look closer."

Wynter stopped and looked back. Quinn had piqued her curiosity despite her anger. "What?"

"It's empty."

"So?"

"So if you have sex with Ransom—"

"You don't get to say his name."

Quinn took a calming breath. "Okay. If you have sex—"

"If?" Wynter's anger rekindled.

"Jesus, Wynter. *When* you have sex with *him,* you can't get pregnant." Quinn locked gazes with her. "His cum disappears when he does. We talked about this, remember? At Lucy's?"

Wynter scanned the empty condom in the baggie, her eyes lightening a little. "How do you know for sure?"

Images of Ransom having sex with her a second time *without* a condom flashed through her head. Quinn briefly contemplated whether to tell Wynter about it but decided against it. One nail in the friendship coffin per day was her limit. "The condom's empty. I don't know what else I can say."

Wynter's eyes darkened again. "It doesn't matter anyway. Ransom's gone. Maybe it's for the best." She pulled the door latch and stepped out of the car, flinging her duffel bag over one shoulder. "Don't call me." She slammed the door and stomped to the front entrance of the trailer.

Quinn watched her go. She was about to yell another apology but stopped herself. She didn't see how it would do much good. Wynter unlocked the door and disappeared inside, slamming it behind her.

Defeated by her own poor choices, Quinn started the VW's engine and backed out of the driveway.

Nolan poked his head out the front door and waved.

Quinn stuck her head out the driver-side window and called to him, "Tell her I'm sorry, okay?" She backed out onto the ring road and drove away, a tumbling cloud of dust and exhaust following her.

Nolan, perplexed, scratched his head and stepped back to the trailer door. He turned to see Cash sitting on the stoop of his trailer across the central field, eating a bowl of cereal. Whatever had just happened, Cash had seen it all.

# Hard To Say
# I'm Sorry

Wynter woke in her room surrounded by all the things she loved. It was a welcome contrast to the unfamiliar bedroom at Quinn's cabin and it made it easier to push the memories of the weekend into the back of her mind. Ransom had been noticeably absent from her dreams and for that she was grateful. But Wynter had a feeling Quinn knew where he was.

She saw that Madeline had unpacked her duffel bag and taken care of her dirty laundry.

*The zees!*

Wynter hopped out of bed and searched her bag, but the gelatin cubes that had proven so useful when drifting in and out of sleep were nowhere to be found. She couldn't remember putting them in her bag, but her good memories of the weekend had faded after finding out about Quinn and Ransom. If her parents had found them, they'd make her life hell. She decided to play it cool and only address it if they came up.

She looked at the clock radio: 11:23 a.m. Wynter had been asleep for the past three hours. Ransom had been notably absent in her dreams again. Instead of slipping into anger, she took a quick shower and pulled on her favorite jeans and a Foreigner T-shirt.

On the kitchen table was a short stack of pancakes and a couple strips of bacon. The note beside it read, "Gone for a walk at Windspeaker. Back later. Love M&N. P.S. Cash called."

Wynter reheated breakfast in the microwave, smothered it with butter and syrup, and dug into the food. It tasted heavenly compared to the processed food at the cabin. It was an accepted fact that Quinn was a bad cook.

As she ate, Wynter's thoughts drifted to Cash. And except for his outburst at the park a week ago, he had always been so nice to her. Why had he called? She decided to find out.

Wynter grabbed her purse and stepped out into the Sunday sunshine, locking the trailer door behind her. She strolled across the field to Cash's trailer and knocked on the door. After a moment of commotion inside, the door swung open. Cash's father Ernie faced her, unshaven with his salt-and-pepper hair sticking up at odd angles. He wore a stained tank top and worn jeans.

Ernie Hawkins worked the night shift as a janitor at the newly opened Walmart in Halston. Wynter had known this but remembered only after knocking.

"Wynter?" Ernie scratched his head.

"I'm so sorry for waking you, Mr. Hawkins." Wynter's cheeks flushed pink with embarrassment.

Ernie waved her off but his effort to look alert failed when a yawn overtook him. "Don't worry about that. What can I do for you?"

"Is Cash available?"

Ernie cast a brief look into the trailer. "Don't believe so. Have you tried Finn's? That boy's always working."

"That was my next guess." Wynter stepped off the stoop. "Thanks. And sorry."

Ernie yawned again and shuffled back into the trailer, shutting the door behind him. Wynter crossed the field toward the Main Street Overpass.

Cash was right where he was supposed to be: operating Finn's register. A customer had just stepped out of the store. Cash saw

Wynter's approach and waved at her. Just as she waved back, he disappeared momentarily from view.

Wynter pulled open the door to the store. "Hey."

Cash leaned against the back wall, arms crossed, as if running the till at a gas station was the coolest thing ever. "Hey Wynter. How you doing?"

"I'm good." Wynter stammered. "My parents said you called?"

"Oh. Yeah. I just wanted to make sure you were okay." Cash flicked his eyes to a car driving up to the empty gas bays, then back to her. "I was eating breakfast on the front steps and kind of saw everything."

"It's bad."

"I'm sorry." Cash nodded as a customer entered the store. "Look, I get off at four and was going to go to Jake's, just to hang out, maybe play some Nintendo. Want to come?"

"Sure." Wynter answered without a second thought.

"Great." Cash beamed. "Meet me here and we can walk. Okay?"

Wynter nodded. Her heart already felt lighter. She waved at him as she turned toward the door.

"Oh, Wynter!" Cash beckoned her to the counter with his index finger and presented her with a cold Coke and a blueberry Hostess Fruit Pie. "To help you feel better."

Wynter accepted the soda and pastry. "You're sweet. Thank you."

"Not half as sweet as that pie." Cash grinned with full knowledge that the line was corny as hell. "See you later."

She waved, stepped back out into the sun, and immediately cracked the seal of the Coke. The first sip cascaded across her tongue and sent a wave of relaxation through her body. Maybe the day could get better.

WYNTER HAD PLANNED to spend the afternoon going through *Eyes Wide Dreaming*. She emptied her duffel bag on the floor before she realized that she had left it at the cabin. And now Quinn had it.

She could feel her anger brewing again, so she turned on the TV to try and distract herself. Madeline and Nolan could only afford basic cable and on a Sunday afternoon in the middle of summer the pickings were slim.

Wynter found herself back in her bedroom. She clipped her Walkman on her waist, threw on her headphones, and pressed play. Foreigner rocked out in her ears. She picked up her Pentax, stepped outside, and looked for subjects to photograph.

It was just what she needed. Between the music and fresh air, Wynter lost herself behind the lens. Before she knew it, it was time to meet up with Cash. She put away her camera and Walkman and headed back to Finn's after giving Madeline and Nolan a quick kiss goodbye.

Cash stood waiting for her on the curb beside the station, surreptitiously chewing a piece of gum. "Hey you. How was your afternoon?"

"Better than my morning," Wynter said as the two of them began their trek to Jake's. "And about that..."

"You don't need to tell me anything, you know."

Wynter nodded. "It's better if you do know, but you have to promise me that you won't get angry."

"Whoa." Cash flashed his brows. "Sounds heavy."

"And you have to promise that you won't say anything to Jake."

"This involves Jake, too?"

"Kind of. He likes Quinn, so..."

Cash glanced at her and nodded, his face serious. "I promise."

"I was up at Quinn's cabin over the weekend."

"Yeah. I called you on Friday. Your mom told me." Cash

stopped. "Want to go through the park or around? It's the same distance."

"Park." Once walking again, Wynter continued. "Ransom was there too, when I was able to find him in my dreams, that is." She decided to leave out that Ransom was in all of her dreams, all but one. "Everything was going great until Sunday morning when I found out that Quinn and Ransom slept with each other."

"Huh." Cash kept his eyes on the path ahead. "The guy gets around."

Wynter looked at him confused, with anger just under the surface. "What do you mean?"

Cash returned her gaze and flushed red from embarrassment. "Oh! I thought you two had—"

"Nope. Still a card-carrying Vestal virgin."

"Sorry." Cash backpedalled. "That came out wrong."

"It's okay," Wynter said. "Anyway, Quinn and I had a huge fight. That's probably what you saw."

Cash shook his head. "That's rough. It doesn't sound like the Quinn we know. Why would she do something like that?"

An image of Quinn holding up an empty condom flashed in Wynter's head. "I don't know."

"I hope you guys work it out."

"Me too."

The two friends walked in silence along 3rd Street, enjoying the day. Their hands brushed against each other once but neither of them acted on it. Cash had even apologized. As they entered Windspeaker Park it began to feel awkward.

"Hey Wynter," Cash began. "Last time we were here, I, uh... I kind of acted like a doof."

"Kind of?" Wynter cast a smile at him, but Cash missed it.

"Okay. I deserved that. I just wanted to make sure you knew I was sorry for, you know, flipping out over your boyfriend."

"I know, Cash." Wynter kicked a stone from their path. "But Ransom might not be my boyfriend any more."

"Oh." Cash looked at her to gauge how serious she was. "Is he really from your dreams?"

"You saw it." Wynter pointed back at the playground. "Right over there."

"I know I did but..." Cash thought about his words carefully. "The more time passes, the more I think I was drunk or something."

"Cash Hawkins? Drunk after one beer?" Wynter laughed. "You weren't drunk."

Cash nodded. "Yeah. I guess not... Not even with Grain Belt." He smiled at her.

"The *friendly* beer," they said in unison, laughing.

Cash stepped onto the pedestrian bridge, Wynter following several steps behind. Even though the structure was solidly built, Wynter could feel the vibration of their footsteps amplify as they walked.

At the midpoint, Cash leaned over the railing and looked down at the Sheyenne River. "Ever feel like jumping? It's not that far."

"No." Wynter hurried past him, intent on getting to the other side as quickly as possible.

Cash ran to catch up. "I think it would be fun."

Wynter shook her head, her fiery hair swaying back and forth. "You're on your own with that."

"Got something against bridges or something?"

"Yeah," she said. "Just don't like them. Don't tell anyone, okay?"

"Okay."

The two pressed on. They'd be at Jake's soon.

"We're in northie territory now." Cash surveyed the streets and the perfect houses lined up in a row. "Here's a secret about me. I've never felt comfortable in this part of town." He ran his hand along the slats of a white picket fence. "Never felt like I fit in."

"I get it," Wynter said. "Maybe it's because we're trailer kids."

"Yeah, maybe."

"But that doesn't mean the trailer is our destiny."

"You're pretty cool." Cash smiled at her and for a moment he looked a bit like Ransom. Wynter's heart skipped a beat.

"Thanks." Wynter dipped her head, her long hair hiding her smile and flushed face.

"Hey..." Cash took a breath. "Can I ask you a question?"

"Um, sure." Wynter didn't know what to expect. Seeking permission to ask a question usually meant the question was loaded.

"What do you like about him? Ransom, I mean."

*Most definitely loaded.*

"I don't know." Wynter took her time answering, not wanting to say the wrong thing. "He's handsome, I mean he came from my head so he's perfect, you know? He's fun to be around too, well, most of the time."

They turned onto Mortimer Avenue. Jake's house was a block away.

"He's fearless and he'll do anything for the experience." Wynter felt herself pulled back into her attraction for Ransom, but the memories of the morning and imagining Quinn with him overrode everything else.

"There's a lot of guys, real guys, who'd love to be your boyfriend." Cash found Wynter's eyes with his. "Guys like me."

Without hesitation, Wynter placed her hands on Cash's shoulders, raised up on her toes, and kissed him on the lips.

Cash stood, stunned, as she pulled away to hide her face. "I'm sorry. I shouldn't have done that."

"That's okay." A subtle smile broke across his lips. "I've always wondered what it's like to kiss you."

Wynter forced a smile and hoped it didn't look as awkward as it felt. She hooked her hair around one ear to distract herself and quickened her pace along the sidewalk.

Cash's smile faded. "I know this doesn't mean we're boyfriend-girlfriend or whatever."

"I'm sorry," Wynter said. "Ransom and I aren't even officially broken up yet. I shouldn't have kissed you but what you said was so sweet."

"Don't worry about it."

"Are you sure?"

Cash nodded. "Secret's safe with me. But if he drops the ball again, look out baby." He flashed a grin that reminded Wynter of Ransom all over again. "And we're here. Have you ever been to Jake's place before?"

"No."

"Get ready to feel out of place."

They both laughed as they walked up to the front door. Cash rang the doorbell.

"Got it!" Jake's voice filtered through the door, his socked feet thumping across the floor inside. He pulled the door open. "Cash... and Wynter!"

Cash raised a brow. "Got room for one more?"

"Um, sure!" Jake peered around the door frame. "Quinn with you guys?"

Wynter and Cash exchanged looks.

"She was busy," Cash said.

"Crap. Could've been a double date." Jake stood aside as Cash and Wynter stepped into the house and took off their shoes. "I've got the NES set up in the games room so we can use the big TV."

"NES?" Wynter gave Cash a confused look.

"Sorry. Nintendo Entertainment System." Jake led them downstairs into a large room with a pool table on one side, shelves of board games along the walls, and a leather sofa facing a large TV with the Super Mario Brothers logo displayed on it. "The NES is state of the art. I got one four months early. My dad's got connections." He picked up a controller from the table in front of the TV. "Who's first? Wynter?"

Cash chuckled at Jake's overt attempt to impress Wynter. He looked at her. "Go for it. I think you'll rock."

Wynter took the controller and sat on the sofa. "Okay. What do I do?"

"Where do I start?" Jake laughed and sat next to her, clearly in his element. "You have to get Mario through the Mushroom Kingdom as fast as possible and save Princess Toadstool."

"Is that it?" Wynter looked at him, then Cash. "Have I just become a video game nerd?"

Cash and Jake laughed as Mrs. Peterson stepped into the room. She stood beside the sofa in high-waisted acid-wash jeans with a pastel oversized button-down shirt. "Jake? I think an introduction is in order." She glanced at Cash and smiled. "Nice to see you again, Cash."

"You as well, Mrs. Peterson," Cash said.

"Oh, sorry Mom." Jake stood. "This is Wynter, Cash's friend."

Mrs. Peterson extended her hand. Wynter took it and they shook firmly. "Good to meet you, Wynter. Will you be staying for dinner?"

Wynter alternated her gaze between Jake and Cash. They were both smiling and nodding. "Um, I think so? But I'll call home to make sure."

"Sounds fine. I'll assume you're staying." Mrs. Peterson strolled back to the door of the games room. "It's nice to see *girls* interested in this..." She waved her hand at Mario on the TV screen. "This video game stuff."

Wynter set the controller down and followed Mrs. Peterson's exit.

Jake looked confused. "Where are you going?"

"I need to let my parents know what's going on."

Jake picked up the cordless phone from its cradle on one of the nearby shelves. "Just use this."

"A cordless phone? Cool." Wynter's eyes widened. "We have

one phone at my place and it's a wired one. So it's habit to go look for it."

Jake handed the phone to her. "Just slide the switch and dial." He shared a glance with Cash. "I can't imagine having only one phone," he whispered.

"You're pretty lucky," Cash said.

"Yeah." Jake tapped Cash's shoulder lightly, a thankful smile on his face. "Thanks for reminding me."

Wynter placed the phone back on its cradle. "It's okay with my parents." She scanned the dozens of games on the shelves. "You really play all these?"

"Some of them. My parents are the board game junkies." Jake looked back at the TV. "I'm more into video games these days." Jake picked up the Nintendo controller. "Want to try?"

"Can I watch you play for a bit?" Wynter looked at Cash for support.

"That's what I would do," Cash said.

"Okay. Just for a few minutes." Jake sat down, excited to share his video game experience with others. "I've been known to play for hours."

"Brag much?" Cash gave Jake a friendly shove.

"If I take longer than a few minutes, you have my permission to take the controller."

Wynter sat next to Cash and Jake as they began to explain the basic game play of Super Mario Brothers. As much as she wanted to pay attention, her mind wondered about Ransom, where he was, if he was okay.

But Ransom heard her. Loud and clear.

○

QUINN AND RANSOM sat facing each other on the chaise lounge, both wearing nothing but bedsheets. They were back on the deck, but without a cabin, her bed, or trees. Instead, the deck floated in the middle of a great expanse of water.

*Lake Gilberg?*

They were adrift with no way to get back to shore. Even with Ransom sitting across from her, Quinn felt unease settle into her. She remembered a short story written by Stephen King the previous year, about teenagers stranded on a raft and terrorized by a strange creature.

Quinn took in the expanse of perfect blue sky, which did nothing to calm her anxiety. "I don't like it here."

Ransom leaned forward and took her hands in his. "Then let's go back."

"I don't know how." Quinn's eyes clouded with concern. "I know I pulled you out of my dream before, but I don't know what I did."

"You didn't do anything." Ransom's clear blue eyes studied her.

She sensed trouble. "What do you mean?"

"You, Wynter, or whoever... you can call me in a dream," Ransom continued, "but I decide if I want to make the leap to reality or not."

"All this time Wynter thought she was pulling you out, but..."

Ransom nodded. "It was me." Gray storm clouds formed behind him, churning in angry swirls. Despite this change, he leaned in and kissed her. "Want to go real?"

"Yeah."

"Hold on." Ransom rocked backward and pulled Quinn on top of him. They tumbled off the chaise, the deck, and finally into the dark, cold water.

Then Quinn woke up.

○

QUINN FOUND HERSELF in her own bed, staring into Ransom's eyes, eyes that still carried trouble. In her dream she had been on top of him but now the situation had reversed. And he was naked under his bedsheet. She didn't like it and his eyes sealed the deal. When he swooped in to give her another kiss, she pushed him away.

"What's wrong?" Ransom's face showed not confusion or hurt, but anger. "I thought you wanted to make out, for real."

The events of the morning swirled in her head, both the passion and the betrayal. She had sworn to never let a boy get in the way of her friendship with Wynter, if there was a friendship left after this morning. Yet here she was, on the cusp again. "I thought I did."

Quinn squirmed out from under him. She placed her hands together at her chin as if praying and rocked gently back and forth. "I've got to make things right again."

She looked around her room, at the movie posters, at the rock and roll glamor shots, her desk, books, and knickknacks, all in hopes that it would ground her in some way.

Quinn had expected a reply from Ransom but received silence back instead. "I think you have to go," she said. "And that means out of my head, too." She faced him. "Did you hear me?"

For the first time since meeting Ransom, Quinn saw that anger was possible in him. He was practically vibrating from it. She touched his arm gently and his body jolted, like she had thrown a switch and shocked him.

Quinn pulled her hand back. "Are you okay?"

"Huh?" Ransom returned her gaze. The darkness behind his eyes cleared, but not entirely. "Uh, yeah. I'm... fine. But you're right. I got to go." He looked around Quinn's room. "What's the easiest way out of here?"

Quinn glanced at the clock on her desk: a few minutes after seven. "My parents are probably watching *60 Minutes*. I can sneak you out the back." She made a motion to stand, but Ransom grabbed her arm and stopped her. He let go just as quickly.

"I'm not mad at you, Quinn," Ransom said. "I could have prevented all this from happening. I just couldn't control myself."

"And I could've stopped you..."

Ransom cast his gaze at the floor. "Do you think Wynter will forgive me?"

"I don't know if she'll forgive *me*."

"I got to try."

"Want me to call her?"

Ransom shook his head as his eyes went dark again. "I already know where she is." He raised the bedsheets around him. "Could I borrow some clothes?"

"I'll see what I can do." Quinn eased her bedroom door open. "Next time dream yourself a designer outfit."

"You're the one who wanted me naked."

"Don't start." Quinn disappeared down the hallway, returning a few minutes later with a pair of track pants and a MAXELL-branded sweatshirt. "Sorry. It's all I could find that wouldn't raise suspicion."

"This is great, thanks." Ransom pulled on the clothes. "How do I look?"

"Honestly? Like a hobo." Quinn rolled up the cuffs of the sweatshirt. It didn't help much.

"It doesn't matter," Ransom said. "Show me the way out."

The two of them crept out of the bedroom and down the stairs, Quinn leading the way. She bypassed the TV room and led Ransom to the back door.

"Good luck," Quinn said, knowing forgiveness was only the first step.

"Thanks." Ransom padded down the back walk in bare feet. He stopped to look back. "Don't fall asleep any time soon, okay."

Quinn nodded. And in a moment, Ransom was gone from view. Whatever Ransom had planned, she hoped it would work.

O

Wynter, Cash, Jake, and Jake's parents finished up their dinners in the back yard. They sat around a picnic table shaded by a large free-standing cantilevered sunshade. An inviting in-ground lap-pool filled with clear, blue water glinted in the evening sun.

Mr. Peterson transferred several hamburger patties from a large stainless steel barbecue to a serving platter and made the rounds. "Any takers for seconds?"

Cash patted his stomach. "No, thank you, Mr. Peterson. I'm stuffed. Lucy's better look out."

"Well, I just cook the patties," Mr. Peterson said. "Miri makes them, and everything else. She's magical."

Mrs. Peterson pushed his shoulder playfully. "We make a good team."

"How about you, Wynter?" Mr. Peterson eyed her plate. "Another burger?"

"I'll split one with someone." She looked at Jake "Interested?"

"I'm no fool." Jake cast a glance at Cash.

"Ha ha. Very funny," Cash said.

"Wynter?" A voice rose from across the back yard, near the side of the house.

Wynter turned in her seat and saw Ransom. Gone were his usual jeans, T-shirt, and hoodie. Instead, he floated in leisure wear too big for his teenaged frame. Her eyes darkened.

"Who's *that*?" Jake asked.

Cash shot him a look, leaned in, and whispered through his teeth. "That's the guy, remember? The one from her dreams."

"The one that—"

Cash glared at him.

Mr. Peterson set the plate of patties down. The concern on his face was mirrored by Mrs. Peterson. "Is everything okay, Wynter? Do you know this boy?"

"I know him." Wynter looked at the rest of the group at the table. "Excuse me for a moment." She slid her chair out and took urgent steps toward Ransom.

Jake squinted in confusion. "Why is he in *bare feet?*"

"Jake, that's enough. Voices carry." Mrs. Peterson leaned forward and spoke in hushed tones. "You don't know anything of that young man's situation."

"I know some things," Cash said to himself.

Wynter and Ransom were out of earshot and looked to be in a heated discussion. She looked back, connected gazes with Cash, then dropped her eyes. Jake noticed the exchange.

Ransom stepped forward, placed his hands around Wynter's waist and pulled her close. He kissed her, sloppy and uncoordinated, as if he was drunk.

Cash stood, knocking his chair over. "Hey! Get your hands off her."

At the same time, Wynter pushed Ransom away and started back toward the picnic table.

Jake placed a hand on Cash's arm. "Easy, dude. Looks like she doesn't take any shit."

"No, she doesn't," Cash said.

When Wynter returned to the table, she grabbed her purse from her chair. "Thank you for a lovely dinner, Mr. and Mrs. Peterson." She looked at Jake and Cash. "Catch you later, guys. I got to take care of some... things."

"Sure you're okay?" Cash asked.

Wynter nodded, then walked back toward Ransom. She stormed past him along the side of the house and he followed.

Mr. Peterson sat back down. "What was *that* all about?"

Everyone looked to Cash. "Ex-boyfriend, probably," he said.

"Well, Wynter's a lovely girl." Mrs. Peterson began collecting dishes. "You tell her next time you see her that she's welcome here any time."

"I'll do that, Mrs. Peterson. Thanks." Cash looked back to the side of the house where Wynter and Ransom had just stood. Anger flowed through his veins. All he wanted to do was run after them and beat the shit out of Ransom. Then walk Wynter home.

"Super Mario? Best two out of three?" Jake did his best to salvage the mood. "Take it out on Bowser?"

"Yeah. You're on." Cash collected his plate and cutlery and carried it inside. But his mind replayed the kiss. He had seen Wynter kiss Ransom twice now. He didn't think he could take it a third time.

○

WYNTER MARCHED DOWN 3rd Street, choosing to stick to the sidewalks instead of cutting through Windspeaker Park. Anger at Ransom mixed with the embarrassment of having her lovely evening interrupted kept her moving at a brisk pace. Rage was a good motivator.

Ransom shuffled along beside her, doing his best to keep up in bare feet. He quickly discovered that when walking without shoes, practically everything is a rock to the foot.

"Come on, Wynter. Talk to me."

Wynter ignored him and cut through the parking lot of Stedford Plaza to get to Main Street. She could see the overpass ahead. Soon she'd be back into her familiar southie stomping ground.

"You can't ignore me forever," Ransom said through heavy breaths.

"I can and I will."

He glowered at her. "I'll haunt your dreams."

Wynter stopped and spun to face him. "You're joking, right?

You *fuck* around on me and expect *me* to take you back. And if I don't, you *threaten* me. Fuck you."

She stormed up the incline to the Main Street Overpass, the place where everything had started almost two weeks ago. At that moment she regretted saving his cheating ass.

"I'm sorry, Wynter. Please."

As she neared the midpoint of the overpass, Wynter turned again. "You weren't in my dreams last night either. Where were you?"

"I was... I—" Ransom stammered, searching for the right words.

"You were with Quinn, right?"

"Yes, but—"

"God, why did I even bother." Wynter resumed walking again.

Ransom chased after her. "We didn't do anything. I mean Quinn didn't want to. I—"

"So *you* wanted to fuck around again and Quinn didn't. That's great." Wynter continued her furious pace down the other side of the overpass. "You better not fall asleep, asshole, because I'm *never* bringing you back."

Ransom's pleas stopped and for a moment she thought he had given up. But his voice rose up again a few seconds later. "Wynter! I'd die for you!"

"You're a dream. You can't die." Wynter turned to see Ransom standing on top of the overpass railing. They both looked down to see the steady stream of traffic barreling down the Interstate. "Quit fooling around, Ransom. You could hurt someone."

"I love you, Wynter," Ransom yelled. "Do you believe me?"

"Get off the railing!"

"I'm just going to have to show you." Ransom looked at the oncoming traffic and spotted an eighteen-wheeler approaching. "Remember. I'm doing this because I love you."

He made a graceful swan dive off the overpass. Wynter leaned over the railing and watched in horror as his body glided head first toward the road below.

The sound of Ransom's head cracking against the pavement was more than she could bear. Wynter screamed and hid behind the railing as his body crumpled in a heap.

A vibrating screech of tires mixed with the repeated blast of an air horn echoed from the eighteen-wheeler. The entire vehicle shuddered on the road as it shot forward with little signs of slowing. Its semi-trailer payload began to snake sideways into the adjacent lane.

Wynter looked over the railing as the truck tractor unit slid over top of Ransom's broken body and under the overpass. Acrid smoke from burnt tires filled the air.

"Ransom!" She crossed Main Street, ran to the end of the overpass, and inched herself down the embankment of the eastbound merge lane.

The truck came to rest just beyond the overpass with traffic piling up behind it. The driver engaged his hazard lights and hopped out of the cab. He spotted Wynter across the highway. "Stay there! Did you see anything?"

Wynter shook her head. The driver disappeared behind the semi-trailer to look for Ransom's body. She stood far enough away to see underneath the semi-trailer and knew at once that his search would be fruitless.

There was no body, no blood, no expected carnage. She sighed heavily in an attempt to shake off the charge of what she had just witnessed. It didn't work. The sound of Ransom's impact with the road still echoed fresh in her mind.

Wynter scrambled back up the embankment and ran home as fast as her legs could carry her, knowing that she had unlocked another of Ransom's secrets. And there was only one person she could talk to about it.

O

WYNTER STEPPED INTO the trailer, her breath coming in quick puffs and her cheeks flushed. Madeline and Nolan snuggled on the sofa in the living room watching *Murder, She Wrote*.

*How would Jessica Fletcher solve* this *mystery?*

"Wynnie? You alright, honey?" Madeline tempered her concern while waiting for an answer.

"I'm fine, Mom. I just ran all the way from Jake's is all."

Nolan exchanged a look with Madeline. "How was dinner?"

"It was good. We had burgers." Wynter walked past her parents to her room and closed the door. She slid to a sitting position, her back against her door, and burst into tears. She cradled her head on her arms.

A soft knock sounded at the door. "Wynnie?" Madeline's voice beckoned her. It took all her will to stop herself from throwing open her door, wrapping her arms around her mom, and spilling her guts about the past twenty-four hours. But that would mean explaining Ransom, and he was still a wildcard.

Wynter swallowed her sorrow and wiped away her tears. "Yeah, Mom?"

"Quinn called earlier," Madeline said through the thin door. "A couple hours ago. I just remembered."

"Thanks." Wynter wanted to blow her nose and wipe her eyes properly, but that would be a dead giveaway that she'd been crying.

"Join us if you want, okay?"

Watching *Murder, She Wrote* was the last thing Wynter wanted to do. What she really wanted was a good night's sleep, free of anxiety, bad dreams, and Ransom. "I think I'll call Quinn back."

She tossed her purse on the bed and examined herself in the mirror. With her red-rimmed eyes, Wynter knew she wouldn't pass the "mom" test. She stepped out of her room and into the bathroom, closing the door behind her.

Wynter dotted her eyes with crumpled toilet paper. She flushed the toilet and blew her nose gently, hoping that the sound of the flush would cover everything else.

She walked the length of the trailer to the kitchen and looked at the phone with its coiled cord. A cordless phone would have been nice, but luckily the handset had come with a long cord.

Wynter carried the handset out the front door to the stoop. The cord bounced and stretched out across the kitchen and over the table, just long enough to reach.

She sat, closed the door, and dialed Quinn on the keypad of the handset. The speaker trilled in her ear and she almost lost her nerve. Mid-way through the second ring, the call picked up.

Silence. Then, "Bug?"

Wynter fought back her tears. "Yeah."

"Oh, Bug." Quinn sputtered back through the line. "I... I'm so sorry."

"I know."

"I wouldn't blame you if you never forgave me," Quinn said. "I'm impulsive. I make bad choices sometimes."

Wynter sighed and smiled ever so slightly. Even that felt good after a very bad day. "You really screwed up."

"Big time."

Wynter paused to collect her thoughts. The dead air on the line combined with everything that had happened earlier weighed down on her and she couldn't bear it much longer. "I thought I could talk to you about this over the phone, but I can't. Can we meet tomorrow? After work?"

"Is this about... you know who?"

"I can't right now, Quinn. Tomorrow, okay?"

"Okay."

Wynter was about to hang up when she heard Quinn's voice filter through the speaker of the handset.

"Wynter?"

"What?"

"Thanks... for calling me back."

"Yeah." Wynter felt her tears rush at her again and she let them fall as she hung up the phone.

◯

WYNTER'S SHIFT AT Shooters began like any other weekday: unlock the security gate, turn off the alarm, turn on the lights, and initialize the cash register. Those tasks should have been evenly shared between Daytona, Hunter, and herself, but she was the only one who showed up each morning.

Most days Wynter ignored their lack of punctuality, but her sleep had been fractured the previous night by irrational fears of whether she would have to face Ransom, if he'd show up at all. She would have appreciated the option of sleeping in, but his threat to "haunt her dreams" remained fresh in her mind and made sleep impossible.

Monday mornings never saw many customers beyond a flurry right at the store's opening. Wynter had figured that the lines at Minit Prints were too long for people who just wanted to buy film. Being the middle of summer further reduced the store's mid-morning traffic to close to zero.

Wynter positioned herself behind one of the glass counters and flipped through the latest issue of *Popular Photography*. She could hear Vinny scolding her in her head, saying that she'd leave fingerprints all over it.

"Fuck you, Vinny," she whispered to herself, but apparently she had spoken loud enough to be heard clear across the store.

"That's the spirit," a familiar voice said.

Wynter looked up to see Quinn leaning against the wall at the entrance to the store in her pink and black FreshWhip uniform. "How long have you been standing there?"

"Not long. I just got here." Quinn pushed herself away from the wall and casually strolled through the store, looking at the displays. "Sorry. I know you said after work, but I couldn't wait."

"It's always about you, isn't it?"

"No. This is about you, actually." Quinn jammed her hands into her pockets. "Can I drag you away from here for a couple hours?"

"I can't just close up shop and leave whenever I want to."

"Why not?" Quinn looked back out of the store. Less than a dozen people wandered the main concourse. "The plaza is dead."

"Vinny would fire me."

"Vinny's dumb, but he's not *that* dumb."

Wynter directed her attention back to her magazine.

"Look." Quinn sighed. "I'm trying to make things right. I wanted to surprise you but maybe that's a bad idea."

"Sorry to inconvenience you." Wynter kept her eyes on her magazine. "I just can't turn the hurt off like a switch."

"I know," Quinn said softly.

Sounds of laughter echoed from the concourse, breaking the wall of silence between the two girls. A moment later Hunter and Daytona strolled into the store, both wearing their Shooters uniforms.

"We're not interrupting anything are we?" Hunter eyed them and grinned. "If so, can we join?"

Daytona slapped him on the shoulder. "Don't be gross."

"Hey Hunter, Daytona."

Wynter looked up to see the gears in Quinn's head begin to turn.

"Wynter and I need to head out for a couple of hours," Quinn glanced at the clock in the corner. "We'll be back by noon at the latest. Cover for her, okay?"

"Did you clear it with Vinny?" Daytona placed her hands on her hips. "He's going to be pissed if he finds out."

"Then don't let him find out," Quinn said. "It's not rocket science."

"It's not that easy."

"But it is." Quinn stepped toward Daytona. "You and Hunter have been late for every single shift you've ever worked here. And you're *still* working here because Wynter covered for *you*."

"That's not true." Daytona hesitated, then looked at Hunter. "Is it?"

"It's probably true enough." Hunter motioned at Quinn and Wynter. "We got your backs."

Quinn beckoned to Wynter and smiled. "Come on. Time's ticking."

Wynter decided to go, not because she wanted to, but to hide the rift between her and Quinn. Daytona and Hunter didn't need to know. She closed her magazine and followed Quinn out of the store.

◯

WYNTER AND QUINN headed for the exit.

"Just a second." Wynter plucked a roll of film out of her purse and made a detour toward Minit Prints. "I need to get this developed."

While Wynter dealt with her film, Quinn paced the deserted concourse, worry drawn all over her face. Moments later they emerged from Stedford Plaza and headed across the sparsely filled parking lot, Quinn leading the way.

"Where are we going?"

"It turned out I get to surprise you after all." Quinn stepped up onto the sidewalk of Main Street and followed it toward downtown Newhaven. "And if you're wondering, he-who-shall-not-be-named didn't appear in my dreams last night."

"I wasn't." After several steps of silence, Wynter added, "He threatened to haunt my dreams if I didn't forgive him. Then he killed himself."

"What?" Quinn froze, her eyes wide in surprise. "But he can't die. He's not real." Quinn's eyes flickered as if she was remembering something.

"That's what I said, but it didn't stop him from jumping from the overpass, then getting run over." The crack of his head hitting pavement replayed in her mind, causing Wynter to flinch. "I didn't sleep at all last night."

"Oh my God." Quinn took a step toward Wynter, then stopped herself, respecting her boundary.

Wynter could tell Quinn wanted to hug her. That's what she would have done before the cabin retreat. And knowing Quinn's intent comforted her.

"So was he..."

Wynter locked gazes with Quinn. "There was no trace of him. He must have drifted away when he died. I just ran home after that. I feel sorry for the truck driver."

"So he drifts away when you sleep, when he sleeps, and when he dies." Quinn worked the details in her head, her eyes falling away fascinated. "Let's go."

Quinn offered her hand and Wynter took it, even though it had only been a day since her betrayal and her head screamed not to. It just felt right.

They continued walking.

"If you die in your dreams, do you die in real life?"

Wynter shook her head. "That's a myth. There's been lots of studies on it."

"Good. That means that Ran... that *he's* probably okay. You're going to have to find him."

"I know."

Quinn snapped her fingers. "I've got your book, by the way. Remind me to give it to you later."

"Thanks," Wynter said. "So where are we..."

Then everything clicked. Just ahead was the Bombshell Salon. The shop's sign hung over the door and front window, lettered in red script with a thick white outline and a curvy caricature of a woman's head with a voluminous hairdo next to it. It could have been transported straight from the 1950s. Maybe it had been.

Quinn looked at her and raised her brows in hopeful expectation. "Manicure? Pedicure too, if you want it? It's the least I can do."

Wynter smiled wistfully. "Okay." Even though Ransom was a figment of her imagination, Quinn's betrayal was real and still stung. Yet, she couldn't ignore Quinn's earnest attempt to make amends.

"Awesome," Quinn said. "Let's go. Mercy's waiting."

"What do you mean? You booked an appointment?"

"Of course. Everyone wants their nails done by Mercy."

Wynter softened. "It's hard to stay mad at you. But I *am* still mad. Just so you know."

"Just a little *less* mad." Quinn pushed open the door, jingling a bell at the top of the doorframe.

"Just a little." Wynter followed her inside, but her head was back at the overpass, replaying the events of last evening and wondering if Ransom was really dead. Soon she would have her answer.

○

BOMBSHELL SALON WAS long and narrow, with full length mirrors on each facing wall. There was space for eight customers at a time, two work areas at the back devoted to Mercy and one other nail technician, and the rest reserved for the stylists. The mirrors served a dual purpose: to help the space feel much larger than it was, and to encourage customers to interact with each other, if only to give each other knowing looks.

Quinn sat next to Wynter in the back corner facing the mirror, allowing them to see everyone else in the salon as Mercy worked on Wynter's feet.

"Is it normally this busy on a Monday morning?" Quinn asked.

"Yup." Mercy nodded. "It's pretty much like this, nine to five-thirty, Monday to Friday." Mercy had her bleached blond hair tied up in a knot, with the strawberry tips sticking up. She looked like an exotic fruit.

She leaned in and whispered, "That's why I want to start my own salon. It's a license to print money. Plus I'm fuckin' good at it." All three laughed.

"Anson told me you were thinking of..." Wynter lowered her voice. "You know, doing your own thing."

"Getting closer every day," Mercy said. "Now if I could just get that lug nut to propose, I'd be set." She glanced at the two girls. "Not that I need a man to get what I want. It's just that he's..."

"A total babe?" Quinn's face lit up.

Wynter laughed and shook her head. "Quinn's got the major hots for Anson." She shared a knowing look with Quinn.

Mercy shrugged. "So does every woman in Newhaven. He can window-shop, I always say. Just as long as he doesn't buy or touch anything or try any free samples. And always comes home to eat, if you know what I mean."

Quinn and Wynter giggled, but for Wynter the friendship still felt raw and strained. Her laughter did not feel genuine and she did her best to hide her discomfort.

After Mercy had finished with Wynter's feet, she wrapped them in a towel with just her toenails exposed, newly painted purple.

"My feet feel *amazing*," Wynter said.

"If you think that feels good, just wait."

With no polish to remove, Mercy got to work on buffing and shaping Wynter's fingernails.

Besides a manicure feeling heavenly, Wynter discovered that she loved to watch Mercy work. "If I had known I was coming here today, I would have brought my camera." Mercy moved with such precision that Wynter imagined she could do the job with her eyes closed.

"But you need both hands to take photos," Quinn said.

Wynter glanced at her. "Details, details."

"Oh, this was a surprise?" Mercy gave her a quick glance. "Like for your birthday?"

"Not exactly." Wynter cast her eyes to the hand Mercy was working on.

Quinn picked up a *Glamour* magazine and casually flipped through it.

Mercy raised a brow and looked at the two girls as a veil of silence descended between them. "I sense a bigger story here but I'm not one to pry." She refocused on Wynter as she pushed back her cuticles with a birchwood stick. "So you're a photographer?"

The change of subject perked Wynter up. "I like to think so. I work at Shooters to help pay for my gear."

"Good for you," Mercy said. "I like seeing young women going for what they want."

"Queen Of Hearts" by Juice Newton floated from the speakers in the corner of the salon.

Quinn looked at Wynter before tossing the magazine on the side of the table. "How long have you and Anson been together?"

"What did I tell you?" Wynter hooked her thumb at Quinn. "One track mind."

"Ha. Ha." Quinn rolled her eyes.

"Seven years," Mercy said without missing a beat. She moisturized Wynter's hands and swiped each nail with nail polish remover.

"Wow," Quinn said. "What's your secret?"

Mercy nodded knowingly. "Ah yes, the secret. I'm going to make you work for it. Take a guess."

Quinn's eyes connected with Wynter's, then she leaned across the table. "Hot sex?"

Mercy weighed the answer, subtly rocking her head back and forth. "That's part of it, but not my number one." She turned to Wynter. "Same purple as your toes, hon?"

"Yes please."

"What's *your* guess?" Mercy continued.

Caught off guard, Wynter blurted the first thing that came to her mind. "Honesty?"

Mercy nodded as she shook a vial of purple nail polish. "That's a big one."

"Trust?" Wynter said.

Mercy loaded the brush with enough polish to completely cover a nail with three broad strokes. She looked at Quinn briefly. "Sounds like Wynter knows the secret."

"There's got to be more to it than that," Quinn said.

"I do have a personal favorite, but I'm sure it's different for everyone." Mercy applied even strokes of polish to Wynter's nails and shook her head. "I don't know if I should even be talking to you two about this."

"Come on, Mercy. Don't leave us hanging." Quinn tapped her fingertips on the table.

"Let me finish the first coat." Mercy continued painting until the nails on Wynter's fingers all matched with an even purple coat. She capped the polish and set her hands on the table. "My secret is to find a guy that loves to kiss. Because kissing can be more powerful than anything else."

Quinn looked deflated. "Just kissing, huh?"

Mercy laughed. "It also helps to be twenty years older. I mean I'm in my sexual prime." She had spoken a bit too loudly and several customers turned their heads, their interest piqued.

Wynter smiled. "Sounds good to me."

Mercy glanced at the clock on her table. "Let's get you finished up. I think—"

Quinn saw Anson step into the salon and all heads turned his way.

"Afternoon, ladies." He tipped his hat, then smiled and waved at Mercy. She waved back.

Quinn sighed. "So Anson likes to kiss, huh?"

Mercy leaned forward and lowered her voice. "Don't go blabbing my secret, all right? I'll know. This place is the hub of town gossip. Okay?"

Both girls nodded.

"Okay. Second coat and top coat coming up." Mercy shook the bottle of nail polish. "Then Anson is taking me to lunch."

"Where is he taking you?"

"Not FreshWhip, you stealer of hearts." Mercy winked at Quinn as she began Wynter's second coat. Joking or not, Mercy had Quinn pegged.

Quinn watched Anson chat up the other customers in the salon while Wynter focused on Mercy's steady-handed brush strokes.

Ten minutes later, Quinn and Wynter pulled open the door to the salon and began their short trek back to Stedford Plaza.

They walked without talking for a couple blocks until Quinn couldn't stand the silence any longer. "I hope I didn't make things worse."

"No, but I need time," Wynter said. "It's been, like, a day."

"Okay." Quinn paused. "I really am—"

"Sorry. I know."

They cut through the plaza parking lot, weaving between the many vehicles.

"Lots of people in the plaza today. More than when we left." Wynter chuckled. "Daytona and Hunter might actually have to work for a change." She pulled open the door to the plaza and let Quinn go through first. A cool, air-conditioned breeze washed over them. "You going to get in shit?"

Quinn shrugged, then looked at Wynter's watch. "We're not late. Deb can't fire me because the plaza got busy."

They reached Shooters first. Wynter held out her nails and admired their purple sheen.

"Thank you for the Bombshell treatment," she said. "I love them."

"You're welcome, Bu... can I call you Bug?"

Wynter nodded.

"Can I give you a hug?"

Wynter nodded again, this time with a small smile.

Quinn wrapped her arms around Wynter and held her tight. "I love you, Bug." She held Wynter for a few moments before kissing her cheek and letting go. "Will you call me later?"

"Yeah."

Wynter headed into Shooters. Hunter and Daytona were in the middle of dealing with customers and could only manage head nods. She was about to step into the back room to deposit her purse when she heard footsteps that could only be made by Vans.

Quinn reappeared at the front of the store and charged back to where Wynter stood. Daytona and Hunter exchanged a glance as Quinn strode past.

Quinn took hold of Wynter's shoulders. "I figured it out, Bug!"

"Figured what out?"

Quinn took a breath, leaned close to Wynter's ear, and shared the secret that would change everything.

# Kiss You When It's Dangerous

Quinn grabbed Wynter's hand and pulled her out of Shooters and into the bustling plaza concourse. Now the customers in Shooters were distracted as well as Hunter and Daytona.

"What?" Wynter saw excitement and even some fear in Quinn's face. "What is it?"

"At the cabin yesterday morning, you said that he-who-shall-not-be-named didn't show up in your dreams."

"Just call him Ransom."

"Okay, Ransom didn't show up."

"Yeah, that's because you were…" Wynter took a step backward. "Why are you rehashing this?"

"I didn't tell you everything that happened." Quinn took a fortifying breath. "On Saturday night, when I was in the kitchen, I kissed Ransom. Just once."

"Yeah, so?"

"Ransom went to bed with you, but he appeared in *my* dreams, in *my* bedroom."

Wynter faced her, upset and confused.

"The *kiss*. I was the last person to kiss Ransom and he appeared in my dreams."

Wynter connected the dots. "Your kiss connected you to him?"

"Yes." Quinn hopped with excitement.

"And you made out with him in your dreams, but it became real."

"It only became real because Ransom wanted it that way."

"You wanted it too, obviously."

"Yes, I admit I'm a horny teenager. But I didn't pull Ransom out. He controls that."

"No." Wynter shook her head. "You're wrong. I've always pulled him out of my dreams."

"You've called him. But he decides if he drifts into reality or not." Quinn took a step toward Wynter. "I think he has to be touching the dreamer for it to work."

Wynter narrowed her eyes at her. "So was Ransom in your head all day yesterday?"

"Until about seven o'clock," Quinn said. "He wanted to make out, but I didn't. I swear. There was something off about him too. Something dark. I gave him some clothes and he left. Then I called your place, but you weren't there."

Wynter stood and locked gazes with her.

"Did you kiss him last night?"

Wynter nodded.

"Then he'll be in your dreams tonight. Maybe you should keep him there."

"Or I just stay awake," Wynter said. "Just like in *A Nightmare on Elm Street.*"

"That didn't end well for anyone." Quinn studied Wynter's face. "Besides, you've got that whole lucid dream thing going on. If anyone can control their dreams, it's you."

"Okay. I'll try and keep him in my head for a night."

Quinn hugged her again. "Call me any time, day or night."

"I will."

Quinn headed toward the food court and Wynter turned back to Shooters. Hunter and Daytona both leaned against the back wall of the store, both with their arms crossed.

"What the *hell* was that about?" Hunter smirked and raised an eyebrow.

"Nothing." Wynter walked past them and deposited her purse in the back room.

"Ha! For nothing, it sure looked like *something*."

Hunter didn't know it, but it *was* something. Perhaps it was everything.

O

DAYTONA AND HUNTER chose to lock up Shooters on Monday night, an uncharacteristic move that Wynter didn't argue with. Maybe they were developing a sense of responsibility. She stepped out of Stedford Plaza to another clear, bright, and warm July evening.

"Can I give you a lift?"

Wynter turned to see Quinn leaning against the exterior brick wall of the plaza, still wearing her pink and black FreshWhip uniform.

"Has anyone ever told you that you look like a licorice allsort?"

"You do. All the time." Quinn shielded her eyes from the sun. "Want a ride or not?"

"Sure."

Wynter expected Quinn to drape her arm across her shoulders, but she didn't. She held back, aware that things weren't back to normal between them yet. It was the right move.

Quinn unlocked the doors to Blue Belle. She had managed a parking spot facing away from the direct sunshine and the front seats were comfortably warm. She reached into the back seat, grabbed *Eyes Wide Dreaming,* and handed it to Wynter.

"Thanks. I've missed this book." Wynter ran her hand across the hardcover. "I know that sounds a bit weird."

"No, I get it." Quinn started Blue Belle's engine. "You don't know what you've got 'til it's gone." And with that the mood was set for the ride to Sven Dwarfs.

Wynter clicked on the radio to KROK. Two teenagers whispered about the virtues of swishing with Close Up mouthwash before the kiss. She rolled her eyes. "That's so cheesy."

"They have a point though," Quinn said. "I'd rather kiss peppermint than coffee and cigarettes."

"Well, when you put it that way…"

The ad transitioned into "Girls on Film" by Duran Duran.

"Shit!"

Quinn shot a look of panic at Wynter and slowed down the VW. "What?"

"Sorry. I just remembered that I have those pictures to pick up at Minit Prints."

"Is that it?" Quinn's body relaxed. "Don't worry about it. I can pick them up on my way home."

"Awesome. Thanks." Wynter opened her purse and pulled out several bills and the photo claim stub. "This should cover it."

"I got it."

"No, please take it." Wynter had accepted the trip to Bombshell Salon as Quinn's penance but wasn't prepared to accept anything else that had financial value. It wasn't about money. She set the bills and the stub on top of the dash.

Quinn sighed in resignation as she rolled into the trailer park and around to Wynter's pad. "Good luck avoiding Ransom tonight. Remember, you can call me any time."

"Got it." Wynter stepped out of the little car and walked toward the front stoop of her trailer.

"Wait!" Quinn turned off Blue Belle's engine, hopped out, and chased Wynter. She wrapped her arms around her. "Be careful."

"I will. But it's just a dream." Wynter studied Quinn's face curiously as she stepped back. "Quinn? What is it?"

"Just be careful," she said. "I don't know if you noticed it with him last night, but I saw darkness in his eyes. I think he's changing."

Wynter nodded. She had noticed something in Ransom as well but had been too angry at the time to address it. She stepped to the front door and unlocked it. "Thanks for the drive home and for getting those pictures."

"Any time, Bug." Quinn half-smiled and jammed her hands in her pockets.

Wynter closed the front door, locking it behind her, and peeked out at Quinn through a side window. She started Blue Belle and drove away.

The trailer seemed quieter than usual. Wynter threw herself on the sofa and flipped on the TV to keep her company while she waited for her parents to come home. Nothing but boring news but at least it was something. She opened her book and began to reread it for the umpteenth time.

But even Wynter's book failed to capture her attention. Her mind kept going back to the previous night, to Ransom, and wondering what her dreams would hold.

◯

WHEN QUINN RETURNED to Stedford Plaza, most of the vehicles in the parking lot had cleared out. She parked and headed for Minit Prints' exterior door, knowing that the main doors to the plaza would be locked by now.

Two people stood in line ahead of her, but the wait to get to the cashier amounted to less than five minutes. To pass the time, Quinn watched the big blue instant photo machine churn out 4"x6" photos from one end in full view of everyone in the store.

She stepped to the front counter and handed the claim stub to the clerk. The young guy dug through his finished bin and pulled out a packet of prints.

Quinn handed him Wynter's cash. "You ever get weird photos come out of that thing?"

The clerk rang in the prints and handed Quinn her change. "We try and pre-screen the negs, but every once in a while a few slip through."

"Like what, exactly?" Quinn was genuinely curious.

The clerk checked his surroundings, leaned forward, and lowered his voice. "We got a picture of a guy fucking a purse once. Just a close up of—"

"Okay I got it." Quinn grimaced. "Maybe you should put a cover on the end. You know, for privacy."

The clerk shrugged. "Maybe."

Quinn held the envelope of photos in her hand. She wanted to open it up and take a sneak peek, but she'd have to break the safety seal in order to do that. It would be better to let Wynter see them first, she decided.

She pushed open the exterior door and stopped dead in her tracks. In the parking stall beside Blue Belle's driver side sat a midnight black Barracuda. Jezebel and Roxy leaned on the front of the hood, passing a joint back and forth.

"Oh shit." Quinn swallowed hard and forged ahead to her VW.

Jezebel took a drag from the joint and handed it to Roxy. "Look who it is, Rox. Isn't that the bitch who cut me off on the highway?"

"Yup." Roxy inhaled and handed the joint back.

"Jesus, you drooled on it. Learn to fucking toke." Jezebel stubbed the joint's ember on her tongue and dropped it into the outside pocket of her jacket.

Quinn dug her keys out of her purse.

"Hey, you prissy bitch, I'm talking to you." Jezebel snorted and spat at Quinn, half of the glob landing on the side of one of Quinn's black Vans. "You could've killed us."

"You could've killed *us*." Quinn positioned her keys at the door's keyhole, but Jezebel slapped them to the ground. As she crouched to pick them up, Jezebel snatched the envelope of photos.

Quinn reached for the envelope, her mind imagining Wynter seeing the opened envelope as another breach of trust. "Come on. Give them back."

Jezebel stood taller than Quinn and it was easy for her to hold the envelope of prints above her head. "I don't think so." With her free hand, Jezebel pulled out a switchblade and flicked it open.

Quinn eyed the sun's glint coming off the blade and backed off.

Jezebel slid the knife under the envelope's seal, cut it open, and handed the switchblade to Roxy. "Time for some show and tell."

Roxy grabbed the knife and bounded off the hood of the Barracuda. "Don't do anything stupid." She sneered, pointing the sharp tip of the blade at Quinn.

Quinn held her ground. Roxy was a wild card most of the time and it was best not to provoke her. At least Jezebel was consistently evil.

"Don't you have something better to do?"

Jezebel laughed. "Actually, I don't." She turned the envelope around in her hands. It was then that she noticed the name on the envelope's label. Jezebel's eyes flicked to Quinn and narrowed on her. "Wait. These aren't yours, are they?"

Quinn crossed her arms and quoted *Late Night with David Letterman,* a detail she knew would be lost on Jezebel. "Apparently there's no off on the genius switch."

"Shut up." Jezebel's words came out in a snarl.

"Yeah, shut up." Roxy took a step forward, her eyes sparkling with excitement.

Jezebel cast an annoyed glance at Roxy and looked at the label again. "*Whiner* LaCroix, huh? Let's see." She dumped the contents of the envelope into her hand. A stack of prints and negatives slid out into her hand.

Jezebel dropped the negatives to the asphalt and twisted the heel of her black Doc Martens into them, shredding the plastic. "Oops."

She began flipping through the photos one by one, flinging them into the road. "*Whiner* sure likes to take photos of boring shit."

"She's more talented than you'll ever know." Quinn watched the prints flutter to the road, most of them image-side down.

Jezebel scoffed as she continued to riffle through the prints. "Wait a second. Who's this?" Jezebel held up a photo of Wynter and Ransom.

Quinn's stomach sank. It was the picture she had taken under the slides at Windspeaker Park. The image was grainy but had enough detail to show Wynter and Ransom at a happier time.

Quinn shrugged. "A friend."

"He was at Lucy's." Jezebel tapped the photograph for emphasis. "I'd like a friend like this, too." She tore the print in half, placed the half with Ransom on it in her jacket pocket, and let the half with Wynter on it fall to the ground.

Jezebel slid off the hood of the Barracuda and approached Quinn. "You tell *Whiner* that we're coming for her. And her *friend*."

Quinn kept her arms tightly crossed against her chest and stared back without saying a word. There was no point in engaging.

Jezebel extended her arm and beckoned. Roxy folded the switchblade into its hilt and handed it back to her.

Jezebel took her spot behind the wheel of the Barracuda and started the engine, revving it into a low grumble. Roxy hopped into the passenger seat and stuck her tongue out at Quinn.

The Barracuda rolled forward a few feet before Jezebel floored the accelerator and laid a strip of rubber across many of the photographs on the ground.

Quinn could hear the two bullies laughing as the menacing black vehicle zoomed out of the parking lot.

"Fuck," Quinn said to herself quietly. She crouched onto all fours and picked up all the prints and negatives, both salvageable and destroyed.

How was she going to explain this to Wynter? She'd have to tell the truth, but would Wynter believe her? Two days ago, the answer would have been "yes" but now Quinn wasn't so sure.

○

WYNTER LAID IN BED. Despite the warm summer day, a chill washed over her body. She pulled her covers up to her chin and stared at the ceiling.

*What if Ransom's a monster?*

She fought a losing battle against sleep and did not have the energy for "what-ifs." After a day and a half of intense emotion and heartbreak, exhaustion had taken its toll.

Wynter struggled to stay awake, but her eyelids hung heavy. She promised herself to close them just for a moment, but seconds turned to minutes. That was all it took. She drifted into what should have been a familiar land of dreams. When she reopened them, her room felt overwhelmingly dark. Wynter imagined a sky of summer blue, but the darkness prevailed.

The sight of Ransom leaning against her desk at the foot of her bed gave Wynter a start. He wore his standard attire of a white T-shirt, jeans, and a black hoodie that melted into the shadows. His arms were crossed against his chest and she could feel his eyes on her, going through her. He showed no signs of injury from his leap off the overpass a day earlier.

"Ransom!" Wynter's words came out in a whisper. "Are you okay?"

"Do you really care?" Ransom's words carried none of their usual warmth.

"Of course." Wynter pushed herself into a sitting position against the headboard and pulled her knees to her chin. "I've been worried."

"Is that why you left me in here?"

"I needed some time. You're not exactly innocent."

Ransom sighed. "If you're talking about Quinn, I'm sorry. You know I live for experiences."

"That doesn't give you the right to do anything you want, whenever you want, with whoever you want." Wynter glared at him. "There's consequences."

He shrugged. "Maybe for you."

"Well maybe I'll just leave you in my head then."

Ransom let his arms fall to his sides and he placed a knee on the end of the bed. "You and I know that won't work. I decide when I leave."

"Then you need to behave." Wynter kept her eyes on Ransom's approach.

"But I don't want to behave." Ransom grinned, but instead of comfort, his smile carried an element of malice. "Behaving isn't fun." He crawled onto the end of the bed. "And I want to have fun. You want to have fun, don't you?"

"Not right now. I need you to leave me alone."

Ransom shook his head slowly back and forth and continued to inch closer.

Wynter backed her way to the opposite corner of the bed. She scanned her bedroom for potential weapons and came up empty. She wished for the first time in her life that she played baseball. A bat would do nicely right now.

"Let's just have some fun, Wynter."

*Wait. This is a dream. My dream. And I control it.*

Wynter grabbed the sheets covering her legs, now heavy and soaked with water, and threw them over Ransom's head, blinding him.

She seized this momentary advantage and hopped off the bed, raced between the bed and her desk, and grasped the doorknob. But it wouldn't budge.

"You don't control everything." Ransom pulled the sheets from his face, his eyes gleaming at her.

"But I'm stronger than you." Wynter kicked the door and it flew off its hinges, crashing on the hallway floor. She turned toward where her parents bedroom should have been but their door was gone.

Without wasting another moment, Wynter ran to the front door of the trailer. Ransom pursued her, hot on her heels. She could hear his frenzied breath as if he was right at her ear.

Wynter reached the front door, yanked it open, and stepped out into thin air. The front stoop had been replaced with steep and rocky scree with no discernible bottom and strong winds whipped up from below. She screamed, lost her balance, and fell forward.

Ransom caught one of her forearms and their hands locked around each other's wrists. "That was close." The grin that had made her so uncomfortable before was back.

"Pull me up, Ransom!"

He loosened his grip briefly, allowing her to slip down an inch further. "Having fun, yet?"

*It's just a dream. Create what I need.*

"Why are you doing this?"

Ransom let her drop another few inches. "I don't want to be in your head. You're boring, Wynter."

His words crushed her soul. Was he just toying with her? Wynter released her grip of his wrist and felt him tighten his grip around hers to compensate.

She reached up with her free hand and tried to pry his fingers off, but his grip was too strong. Wynter imagined a Ginsu steak knife and felt the hilt materialize in her free hand. She plunged it into Ransom's arm.

Shocked, he released her wrist. Wynter plunged toward the scree below. She landed on her back and began to slide into the depths.

"Not so fast." Ransom leaped from the front door of the trailer, his feet digging into the loose rocks. With sliding steps, he ran down the steep slope in hot pursuit. After he had closed the distance between them, he kneeled and slid between Wynter's protesting legs. He scrambled toward her as they both sailed off the rocky ledge and into oblivion.

○

WYNTER AND RANSOM landed beside the foot of her bed with a loud thud. The bedside lamp was already on the floor. She scooted away from him, righted the lamp, and turned it on.

She looked him up and down in the warm glow of the lamp. "You've changed."

"I just like the real world better than the one in your head." Ransom smiled. "No comparison, really."

"Except you hurt people for real." Wynter drew her knees close.

The sound of her parents' bedroom door opening, followed by a series of rapid knocks, filtered through her door.

"Wynnie?" The concern in Madeline's voice was clear, even through the door. "Are you okay?"

"Wynter?" Nolan knocked on the door again. "We're coming in."

Wynter looked at Ransom, her fear dissolving into a small, satisfied smile. "I'm in shit now."

Madeline and Nolan burst into the room. Wynter and Ransom

stood. He pulled his hoodie over his head and took his place beside Wynter, but he kept his distance.

Madeline glared at both of them, her nostrils flaring, her concern bubbling over into anger. "Who is *this?*"

"Mom, I—" Wynter couldn't find the words to explain who Ransom was and how he got here. But Madeline didn't give her a chance. Her fury cut her off.

"A boy? In your room? At this hour?" When Madeline got angry, there was never a shortage of questions. Nolan placed his hand on her shoulder, but she shook him off. "You know the rule, Wynnie."

Wynter nodded.

All four of them stood in a stand-off until Nolan broke the silence. "What's your name, son?"

Ransom peeked out from under his hoodie at Nolan and Madeline, then glanced at Wynter. His eyes blazed bright blue again. "I'm sorry," he said, then bolted for the bedroom door, pushing Nolan aside.

Nolan fell backward against the bedroom's back wall but regained his balance quickly enough to see Ransom run to the kitchen, pull open the front door, and disappear outside.

"I'm going to go lock the door." Nolan left Madeline and Wynter alone.

"Who *was* that, Wynnie?" The concern was seeping back into Madeline's face. "How did he get in your room?"

Wynter remained silent but couldn't stop the tears. Madeline took Wynter in her arms.

"Oh, Wynnie. You gave us quite a scare."

Nolan returned and leaned in the doorway. "Not a trace. That boy runs like the wind."

Madeline released Wynter but held her shoulders firmly. "There will be consequences, Wynnie. We love you but the rules are there for your safety." She kissed Wynter's forehead. "Back to bed, okay."

Wynter wiped her face with her sleeve and slipped under the covers. Nolan shuffled over and gave her a kiss on the cheek.

"It'll be okay by morning," he whispered. "Cooler heads will prevail." He followed Madeline out and closed the door.

Wynter wanted to sleep, but sleeping would lead to dreaming. Ransom would return to her head and this whole nightmare would begin again.

She decided Ransom had to go. But how?

○

THE TRAILER HAD fallen quiet again, but sleep was eluding everyone. Madeline rested her head on Nolan's shoulder and draped her arm across his chest.

She blinked in the darkness and whispered, "Do you think Wynnie's asleep?"

Nolan raised his free arm and tucked his hand behind his head. "I don't know. After that, I'm not sure I would be either."

"*That* being what, exactly?" Madeline waited for an answer but heard only Nolan's steady breathing. "Are you thinking what I'm thinking?"

"The smell?"

"Yeah, like ozone, but not quite." Madeline propped herself up on her elbow. "Like with your..."

"Grandmother," Nolan said. "Yeah."

"The power of summoning."

"It's possible. As far as I know, my parents couldn't do it, and I could never control it the way I wanted to. Believe me, I tried." Nolan sighed deeply. "It would have been helpful as a Native American teenager."

"Can it skip generations?"

"Maybe, but I just don't know for sure," Nolan said. "If you believe the stories my parents passed down to me and my brothers and sisters, my grandmother's powers were more a curse than a blessing. They drove her mad. Some believe that's why she jumped."

"Oh, God. I'm sorry, hon." Madeline hugged Nolan's chest. "I shouldn't have brought it up."

"No, it's best that we talk about this. I don't want it to get away from us, or for Wynter to suffer the same fate." Nolan ran a finger down the curve of Madeline's shoulder. "The sooner we deal with this the better."

In the silence, Nolan could tell that Madeline's gears were turning. "I was thinking we could ground her, but if she can summon people..."

"Right. Grounding won't work," Nolan said. "Wynter needs to be honest with us. That's the only way to move forward."

"So, that boy could have been summoned? From where?"

"From her head. Her dreams." Nolan shifted onto his side so he could just discern Madeline's face in the darkness. "I bet her dreams are incredible."

"She didn't look guilty, though." Madeline replayed the scene in her head. "It was more like she was scared."

"But scared of that boy? He seemed innocent enough."

"He had something to hide," Madeline said. "Otherwise, he wouldn't have run."

"You're probably right."

Nolan and Madeline settled into their own pillows.

"Do you think Wynnie could die from this?"

"We won't let it get that far. We'll bring in somebody to help if we have to." Nolan yawned. "Maybe a healer from Standing Rock. But there might be problems."

"Like what?"

"The tribe may not accept Wynter's blood quantum."

"Surely they'd make an exception if it was a question of life and death."

Nolan sighed. The night had been exhausting. Contemplating

one more problem frayed his nerves. "Hard to say. I don't want to jump to conclusions."

Madeline fell silent but reached for Nolan's hand in the darkness.

"Let's agree to keep our eyes on her. Sound good?"

"Okay."

Madeline and Nolan kissed each other good night. Nolan pulled the covers up and was asleep in minutes, but Madeline's thoughts swirled in her head. Their talk had done nothing to quell her fears.

"Nolan? Hon?" Madeline woke Nolan up.

"What? What is it?"

"I think we should talk to Wynnie."

"Right now?" Nolan rolled onto his side to face her. "Can't it wait until morning?"

"No. No, I don't think it can."

Nolan sighed. "Okay. Let's talk to her."

They both slipped out of bed and walked to Wynter's bedroom.

◯

RANSOM RAN AS fast as his legs would carry him, across Sven Dwarfs's grassy field and onto Jones Avenue. His legs felt brand new, full of power, and his speed made wind whistle at his ears. He loved the real world.

He needed to find Quinn fast, before Wynter fell asleep again and made him drift. Going back into her head was one power he had no defense for, unless he could kiss someone else. And Quinn knew how to party.

Once he found Main Street, a memory clicked. Ransom retraced his path over the Interstate toward Quinn's house.

Engine noise rose up from behind. The vehicle's headlights cast stretched shadows of Ransom's legs in front of him. A black

Barracuda flew past and a hand clipped his shoulder, knocking the hood off his head.

A blond girl pulled her arm back through the passenger window and twisted her head around. Her wind-blown hair concealed her face. "Watch it, idiot!"

Ransom continued running along the sidewalk of Main Street. The Barracuda, now a few hundred feet down the road, slid to a stop with a teeth-shattering screech and a plume of pungent smoke. Its taillights burned red like the eyes of a devil. The vehicle accelerated in reverse until it met Ransom's stride again, then followed him.

Jezebel leaned toward the passenger window. "Hey, hot stuff. Where you going?"

Ransom looked into the car as he ran. He recognized the two girls immediately. On the dashboard, he saw himself in the torn half of a photograph. He slowed to a walking pace, his hands on his hips.

"You...," he said between breaths. "I've seen you two before." He stopped and Jezebel slammed the brakes. Ransom snapped his fingers and pointed at her. "Lucy's, right?"

"Good memory."

Roxy traced his body with her eyes. "Wonder if he's good at anything else?"

"You also tried to run us off the road," Ransom said.

Jezebel shrugged. "Yeah, sorry about that. What can I say? I'm a flirt." She licked her lips. "What're you doing out so late?"

"Nothing special."

Jezebel's eyes wandered over his face. "What's your name?"

"Ransom."

"Handsome Ransom." Roxy giggled.

"Want to have some fun... Ransom?" A sly smirk slid across Jezebel's lips. Roxy covered her mouth and stifled a snicker.

"What do you mean by *fun*?"

"You know…" Jezebel leaned across the center console, pulled Roxy toward her, and kissed her, their tongues mingling. "Fun."

Ransom alternated his gaze between the two girls. "Okay, I'm up for some fun." He rested his forearms on the car door. "Who's first?"

Roxy squirmed, moved up to the window, and puckered her lips.

"Not so fast, bitch." Jezebel pulled her back into her seat. "You'll get some soon enough." She shifted her eyes to Ransom. "Come around to my side."

Roxy's eyes fell only for a moment. Soon they were back following Ransom as he strutted around the front of the car, crossing the Barracuda's headlight beams. "His ass is fine."

Ransom stared at Jezebel. She beckoned him with a curled index finger. A kiss would mean he'd get to live in their world for a while and he had no problem with that. He leaned in and they kissed. Jezebel worked her tongue again. Always a quick learner, Ransom reciprocated. Roxy watched, moistening her lips with envy.

Ransom and Jezebel parted, but both appeared energized by the kiss.

"You're fucking *magic*." Jezebel nibbled her bottom lip. "Want to get high?"

Ransom shifted his gaze between Jezebel and Roxy. Two girls wanted him instead of one and he was free from Wynter and her power to drift him. He nodded.

Roxy opened the passenger door and pushed the seatback forward.

"Here's to new experiences." He ran around the Barracuda and jumped into the back seat. Roxy hopped back into the passenger seat.

Jezebel floored the gas, pulled the steering wheel hard left, and made a fast U-turn. She sped toward the Main Street Overpass.

"Where are we going?" Ransom sat forward and rested his elbows on the seatbacks.

"You'll see." As Jezebel turned onto the merge ramp for the Interstate headed east, she exchanged a knowing look with Roxy.

Roxy giggled in response.

Ransom had no idea what to expect and it was exactly what he was looking for.

○

CASH LAID IN bed unable to sleep. He kept replaying Sunday night in his head, how Ransom appeared out of nowhere, how Wynter ran to him even after his betrayal. And that kiss. It didn't make any sense.

Ernie rattled around in the trailer, preparing for his night shift at Walmart. Cash knew the ruckus wasn't intentional, but the walls in the trailer were thin. There would be no sleep until he left. Cash rolled out of bed, threw on his jeans and yesterday's T-shirt, and stepped out into the common area.

"Sorry, son. I'm running late. Did I wake you?"

Cash shook his head. "I was having trouble sleeping anyway."

Ernie glanced at his watch, an old wind-up Timex that his father had given him. "Anything on your mind? I can spare a few minutes."

"It's okay. We can talk later." Cash gave his father a hug and a pat on the back. "You don't want to get fired."

Ernie waved him off. "It's not the end of the world if I get fired." He paused and gave him a sideways look. "Girl trouble?"

"Dad. Go." Cash could feel the heat of embarrassment forming under his T-shirt.

"I know I raised you right." Ernie looked at him and patted Cash's cheek. "They're missing out." He grabbed his coat, wallet, and keys.

"Thanks, Dad." Cash saw Ernie to the door and watched him drive their Honda Civic down the trailer's gravel driveway. After the dust settled, Cash stood on his front stoop and took in the expansive night sky. He may not live in a big house with all the bells and whistles, but his life was pretty good, all things considered.

Across the field, a dim glow illuminated one of the windows in Wynter's trailer. Odd. Cash knew that Wynter's parents did not work nights. Most trailer windows were dark by eleven-thirty on a weekday.

Cash pulled on his shoes and tucked the laces into the sides. He closed the door and stepped down to the field.

The front door to Wynter's trailer burst open and a young person ran across the field, toward the Main Street Overpass.

Cash ducked beside the end of his trailer, out of the light from the front stoop, his eyes locked on the runner. There was no long red hair trailing behind, unless it was concealed in the... black hoodie.

*Ransom?*

Moments later, Cash saw Nolan appear at the front door of the trailer in shorts and a T-shirt. He scanned the field, then stepped back into the trailer, closing the door behind him.

Cash slipped behind his trailer and ran after the unknown figure. He wasn't sleeping anyway. The exercise might do him some good. He hopped the fence at the side of the property and raced down Jones Avenue.

A familiar rumbling rose up from behind. Cash ducked behind a shrub, shifting his position as the black car rolled past him. When it was far enough ahead, he resumed his pursuit.

Worried about losing the mystery runner, he ducked diagonally through two yards, in hopes of gaining some ground. He could hear his math teacher in his head praising him for choosing the hypotenuse as the shorter distance.

Cash hopped the final fence, trailing just behind the Barracuda.

Looking to his left, he saw the runner crossing the Interstate. He crossed Main Street, ducking to avoid discovery, and chased both the Barracuda and the runner. Adrenaline in his veins mixed with the energy of the night propelled him forward.

By the time Cash had crossed the overpass, the Barracuda had stopped and reversed back to the runner. His hood was off, revealing blond curls. It had to be Ransom. They appeared to be having a conversation.

Cash hopped the end of the overpass railing and slid far enough down the off-ramp to conceal his body but high enough to give him a direct line of sight on his suspects.

Ransom walked around the front of the Barracuda, then leaned into the open driver's side window.

"What is he doing?" Cash whispered to himself, but it was soon obvious that he was kissing Jezebel. Surprised, he found his heart aching for Wynter. She deserved better. "This asshole *really* gets around."

Ransom ran back around the car. Roxy held the door open for him as he climbed into the back seat. Roxy hopped back into the car and had barely closed the door before the Barracuda peeled out, spinning into a tight U-turn.

Cash ducked under the overpass railing until the Barracuda was even with him. He poked his head up and confirmed it was Ransom in the back seat, grinning ear to ear with those perfect teeth. He followed the black car's headlights as it crossed the overpass, turned left onto the on-ramp, and accelerated to merge onto I94 East, toward Halston. It was the same route his dad had taken to work twenty minutes ago. This time, he had no idea where they were going and no way to follow.

Cash walked home using lit side streets and sidewalks. Part of him expected Jezebel to roll up on him but he was met with the silence of a Monday night in Newhaven. The summer air cooled him down. By the time he returned to his trailer, the light in

Wynter's trailer was out. He hoped she was asleep and dreaming but had a strange feeling that she wasn't.

Cash undressed and slipped back into his bed. After everything that had happened to Wynter, this new development would devastate her. But he had to tell her, and the sooner the better. That's what friends did.

Despite his exhaustion, Cash found himself chasing sleep as the minutes ticked by. When the clock beside his bed struck midnight, he had had enough. He pushed the covers off and pulled on his clothes.

Cash walked to the living room, picked up the trailer's only phone and dialed.

◯

QUINN ARRIVED AT Cash's trailer twenty minutes later with Jake in the passenger seat of Blue Belle. Both looked like they had been yanked from their beds by their feet. Cash waved at them from the front steps of his trailer.

Quinn slammed the door of the VW and trudged toward him. "This better be good."

Jake slid out from his seat and positioned the viewfinder of his JVC camcorder to his eye.

"What're you doing?" Cash held up his hand. "No. Shut it off."

Jake smiled behind the camera. "If Quinn kicks your ass, I want to get it on video." The red recording light lit up.

"And I just might," Quinn said. "So what's so urgent?"

"Ransom's with Jezebel and Roxy."

Quinn's eyes narrowed. "What do you mean *with*?"

"I saw Ransom bust out of Wynter's trailer earlier tonight," Cash said. "So I followed him. Jezebel pulled up, they kissed, and the three of them drove off toward Halston."

"They *kissed*?" Quinn's eyes bugged out and she began to pace. "Oh shit. This isn't good."

Cash exchanged a look with Jake. "It's just a kiss. What's the big deal?"

"It's *not* just a kiss." Quinn glared at Cash, then at Jake and his red record light glowing back at her. "Yeah, shut that thing off."

"Okay, okay." Jake stopped recording and lowered the camera.

"What do you mean, Quinn?" Cash hopped off his front stoop and approached her.

"Sorry. I forgot you guys don't know the latest," Quinn said. "Wynter and I figured out that the last person to kiss Ransom gets him in their dreams."

Jake looked at Cash, confused. "What the hell is she talking about?"

"I told you about the dream guy, last Friday remember?"

Jake shook his head. "I didn't think you were serious." He turned to Quinn. "So when you say someone 'gets Ransom in their dreams,' what do you mean?"

The three stood closer together and Quinn continued. "Wynter's mega into lucid dreaming, like when you can control your own dreams, okay? Somehow, she developed the ability to, like, pull a guy out of her dreams into the real world."

"No shit." Jake was all ears. "And this guy just walks around, even though he's from a dream?"

"Yeah," Quinn said. "A literal dream walker."

"A dream *waker*, more like." Jake formed an enthusiastic grin. "I'd like to get *that* on video."

Quinn nodded. "You might get your chance." She looked at Cash. "He drifts away when he or his host sleeps, or if he dies. But he doesn't *really* die. He just jumps out of the next dream of—"

"The last person who kissed him." Jake raised his brows at Quinn. "He's immortal. Like Connor MacLeod in—"

"*Highlander*," Quinn and Jake said in unison.

"Kind of, yeah." Quinn eyed Jake, her eyes sparkling.

"Wicked movie," Jake said. "I love the scene when Kurgan got his…"

Cash stared at him and raised his brow. Jake took the cue and stopped talking.

"To be continued," he said.

"I like a guy who knows their cinema." Quinn glanced back at Wynter's trailer. A vast expanse of stars dotted the sky. "Anyway, you see how this could be a problem? Jezebel controlling an immortal?"

"Yeah." Cash followed Quinn's gaze across the field.

"It might even affect Wynter's mental health… with a piece of her in that psycho." Quinn cringed subtly and Cash noticed. Their eyes connected briefly but a moment was all that was needed. Quinn knew that Cash knew of her betrayal.

"A piece of her?" Jake furrowed his brow in confusion.

"She created Ransom," Quinn said. "He's a part of her."

"Right. I get it."

"It's past midnight, guys." Cash faced Quinn and Jake. "We need to tell Wynter. And figure out how to get Ransom back." He started across the field. "Let's go."

The three of them crossed the field to Wynter's trailer.

"Who's going to…" Quinn trailed off as Cash marched up the steps to Wynter's front door and knocked on it several times.

Cash rejoined Quinn and Jake at the foot of the steps. "I figured I'd knock since I'm practically her neighbor."

"Better you than me this late at night," Jake said.

"Shit, someone's coming." Quinn shifted uneasily on her feet. "Nolan's going to kill us."

The door to Wynter's trailer opened a crack first, then wider as Nolan stuck his head out of the door. "Cash?"

"Hi, Mr. LaCroix." Cash offered a small, awkward wave. "We need to talk to Wynter."

Nolan eyed the three teens for a moment, then opened the door to let them in.

"He didn't even ask why," Jake whispered to Quinn.

"Yeah. Something's up."

After Cash, Quinn, and Jake were inside, Nolan closed the door and locked it. "How did you know?"

The three teenagers looked at each other and shrugged.

"I swear you teenagers are all psychically linked." Nolan led the group down the hall and into Wynter's bedroom.

Madeline sat next to Wynter, holding her hand, their backs against the wall at the head of the bed. Wynter's eyes looked puffy and red, as if she had been crying recently. The lamp beside the bed cast a warm glow through the room and helped elevate the somber mood.

"Oh, Bug!" Quinn ran to Wynter and threw her arms around her. Wynter hugged her back. Fresh tears seeped from the corners of her eyes as Quinn sobbed into her shoulder.

Jake leaned toward Cash and whispered, "What's going on?"

"It's okay," Cash whispered back.

Quinn and Wynter released each other. Madeline offered them both tissues, then slid off the bed and walked around to join Nolan. Wynter offered Quinn the spot next to her on the bed, which she gladly accepted.

Madeline looked at Quinn, then Cash and Jake. "How did you all know to come here tonight?"

Cash's eyes flicked to Quinn, then to Madeline. "I was seeing my dad off for work earlier and I saw a person run out of your trailer. At first, I thought it was Wynter, but..." He smiled as his gaze drifted to Wynter. "No trademark red hair." Cash looked at Quinn, then Jake, and shrugged. "I called Quinn and Jake over because I thought if Wynter had had a scare, some friendly faces might help."

Nolan placed a firm hand on Cash's shoulder and gave it a pat. "You're a good friend."

"Thanks, Mr. LaCroix."

"Okay, my dear," Madeline said. "I think that's our cue. Wynnie's in good hands." She shuffled out of the bedroom.

Nolan followed but pulled Cash aside. "You need to find that boy."

"Yes, sir." Cash looked at Nolan, his eyes serious. "How much did she tell you?"

"Enough," Nolan said. "Even as a dream, that boy's still a vital part of Wynter. She'll die without him."

Cash swallowed hard. "I'll do my best to find him, sir."

Nolan nodded. "I know you will." He disappeared from Wynter's bedroom and into his own.

Cash closed Wynter's bedroom door.

Jake stared at him intently. "Are we in shit?"

"No, but we got to get Ransom back to Wynter."

Wynter crossed her arms against her chest. "What if I don't want him back?"

"Your dad said that you'd die without him," Cash said. "What's *that* all about?"

"According to my parents, I have the power of summoning." Wynter waved her hands and wiggled her fingers as if performing a magic trick. "Apparently my great grandmother had it and it drove her mad."

"The power drove her mad?" Jake asked. "How, exactly?"

"No one knows for sure, but she ended up jumping off a cliff or a bridge or something."

"So she never got to reunite with her dream... person?" Cash exchanged a quick glance with Quinn. "Damn."

"Well, you've got the power of *something*, Bug." Quinn pulled her knees to her chest and motioned at Cash.

Wynter noticed. "What's going on? The last thing I need right now is more secrets."

"I didn't tell your parents the whole story." Cash looked over his shoulder to make sure the door was closed. "I followed

Ransom. He met up with Jezebel and Roxy and they drove east, toward Halston."

"You forgot the most important part," Quinn said.

"Yes." Jake held up his index finger. "They kissed." He sat on the floor with his back against the wall. Cash joined him.

"Oh shit." Wynter covered her mouth.

"Quinn reacted the same way," Cash said. "Except she swore like a sailor."

"Fuck you. Did not." Quinn glared at him playfully.

"Jezebel, huh?" Wynter shook her head. "Figures. Ransom became an asshole after he lost his virginity."

Quinn hung her head. "You're never going to let me forget that are you?"

"Never!" Wynter grabbed Quinn's shoulders and shook them playfully.

Jake furrowed his brow. "I don't understand girls."

"They are a mystery." Cash turned to Quinn and Wynter. "It's going to be a bitch getting Ransom back. Once Jezebel figures out how things work, and she will, she'll guard him like Fort Knox."

"At least my dreams will be free of him for a while," Wynter said. "I might actually get some sleep."

"Oh, shit!" Quinn covered her mouth with her hand and glanced sheepishly at Wynter.

"What?"

"Your photos," Quinn said. "I'm sorry."

Jake leaned toward Cash. "You know what they're talking about?"

Cash shrugged and shook his head.

"When I picked up your photos at Minit Prints, Jezebel pulled a knife on me in the parking lot," Quinn said. "She destroyed the negs and everything, except a picture of Ransom." She faced Wynter with worry etched on her face. "I'm sorry."

Wynter nudged Quinn's shoulder with her own. "It's okay. I don't think there was anything good on that roll anyway."

"I'll buy you a new roll of film."

"Don't worry about it," Wynter said.

Jake turned on his camcorder, placed the viewfinder to his eye, and hit the record button. "This is Jake Peterson, Action Five News. I'm at Sven Dwarfs Trail'r Park where a group of teens are planning to rescue Ransom the dreamwaker."

Wynter leaned into Quinn. "Dream*waker?*"

"Yeah, that was Jake's idea."

"I like it."

Quinn nodded and stole a glance at Jake. "I like it, too."

Jake turned the camera to Cash. "Cash Hawkins, Newhaven's preeminent gas jockey, leads the rag-tag team of teens. Mr. Hawkins, tell us your plan."

Cash held his hand up and blocked the camcorder lens. "Come on, Jake."

"Come on Jake? I don't think I like that plan." He aimed the camcorder toward the head of the bed. "Wynter LaCroix, local photographer blessed with the power of summoning, do you have any thoughts on the matter?"

"I think we should sleep on it."

Jake zoomed in to Quinn's face. "Quinn Benoit, movie critic for the *Newhaven Register,* any final thoughts?"

"I think I'm going to kick your ass if you don't put that camera down." Quinn scooted off the bed toward Jake.

He flipped the camcorder on himself. "This is Jake Peterson, Action Five News, signing off." He stopped the recording just before Quinn reached for the camera. She lost her balance and toppled on top of him. Everyone burst out laughing.

"Shh," Wynter said. "My parents are pretty cool but even they have limits."

Quinn backed up onto her knees. "Is it off?"

Jake nodded, suddenly red-faced and tongue-tied.

"Good." Quinn brushed herself off.

"So, what's the plan?" Cash smirked and looked around the room.

"I was serious. We should sleep on it," Wynter said. "Then we can meet at Finn's tomorrow at eight. Sound good?"

Jake groaned. "Isn't that a little early?"

"Says the guy who doesn't have a job." Cash gave him a playful shove.

"I mean *awesome*. Sure. Eight o'clock in the morning sounds *great*."

Quinn leaned over the bed to give Wynter a hug goodbye. "See you in eight hours, Bug." She kissed her cheek. "Let's go, guys."

Wynter followed Quinn, Cash, and Jake to the front door and waved them goodbye. After locking up, she slipped back under the covers, ready to get a good night's sleep.

But sleep had other plans.

○

Jezebel threw Roxy the keys to the room and pushed Ransom against the stucco wall, pressing her mouth to his. Roxy juggled the keys with one hand and a brown paper bag in the other.

Jezebel took a short breather. "What's the holdup? It's getting cold out here."

"Really?" Roxy jiggled the key into the doorknob. "Looks pretty hot to me."

"Ha ha. Trying hard to be funny and failing majorly." Jezebel's hand found Ransom's crotch and gave it a squeeze. "For fuck's sake open the door already."

The doorknob clicked open. Jezebel pushed Ransom past Roxy and they both fell back onto the bed, kissing, their hands tugging at each other's clothes.

Roxy hung a "Do Not Disturb" sign on the door and locked it. Jezebel had asked the clerk at the front desk for the cheapest room they had, and this room delivered. One twin bed, a chair, a table with a small TV, a push-button phone sitting atop a tattered phonebook, and a bathroom-shower combo that looked like it hadn't been cleaned since the turn of the decade. The carpet was threadbare and the wallpaper cracked and peeled from the corners.

Roxy kicked off her shoes to reveal bare feet with pink-polished toenails. She set the paper bag down on the table and pulled out a forty ouncer of rum and two six-packs of Coke. She glanced behind her. Jezebel and Ransom kneeled on the bed, facing each other. Jezebel pulled off his hoodie and T-shirt.

Roxy removed a can from the six-pack, cracked the seal and took a long drink. After twisting the cap off the bottle of rum, she topped up the can with Captain Morgan's finest and set the can on the table. She dug into one of her tight jean pockets, pulled out a small plastic pouch of green shamrock-shaped pills, and placed them beside the soda can.

She peeled off her red T-shirt and jeans, and picked up the pills. "Who wants a shamrock shake?" Roxy shook the bag, jostling the pills inside.

Ransom gazed over Jezebel's bare shoulder and licked it. "What's a shamrock shake?"

"Take one and find out." Roxy took out a pill, placed it on her tongue, and washed it down with a swig of rum and Coke. "Yummy." She shook two more pills into her palm, set the bag aside, and grabbed the Coke can.

She held them out to Ransom and Jezebel. Before Jezebel could stop him, Ransom had taken one of the pills and washed it down with a swallow of Roxy's concoction.

"What the fuck, huh?" Jezebel took the pill and the soda can. "Top me up."

Roxy poured more rum into the soda can. Jezebel placed the shamrock pill between her teeth and took a long pull on the can.

Then she poured some of the rum and Coke over Ransom's shoulder and licked it.

His eyes followed her tongue as it traveled along his bicep. "What's in those pills?"

"It's just speed," Roxy said. "Makes you go fast."

"We're going to be up all fucking night." Jezebel unbuttoned her skin-tight jeans and pulled off her T-shirt.

"Fine by me." Ransom watched Jezebel undress.

Roxy kneeled on the bed behind Ransom, pressed her body against his back, and ran her hands down his chest. "We're going to be up *fucking* all night."

"Even better." Ransom faced Roxy, pulled her toward his body, and kissed her. He helped her take off her bra.

"You're right, Jazz," Roxy said, breathless. "He tastes magical."

Jezebel threw her arm around Ransom's neck. For a moment, it looked like a sleeper hold. "Take off his pants."

Roxy unbuttoned the top of Ransom's jeans and unzipped his fly. She raised her brows and smiled. "You're not wearing underwear."

Ransom shrugged. "What's the point?" He winked at her.

Jezebel pulled him backward onto the bed, straddled him, and kissed him.

"I don't have condoms."

"We're on the pill so we don't need fucking condoms." Jezebel removed her bra and placed his hands on her bare breasts. "Now shut up and make me cum."

Ransom had become Roxy and Jezebel's living sex doll and neither of them wanted to share. But with the shamrocks and the rum taking effect, they spent the entire night tag-teaming him in every way they could think of.

Ransom followed their lead and gained both experience and an education. As the rising sun broke through into morning, the three of them collapsed on the bed in a naked, exhausted heap.

○

WYNTER WAS UP, showered, dressed for work, and in the kitchen by seven-thirty in the morning. Madeline and Nolan sat at the kitchen table, sharing the morning's newspaper. They exchanged a curious glance.

Madeline sipped her coffee. "You get everything sorted out last night, hon?"

Wynter pulled open the cupboards one by one like the kitchen was brand new to her. She found a cup and splashed some coffee in it, drank, and set the cup down.

Madeline turned in her chair. "Wynnie? Are you okay?"

"What, Mom?" Wynter looked confused for a moment, then smiled. "Oh yeah, got lots of sleep. Even had good dreams for a change. The coffee's great, by the way. Is it instant? I'm meeting Quinn and Cash and Jake at Finn's at eight and I don't want to be late."

She slipped on her shoes and hastily tied them, grabbed her purse, and opened the front door. "See you guys later. Bye." The front door closed, leaving Madeline and Nolan in silence.

Nolan raised a brow at her. "Now that was weird."

"Weird doesn't even cover the half of it. First, she summons a boy from her dreams, then her friends appear out of nowhere. Now this." Madeline sipped her coffee. "Something's going on, Nolan. I can feel it in my bones."

"But she's always come to us when she needed to. Last night was evidence of that." Nolan set his paper down. "She was probably just excited to see her friends."

"I hope you're right." Madeline stepped to the sink. Wynter's mug, still half filled with coffee, sat precariously close to the edge of the counter. Spilled coffee surrounded it in random pools. Wynter was never this messy.

She grabbed a rag, cleaned up the spills, and placed the mug in the sink. Although she tried, Madeline couldn't shake the worry forming in her gut.

# Every Breath
# You Take

CASH STOOD BEHIND the cash register at Finn's. Through the window he spotted Wynter marching headlong across the street, her red hair floating behind. Her walk said she had something important to say. The clock next to the register read ten minutes to eight.

*Definitely not late so what's with the urgency?*

Wynter pushed through the door and walked right up to the counter, then turned and walked part way down an aisle before returning to the counter. "Hey, Cash. How're you doing?"

"Pretty good I—"

Wynter began to pace. "Did you think of a plan? We need a plan."

"Not really. I wanted to talk with you guys about—"

"I dreamed of highways and motels, over and over. It was mega lame."

Quinn rolled into one of the two customer parking spaces at Finn's and stepped out. Jake tumbled out of the passenger side, his Nintendo baseball cap firmly set on his head.

"Good for you, Jake," Cash said to himself, smiling.

"You say something?" Wynter rocked herself up to the front counter, fluttering her eyelashes seductively.

Cash studied Wynter's face and tried to get a good look at her eyes, but she resumed her pacing before he could get a lock. "Hey Wynter, are you okay?"

"What? Yeah."

"Want your regular? Coke and a fruit pie?"

She grabbed a bag of chips and held it in front of her face. "How come we haven't fucked?"

Cash's eyes bugged out. "What?"

"Never mind." Wynter put the chips back on the shelf.

Quinn and Jake strolled into the store and waved.

"I figured since we lived so close together that Quinn might be able to give me a ride," Jake said.

"Didn't ask, actually." Cash's brain was still trying to process Wynter's comment. "Good idea though." He waved them over. "Wynter's acting really weird."

"Quinn?" Wynter poked her head around the end of the first shelf. "Queenie!" She ran and wrapped her arms around her and planted a kiss on her cheek.

Cash stepped back from the counter. "See what I mean?"

"Did you say Coke? No. No Coke." Wynter waved her hands emphatically. "It's weird. It's like I've drunk a gallon of Coke already. Or coffee. Speaking of Coke, has anyone done coke?"

Quinn held Wynter by the shoulders. "Bug, what are you talking about?"

"What did you dream about last night, Queenie?"

Jake shot Cash a wary look. "It's like she's high on something."

"I dreamed of highways and motels, highways and motels." Wynter grabbed a handful of her hair. "Then it's sheyenne sheyenne sheyenne. Sheyenne this, sheyenne that."

Quinn looked at Cash. "Do you have any water?"

"On it." Cash grabbed a paper cup, filled it with water from the tap beside the coffee maker, and handed it to Quinn.

"Here, Bug. Drink this."

Wynter took the cup and drank it in several gulps. Quinn

handed it back to Cash and he refilled it. Wynter drank the second cup just as fast.

Quinn and Jake stepped back to the counter next to Cash. All of them watched Wynter in silence as she tried to shake off whatever had ahold of her. The water seemed to have had a calming effect.

"Whoa, guys." Wynter clutched her head. "Sorry about that."

"No need to apologize," Cash said.

Quinn scanned Wynter's face for clues. "Are you feeling better?"

"Yeah." Wynter furrowed her brow and shook her head. "Sorry. We wanted to come up with a plan and I, like, flipped out."

"Don't worry about it." Quinn looked to the others. "We all slept on it. Any ideas?"

Cash shrugged. "Other than heading east and watching for a black Barracuda, I got nothing."

"That's not going to work too well," Quinn said. "It's about an hour to Halston from here and it's, like, ten times the size. And that's assuming they're actually in Halston."

"All I have is my dreams from last night." Wynter handed the paper cup to Cash. "Thanks." She could feel embarrassment creeping up her neck.

"Wait." Jake reseated his baseball cap. "You said Ransom is from your dreams. He's part of you, right?"

Wynter nodded.

"Maybe you're *still* connected to him."

Cash leaned onto the counter. "Keep talking."

"Maybe it works kind of like vampires." Jake began to pace as he worked through the idea. "Wynter, you're the 'elder,' and you know where all your 'lower-ranking vampires' are." He air quoted the words. "Of course that 'lower ranking vampire' is Ransom."

Quinn watched Jake and a small smile formed on her lips.

"But I don't know where Ransom is," Wynter said.

"Maybe you do and just don't know it." Jake raised a brow.

"You were going on about highways and motels," Cash said.

"And sheyenne this and that," Quinn added.

"But what does that mean?" Cash asked. "The Sheyenne River? The Grasslands?"

"What about Sheyenne Motel?" Jake cast his gaze at the others, one at a time. "Does a place like that exist?" He settled on Cash. "Do you have a phone book for Halston?"

Cash shook his head. "Nope. Just Newhaven."

"Well, seeing as I'm the only one here who's not *gainfully employed*..." Jake shot a smirk at Cash. "I got an idea, but I need to do some research first."

"What's your idea?" Cash called back at him.

"Patience, grasshopper." Jake looked at Quinn and Wynter, but mostly Quinn. "How about we meet at the FreshWhip at five o'clock?" Jake was out of the store before anyone could respond.

Cash shook his head and chuckled. "Always about the big reveal."

Quinn gave Wynter a once-over, then said to Cash, "So five o'clock's good for you?"

"I'm off at four anyway, so yeah."

The two girls headed for the door.

"Oh!" Cash dug under the counter for something. "Wait." He grabbed a can of Coke from the cooler and handed it to her with one hand, a blueberry Hostess Fruit Pie in the other.

Quinn gave him a sideways glance. "Aren't you forgetting something?"

"Sorry Quinn. Wynter and I have an arrangement." Cash winked.

"I'll bet."

Wynter gave Quinn a playful jab and dragged her out of the store. "Thanks, Cash. Next time let me pay, okay?"

With the girls already out of earshot, he said to himself, "Ain't going to happen." He smiled and waved as he watched the two girls pile into Blue Belle, back out of the parking stall, and drive toward Stedford Plaza.

Cash stepped back behind the front counter and waited for the next customer to arrive, but his thoughts remained on Jake and what his big reveal would be.

○

ROXY GROANED AND cracked her eyes to a squint. Her temples throbbed and the room was a mess. Soda cans, clothes, and sheets lay strewn everywhere. Even with the curtains drawn, the rotted fabric allowed the afternoon sunshine to cast radiating beams across the room. The brightness made her head pound more.

*We partied hardcore apparently.*

The night was a blur and despite the disarray of the room, Roxy had a difficult time recalling specific details. But she didn't forget Ransom.

Roxy surveyed the room but Ransom's hoodie, T-shirt, his jeans—

*oh, those jeans!*

—were absent.

*He must be in the bathroom.*

Jezebel was still asleep in a swirl of sheets. Roxy sat up, stretched, and rubbed her eyes. She tiptoed around the room to avoid waking Jezebel, collecting her clothes as she went. She pulled on her panties, fastened her bra, and crept to the bathroom, expecting to see Ransom inside.

But he wasn't there.

"What the fuck?" Roxy pulled on her red T-shirt and wriggled into her jeans. She exited the bathroom and made a beeline for the door. Her foot struck an empty can and catapulted it across the floor, clattering as it went.

Jezebel moaned and pulled sheets over her head. "Keep it the fuck down."

Roxy unlocked the door and stepped out into the afternoon

sun. She winced, shielded her eyes, and scanned the parking lot. The Barracuda was right where it should have been, but Ransom was nowhere to be seen.

"Shut the damn door!"

A partially filled soda can hit Roxy on the shoulder and splashed Coke on her T-shirt. "Don't be an asshole." She closed and locked the door. "He's gone."

"Huh? Who?"

"Ransom." Roxy sat on the chair near the bed. "Remember? The guy we did last night?"

"Oh yeah." Roxy could hear the smile in Jezebel's voice. "He was fine."

"Wait." Roxy stepped to the door, her brain straining against the fog of the previous night. She touched the doorknob. "He doesn't have a key."

"Fuck, I'm hungry," Jezebel groaned.

"If he doesn't have a key, then how did he lock the door...?"

"Stop talking and get me some breakfast." Jezebel crawled out of bed trailing sheets behind her. "I'm going to take a bath." She disappeared into the bathroom, but called back, "The next time I see you, you better have food."

"Or what, bitch?" Roxy said under her breath. She found Jezebel's jeans and pulled some cash from the pocket plus a little for herself. Jezebel was horrible at math and high half the time. She'd never know the difference.

Roxy grabbed the room key, unlocked the door, and stepped back out into the bright sunshine. Her head felt a little better, but the sooner she had food in her stomach the better.

The motel sat a block away from Zoey's Fast Fill, a full service gas bar and convenience food store. Roxy took her time. She was in no hurry to get back to the room to face more of Jezebel's unhinged outbursts.

Once inside the store, Roxy loaded up on donuts, snacks, Tylenol, and more Coke. Unable to wait, she found some shade and ate a Slim Jim, a donut, three Tylenol tablets, and washed it all down with one of the cans of Coke. What she really wanted was a fresh crisp apple, but Zoey's didn't sell fruit.

Once back in the room with the door locked, Roxy peeked into the bathroom. Jezebel had fallen asleep.

*Don't wake the lion. Although drowning her might be okay.*

Roxy stifled a giggle and crept back to the room. She set the groceries on the bed, grabbed another can of Coke, and opened it as quietly as possible. She turned on the TV with the volume low and reclined on the bed.

As she sipped her soda, the soap opera *Santa Barbara* droned across the room. Roxy closed her eyes and imagined what it would be like to live on the "American Riviera" as a member of the Capwell family.

Roxy's life was comfortable; she was a northie after all, with parents that earned a good living, but she couldn't help but dream of being even richer. To live by the Pacific Ocean would be a dream come true.

A shriek rose from the bathroom followed by a frenzy of splashing.

Roxy sat up and knocked her can of Coke on the floor. "Jazz?" She hopped off the bed and was at the bathroom door in seconds. "Jezebel?" She eased the door open just enough to get a peek.

Ransom was in the tub on top of Jezebel, fully clothed. They were kissing, with Jezebel's hands wrapped around his neck.

"Quit fucking staring," Jezebel said. "Now get out."

Roxy pointed at Ransom. "But how is he here? The door is locked."

"I'll tell you how," Ransom said with a mischievous smile.

"Right now, I don't care." Jezebel waved her off and went back to kissing Ransom.

Roxy closed the door.

"Wait." Jezebel's voice filtered through the door.

Roxy stuck her head back in. "What?"

"The food. Leave it in here." Jezebel tugged at Ransom's wet hoodie.

Roxy walked back to the bedroom and reserved some of the snacks for herself. She deposited the rest in the bathroom. Jezebel paid no attention, instead focusing on working Ransom's jeans off.

*Sometimes Jezebel could be such a bitch.*

It must have been past four o'clock. *Santa Barbara* had been replaced by some boring afternoon movie and even though Roxy didn't care for the subject matter, she turned up the volume and watched it anyway. Anything to drown out the noises emanating from the bathroom.

Without a clock, Roxy had no idea how long Jezebel and Ransom were in the bathroom. She dozed off again before their laughter brought her back to reality.

Ransom and Jezebel stepped out of the bathroom wearing towels around their bodies. "We should order a pizza." She looked at Ransom. "Fuel up for round two."

"Don't you mean round three?" he said.

"Shit, yeah." Jezebel kissed him. "The TV's fucking loud enough." She flicked it off. "You going deaf, Rox?"

Roxy crossed her arms against her chest. "Not everyone likes to listen to you fuck."

"Aww. Is Roxy jealous?" Jezebel's eyes went dark.

Roxy stared back at her, a scowl on her face.

Ransom sat on the bed and massaged one of Roxy's feet. "There's enough of me for both of you." He looked at Roxy and grinned. "Variety is the spice of life."

"I like you better when you don't talk." Jezebel laid down on the bed.

"So, Ransom," Roxy began. "How did you get in here?"

"Jezebel dreamed of me, and I took that opportunity to become real."

"Bullshit," Jezebel said. "You must have snuck into the room and surprised me. Or you hid somewhere."

"Nope." Ransom grabbed a Slim Jim and gnawed on it enthusiastically. "Man. The sex and the food keep me coming back."

"You're from Jezebel's dreams?" Roxy hopped off the bed and checked the door. It was still locked. "Impossible."

Ransom tugged on Jezebel's towel. "Were you dreaming of me just before you woke up?"

Jezebel pulled the towel back. "Yeah, but that doesn't prove anything."

"We were making out on the hood of your car."

Jezebel shot a quick glance at Roxy.

"While Roxy was driving down an empty highway."

Jezebel propped herself up on her elbows. "No fucking way. How did you do that?"

"I was there. In your dream." Ransom's eyes blazed a bright blue. "Now I'm here. And I want more." He looked back at Roxy and smiled. "From both of you."

Roxy felt desire wake up within her. "So, you're real... but not real?" Roxy paced the room keeping her eyes on Ransom.

"Did I *feel* real last night?"

A small grin spread across Roxy's lips.

"Fuck, yeah." Jezebel flopped back down onto her pillow. "You fucked the shit out of me. So where did you go?"

"I disappear into the mind of the last person I kiss," Ransom said. "Either when I sleep or when that person dreams, whichever comes first."

"So we need you awake." Roxy placed a shamrock on her tongue and took a swig from her Coke. She placed a green pill in Jezebel's palm and Jezebel popped it into her mouth without hesitation. "Oh look, we have one more left."

"Keep it in reserve," Jezebel said. "We got to keep him on a short leash."

Ransom tilted his head and narrowed his eyes at her, no longer a vibrant blue but dark, almost black. "Don't be a bitch."

Jezebel sat up. "What'd you call me?"

Ransom grabbed the plastic bag from Roxy and extracted the last shamrock pill. He placed it on his tongue and swallowed. "I said don't be a bitch." He laid a trail of kisses up Jezebel's legs. "You're more fun when you're not a bitch."

"Stop talking." Jezebel grabbed Ransom's head by his hair and pulled him on top of her. "Rox, call Monty. You know why. Then get out."

*Selfish bitch.*

Roxy scowled, slipped some cash out of Jezebel's pants pocket, and went to the phone. She punched in Monty's number, waited, then dialed the number to their room and hung up.

Ransom tugged at Jezebel's towel as he kissed the swell of her breasts.

Jezebel pushed him aside. "What are you waiting for?"

"He has to call me back," Roxy said. "That's how it works, remember?"

Ransom looked back at Roxy and extended his hand. "Come join us."

"Fuck that." Jezebel bit Ransom's ear, hard enough to get his attention. "She's going to wait outside."

The phone rang and Roxy picked up. "Hey. Yeah, it's Roxy... We need some shamrock... um, six." Roxy covered the mouthpiece. "He says it's going to be sixty."

"Yeah, whatever," Jezebel said between kisses. Ransom's hand crept under her towel.

"Yeah, our usual spot, room 123... Don't freak, we got cash." Roxy hung up.

"Now get out," Jezebel said.

"I heard you. Don't wig out."

"Roxy." Ransom looked back at her at the door. "I won't forget about you."

Jezebel spun Ransom's head around to face her. "Not if I can help it."

Roxy scoffed and stepped out of the motel room into bright sunshine again. Maybe it was better this way. Her headache was gone and the sun felt good on her skin, but she could feel the speed beginning to kick in.

She wandered over to Zoey's to buy a magazine and a snack. If she was going to have to wait outside, she may as well entertain herself with something other than the sounds of teenaged sex.

O

BY THE TIME five o'clock rolled around, Wynter could barely keep a thought in her head. She felt jittery and when she wasn't pacing the floor of the store, she was doodling on any piece of paper she could get her hands on.

Daytona and Hunter thought she had drunk too much coffee, but except for the mouthful she had swallowed at the trailer, her system had remained caffeine free. The can of Coke Cash had given her couldn't have made her feel like this, could it?

Wynter collected her purse. "You guys get to lock up tonight, okay?"

"The way you're acting today, you'd probably screw something up," Daytona said, her hands on her hips.

"I couldn't possibly remain in the store, *alone*, with Daytona." Hunter winked and slid his hand over her backside.

"Nope." Daytona swatted him away. "Be good and stop harassing me."

"Yes, my master... I mean mistress." Hunter grinned, seeming to have no intelligent thought in his head.

Wynter trudged out of the store and into the main concourse of the plaza, headed for the FreshWhip stand.

Quinn had reserved a table in the food court. Cash and Jake were already there, Jake's camcorder set carefully on the table.

Wynter skipped quickly to the table and sat down. "Sorry I'm late."

Quinn glanced at the guys, then back at Wynter. "It's, like, two minutes after five. That's not late."

"Okay." Wynter took out a pen from her purse and began doodling on the table. "Did you guys have a good day? I couldn't wait for mine to end. It was pretty dead and I had nothing to do really."

Cash raised a concerned brow and looked at Quinn.

"You feeling okay, Bug?" Quinn placed her hand gently on Wynter's shoulder. "You're acting strange again."

"I don't know what's going on. Been doodling all day." Wynter moved the pen from the table to her hand, rolling the inky tip across the skin of her palm in broad strokes. "It's just like my brain's going and going and going and..."

Quinn gave Wynter's arm a gentle squeeze.

"Well, I have some news." Jake sat, his knee vibrating under the table.

"Oh yeah. Your secret idea." Cash sat back and crossed his arms against his chest. "*This* grasshopper is waiting."

"I went to the library to see if they had a phone book for Halston," Jake began.

Quinn leaned on the table, her attention divided between Jake and Wynter. "And?"

"And they did have a phone book for Halston."

"I think you need to get to the point, Jake." Cash glanced at Wynter as her pen strokes began to move up her arm. Her lips moved like she was speaking a silent prayer. "At least for Wynter's sake."

"Way to steal my fire."

"I promise we'll be impressed." Quinn smiled warmly at Jake and that perked him up.

Jake pulled out a folded piece of paper from his back pocket. "After what Wynter told us this morning—"

"I remember. I can remind you guys if you want." Wynter continued doodling. "Dotted lines and hotels and highways, always going fast..."

"Exactly." Jake gave Wynter a wary eye and continued. "I wanted to know if there were any motels or hotels off the main highway that had 'sheyenne' in the name."

Cash nodded. "I literally see where you're going with this."

"I got a map and followed I94 east and cross-referenced the towns with the yellow pages of Halston and the surrounding area." Jake unfolded the paper and smoothed it out on the table. "Then I found this." He presented the paper to Cash.

"It's a photocopy of the yellow pages." Cash sighed. "What am I looking at?"

Jake pointed to one of the smaller ads lining the left side of the page.

"Wait, is this right?"

"I'm not making this shit up," Jake said.

"What?" Quinn alternated her gaze between the two boys.

Cash turned the paper around and slid it across the table to her. "Left side, middle-ish."

Quinn's eyes widened. "The Shey-Inn? Holy shit. Hey Wynter you got to see—" Her face turned ashen. "Guys. Look."

Jake and Cash stood and crowded behind Wynter. On the table, her palm, and forearm were doodles of what looked like grass blades, clustered in groups of three and curved to the right. The logo for the Shey-Inn had the exact same clustering of grass blades.

"I think we found our place," Quinn said. "Nice detective work, Jake."

He grinned back at her. "Thanks."

"Stakeout!" Wynter dropped the pen on the table. "We can be just like the police. We can take photos and everything. Wait! I know what we need." She burst from her chair and ran back toward the main concourse.

Quinn picked up Wynter's purse. "She's headed to Shooters." Jake grabbed the strap to his camcorder and followed Cash and Quinn.

By the time they arrived at the store, Wynter had a box under her arm, the word "PENTAX" written on the side in bold red capital letters. She held two boxes of film in her other hand.

"We need a telephoto lens, and this is the best." Wynter vibrated with excitement.

Jake held up his camcorder. "Don't forget. This baby has a zoom lens."

Daytona stood by the partially closed security gate, one hand on her hip. "You better not break it. Vinny'll have our asses."

"Quit worrying." Wynter waved her off and started toward the plaza exit. "Let's go. We need to swing by my place and get my gear."

Once outside, they piled into Blue Belle, everyone still in their work clothes, except Jake. Quinn drove to Wynter's trailer. Her parents weren't home yet, which made their lives easier.

Wynter hopped out. "Back in a flash." She unlocked the front door and disappeared inside.

"She's tripping majorly," Cash said.

Quinn glanced at the guys through the rear view mirror. "But on what?"

Less than five minutes later, Quinn merged Blue Belle onto the Interstate heading east. Wynter unloaded her SLR from her camera bag, attached the telephoto lens, and loaded a roll of film.

"Isn't this exciting?" Wynter squirmed in her seat and looked back at Cash and Jake. "And this lens is choice. It's going to take great pictures."

Cash leaned forward. "What makes it great?"

As Wynter chattered about lens speed and focal length to Cash,

Jake caught Quinn's eyes in the rear view mirror and smiled at her. He opened his mouth to say something, then reconsidered.

The little blue VW Beetle sped east toward an unknown fate.

○

Roxy had stretched out on the hood of the Barracuda, using the windshield as a backrest. She nursed a bag of Hostess Salt and Vinegar potato chips and a Coke. If Jezebel had seen her, she probably would have killed her, but at that moment Roxy didn't care. Part of her wanted to get caught. She'd take the opportunity to beat Jezebel's ass. Or at least try to.

Roxy tapped her shoes on the hood of the Barracuda. "Where the fuck are you, Monty?"

Reliability was not Monty's middle name. Although he always eventually arrived where he was paged to, he could be hours late. Jezebel had long suspected that he committed the cardinal sin of a drug dealer: getting high on his own supply.

"He must really love Tony Montana," Jezebel had said. "Doesn't he remember how that movie ended?"

She flipped through the latest *Seventeen* magazine. Roxy had always had a thing for Michael J. Fox, ever since she saw him in *Family Ties*. And she was one of the first in line to see *Back to the Future* when it came out a year ago, despite Jezebel's insistence that the movie was shit. When she made it to California, one of the first things she promised herself was to attend a live taping of the show.

Monty rolled up in his silver Fiat X1/9. He wore his signature mirrored sunglasses and a worn Doobie Brothers T-shirt. Roxy thought the little sports car looked clunky and awkward, an opinion that Jezebel surprisingly agreed with. It was no comparison to the Porsche 928 that Tony Montana drove in *Scarface*.

He backed into the parking space next to the Barracuda, killed the engine, and combed his hair back. "Hey foxy Roxy. Your knight in shining armor has arrived." He grinned at her, looking like the Cheshire Cat.

"Oh, *please*." Roxy barely glanced at him. The profile she was reading on Michael J. Fox was more important. "You got my stuff?"

"Hey, I always deliver." Monty's eyes traced a line down Roxy's body. "I took the top off 'cause the weather's been so good. Like it?"

Roxy had no patience for Monty at the best of times, and today was no exception. She set the magazine down and dug out the cash from her pocket. "Here. Where's the stuff?"

Monty hopped out of his car. "Not so fast. Where's Jezebel?"

Roxy's eyes flicked toward the room. "Busy."

"We should get busy too. I'll get a room."

She could feel his gaze all over her body and it made her sick to her stomach.

"I bet you'd look good with *your* top off." Monty narrowed his eyes. "I'd give you a discount."

"Are you for real? Just give me the shamrocks."

Monty took the cash and handed Roxy a little plastic bag with six green pills in it. "Here you go, you fuckin' dyke."

"You talk to all your customers like that?"

Monty brushed her off and strolled to the door to room 123.

"Wait, where are you going?"

"I want to talk to Jezebel." Monty knocked on the door. "Need to take a piss, too."

"Don't be an idiot," Roxy said. "What part of 'she's busy' don't you understand?"

When the door didn't open, Monty pounded on it, rattling the door in its frame.

Roxy slid off the hood and tried to push Monty away from the door. "She'll kill us."

Monty pulled up the hem of his T-shirt and displayed the handle of a .38 snubnose sticking out of the waist of his jeans. "You, maybe."

The door eased open. Ransom stood in the void wearing nothing but a towel, his skin covered in a sheen of sweat.

"I thought you said Jezebel was in there." Monty tried to peer over Ransom's shoulder.

Ransom glanced at Roxy, then back at Monty. "She's busy."

"See?" Roxy looked at Ransom and watched a bead of sweat roll down his chest. "I tried to tell him, I swear."

"Who is this joker?"

"I'm Ransom. And you must be the dealer."

Monty scoffed. "What kind of name is *Ransom?*"

"Roxy, you got the stuff?"

Roxy nodded.

Ransom winked at her, then faced Monty. "I guess your business here is done." He tried to close the door but Monty jammed his foot beside the door frame, stopping it.

"I need to take a piss."

"Not here." Ransom motioned toward Zoey's Fast Fill. "Try the gas station. Move your foot."

Monty tried again to look past Ransom, but the rest of the room was dark. "I got a gun."

Ransom returned Monty's heated gaze with a cool one of his own. "What are you going to do? Shoot us? That's not very good for business if you ask me."

"No one's askin' you." Monty backed out of the doorframe. "Look. I got somethin' for Jezebel. Somethin' new."

"Give it to Roxy." Ransom shut the door and locked it.

Monty scowled. "I don't like your new friend."

"I'm quite sure he feels the same way about you," Roxy said. "You got something for Jezebel. I'll make sure she gets it."

Monty pulled a small plastic bag from his pocket, smaller than the one he had given Roxy earlier. Within the small bag sat a small yellowish nugget, almost like a chunk of quartz.

Roxy squinted at it. "What is that?"

"You've done coke, right?"

"Who hasn't?"

"This is the future," Monty said. "Rock cocaine. You smoke it. The high is un-fuckin'-believable." He handed her the bag.

"I don't have any cash to buy this."

Monty chuckled and walked back to his car. "Who said anythin' about *buyin'* it? That one's on the house." He slid into the driver's seat and started the engine. "Later, foxy Roxy. Keep in touch."

Monty floored the gas and laid a strip of rubber the length of the parking lot.

Roxy examined the single rock, turning the little bag over in her palm, then shoved it into her pocket. She picked up her magazine and continued reading, pacing in front of the curtained window. Free drugs? From Monty? She'd deliver the new product to Jezebel, but something didn't feel right.

○

QUINN PILOTED BLUE BELLE into the city limits of Halston, keeping her eyes on the passing buildings as much as she safely could. Cash and Jake picked up the surveillance slack and Wynter sang off-key to the songs on the radio. She had her camera in her hand, the new lens attached and ready to go. She practiced framing moving targets.

"What was the address?" Cash leaned next to Jake to look at the photocopy.

"3023 Sheyenne Road."

"Seriously?" Quinn cast a quick, casual glance at the two boys in the back.

"Check it yourself if you don't believe me." Jake handed the paper to Cash.

"Huh. Shey-Inn on Sheyenne," Cash said. "But where the hell are we? And where's Sheyenne Road?"

"Wynter, there's a map in the glove box." Quinn glanced at Wynter. She was singing along with Cyndi Lauper and "Time After Time." Quinn knew there was no stopping her. She shook her head, motioned to Cash and Jake, and pointed. "Guys. Map. Glove box."

Cash seized the opportunity to lean forward between the front seats. As he moved past Wynter, he took in the fragrance of her hair. He smiled at her and Wynter pointed her camera back at him, pretending to take a picture and continuing to sing. Badly.

Jake caught the move and nodded approvingly.

Cash opened the glove box. An avalanche of "girl stuff" tumbled out of the compartment and into the footwell, including tubes of lipstick and lip gloss, a couple of tampons, sunscreen, napkins, and assorted plastic cutlery. Jammed in the back was the map. He grabbed it and sat back in his seat next to Jake.

"Smooth, Hawkins," Jake whispered.

Cash unfolded the map. "What?"

Jake sniffed Cash's hair. "Gee, your hair smells terrific."

Cash pushed him back, speaking in hushed tones. "Shut up, man. I couldn't resist. Now help me find out where we are."

Not many roads crossed the highway, and it didn't take long for Cash and Jake to find the location of Shey-Inn.

"Quinn, take exit 161," Jake said. "Continue going south and it should be on your right."

Quinn followed Jake's instructions off the Interstate. Sheyenne Road bordered Halston's city limits and the buildings reflected the lack of population density. Most were industrial and no more than two stories tall.

The little blue VW Beetle had just passed Zoey's Fast Fill when

Cash thrust his arm between the seats, pointing forward. "There it is! Just past the gas station."

The Shey-Inn was a modest two-story motel with two wings that joined in the shape of an "L." The second floor rooms were accessible by stairs at both ends and at the apex where the two wings joined. The entire structure was covered in uninspired white plastic siding, which did nothing to improve the motel's lack of character. The only splash of color was the branded red Coca-Cola vending machine by the office.

"Jesus." Quinn scanned the building as they approached. "If you want to get murdered, this is the place." She nudged Wynter. "We're here."

Wynter lifted her camera to her eye and aimed it at the cars in the parking lot. "Barra-barracuda." She took a picture.

"Shit, you're right," Cash said. "And that's Roxy lying on the hood."

Jake craned his head to get a look as Quinn pulled into a parking stall furthest from the motel. Wynter unbuckled herself and crawled into the back seat. Cash's eyes widened, unprepared for Wynter's impulsive move.

"Stakeout time." Wynter grinned at Cash, then hunkered down, kneeling on the back seat and resting her forearms on the ledge at the back window. She aimed the camera through the back window. "Quinn, you need to clean the glass back here." She adjusted the camera's settings.

Quinn hung her elbow out the window. "I'll get right on that."

Jake sized up the back seat. "Two's company but three's a crowd." He squeezed between the front seats, soon sitting next to Quinn. He collected the items in the footwell that had fallen from the glove box and returned them. "Evenin', ma'am." Jake tugged at the brim of his baseball cap. "This seat taken?"

Quinn flicked her eyes over him, her lips curling in subtle amusement. "It is now."

*What am I doing? Flirting with a nerd?*

Jake offered a raised brow and a sweet smile. "Come here often?"

"Um…" Quinn knew this wasn't the time or place for come-ons, even if in jest. They had a job to do.

Cash saved Quinn the embarrassment of having no snappy comeback for Jake. "Look who just rolled up. And he's still driving that shitbox Fiat."

"Monty." Wynter focused the telephoto and snapped a picture. "Quinn, this back window is—"

"Dirty, I know," Quinn said. "I can't clean it without blowing my cover. Monty knows all the girls." She turned to Jake. "Can you take care of it?"

Jake nodded. He held his camcorder to Quinn. "Could you hold onto this for a second?" She nodded. He removed his baseball cap, popped open the glove box, careful to not let everything spill out again, and grabbed a Burger King napkin. "The King would approve."

He eased the passenger door open and stepped to the back of the Beetle. "Get down," he whispered through the glass to Wynter and Cash. They ducked as he got to work.

Jake spit on the napkin and wiped away the dirt on the bottom half of the window. He walked around to the other side and repeated the action. Jake returned to the passenger seat and pulled the door closed as quietly as possible. "All done," he said, pulling on his cap.

Wynter and Cash resumed their surveillance.

Quinn looked at Jake through the viewfinder of the camcorder. "Did you just use *spit* on Blue Belle?"

"Only the best spit." Jake said, suddenly serious. "Premium quality."

Quinn scrunched her brow. Jake kept her guessing and she liked that. She handed the camcorder back to him. "You're weird."

"Thank you, ma'am."

"And quit it with the *ma'am* stuff, okay?"

"Yes, ma—"

"Hey, guys. We got some action." Cash nodded toward the motel. Monty and Roxy were arguing as he pounded on the door.

Quinn and Jake both twisted in their seats to look out the back window and came very close to bonking heads. Jake caught the scent of Quinn's hair, glanced at Cash, and offered a subtle nod of understanding. He raised the camcorder's viewfinder to his eye and tried to shoot through the window, but Cash and Wynter blocked his shot.

"Ransom!" Wynter aimed and focused. "He's at the door."

"In nothing but a towel." Cash watched Wynter take pictures excitedly. He dropped his head and tried to hide his disappointment, but it was obvious to Quinn and Jake.

"At least we know for sure they have him," Quinn said.

"And he's probably knocking boots with Jezebel." Jake's words were out before he could stop them. He glanced at Quinn and winced.

Wynter either didn't hear Jake or chose to ignore his comment. She continued to stare down the lens at Roxy, Monty, and Ransom at the door to the motel room.

"So what do we do now?" Cash sat and faced Quinn and Jake. "Bust into the room, get Wynter to kiss Ransom, and leave?"

"I think we're going to need a better plan than that," Quinn said. "Jezebel's a loose cannon, even more than Roxy."

Wynter set her camera down and faced the others. "Let's just watch them for a while and see what happens. I'm hungry. Is anyone hungry?"

"I could eat," Jake said, "but we should wait until the coast is clear. Like when it's dark."

"But that's..." Wynter glanced at her watch. "Like, four hours away. I won't last that long." She went back to her camera.

"We got to deal with our parents first. And soon," Cash said. "Or they're going to have the police out hunting for us."

Quinn shrugged. "Must be nice having parents that give a shit. Although, I wouldn't mind Anson out searching for me."

"If it makes you feel any better, *we* give a shit about you, Quinn." Jake gave her a genuine smile and it melted Quinn's heart, just a little.

"Let's give it an hour, tops," Cash said. "Then we sneak to Zoey's, call home, and get some food. Sound good?"

The sound of Monty's X1/9 peeling out of the parking lot distracted all of them, but Cash didn't need an answer to know that they were all in.

It turned out they didn't need to wait an hour. Roxy unlocked the door and stepped back into the motel room. Wynter and Jake grabbed their cameras and joined Quinn and Cash as they slipped out of Blue Belle. The friends skulked toward Zoey's, setting the next phase of their plan in action.

Quinn, Wynter, Cash, and Jake had no way to know that ten minutes later, Roxy would step out of the motel room again. Her destination: Zoey's Fast Fill.

○

WITH THE EXCEPTION of a green shingled roof, the exterior of Zoey's Fast Fill matched the uninspired architecture of the Shey-Inn. But the buildings didn't need to look pretty. They were built for function, not form.

Four gas pumps did brisk business under a free-standing overhang lit by fluorescent lights and a single pay phone was bolted to the exterior wall next to the corner of the building, near the main doors. A tattered phone book hung underneath.

Cash pulled out his wallet. "What do you guys want, besides the usual snacks and drinks?"

Wynter and Quinn looked at each other and spoke in unison. "Hot dog?" They both laughed.

"You got it. Jake?"

"Let's look around a bit first."

"We're going to call our parents." Quinn split from the group and headed to the pay phone, Wynter following close behind. Cash and Jake pulled open the double doors to Zoey's and stepped inside.

Quinn dug into her purse for a quarter, lifted the handset, and plugged the pay phone's coin slot. After listening for a dial tone, she punched in her phone number and waited.

"I bet it'll go to the answering machine," she said.

Wynter stood close enough to hear the line trilling in Quinn's ear. Then a *click*.

Quinn let the handset go slack in her hand. "What did I tell you? You've reached the Benoit residence, blah blah blah." She raised the handset to her head when the extended beep sounded through the speaker. "Hi. This is your bodacious daughter calling. I'm going to be staying at Wynter's place tonight. Her mom says it's okay. I'll be home tomorrow after work. Bye." She pressed the cradle switch to hang up the call and passed the handset to Wynter.

"So you don't have to ask permission?" Wynter raised a brow.

Quinn shrugged. "I guess that's one of the perks of having parents that don't care."

Wynter deposited her quarter and dialed. It rang twice before someone answered. Quinn could tell from the filtered voice and a few select words that it was Madeline on the other end.

"Hi, Mom."

Quinn leaned next to the handset. "Hi Mrs. LaCroix!"

Wynter waved her off, giggling. "Yeah, that was Quinn." She paused to listen. "Work was okay."

As Wynter talked, Quinn looked back at the doors to Zoey's as customers came and went. Her eyes drifted past the gas pumps and across the parking lot. Her stomach dropped when she thought she saw Roxy strolling toward the store. She tugged at Wynter's sleeve.

"Quinn, stop. I'm almost done."

Quinn whispered into Wynter's ear, "What was Roxy wearing? Do you remember?"

Wynter swatted her away while the girl with the red T-shirt and shoulder-length blond hair moved closer.

Panic rose up in her gut and Quinn wasted no time. She grabbed Wynter's camera and aimed it at the girl.

"Just a second, Mom." Wynter covered the receiver and turned on Quinn, both of them tethered together by the camera strap. "Stop! What's wrong with you?" She tugged on the strap, but Quinn held onto it a moment longer.

She focused the lens and hoped she was wrong. But the girl had short bangs, the sides curled back, and a part right down the middle. It was Roxy.

Quinn let go of the camera. "Bug! It's *Roxy*," she whispered through clenched teeth.

"Where?" Wynter craned her head to look but Quinn pulled her back.

"We got to *go*," Quinn said. "With your red hair and my pink shirt, we're completely obvious. If she sees us, we're screwed." She made a quick glance backward. "Tell your mom the pizza's arrived."

"What pizza?"

Quinn glared at her as her whisper rose in volume. "BUG! Let's GO."

Roxy was less than fifty feet away.

"Mom, our pizza's arrived. I'll call you tomorrow, okay?" Wynter paused, then said, "Yes, I'll be safe. Love you. Bye." She managed to press the cradle switch and end the call before Quinn pulled her around the side of the building.

Roxy casually glanced in their direction as she pulled open one of the double doors leading into Zoey's. She stopped and looked back at the pay phone. The handset hung by the end of its cable, swaying back and forth even though there was no breeze.

Quinn and Wynter ran along the side of Zoey's past a row of ice machines to the back, where a line of trees and shrubs bordered the parking lot. They jumped the curb, dropped to the ground, and hid in the shadows of a large bush.

"What about the guys?" Wynter held her camera to her eye.

"They're on their own." Quinn said between breaths.

"Shit," Wynter whispered and pointed. "Look."

Back at the side of the building, just in front of the ice machines, Roxy poked her head around the corner, then went back to the front of the store.

"See?" Quinn looked at Wynter. "She saw us."

Wynter pressed the shutter. "She saw *something*."

"Too close for comfort." Quinn followed the line of foliage to Sheyenne Road. "Let's get back to the car."

○

THE INTERIOR OF Zoey's focused on two types of customers. Those who preferred a hot prepared meal, usually travelers staying at the Shey-Inn, sat in the cafe, a nondescript greasy spoon with an extra helping of grease. Everyone else bought convenience food, snacks, and beverages by the armload. At the end of the day, each side did comparable business.

Cash and Jake pulled open the doors and grabbed a plastic basket. The smell of roasting hot dogs made Cash's stomach growl. Jake followed Cash to the back of the store.

"Damn, those hot dogs smell good."

"Let's leave those to pick up last," Cash said. "So they might still be warm when we get back." He opened a windowed refrigerator, hooked his fingers around a six-pack of Coca-Cola, and placed it in his basket.

"Wynter loves Coke, right?"

"Everybody loves Coke." Cash smiled sheepishly. "But yeah, it's Wynter's fave. That and..." He grabbed a Blueberry Hostess Fruit Pie. "It's not time for breakfast, but what the hell. Call it dessert."

Cash topped his basket with two bags of Dakota Style Original Kettle Chips. Jake grabbed a bag of Tostitos and a jumbo package of Sour Patch Kids.

He hooked a thumb at the hot dog warming carousel. "You think one each will be enough?"

"Yeah." Cash dug out his wallet. "I'm going to get in line to pay."

There were three people ahead of Cash in the line to the cashier. He glanced over at the restaurant side. Almost every seat was filled. The food and soda in his basket weighed down on his arm. He felt like crossing sides and ordering a burger with fries.

The subtle squeak of the front door caught his attention. Cash turned to see Roxy pulling open the door. He was in full view and there was nowhere to run.

But Roxy paused, looked to her right, and let go of the door. She had seen something.

*Or someone. Wynter and Quinn?*

Cash seized the moment and ducked out of the line back to where Jake was finishing packaging the hot dogs. "We got to get the hell out of here."

Jake had a puzzled look on his face. "What?"

"Roxy's here."

"Oh shit." Jake looked toward the entrance. "And there's only one way out."

"Bathroom! Stay here." Cash ran to the front counter, past the people in line to pay. "Excuse me! Can I get the bathroom key?"

"Back of the line, kid," one customer said.

"It's an emergency."

The cashier, who was trying hard to capture a Madonna in *"Lucky Star"* vibe with her black and silver pixie goth outfit, glanced at him and snapped her gum, annoyed. "It's occupied."

"Shit." Cash muttered.

"Apparently not," said another customer and the people in line began laughing, including Miss Lucky Star.

Cash scanned the front bank of windows and spotted Roxy walking back to the main doors. He had maybe six seconds to react. He rejoined Jake. "Bathroom's not an option. Follow me."

He pulled Jake around the corner into a short hallway that led past the bathroom to the stockroom. Cash pushed through the swinging double doors and both of them hid behind a shelf full of boxes.

Jake looked at Cash with wild excited eyes. "Did she see you?"

"I don't think so."

Then a voice rose behind them. "Hey. You're not supposed to be back here."

The two teens spun around to face a young woman wearing a Zoey's Fast Fill apron. She gripped a dolly with boxes of food stacked on it.

"Uh, yeah. We know. We're..." Jake stammered. "We're not trying to steal anything. We're..."

The woman rocked the dolly upright and rested her elbow on the handle. It was clear to Cash that she didn't believe them.

"We're hiding..." Cash squinted at her name tag. "Gloria, we're hiding... from our stepfather." He peeked back through the small window in the stockroom door. "Please. We promise to pay for all this stuff after he's gone."

"He'll beat us again," Jake added.

Something changed in Gloria's eyes, like maybe she'd been in the same position once. She stepped to a phone on the wall and began to dial.

"Wait." Jake took a step forward. "What are you doing?"

"I'm calling the cops."

Cash reached out, calm but with purpose, and pressed the cradle switch. "No, don't. *Please.*"

Concern mixed with confusion filled Gloria's face. "Why not?"

"Uh..." Cash exchanged a panicked look with Jake, then faced Gloria again. "Because he *is* a cop. It'd be like handing us over to him." He peeked through the window in the door and spotted Roxy in line to the cashier, with one customer ahead of her. It wouldn't be long until Roxy was out of the store. "Let us hang out here for ten minutes. Please."

Gloria sighed. "Okay. You guys stay right here. And don't move." She moved to the window in the door, her eyes narrowing. "Which one's your stepfather?"

Jake and Cash exchanged looks.

"We can't tell you." It didn't take a lot of effort for Cash to look scared. He was halfway there already. Lying about their situation added to the realism. "If he found out you knew what he's done, he'd..."

Gloria's brown bangs couldn't hide the worry and anger building in her eyes. "He'd *what?*"

Cash swallowed hard. "He'd do something bad."

Gloria believed him.

"There's something you *can* do, though," Jake said. Cash looked at him, alarmed. "It's okay." He slid the strap for his camcorder off his shoulder, turned it on, pressed record, and handed it to Gloria. "Could you take this video camera and do a walk-through of the store? Then we can look at it after and know for sure that he's gone. It's already recording."

Gloria took the camcorder without question. "I've always wanted to try one of these things out." She looked at Cash and Jake. "Don't move."

They both shook their heads.

"We won't," Cash said.

Gloria pushed through the stockroom doors. Jake heaved a sigh of relief.

"Don't get too relaxed." Cash slid down the wall to a sitting position. "We're not out of this mess yet."

The two sat in the gloom of the stockroom, their full baskets of snacks beside them.

"I hope Quinn and Wynter like cold hot dogs."

"At this point, I don't care," Cash said.

Gloria pushed through the stockroom doors, followed by Miss Lucky Star. "This is Louise, my manager. You recognize these guys?"

Louise chewed and pointed to Cash. "You're the one who needed to use the bathroom."

Cash stood up and brushed himself off. "Yes, ma'am."

"*Ma'am?* Awesome." She laughed and held up the bathroom key tethered to a license plate with "ZOEYS" written on it. "Still need to use it?"

"No ma'am."

"Didn't think so." Louise snapped her gum. "You going to pay for all that?"

Jake and Cash nodded.

"Let's get on with it, then." Louise left the stockroom for the front of the store.

Gloria handed Jake's camcorder back to him. "Cool gadget."

Jake stopped recording and cued up the video in the viewfinder. "It's state of the art, as far as consumer camcorders go." He pressed play and reviewed the video.

Cash picked up his basket. "We good to go?"

Jake gave Cash a "thumbs up" and powered down the camcorder.

"She's your *manager?*" Jake raised a brow.

Gloria rolled her eyes. "Tell me about it."

Jake shook his head. "Thanks for helping us. We really appreciate it."

"Where are you headed now, if you don't mind me asking?"

Jake looked back at Cash. "We're headed... north, to Cooksville. Our real dad lives there."

"Travel safe, okay?"

"Yeah, we will." Jake joined Cash at the front of the store and paid for his snacks.

With their food and beverages in bags, Cash and Jake pushed through the double doors to the outside. Jake glanced back and saw Gloria watching them from the stockroom. He waved and she waved back.

"Jesus, it feels like we were in there for hours," Cash said. "Maybe we should take the road back instead."

"Good plan."

Jake and Cash crossed underneath the gas pump overhang to the road next to it and continued on their way back to Blue Belle.

"Child-beating stepfather cop." Jake chuckled. "We could be actors."

"Yeah, maybe." Cash reached into Jake's bag, pulled out a hot dog, and took a bite. He couldn't wait for mustard or ketchup.

"Gloria was nice, huh? But Louise? What a ditz."

As Jake rambled, Cash's thoughts drifted to Quinn and Wynter and whether Roxy had spotted them. "There's the car," he said. "Let's go find out if our mission has been compromised."

Jake and Cash quickened their pace toward Blue Belle, both eager to share their recent adventure.

○

ROXY DUG OUT her key to the motel room like she was on autopilot. This had been her third trip. Fourth? She had lost count. Her mind kept going back to that moment outside Zoey's when she swore she saw Quinn and Wynter standing at the pay phone. The more she played it back in her head, the fuzzier the memory got until all she remembered seeing clearly was the handset hanging down, a steady dial tone buzzing from the speaker.

She stepped into the motel room, locking the door behind her. Roxy set the snacks on the table and slipped off her shoes. She wanted to relax on the bed, but Ransom and Jezebel were going at each other again, any remaining modesty lost. Roxy had been a willing participant the first time, almost twenty-four hours ago, but now it felt one-sided. She had become more of a servant than a sidekick and she was getting tired of it fast.

She pulled the chair over to the TV and turned it on in hopes that some Tuesday night primetime shows would be able to save her. *The A-Team* had just started and if she sat close enough, the TV's volume could almost drown out the sounds of sex behind her. But almost wasn't enough.

"I'm going to order a pizza," Roxy announced to the room so she could hear her own voice over the noise. She opened the phonebook and flipped to the yellow pages, narrowing her choice to Pizza Zip. "Fast, hot, and fresh." She glanced at Ransom on top of Jezebel on the bed. "That sounds about right."

Roxy dialed and ordered a large pepperoni and mushroom, even though Jezebel hated mushrooms. At that moment she didn't care. Her stomach protested louder than Jezebel's complaint in her head.

She shut off the TV, grabbed her *Seventeen* magazine, and sequestered herself in the bathroom, cutting the amorous din to a minimum. She threw all the remaining towels into the tub and used them as a backrest. Roxy flipped open the magazine, all ready to read about the "cool attitude clothes" for summer.

Less than twenty minutes later, Roxy heard Jezebel yell, "Get the goddamn door!" Pizza Zip had lived up to its name.

Roxy leaped out of the tub and headed for the door. "You guys paralyzed or something?"

"We're not exactly decent." Jezebel and Ransom lay tangled

in a sea of sheets. They didn't bother covering themselves up as Roxy opened the door.

The Pizza Zip delivery guy stepped into the room, his eyes going wide when he spotted Jezebel's naked backside. Roxy pushed him back. Despite her annoyance at Jezebel, something she knew would pass, she always protected her. But Jezebel's callousness had been chipping away at her loyalty.

Roxy eased the door to a crack. "Sorry. Peep show's over. How much?"

"Twelve bucks." The delivery guy craned his neck to try and see into the room. "What's going on in there?"

"You want a tip?" Roxy pulled a stack of bills from her pocket. "Yeah, course."

"Stop asking questions. You'll live longer." Roxy gave the delivery guy twelve dollars and took the pizza box from him.

"What about my tip?"

Roxy cocked her head. "Weren't you listening? The tip was 'stop asking questions.' " She stepped into the room, slammed the door closed, and smiled upon hearing the delivery driver cursing outside. She dropped the box on the table.

The smell of the pizza roused Ransom from his sex-induced exhaustion. He sat up and Jezebel pulled him back down. She balanced her chin on his shoulder.

"There better not be mushrooms on that."

"You can pick them off," Roxy said.

Ransom spoke lightly into Jezebel's ear, but loud enough for Roxy to hear. "I'll eat your mushrooms."

She smiled at him. "Promise?" Ransom had a strangely calming effect on Jezebel. She appeared softer and easier to be around, almost normal.

Roxy rolled her eyes as she tore the lid off the pizza box and placed a few slices on it. She switched the TV back on. *The A-Team* still had work to do. If Michael J. Fox was her number one, Dirk Benedict would be on her top ten, even if he was a little old.

The three of them ate pizza and junk food, drank rum and Cokes, and channel-surfed into the wee hours of the morning. Roxy had been watching Jezebel and Ransom fade over the past few hours. It turned out there was a limit to Jezebel's stamina. Roxy decided it was her turn to be with Ransom before it was too late.

She pulled out her little bag of shamrocks and popped one into her mouth. She wasn't going to let sleep steal her chance at some one-on-one time with Ransom. Roxy nudged the bed with her foot, showed the bag to Ransom, and batted her eyelashes. "Want one?"

Half asleep, Ransom scooted across the bed and swallowed the pill without hesitation.

Jezebel cracked her eyes at Roxy. "What are you doing with those?" Her gaze shifted to Ransom. "Did you give him another one?"

"So what if I did?"

"Bitch. He's mine," Jezebel hissed, her soft edges gone. "You keep your hands off. And give me those pills."

"Ladies." Ransom had perked up and tugged on the towel around his waist. "There's plenty of me. You don't have to fight."

"There's plenty of you for *me*," Jezebel said. "No one else." She pulled him next to her. "Help me sleep." Ransom positioned himself behind Jezebel, spooning her and stroking her shoulder.

Roxy turned off the TV, turned the chair around, and propped her legs up on the bed. She stared at Jezebel and Ransom as the shamrock's speed began to take effect, sending her mind into a buzz of impulses that she found hard to control.

*Ransom must be feeling this too.*

Roxy watched Jezebel's eyelids droop, flick open, then droop again. Sleep was winning blink by blink and when it did, Roxy would take what she had been waiting for. She'd earned it.

She stood and retrieved her magazine from the bathroom. Ransom's eyes were on her when she returned.

"She's out," he said.

"Oh yeah?" Roxy flipped open her magazine and turned through the pages absently. "Are you sure?"

"Watch." Ransom kissed Jezebel's bare shoulder and stroked her arm, all the while keeping his eyes on Roxy. Jezebel remained asleep and unmoving, her breathing calm and steady.

Roxy tossed the magazine onto the table and kneeled on the floor next to Ransom's side of the bed. He rolled away from Jezebel's back, watching Roxy's every move. His eyes burned brightly.

"Can I ask you a question?"

Ransom smiled. "Sure, but don't take too long."

"You could be with any girl you want," Roxy said. "Why Wynter?"

"She..." Ransom's eyes flickered with hesitancy. "She created me."

"What do you mean?"

"I came from her dreams." Ransom locked gazes with Roxy. "I'll always be connected to her. You're just borrowing me."

"Lucky me." Roxy placed a hand on Ransom's foot and traced a line up his leg, over the towel tucked around his waist, and to his well-defined abdominals. She opened her hand and let her fingers roam, her pinky dipping beneath the tucked towel, searching.

Ransom watched his body stir under the towel. He turned to Roxy. "*You* do that to me, Rox. Jezebel's like a bull in a china shop. You're more subtle."

"What was that you were saying about variety?" Roxy ran her hand up Ransom's chest, leading her fingers along his collarbone.

"It's the spice of life."

"I like spice." Roxy pulled off her T-shirt and squirmed out of her jeans. She planted her lips just above Ransom's navel and laid kisses up his chest.

Ransom reached forward and worked at Roxy's bra clip with

one hand, but even he wasn't that dexterous. She reached behind her back with both hands and unhooked the clip. The bra slid off her shoulders to the floor.

"Hurry," Ransom said.

Roxy continued laying kisses on Ransom's chest. "Why?"

"We don't have much time. If Jezebel dreams..."

"You disappear, right?"

"Right." Ransom gazed at her with a mix of panic and excitement.

Roxy stood and slid off her panties. She climbed onto the bed, keeping one wary eye on Jezebel, and carefully straddled Ransom. She placed her hands on his chest and leaned in to kiss him.

"Oh *shhhit,*" Ransom whispered as he glanced at Jezebel sleeping beside them. In an instant flash of blue light, he was gone.

Caught by surprise, Roxy tumbled forward, her hands breaking her fall. A whiff of ozone hung in the air for a second or two.

"Fuck me," she muttered to herself. "Just my luck." She collapsed onto the bed, naked and disappointed.

"Roxy. What did you do now?"

Jezebel must have woken up the instant Ransom disappeared. A short-lived bolt of fear washed over Roxy's body. What did she know? She chose to remain silent.

Jezebel rolled over and propped herself up on her elbows. "Where is he?"

"You mean Ransom?" Roxy huffed. "You've been fucking him for hours and you don't even know his name."

Jezebel scanned Roxy's naked backside. "Did you just *fuck* my man?"

"Do you see Ransom anywhere?"

Jezebel bounded off the bed and peered into the bathroom.

"Besides, he's not *your* man." Roxy collected her clothing and began to dress. "If he's anything, he's *ours.*"

"Bullshit." Jezebel returned to the bed. "Where is he?"

"You know how it works. I guess he's stuck in your head." Roxy pulled on her jeans and T-shirt. "He just – *poof* – disappeared, just like he said he would. You must have been dreaming because I didn't get a chance to kiss him." She scowled at Jezebel and lowered her voice to conceal her anger. "I won't wait next time."

"If there's a next time, I'll beat your ass so bad you'll never get a date again." Jezebel hunted for her clothes amid the mess of sheets around the bed and slipped on her panties and bra. "Give me the pills."

"They're on the table."

Jezebel wrangled her jeans on and picked up the baggie of shamrocks. "I can't believe you wasted one on an imaginary fuck boy. Maybe he's better off in my head for a while." She placed one in her mouth and shoved the remaining three into her front pocket.

"Oh, and there's this. Solid cocaine. Monty called it rock." Roxy pulled out the small off-white pebble from its tiny bag and handed it to Jezebel. "He says you smoke it."

"*Smoke* cocaine?" Jezebel laughed as she shoved the rock of cocaine back into the bag and into the same pocket. "Sounds like a great way to die."

"He says the high is amazing."

"Monty says a lot of things. Most are bullshit." Jezebel found her keys. "Let's get the hell out of this dump."

Roxy grabbed her *Seventeen* magazine, bagged up the unopened cans of Coke and snacks, and followed Jezebel out of the room.

"Can't believe you read that shit."

"I couldn't resist." Roxy held the magazine up to Jezebel. "It's got Michael on the cover."

"Ah, Marty McFuck." Jezebel unlocked the Barracuda and dumped herself behind the steering wheel. "Shit movie." She cranked the ignition and the muscle car shuddered to life.

Roxy deposited the Coke and snacks in the footwell and took

her usual place riding shotgun. Jezebel reversed, then peeled out of the parking lot, waking the entire complex prematurely from their slumber.

The rising sun had just breached the horizon. As Jezebel drove north on Sheyenne Road toward the western on-ramp to the Interstate, Roxy found herself wondering if Ransom would remember where they left off. He was more than an object to her.

Both failed to see the little blue Volkswagen Beetle flip on its headlights in the Shey-Inn parking lot.

○

"THE SUSPENSE IS KILLING ME." Jake balanced his chin on the backrest of the front passenger seat, his eyes half open. "We got any more Cokes?" His head bobbed when he spoke.

Quinn balanced her arm casually on the driver's seatback and rested her chin. Their poses almost mirrored each other.

"Nope." Cash sat in the back seat, with Wynter beside him aiming her camera at room 123.

"Coke's my absolute favorite." She squinted through the viewfinder. "What's yours?"

Cash shrugged. "Um, I never really thought about it. I'll drink practically anything."

"Come on, you got to have a favorite." Wynter looked at him. "What about your *least* favorite soda? Hey look, guys. The sun's coming up. It must be, what, 5 a.m.?" She brought her watch closer to her face to see it in the low morning light. "Close. Quarter after."

"Yakety-yak alert," Jake said.

Quinn swatted him with her free hand. "Be nice."

"Sorry. But it's just like before. Like she's on speed or something." Jake sat up and turned on his camcorder. "I can't take it anymore. I'm going in. Cover me." He burst out of the Blue Belle and crouch-ran toward room 123.

"Wait!" Quinn protested. "Jake!"

But Jake was out of earshot within seconds. Everyone else in the car jolted awake on adrenaline.

Cash's eyes followed Jake across the parking lot. "What the hell is he doing?"

"I don't know, but I'm getting some great shots." Wynter focused, snapped a picture, and advanced the film.

"He better not fuck things up," Quinn said. "We don't need another loose cannon."

Jake squatted at the back bumper of the Barracuda. He aimed his camera back at the VW, then at room 123. On tiptoes, he advanced between the Barracuda and the truck parked next to it, aiming his camcorder at the curtained window.

"Jesus," Cash said. "He's trying to see inside."

"I can't watch." Quinn placed her hand over her eyes, then split her fingers so she could see.

Wynter continued taking pictures. "This is awesome. Jake is so brave."

"There's a fine line between brave and stupid," Cash said. "And I think he just crossed it."

"Oh, shit. Look!" Quinn pointed at the door to room 123 as it cracked open. Jake stumbled backward and managed to hide behind the hood of the truck just before Jezebel and Roxy left the room.

Jake peeked through the windows of the truck's cab and watched Jezebel and Roxy pile into the Barracuda. Jezebel wasted no time starting the engine and backing out of the parking stall. He circled the truck as they left to maintain his cover. From the truck's back bumper, Jake aimed his camcorder at the back of the Barracuda as it peeled out.

Once the Barracuda turned onto Sheyenne Road, Jake ran back to the VW. Quinn had already started the engine. He leaped into the passenger seat and fastened his seat belt. "Did you see that? Got some fucking awesome shots. How about you, Wynter?"

"Yeah, I can't wait to get my pictures developed." Wynter framed Cash in her lens and took a picture. "There's some real beauties, I'm sure." She squinted through the viewfinder and aimed the telephoto lens at targets beyond the VW's windows.

"Such an idiot." Quinn waited until the Barracuda drove by before switching on her headlights and backing out of the stall.

"What?" Jake looked at her, surprised. "I was careful."

Quinn laughed mockingly. "If you were being careful, you would have told us what you were going to do."

"I did tell you. 'I'm going in.' Remember that?"

Quinn turned onto Sheyenne Road, taking the same route north as Jezebel had moments earlier. "You said that as you left. We were completely unprepared."

"Sorry. Just trying to liven things up." Jake set his camcorder down in the footwell and crossed his arms tightly across his chest. "We've been staring at nothing for hours. Chill out."

"What if Jezebel or Roxy saw you?" Quinn cast him an angry look.

"They didn't."

"But what if they did?"

"I don't know." Jake searched for words, unprepared to defend himself. "I'd make something up. I'm good at that."

"They're not idiots," Quinn said. "They're psychopaths. Jezebel for sure."

Jake fell silent for a moment. "Okay. I'm sorry. We're a team. We need to work together."

At five-thirty in the morning, the traffic on the Interstate was light. Quinn accelerated down the on-ramp, the rising sun casting sliding streaks of orange through the VW's back window and onto the interior.

"You know, we all missed something." Cash spoke calmly from the back seat.

Quinn eyed him in the rear view mirror. "What are you talking about?"

"Ransom never left with them," he said. "Jezebel and Roxy left alone."

"Shit." Wynter dropped her camera to her lap and stared at Cash. "He's in her head. And the longer he's there, the more he's going to want to stay."

Quinn focused on a hulking black mass with a pair of red tail-light eyes floating on the Interstate about a quarter of a mile ahead. "Don't worry, Bug. We'll get Ransom back." She floored the gas pedal and propelled Blue Belle forward faster than she had ever driven her.

Jake switched on the radio. Prince and The Revolution belted out "Let's Go Crazy." He looked at Quinn. "Some driving music, my lady?"

Quinn smirked at him and nodded.

"What's the plan?" Jake glanced back at Wynter and Cash. "When we catch up to them?"

"I don't know," Quinn said.

"I need Ransom back in *my* head. *My* head." Wynter worked herself into a panic. "He's a part of *me,* not Jezebel."

Cash reached for Wynter's hand and gave it a gentle squeeze. "It'll be okay. We'll get him back." He locked gazes with Quinn in the rear view mirror. "Just follow them."

The black devil with the fiery eyes drew closer. Blue Belle was gaining ground.

○

ROXY SPOTTED THE Volkswagen's headlights in the side mirror, approaching fast. She twisted in her seat to look out the back window. Recognition was instant, even at 5:45 a.m. "I fucking *knew* it!"

Jezebel looked at her with a scowl. "What?"

"I thought I saw those two bitches at Zoey's," Roxy mumbled to herself.

"What are you talking about?"

Roxy motioned at the rear view mirror. "Someone's been following us."

Jezebel framed the VW Beetle in the back window of the Barracuda. Her eyes narrowed and her jaws tightened. "And *they're* chasing *us?*" She glanced at Roxy and crunched her brow. "Wait. You saw them at Zoey's?"

"Yeah, last night. Thought I was seeing things because they just disappeared."

Jezebel's mouth curled into a sly smirk, a telltale sign that her devious gears were turning. "I think it's payback time."

"Most definitely."

Jezebel rechecked the Beetle's position in the rear view mirror, then pulled into the left lane of I94. She slammed on the brakes. The Barracuda billowed blue smoke from its tires as it slowed.

Roxy watched as the Beetle shot past, breaking through the acrid cloud to become the pursued. "You're not going to outrun them?"

"I've got a better idea." Jezebel switched back into the right lane and accelerated. Ahead, the Beetle's engine buzzed and strained like the insect it was named after. Outrunning the Barracuda would be impossible.

The distance between the two cars closed until the Barracuda was within inches of the Beetle's back bumper. The little car had nowhere to go.

Jezebel gave the engine more gas. The Barracuda's front bumper hit the back of the VW and bounced it forward, causing it to swerve and nearly lose control.

Roxy sat up, alarmed. "Jesus. Don't kill them."

Jezebel narrowed her eyes. A smile that oozed evil spread across her face. She moved into the left lane and pulled up even with the blue Beetle. "Roll down your window."

Roxy did as instructed. In the Beetle, Quinn alternated her panicked gaze between the road ahead and the Barracuda. Wynter reached forward and lowered the Beetle's window.

Roxy spotted Jake with his video camera aimed at her. "That guy's got a video camera!" She saw Wynter raise a camera with a long lens. "They both got cameras!"

"Whatever, they'll be blurry as shit." Jezebel held the steering wheel with one hand and leaned across the center console, pointing with the other. "You're fucking dead!"

Roxy joined in. "Hear that? We're going to take you out."

Jezebel nudged the Barracuda right and tapped front fenders. The Beetle appeared to jump right in response.

"Do it again, Jazz!" Roxy vibrated with excitement.

"On it." Jezebel drifted right again and didn't let up. She forced the Beetle past the shoulder's rumble strip and into the surrounding grassland where it slid sideways, spun around, and rolled to a stop facing backward.

Roxy leaned out the passenger window, her hair flying everywhere. "Suck on that, bitches!" She fell back into her seat and gave Jezebel an appreciative eye. "You're fucking bad to the bone."

"Tell me something I don't know." Jezebel smirked and floored the gas pedal, leaving the little Beetle behind in their wake.

○

"SHIT, QUINN. THEY'RE GAINING ON US." Cash watched the Barracuda's frenzied approach through the back window. Wynter snapped photos and Jake had his camcorder rolling.

"I'm flooring it." Quinn's eyes flicked to the rear view mirror and the black muscle car framed within it. "I don't think Blue Belle can go any faster."

The Barracuda barreled up to the back of the Volkswagen, backed off for a second, then rammed the little car.

Wynter screamed. "They're going to kill us!"

Jake steadied his camcorder on the seatback. "Jezebel isn't *that* stupid, is she?"

"Never underestimate her." Cash exchanged looks with Jake. "Remember? At the Starlite?"

Jake nodded.

"What are you talking about?" Quinn gripped the steering wheel with white-knuckled fists.

"Jezebel tried to kill us a couple weeks ago," Jake said matter-of-factly.

The Barracuda pulled out into the left lane and barreled up next to the Beetle.

"She's rolling down the window," Quinn said. "Bug? Can you roll down mine? I don't want to take my hands off the wheel."

Wynter placed her camera on the back seat, unbuckled her seat belt, and reached between the driver's side door and Quinn's seat. She gripped the window crank and turned it furiously. The window pane descended into the door, replaced by a blast of cool, early morning air.

Wynter went to grab her camera, but it wasn't on the seat. Cash had it cradled in his lap. He smiled and returned it to her. "Didn't want it to get broken."

She took the SLR and advanced the film. "Thanks." Wynter smiled warmly at him for only a moment before she returned to her role as photojournalist.

Jezebel yelled something at them, but the engine and wind noise drowned her out. But Roxy's threat came through loud and clear.

"Apparently they're going to take us out," Quinn said. Before anyone else could respond, the Barracuda hit the VW's left fender.

Quinn steered away, then overcorrected and caused the car to swerve. "Fuck that. No one hits Blue Belle and gets away with it."

In seconds, the Barracuda was on top of them again. Quinn steered right to avoid damage to Blue Belle's fender and side panels, but the black car continued its assault.

"They're going to force us off the road!" Cash looked back through the rear window, looking for other traffic. But the Interstate was deserted.

The VW's wheels hit the shoulder's rumble strip and rattled everything in the car that wasn't tied down.

"HOLD ON!" Quinn braced herself against the steering wheel. The front right wheel, then the left, slid onto the grass and down the side of the highway bed. The VW slid sideways for a few seconds before two loud *bunys* sounded from underneath.

The car spun backwards, moving through the grass at fifty-five miles per hour. Quinn yanked the emergency brake and jerked the car to a stop.

"Everyone okay?" Quinn spoke through heaving breaths.

"Yeah." Wynter's words came out in a whisper.

Jake glanced back at Wynter. "They did want to kill us."

"What did I tell you?" Cash tapped on Jake's shoulder. "I need to get the hell out of this car."

Jake left his camcorder in the footwell and opened the passenger door. He stepped out and sat in the grass, his head between his knees and his hands clasped over his head. Cash flipped the seat forward and followed him out, choosing to work off his adrenaline by pacing in the grass beside the car.

Quinn slid out from behind the steering wheel to examine the damage. The left front fender was scratched and gouged with black paint. The rest of the left side of Blue Belle somehow escaped damage. Except for the tires.

"Uh, guys," she said. "We got a problem."

Wynter stepped out of the driver's side door, immediately seeing what Quinn was talking about. "Shit."

Cash wandered around the back of the VW to where Wynter stood and groaned.

"Both tires on the left side blew out," Quinn said. "And I only have one spare."

"Fuck." Cash grabbed his hair with both fists. "I'm going to be late for work. Finn's going to shit."

"Don't have a cow." Wynter trudged to the driver's side door, pushed the seat forward, and searched the back seat. She returned with the map and unfolded it on the front hood. "We're probably around here." She pointed at a spot on I94 just west of Halston. "There's a rest stop a few miles down the road." Wynter ran her finger along the Interstate. "Here. It'll have a pay phone."

"Who you going to call at this hour?" Cash harrumphed. "Your parents?"

Wynter placed her hand on her hip and looked at him sideways. "I'm not stupid. I want to live to see tomorrow." She cast a mischievous smile at Quinn. "I was going to call Anson."

Quinn emitted a small squeal of approval as she clapped rapidly. "Oh yes. Call Anson. Great idea."

"Okay. I'll be back soon." Wynter grabbed her camera and headed west along the highway shoulder.

Quinn trudged over to Cash. "Follow her, you twit," she said through clenched teeth.

Cash nodded and trotted off to join Wynter.

Quinn took a spot in the grass next to Jake. "Looks like we're holding down the fort." She expected a snappy comeback but was met with silence. "Jake? You okay?"

Jake dropped his hands from his head and wiped tear tracks from his cheeks with a quick twist of his wrist. But it wasn't quick enough to prevent Quinn from noticing.

"Don't tell anyone I was crying, okay?"

Quinn locked gazes with Jake. "I promise." She laid her head on her knees and studied the lines of Jake's face outlined by the morning light.

Jake pulled out a strand of prairie Junegrass by the root and peeled away the leaves on the side, one by one, until he had exposed the central trunk. He spun it between his fingers, then presented it to Quinn. "Does this look like a tree or a bush?"

Quinn furrowed her brow for a moment. "It's grass, you goof."

Jake shook his head and pointed at the spikelets at the tip. "This part. Tree or shrub?"

"Um, tree?"

"Nope." Jake smiled and ran his pinched thumb and index finger up the trunk, collecting the spikelets into a tight bundle as he went. "It's a bush."

"You learn that in kindergarten?"

"Probably." Jake's smile faded. He threw the grass pieces away and reseated his baseball cap. "When I was in kindergarten, or maybe Grade One, a big truck almost wiped out my whole family."

Quinn opened her mouth to reply but thought better of it.

"It was around Christmas, I think. We were coming back from visiting my grandparents in Steelworth. I remember the weather was bad, but you could still see traffic on the highway. Lots of blowing snow. Everything was going fine until my dad spotted an eighteen-wheeler lose control ahead." Jake took a breath. Even recounting the memory was triggering him.

"My dad must have tapped the brake at the wrong time or something, because we started to slide and spin. There was no stopping it. My mom and my sister were screaming. And as the truck slid toward us, the trailer swung across the highway."

Jake paused in thought. "It was a lot like that scene in *The Dead Zone,* with the tanker. Have you seen that movie?"

Quinn nudged his shoulder. "Who do you think you're talking to? Of course, I've seen it."

"Well, I thought I was going to die. I plugged my ears and

closed my eyes, and somehow the trailer missed us. We ended up in a ditch."

"I can't imagine how scary that was for you." Quinn kissed him lightly on the cheek.

Surprise lighted his face. "Thanks."

"You know, Johnny was driving a Beetle, too."

"Johnny?"

"The main character in *The Dead Zone*."

Jake let out a genuine laugh. "Only you'd know a detail like that." He faced her. "Since we're dishing, what's the deal with your parents?"

Quinn shrugged. "I don't know. They're just wrapped up in their own lives, I guess. I don't think they ever wanted to have kids. I've practically raised myself."

"Not to diss parents as a concept, but you've done a great job."

"You're sweet."

The two of them sat in silence, watching the odd car zoom past, racing the sun westward.

Jake stood and stretched. "I don't know about you, but my butt's going numb." He began to offer his hand to help her up, but Quinn was on her feet already.

"Let's wait in the car. More comfortable." She slid behind the steering wheel.

Jake touched his cheek where Quinn had kissed him moments earlier, a small smile expanding across his face. And as much as he enjoyed connecting with Quinn, he hoped Wynter and Cash would return soon. Jezebel and Roxy had to be stopped.

◯

WALKING ALONG THE greenspace separating the east and westbound lanes of I94, Cash and Wynter arrived at the Red River Rest Stop in just under an hour. The stop offered both covered and uncovered picnic tables, a bathroom, a collection of vending machines, and dozens of trees.

The parking lot was deserted. Traffic had picked up in the hour that they had been walking but apparently no one chose that morning to use the rest stop.

"Rest stops are creepy, with or without people." Wynter aimed her camera at the empty parking stalls, focused, and took a picture.

"I think I prefer them without." Cash eyed her curiously. "How are you feeling? Has your brain slowed down a little?"

"I think walking helped, but I still feel a bit weird," Wynter said. "I don't know what was going on." She looked at him self-consciously. "I hope I wasn't too annoying."

"No. Actually, it was interesting to see you raw and uncut."

"Oh, God." Wynter covered her face with one hand. "I'm embarrassed now."

"Don't worry about it." Cash spotted a pay phone beside the bathroom building and jogged over to it. "Damn."

"What's wrong?"

Cash held open the metal phonebook cover that hung underneath. Half the pages were shredded.

"That's okay." Wynter tapped her temple. "I got the number memorized."

"Um, that's... weird."

"My mom and Anson go way back. She made me memorize it for occasions just like this."

"Remind me to thank your mom later."

Wynter glanced at her watch. "Should I call the station or his house?"

"You know *both* numbers?"

Wynter shrugged and smiled.

Cash dug out a quarter and tossed it into the air. "Heads, call the station. Tails, his house." He caught the coin and flipped it onto the back of his hand. Cash removed his hand to reveal George

Washington's profile. He handed the quarter to her. "Station it is."

Wynter picked up the handset, dropped the quarter in the slot, and dialed. The line trilled once before someone answered. "Hi. Could I please speak with Sheriff Jacobs please? You can tell him it's Wynter LaCroix."

She covered the receiver and whispered at Cash. "They want to know what the problem is."

Cash shook his head. "I don't know. Car accident?"

Wynter returned the handset to her ear. "It's an emergency... Car accident."

Cash whispered, "Can I listen too?"

Wynter nodded and rotated the handset so the speaker faced forward. Cash positioned his head next to hers. Even after almost a day of no sleep, Wynter's hair still held a faint scent of roses.

"No, everyone's okay," Wynter said. "I just need to—"

Anson's filtered voice crackled over the line. "Wynter? What's this about a car accident?"

"It was Jezebel. She ran us off the road."

"But you're okay?" Anson's commanding voice carried even over the phone. Quinn would have swooned if she had been there.

"Yes. We're all fine," Wynter said. "But we're going to need a tow truck."

"Okay. I'll arrange it." Sounds of papers rustled in the background. "Where are you?"

"Red River Rest Stop, along—"

"I94, right, I know it," Anson said. "Why so far out of town?"

Wynter covered the receiver and glanced at Cash for suggestions.

"Don't tell him anything else," Cash whispered.

"Is someone with you?"

She uncovered the receiver. "Cash is here."

"Okay, hang tight," Anson said. "Don't go anywhere. I'll be there in about twenty."

"Thanks, Anson. Oh, wait."

"What?"

"Don't tell my parents."

Anson paused, his reluctance was clear. "Wynter, you know I'm obligated to—"

"Please. Just wait until you hear the details." Wynter heard the early morning background noise of the station in response. "Anson?"

"Okay. See you soon."

The line clicked and Wynter hung up the handset. "I hope he's not pissed."

"No, I don't think so," Cash said. "He's just concerned." He looked back at the vending machine enclosure and dug into his pocket for some change. "Want something to eat?"

"Sure."

As Cash ran toward the vending machines, Wynter found an uncovered picnic table that faced east and sat down. She closed her eyes and let the sun warm her skin.

Cash returned with two bags of plain Hostess potato chips and handed one of the bags to her. "Sorry. They didn't have fruit pies."

Wynter laughed. "This is fine, Cash. Thanks."

Except for the traffic, the crunching of chips, and the occasional bird call, the two ate in silence, slipping into their own thoughts. It never once felt awkward.

Anson rolled into the rest stop's parking lot and tooted his horn at them. Wynter collected her purse and camera, and Cash threw the chip bags into the garbage.

"Your chariot awaits." Anson sipped from his travel mug, his dark Ray-Bans riding high on the bridge of his nose.

"You ride shotgun," Cash said to Wynter as he pulled open the passenger door. Warm air infused with the smell of coffee flooded his nostrils and made his stomach growl.

"Oh, coffee." Wynter sighed. "I'd kill for a cup."

"How about a sip?"

"Most definitely," Wynter said.

"Cash? How about you?" Anson eyed him through the rear view mirror.

"I won't say no to a sip, sir."

Anson passed his thermal mug around and Wynter and Cash each sampled the brew. He studied their faces as they drank. Wynter handed the mug back and Cash hopped onto the back bench seat, buckled himself in, and closed the door.

"Okay. I call bullshit," Anson said. "Who's going to start telling me the truth?"

"What do you mean?" Wynter's eyes flicked to Cash and back.

"Wynter, your pupils are as big as saucers." Anson threw the SUV into park. "It's daylight. What are you on?"

"Nothing, I swear." Wynter looked at Cash.

"It's true, sir," Cash said. "I've been with her for the entire night."

Anson's gaze shifted between the two. "The entire night, huh?" He shifted back into drive and merged back onto the highway. "Where?"

"We were at the Shey-Inn, sir. In Halston."

"Forget the *sir* business, okay?"

"Okay, s... okay." Cash said.

"There was a party there," Wynter added. "We were drinking and instead of driving home right away, we waited in the car."

"Who's *we?*" Anson's eyes alternated between traffic, Wynter, and Cash in the rear view mirror.

"Quinn, Cash, Jake, and me," Wynter said. "Quinn was driving."

"So, you went to a party in Halston... on a Tuesday night." Doubt seeped into Anson's voice. "Halston can be rough, especially in that part of town."

"I know." Wynter fidgeted with the aperture knob on her camera.

"Where did the accident happen?"

Wynter shrugged and turned to Cash for help.

"We walked for about an hour, so maybe four miles?" Cash thought for a moment. "Couldn't be more than ten minutes."

Anson noted the odometer. "Why would Jezebel want to run you off the road?"

"I don't know," Wynter said. "She hates me, I guess."

"She hates everyone." Cash leaned forward as far as his seatbelt would let him. "Everyone except Roxy, that is."

"Was Roxy with Jezebel last night?"

"Yes." Wynter thrummed her fingers on her legs.

"You left that detail out," Anson said. "Seems pretty important to me. In fact, I'm getting a sense that you're leaving a lot of shit out." He shot a pointed glance at Wynter. "I can't help you if you're not straight with me."

"Okay." Wynter let out a shaky breath. "You remember Ransom?"

Anson caught Cash in the rear view mirror flicking his eyes forward in surprise. "The handsome one you and Quinn were with at Lucy's last Saturday?"

"That's the one. He's... he's my boyfriend. Jezebel stole him. We were going to steal him back." Wynter hung her head and looked back at Cash, hoping her hair would shield her eyes. Cash gazed out the passenger window, his expression unreadable.

"And Ransom was at this party?"

"He was."

"It was more like a stakeout, sir," Cash said. "Sorry. And there was no drinking."

"First you said you were drinking. Now Cash says you weren't. Which is it?"

Wynter faced forward and put her hands over her face. "There was no drinking. And it wasn't a party. They were having a threesome. At least that's what we think they were doing."

"Oh-kay." Anson sighed and stroked his beard. "I can't say I've ever started a Wednesday morning quite like this before."

"There they are," Cash said. "Just up ahead."

A tow truck from Halston had already arrived and was hooking up a tow bar to Quinn's Beetle. Anson drove on until he reached the nearest emergency crossover. He performed a U-turn, merged back onto the westbound lanes of I94, and pulled the SUV over behind the tow truck.

Anson killed the engine and placed the SUV in park. "Stay in the car." He stepped out, closing the door behind him, and made a line for Quinn and Jake.

Wynter looked back at Cash. "What's he doing?"

"Probably seeing if their story checks out with ours." Cash undid his seat belt and positioned himself just behind the center console. "I hope it matches up."

Wynter did too.

○

DAVE FROM FAR GONE TOWING in Halston had pulled Blue Belle out from the grassy ditch and hoisted her up on her front wheels, the driver's side tire still shredded. He had swapped out the left rear tire for the spare so the little car could roll properly.

Anson parked his SUV behind the train of vehicles and turned off the engine.

"Look who's back." Jake waved at Wynter, Cash, and Anson behind the windshield. Wynter and Cash didn't return his wave. "Wynter looks terrified. You think Anson's pissed off?"

Quinn wasn't listening. Instead, she focused on Anson as he stepped out of the SUV and closed the door. She released a sigh as she watched Anson shake Dave's hand and exchange pleasantries.

Jake studied Quinn and took mental notes. "All I got to do is become Sheriff of MacLeod County. And grow a beard. Check." He spoke loud enough for Quinn to hear.

"Did you say something?" Quinn managed to tear her eyes away from Anson to for a moment look at Jake.

"Just noting how high the bar is set."

"What?" Quinn returned a perplexed look before she settled her gaze back on Anson again. He shook Dave's hand again and set off toward them, his cowboy boots crunching in the gravel of the shoulder. Dave trudged back to the cab of the tow truck and pulled himself inside.

Anson tipped his campaign hat at Quinn and Jake and took off his Ray-Bans, hooking the temple tip into the V of his short-sleeved button-down uniform.

"Morning Quinn, Jake." He took a moment to survey the Volkswagen.

"Good morning, Anson." Quinn stepped toward the police SUV, but he stopped her. "Are they okay?"

"They're fine." Anson scrutinized Jake and Quinn as he took out a notepad and a pen. "Why don't you tell me what happened."

Quinn and Jake exchanged a glance. "Well, I was driving—"

Anson's body blocked Quinn's view of the SUV, but Jake could see Wynter holding a piece of paper against the front windshield. On it was the word "TRUTH!" in black capitalized letters. Jake leaned in to Quinn's ear and whispered, "Tell the truth."

Quinn stared at him like he was crazy. He widened his eyes and nodded in return.

"Hey. Mr. Peterson." Anson took a step toward Jake and poked his chest. "I've got no patience this morning for secrets, got it?"

Jake nodded.

Quinn managed a glimpse of Wynter and her sign in the SUV's window, and everything clicked.

Anson furrowed a brow and glanced over his shoulder. Wynter sat peacefully in the front of the SUV. He faced the two teenagers again. "You were saying?"

Quinn swallowed, her throat all at once bone dry. "We were following Jezebel and Roxy. They slammed on their brakes so they could get behind us and forced us off the road. She ruined two tires and scraped up the fender."

Jake ran his thumb under the camcorder's strap hanging from his shoulder. "I got the whole thing on video."

Anson jotted down notes. "Why were you following them?"

"We…" Quinn searched for the words to begin.

"They abducted Wynter's boyfriend," Jake said.

"Abducted?" Anson watched Jake's reaction. "Sure about that?"

"Look, Sheriff Jacobs. Quinn, Wynter, and Cash are my friends. That's what they told me and I trust them."

"Is it possible that *this boyfriend* just changed his mind?"

"His name is Ransom."

Anson gave Quinn a curious glance and wrote down the name, underlining it twice. "Is it possible *Ransom* changed his mind? Teenagers have been known to do that from time to time."

Quinn looked away, rolling her eyes.

"I guess anything's possible," Jake said. "But to me it sounded like they were pretty devoted to each other."

Quinn shifted on her feet uneasily. "We were waiting for them—"

"At the Shey-Inn." Jake should have felt Quinn's glare, but he missed it completely. Instead, he smiled broadly at Anson.

Anson looked up at the two of them. "You waited all night?"

"Yeah," Quinn began. "Wynter was really upset."

"I'm glad my teenaged days are over." Anson tucked his notepad and pen away. "You said you recorded it on video? I'd like to see it."

"For sure." Jake turned on the camcorder. "What part?"

"Where Jezebel ran you off the road."

"Coming right up." Jake placed his eye to the viewfinder and rewound the video to the correct spot. He handed the camera to Anson. "No sound unfortunately. I didn't bring headphones."

Anson looked into the viewfinder with one eye and closed the other.

Jake was beaming, clearly in his element and happy to help. Quinn had been annoyed earlier but she couldn't maintain it. Jake could be adorable at times.

"You know…" Quinn stepped closer to Jake. "You shouldn't finish other people's—"

"Sentences?" Jake laughed nervously. "Yeah. Sorry. I do that when I get excited."

"Some people might find it—"

"Annoying? Yeah." Jake looked at Quinn with an intensity that he hadn't quite planned. "Do *you* find it—"

"Annoying?" Quinn smirked at him. "I'll get back to you."

Anson lowered the camcorder from his eye and handed it back to Jake. "It's pretty clear that Jezebel was in the wrong, even though the video is pretty shaky—"

"Sorry," Jake said. "We were all, like, freaking out."

"I get that. One thing stood out, though." Anson shifted his attention between the two. "Ransom doesn't appear to be in Jezebel's car."

Jake and Quinn exchanged a concerned look. "I don't know. He was in it when we left the Shey-Inn. I'd have to look at it myself."

"Maybe he was lying on the back seat," Quinn said.

"Why would he be doing that?" Anson asked.

Quinn shrugged. "I don't know. Maybe he was tired? I've met him only a few times. He's weird. But in a way, Wynter's weird too. In a good way."

Dave hopped out of his tow truck and called over the hood. "Can we get this show on the road? I got calls backing up."

Anson gave him a thumbs up. "Right. Follow my lead."

Dave nodded and got back into his truck.

"Let's get you and your car back to Newhaven." The three of them walked back to the police SUV. Jake hopped into the back next to Cash. They bumped fists and began to chat in subdued voices.

Wynter burst out of the passenger seat and hugged Quinn, then whispered in her ear, "What did you tell him?"

"Later," Quinn whispered back. "Bug, that sign was brill."

"I was so worried for you guys."

Anson called across the passenger seat. "In the car, please, ladies."

The two giggled as Quinn took a seat next to Jake in the back and Wynter hopped into the passenger seat next to Anson. "Quinn? Do you want to sit up front?"

Quinn nibbled her lower lip. She flicked her eyes at Jake, then back at Wynter. "No, I'm okay back here."

Anson started the SUV and turned on his light bar. He rolled past Blue Belle and the tow truck on the shoulder, slowly at first to allow Dave to merge and accelerate to highway speed behind him.

"One more question for you, Quinn." Anson glanced at her through the rear view mirror. "Do you want to press charges against Jezebel?"

Wynter twisted in her seat to look back at her, eyes wide, waiting for her answer. Cash and Jake had stopped their talking and were all ears.

The spotlight was on Quinn. Everyone was waiting on her answer. A sly grin spread across her face and she nodded at Anson. "Let's do it. Let's make that bitch pay."

# A Criminal Mind

LIKE A TRUE southie, Jezebel rolled the Barracuda onto the front lawn of her house, or the "driveway" as her mother Frankie liked to call it, next to Frankie's orange Pinto. Jezebel called it the "Piñata From Hell," a name Frankie hated.

"It's filled with garbage and you can break it apart with a stick," Jezebel had said to her. "It's a perfect name."

"Well, it gets me to work and back and doesn't suck gas." It was Frankie's stock response. Creative comebacks were not her strong suit.

Frankie had relied on her looks to get her through her shifts at the Itty Bitty Bar, the only bar in Newhaven to feature topless dancers. The predominantly male clientele had nicknamed the place the Itty Bitty *Titty* Bar, a name they deemed clever as hell. And Frankie's 1 p.m. to 1 a.m. shift allowed Jezebel more freedom than a seventeen year old girl should have.

Jezebel turned to Roxy. "We sure got those assholes good, huh?"

Roxy nodded, her enthusiasm in short supply. "Stellar."

Jezebel killed the Barracuda's engine and cut off Freddie Mercury singing Queen's "Another One Bites The Dust" mid-verse. "End of the road, Rox."

Roxy's face fell. "What? I got to walk?"

"Yeah. I got some unfinished business." Jezebel tapped her temple and smiled devilishly. "Fuck him if you got him... and I got him."

"It's *smoke* 'em if..." Roxy reconsidered. "Never mind." She pushed open the passenger door and stepped out. Scratches of light blue paint stretched along the right front fender. "Call me later." She closed the door and began her walk across town as Newhaven started its Wednesday morning.

Jezebel locked the Barracuda and walked around to the side of the run-down bungalow. She hated entering through the front door. It felt like she was on display for all the world to see, on a rotted stage that threatened to collapse at any moment. It was too similar to her own life.

Jezebel let herself into the house through the side door. Her room was in the basement, giving her easy access and maximum privacy. But the food was upstairs as was the only bathroom in the house. She didn't live in luxury like Roxy did, with en-suite bathrooms and a fridge on every goddamn floor.

She threw her purse and jacket on her bed and climbed the plywood stairs to the main level of the house. Jezebel smelled coffee brewing, which meant Frankie was up. Hopefully she hadn't brought some loser home with her.

No such luck. When Jezebel entered the kitchen, she stood face to face with an unshaven guy holding two cups of coffee and wearing one of Frankie's floral wraps. It was far too small for him, barely covering his junk.

"Well, *hello*." The guy raised his brow and made no effort to hide his lascivious stare. "Who are *you*?"

Jezebel grabbed a box of Cinnamon Toast Crunch from one of the cupboards. "Fuck off, asshole." She returned to the stairs and descended back to the basement.

The guy's voice filtered through the floor. "There's always room for one more." A pause, then both a man's and a woman's laughter rose up.

Jezebel scowled. "Gross." She flipped open the box of cereal and shoveled in handfuls of bite-sized cinnamon toast. Tossing the box aside, Jezebel closed her eyes and hoped that the shamrock she had taken earlier had worked its way through her system.

The mattress upstairs began to squeak. Jezebel buried her head under her pillow to escape the sounds of Frankie and her douchebag of the week. But it was no use. She was still feeling the aftereffects of the last shamrock. Sleep was going to take a bit more coaxing.

Jezebel trudged back upstairs to the bathroom. She rummaged through the medicine cabinet and found Frankie's Valium buried in the back of the shelf. She shook a pill out and swallowed it with a handful of water.

She stepped to Frankie's door and listened, her nose almost touching the dirty, cracked paint. Jezebel could hear Frankie's moans and it turned her stomach. She pounded on the door.

"Knock it off! All right?" Jezebel was met with silence. "Fucking assholes." As she returned to her basement dwelling, she heard Frankie's shrill laugh and her moans soon echoed through the house again.

Jezebel closed her eyes, mustered all her concentration, and imagined Ransom naked instead. She could feel the warmth of the Valium taking effect, counteracting the shamrock stimulant she had taken earlier. A smile formed on her lips as she drifted off into a deep and unfortunately dreamless sleep.

◖

ANSON ROLLED INTO the gas bay of Finn's, Dave's tow truck right behind. He hopped out, motioned for Dave to wait, and approached the garage. Finn was already on his way out of the store.

Cash watched Anson and Finn talk. "I bet Finn's pissed. I was supposed to open up this morning."

"Don't worry," Wynter said, looking back at her friends. "Anson has our back."

"I don't know. Finn doesn't forgive and forget that easily."

Anson trotted to Dave's open window and pointed to the garage. Dave returned a thumbs up and backed Blue Belle into Finn's garage like the vehicles were on rails. He positioned the little car over Finn's sole hydraulic lift and began the process of uncoupling the Volkswagen from the towing harness.

The four friends climbed out of the SUV. Cash could see Finn pacing inside the store.

Anson faced them. "Quinn, if you're serious about pressing charges against Jezebel, I need evidence. Wynter's photos, Jake's video, and a written account of the offense."

"So don't include anything that came before?" Jake fiddled with the hand strap of his camcorder. "Like the stakeout and all that?"

"Obviously keep all photos and videos, but Jezebel didn't know you were watching her," Anson said. "As far as she's concerned, you guys just showed up, following without any ill intent. There's no good reason why she did what she did."

"Except that she's a psychopath," Quinn said as she hooked her elbow with Wynter's.

"That's up to others to determine." Anson shifted his gaze among the four teens. "The sooner you can get evidence to me, the quicker I can act on it."

"We could drop by after work," Wynter said.

Anson nodded. "That works."

Cash glanced at Finn in the store, watching them with every step. "Should be okay."

"Works for me, too." Quinn gave Jake an expectant look. "How about you?"

"Yeah," Jake said. "I'll use the time to make a dub of the video and transcribe it. Since I'm an unemployed bum and all, I've got tons of free time."

Quinn gave him a playful shove.

"Good. Five-thirty at the station. Sharp." Anson walked over to Dave's truck to see him on his way. Then he hopped into the SUV and headed up 3rd Street, toward Main Street and the police station.

"I'll be back in a bit." Cash pulled open the door to the store and let it close behind him. "I'm sorry I was late—"

"Everything okay, then?" Finn looked at him the way his dad did sometimes, concern without anger.

Cash nodded.

"Glad you're okay, son." He motioned at the baseball bat hanging by the door to the garage. "If you need to borrow Ciara to beat some skulls, she's yours."

"Thanks," Cash said. "I'm going to have to go to the police station after work to make a statement. Might have to leave a bit early. Is that okay?"

Finn waved him off. "Yeah, yeah. Whatever you need."

"I'll be back in a second." Cash stepped out of the store and rejoined Wynter, Quinn, and Jake. "It's all good. I'll see you guys at the station after work."

The group split up. Cash returned to the store and Jake, Quinn, and Wynter headed to Main Street and the Stedford Plaza parking lot.

"We're going to get Wynter's film developed," Quinn said. The three of them cut across the parking lot toward the exterior door of Minit Prints. "They open at eight-thirty."

"Well, I better split, then. I've got work to do." Jake tipped his baseball cap at them. "But I'll be back!" He spoke in a terrible Arnold Schwarzenegger accent.

"Fuck you, asshole!" Quinn tried her own Schwarzenegger accent, equally as bad.

Jake doubled over laughing. "See you guys at the station later."

Wynter gave Quinn a perplexed look. "What was that?"

"We were just quoting lines from *The Terminator*," Quinn said. "Remember? We watched it at the cabin?"

Wynter returned a blank expression.

"You know. Come with me if you want to live?"

That line twigged a memory for Wynter. "Oh, the one about a time-traveling robot who kills everyone? With that muscle-bound guy?"

"Schwarzenegger. He was the cyborg, but yeah."

Wynter shook her head. "You and Jake are made for each other."

"Shut up." Quinn smiled and looked in the direction Jake had gone. He was now out of her line of sight.

A clerk unlocked the door to Minit Prints.

"Let's get your film developed."

Wynter pressed a release button on the bottom of her camera and hand-wound the film back into its canister. She popped open the back of the K1000 and dumped the canister into her hand.

Quinn pushed through the exterior door, Wynter right behind, and walked straight up to the counter.

Wynter presented the canister of 35mm film. "Can you have this ready by the end of the day?"

The clerk looked around the empty store. "As you can see, we're pretty busy. But I could have it ready for you before the plaza opens." He winked at her.

"Would that cost extra?"

"Only if you put a rush on it." He lowered his voice. "A waste of money, if you ask me."

"Great." Wynter slid the canister across the counter. The clerk dropped it into a paper envelope, took her name, and handed back a claim stub. "Thanks."

"Nice camera," the clerk said. "The K1000 rocks."

"Yeah." Wynter returned outside with Quinn.

"Someone's got a secret admirer," Quinn said.

"Get out. Really?"

Quinn nodded. "I was watching. There was a vibe."

"Whatever." Wynter flipped the claim stub around in her hands. "You think this'll be enough to get Jezebel sent to juvie?"

"And pay to fix Blue Belle? It better be."

But deep down, Wynter felt doubt creep in and it scared her. Jezebel had been able to take Ransom away from her so easily. What else could she take?

○

WHEN CASH ARRIVED outside the Newhaven Police Station at quarter past five, Jake was already there waiting, sitting on the front steps. He had a manila envelope next to him crammed with papers. His camcorder hung over his shoulder as he worked on a miniature Rubik's Cube.

"How long have you been here?"

Jake shrugged. "I don't know. Fifteen minutes maybe?"

Cash sat next to him and picked up the envelope. "Mind if I take a look?"

"Sure, but leave the VHS tape in there. I don't want it to get dirty."

Cash slid the papers out carefully and began to flip through the neatly handwritten notes. "This is mega detailed, man."

"Too much?"

Cash shook his head. "Nah. Anson lives for this shit. Let's give him as much evidence as possible." He collected the papers and inserted them back into the envelope.

Jake held up the little Rubik's Cube. "These fucking things were invented by the devil, I swear." Frustrated, he jammed the toy into his pocket.

"The Dreamwaker crew is now complete."

"What?" Jake followed Cash's sight line and saw Quinn and

Wynter strolling toward them. "The Dreamwaker crew. That's good."

"We're lucky to be hanging out with two awesome girls." Cash waved and Quinn and Wynter waved back. "If you haven't noticed, Quinn likes you, man. Don't screw it up."

"What about you and Wynter?"

"I'm working on it," Cash said. "But there's one little problem."

They looked at each other and spoke in unison. "Ransom."

"Hey guys. Look what we have." Wynter held up a packed Minit Prints envelope.

Cash smiled. "How'd they turn out?"

"A lot are motion-blurred, but a few are really good," Wynter said. "Should be good enough for Anson."

"Hey." Quinn's eyes took in the two of them, but focused on Jake. "You changed your shirt."

"I wore it just for you." Jake's black T-shirt featured the words "THE TERMINATOR" across the top in red futuristic letters, "I'LL BE BACK!" at the bottom, and Arnold Schwarzenegger's emotionless mug behind black sunglasses screen-printed in the center in stark white and red ink.

Quinn grinned at him. "I approve."

Cash stood. "Let's head in." He ascended the steps and held the door for the others.

The teenagers approached an officer writing notes behind the front desk. The nameplate attached to her uniform read, "LOWELL."

"How can I help you folks?"

"We'd like to speak with the Sheriff," Wynter said. "He's expecting us."

Officer Lowell pulled out a pad and pen. "Name?"

Quinn stepped up next to Wynter. "Quinn Benoit."

Lowell jotted the name down. "One moment." She walked briskly past a central grouping of open desks to the back offices, knocking on one of the doors. The officer poked her head in, passed the message, and returned to the front desk. "Take a seat. He'll be out momentarily."

Wynter, Cash, and Jake took their place on a nearby bench. Quinn remained standing at the front desk. Officer Lowell returned to her notes but gave Quinn a curious look.

Quinn noticed. "I'd rather stand, if that's okay."

"Suit yourself." Lowell continued writing her report.

Across the station, Quinn saw Anson leave his office. He tipped his hat at her as he approached.

"Quinn." Anson glanced to his right and saw the rest of the group. "Cash, Wynter, and Jake. Long time no see. What have you got for me?"

"Wynter's got some photos." Quinn waved her over. "And Jake's got... what have you got for Anson?"

Jake approached the front desk clutching his envelope. "It's the video you watched earlier, all of it, and described in detail."

"Mega detail," Cash added for emphasis.

Jake and Wynter pushed their evidence across the desk. Anson opened the package of photos, flipped through several of them, then examined Jake's writeup.

"This is great, guys," Anson said. "It's really going to help. I'll head out in five and pick her up."

"Can we come?" Quinn gave Anson a hopeful look. "Like a ride-along?"

"Sorry, but this morning was as close to a ride-along as you're going to get." Anson glanced past the foyer toward the front doors. "You're welcome to wait if you want. But no funny business. Understand?"

Quinn deflated but nodded. She turned to Wynter, Cash, and Jake. "We're waiting."

Cash shot a look at Jake that said "Don't argue."

"Then we wait outside," Wynter said. "Let's go."

Anson watched the teens file out through the front door.

Officer Lowell set her pen down on the desk between them. "Do they have a case, Sheriff?"

"Oh yeah." Anson collected the evidence and brought it back to his office. He secured his gun belt around his waist, equipment he preferred not to wear if he had a choice. But this was Jezebel. A wild card. Anything could happen.

○

Jezebel sat up and swung her legs off the edge of the bed. Her head ached from lack of sleep, even though it felt like she had been asleep for hours. As her eyes adjusted to the sunlight beaming through the window, she realized the bed wasn't her bed. The mattress looked and felt different. So did the room. Instead of bare unfinished joists above her head, a solitary light bulb hung from the center of a finished ceiling.

She was back at the Shey-Inn, room 123. As much as Jezebel had enjoyed her twenty-four hour interlude with Ransom, she wanted her own room back. If it came with Ransom, that would be a bonus.

Her stomach growled, then something rapped on the window. She turned to see a figure in the window, backlit by the sun. Jezebel approached the glass and as her eyes adjusted to the contrast and brightness, she saw Ransom scowling at her from the other side.

"Let me in. Now," he said. "I've been waiting for hours."

Jezebel surveyed the room. As a replica of room 123, it was a poor one. There was no door and other than the bed and a chair, all of the furniture was gone. She picked up the chair by its back and carried it to the window.

"Step back." Jezebel didn't give Ransom time to get out of the way before she swung the chair against the pane of glass. One of the legs cracked as the chair bounced back from the glass with an echoey thump.

"What the hell?" She swung the chair three more times, reducing it to a pile of kindling. The glass remained unbroken.

Ransom motioned to his right. "Why not use the door?"

"I would use the door if this room had one, but it—" Jezebel looked to her left. The door to the room stood where there used to be nothing but wall with cracked and peeling wallpaper.

"What the fuck? There was no door here a second ago."

"You wanted a door, and a door was provided," Ransom said. "You control your dreams."

Jezebel pulled open the door. Ransom stood opposite the threshold. She reached out for him and her hands entered what felt like Jell-O, his visage distorted as if she was looking at him through a dish of water.

"What the hell is going on?"

"It's the Valium," Ransom said. "There's still some in your system, but not enough to stop you."

Jezebel cast him a look of uncertainty. "How do you know—"

"I know what you know. After all, I'm in *your* head."

"I think I prefer you out of my head."

"Then grab me and pull me out." Ransom raised his eyebrows at her and shrugged.

Jezebel reached across the threshold and pulled Ransom through the doorway. Their world tumbled and turned, both coming to rest on the floor next to the bed. She looked up and saw joists running in parallel, sixteen inches on center, instead of a stained drywalled ceiling.

"Home sweet home," Jezebel said. Ransom began kissing her neck, but she pushed him away. "Food first. I'm fucking starving."

"Deal." Ransom hopped to his feet and offered his hand to Jezebel. She took it, pulled herself up, and led the way up the stairs to the kitchen.

"Bacon and eggs?" Jezebel was already rummaging in the refrigerator.

"Excellent."

Jezebel placed the bacon and eggs on the counter and pulled out a frying pan. "You know what I know, so go to it."

Ten minutes later Ransom presented her with a plate of bacon and scrambled eggs, a little overcooked but definitely edible. Jezebel had taken one bite of bacon when she heard the sound of a vehicle out front.

She ran to the front door and placed her eye to the spyhole. A white police SUV had pulled up behind the Barracuda and Anson wearing his brown campaign hat stepped out.

Jezebel tiptoed back to the kitchen. "It's the cops," she whispered into his ear. "Stay here and don't make a sound."

Ransom kissed her and smiled.

"You want to get your ass kicked? Keep being an idiot." Jezebel glared at him. "Quiet."

She stood just down the hall and waited.

O

WOODPARK AVENUE JOINED Main Street and ran right through the middle of southie territory. All the homes looked as if they had come from a 1950s time capsule. Unkempt yards surrounded small run-down houses, most with a single floor and unfinished basement. Jezebel and her mom lived in the epicenter of squalor.

Anson rolled the SUV to a stop on the front lawn. Instead of following the well-worn tire ruts, he parked his SUV sideways behind Jezebel's Barracuda. If she decided to bolt, she'd have to go by foot. From his position behind the wheel, he could make out the scratches embedded with blue paint on the Barracuda's right fender.

He pulled a Canon Sure Shot camera out of the center console and stepped out of the vehicle. He framed the scratches in the viewfinder and took several pictures, then did a walk-around of the Barracuda, looking for other evidence.

Returning to the SUV, Anson cast his eyes up at the house. He spotted a curtain moving inside. "I got you, Jezebel." He returned the camera to the center console.

He picked up the radio handset. "Anson to dispatch."

A second later, the radio crackled back, "Dispatch, go ahead."

"Arrived at 146 Woodpark Avenue," Anson said. "I'm about to take the suspect, Jezebel Caine, seventeen years old, into custody. Anson out."

"Ten-four, Sheriff."

Anson reseated the radio handset and retrieved an envelope from the front seat. He noted the clock on the dashboard read ten minutes after six. It was going to be a long night.

The wooden steps to the front door were old and rotten, badly in need of repair. They creaked under his weight as he ascended to the small porch landing.

Anson knocked on the door then cleared his throat. Jezebel wouldn't be talking her way out of this one.

○

ANSON'S FIRM KNOCK set Jezebel into action. She padded on sock feet to the front door and wiped her sweaty palms on the front of her jeans. Something hard sat in her pocket.

*The drugs.*

"Fuck," she said under her breath. "Just a sec." She ran back to the kitchen, dug the shamrocks and the rock cocaine out of her pocket, and jammed the baggies into Ransom's.

"Stop, you're exciting me."

"Be serious," Jezebel hissed. "It's only temporary. And *don't* swallow any of them. Now keep quiet." She headed back toward the front door.

A second round of knocks echoed through the entryway of the Caines' small house.

"Jesus Christ, I said wait a second." Jezebel disengaged the deadbolt, opened the door, and stepped onto the porch. "Sheriff Jacobs. What an unexpected surprise."

Anson tipped his hat. "Miss Caine."

"Is this a social call?" Jezebel fluttered her eyelashes at him.

He ignored her flirtation. "Afraid not. Is your mother home?"

"No. She works the closing shift at the Itty... Bitty... *Titty*... Bar." Jezebel tugged at the bottom hem of her T-shirt to emphasize her words, stretching the fabric around her body in all the right places.

"So, you're alone?"

Jezebel nodded. "All by my lonesome. What's this about, Sheriff?"

"In this envelope is a warrant for your arrest."

"Arrest?" Jezebel's eyes darkened and her smile faltered. "For what?"

"Aggravated assault with a motor vehicle." Anson removed a warrant from the envelope and handed it to her. "Read it carefully."

"I don't need to." Jezebel ripped up the warrant and scattered the pieces onto the porch. "It's bullshit anyway."

"We'll see about—"

The sound of something metal hitting the floor echoed from the kitchen. Anson's hand instinctively went to the butt of his gun.

"I thought you said you were alone."

Jezebel gritted her teeth and shook her head. "Fucking *idiot!*"

"Show yourself." Anson shot an annoyed look at Jezebel.

"Just do it," Jezebel called back.

Ransom stepped out of the kitchen and into the hallway, timid at first. When he saw that Anson's gun was still holstered, his confidence returned. He strolled up next to Jezebel and placed his hand on her shoulder. She pushed it off.

"You had one job, asshole." Jezebel whacked Ransom across the chest.

"What? It wasn't my fault," Ransom said. "Get better magnets for your fridge."

"I know you." Anson pointed at Ransom. "You're developing quite a reputation in our town. Too bad it's not a favorable one."

"Can't be all things to everybody." Ransom chuckled smugly.

"Face the wall and spread your legs. Both of you." Anson turned Jezebel around, but she pushed back.

"Get your hands off me," she hissed.

"Watch it." Ransom stepped toward Anson, anger building behind his eyes.

"Back up and face the wall with your hands up. Now." Anson saw the hilt of a switchblade sticking out of Jezebel's back pocket. "I'm going to frisk you both. No funny business."

Jezebel laughed. "Just an excuse to feel me up."

Anson pressed Jezebel into the wall. "Get over yourself." Reaching around from behind, he quickly ran his hands over the front of Jezebel's body, then the back. He plucked the switchblade from her back pocket. "One concealed weapon." He slid it into his shirt pocket.

"Concealed? Such bullshit."

Anson brought out a pair of handcuffs and secured Jezebel's hands behind her back. "Don't move." He kicked Ransom's feet further apart and ran his hands over his T-shirt and jeans. His left hand ran over a distinct bump in the denim.

He leaned into Ransom's back. "Empty your left front pocket into my hand."

Ransom dug into his jeans and pulled out the baggies, dropping them into Anson's open palm.

"Oh, look. Monty's lucky charms. We already got him cooling

his heels." Anson pocketed the drugs, brought out his second pair of handcuffs, and locked Ransom's hands behind his back.

"Fuck." Jezebel sighed in exasperation and banged her forehead against the wall.

"Possession of a controlled substance, huh?" Anson chuckled. "Must be my lucky day. Two arrests for the price of one." He grabbed Jezebel and Ransom by the back of their jeans and directed them down the steps to the SUV.

"The warrant wasn't for drugs, you asshole." Jezebel resisted momentarily, then relented. "I know my rights."

"So you're saying those drugs I found on Ransom are actually yours?"

Jezebel hesitated. "Uh, no. They're his."

"Fuck you," Ransom said under his breath.

"That warrant included *any* items which may be connected to a violation of North Dakota Criminal Law." Anson walked them to the back seat of the SUV and escorted them inside. "Aggravated assault with a motor vehicle *and* possession of a controlled substance. You're both going down." He closed the door, cutting off Jezebel's barrage of profanity.

Anson hopped behind the wheel. Jezebel raised her feet and began stomping on the seatback in front of her. The plexiglass divider flexed under her repeated kicks.

"If you want to add destruction of town property to your list of charges, keep it up."

Jezebel glared at Anson through the rear view mirror, her face red with rage. Ransom tried to console her, but she shook him off. "Fuck you."

Anson grinned as he started the SUV and headed back to the station. He was one step closer to making Newhaven a little bit safer.

WYNTER, CASH, AND JAKE sat on the front steps to the police station. Jake had his miniature Rubik's Cube out and was madly trying to align the colored squares.

Quinn paced on the sidewalk in front. "What's the time, Bug?"

Wynter glanced at her watch. "Just past six-thirty."

"What the hell is taking so long?" Quinn raised her voice to the sky.

"I just want to go home and get out of these clothes," Wynter said. "And take a shower."

Cash nodded. "I think we all do."

"Especially me!" Quinn pointed at her pink FreshWhip uniform.

"Hey! I got a side completed." Jake held up the Rubik's Cube to show one red side.

"Nice. One down, five to go." A vehicle in the distance caught Cash's eye. It was Anson's SUV. He nudged Jake. "Perp walk time. Get your camera out."

Quinn spun to face Cash. "What?"

Cash motioned behind her. "Anson's back."

Jake crammed the little Rubik's Cube into his pocket and turned on his camcorder. He stood, placed the viewfinder to his eye, and framed Anson's approach.

"Finally." Quinn fumed as if she was ready to breathe fire. "That bitch is going to pay."

Anson parked in his reserved stall and eyed the group from within the SUV. His face looked like carved stone. He stepped out and opened the passenger door. Jezebel stepped out followed by...

"Ransom!" Wynter jumped up and stood next to Quinn. "He's back."

"Yeah, but he's got handcuffs on," Quinn said. "That's not good. I know he's a part of you, but remember how he treated you the last time you saw him."

"I can't help it." Wynter sprinted toward Ransom. "You're back!"

He watched her approach and his hardened face softened.

"Stay back, Wynter," Anson warned.

Wynter either didn't hear Anson or chose to ignore him. "I've missed you so much."

Jezebel glanced at Ransom and saw the look of adoration on his face as Wynter approached.

"Wynter! Stop!" Anson had begun to redirect Jezebel and Ransom out of Wynter's path when Jezebel exploded with fury. She raised one leg and kicked Wynter in the gut.

Wynter screamed and crumpled to her knees, clutching her abdomen. Quinn ran to her side, then turned and yelled back, "I hope you rot in jail!"

Jezebel laughed as Anson pushed her forward. Ransom craned his neck to look back at Wynter, his eyes full of concern.

Jezebel head-butted Ransom's chest. "Eyes on me, asshole. Or you're not getting out again."

Ransom settled his noticeably cooler gaze back on Jezebel.

Anson passed Cash and Jake, lowered his voice, and motioned at Wynter and Quinn. "Get them to cool it." He placed his hand over the camcorder's lens. "Show's over. But don't leave yet. Give me ten minutes." He escorted the two teenagers into the station.

Quinn helped Wynter to her feet and joined Cash and Jake. All of them wanted to see Jezebel go down in flames and this was a good start.

○

UNLESS SPECIAL CIRCUMSTANCES required extra staff, the Newhaven Police Station ran on a skeleton crew. On weekday evenings Deputy Sadie Buckley took over dispatch and offered backup when needed. She was the first Black deputy hired at the station and had been working alongside Anson for the past four years. Small town life suited her.

Newhaven was rarely a hub of law enforcement excitement, but Sadie had come to learn that when Jezebel Caine graced the station with her presence, it was best to keep herself on stand-by.

Anson led Jezebel and Ransom to the station's two holding cells. Each cell had a low bench that lined the inner walls. "Sadie, grab the keys. We got two hot heads."

"Jezebel Caine and... a new face." Sadie pulled keys from a lock box at the back of the office.

"Says his name is Ransom," Anson said. "No last name. No address. He's like a ghost."

"You're not far off," Jezebel said under her breath.

Ransom looked at her, expressionless.

"What, you're not still angry are you?" Jezebel continued.

"You say something?" Anson stopped at the first cell.

Jezebel shook her head slowly. "Nope."

Anson waited for Sadie to unlock the first holding cell, then he uncuffed Jezebel and pushed her inside, firmly but without excessive force. Sadie closed the cell door and it locked automatically.

"Look who the pig dragged in," a voice from the next cell said. "Handsome Ransom."

"Watch it, Monty," Anson said.

Monty spat on the floor. "You can't hold me for speedin'. My lawyer will have me out within the hour. Then I'll sick her on your fuckin' asses."

"Monty, shut the fuck up." Sadie opened the second cell. "Back against the wall."

Anson removed Ransom's cuffs and ushered him into the cell, closing the door behind him. Jezebel stepped to the set of bars that acted as the common divider between cells.

"Want me to start the paperwork?" Sadie removed a pen from her breast pocket and clicked the end.

Anson lowered his voice. "Hold off for a moment. I'll be right back." He headed toward the front entrance of the station.

"Hey, you." Jezebel curled her index finger at Ransom through a gap in the bars. "Get your ass over here."

Ransom did as he was told.

"You're fuckin' pussy-whipped, bro." Monty feigned disinterest, but kept his eyes on Jezebel in the next cell.

Jezebel pulled Ransom's face to the bars with one hand and kissed him.

"Break it up, you two." Sadie tapped the bars with her night stick.

Jezebel ignored her and pulled Ransom's hips to the bars by the waistline of his jeans. She unzipped his fly and plunged her hand into his pants.

"You don't listen too well, do you?" Sadie stowed the nightstick and grabbed a set of handcuffs from her belt. She unlocked Jezebel's cell, slapped a cuff on one of her hands, and dragged her to the opposite side of the cell.

Jezebel erupted. "Get your fucking hands off me ni..." She glared at Sadie.

"Don't say it." Sadie shook her head slowly.

Jezebel narrowed her eyes to angry slits and scowled. "Bitch."

Sadie stood average height and weight, but everyone in town knew she didn't stand for any crap. Jezebel could talk tough, but she knew she was no match for Sadie.

"Sit down..." Sadie locked the other cuff to the bars. "And shut up."

Jezebel sat on the bench. "I want my fucking phone call."

Sadie returned to her desk and ignored her.

Ransom zipped up his pants and took a seat next to Monty. "I'm not pussy-whipped, *bro*. I just know a fine piece of ass when I see one."

"Word." Monty gave Ransom a once-over. "I may have misjudged you."

"You talking about me?" Jezebel called from the next cell.

"Who else?" Ransom said without looking at her.

Monty lowered his voice. "Just so you know, I'm always lookin' for good people to *network* with, if you catch my drift. I got lots of interesting products and could use some soldiers."

"Noted." Ransom cast his eyes past the bars of Jezebel's cell and waited for Anson to return.

○

ANSON STEPPED OUT of the station. Wynter, Quinn, Cash, and Jake stood up as he approached.

Quinn gave him an intense stare. "Well?"

"Wanted to make absolutely sure you wanted to press charges."

Quinn didn't hesitate. "Hell, yeah I do."

"If found guilty Jezebel could face up to six months in juvenile detention and fines."

"If? What do you mean if?" Quinn took a step forward, the tone of her voice rising. "We've got all that evidence. She's guilty."

"She still has to face a judge," Anson said. "Or she could just be fined without any jail time."

Quinn shook her head. "No. I want her ass in jail."

Anson glanced at Wynter, who in turn exchanged looks with Cash and Jake. Quinn noticed.

"What?"

Wynter pulled Quinn aside and spoke quietly in her ear. "Jezebel has Ransom. If I'm ever going to get him back, she needs to be out. I can't wait six months. I'll be insane by then... or dead."

Quinn struggled between her desire for justice and her need to protect Wynter. In the end, friendship won out. "She needs to pay."

Wynter locked gazes with Quinn. "She will."

The two girls rejoined Cash, Jake, and Anson.

"Okay. No jail time," Quinn said. "But she needs to pay for all the damage to my car."

"I talked to Finn. Both tires need to be replaced, plus scratches and dents buffed out and repainted." Anson did a mental calculation in his head. "Three hundred fifty dollars should cover it."

"Make it four fifty," Quinn said. "Extra for mental anguish."

Anson regarded her with concern. "You sure about this?"

Quinn shifted her eyes from Anson to her friends. "Yeah."

"Okay. I'll make it happen. Now go home," Anson said. "You all look like zombies. Smell like them too."

The four friends watched Anson bound back up the steps to the station.

"Sleep is looking pretty damn good to me right about now," Jake said.

"I feel like we need a reward of some kind." Wynter cocked her head at Quinn. "Starlite?"

"Sleep or Starlite?" Quinn yawned, accentuating her words. "Sleep, hands down."

"What about tomorrow? Or Friday?"

"I could do Friday," Cash said. "We could really cut loose."

Jake's eyes lit up.

"No Donkey Kong." Cash waved his finger at him. "Step away from the arcade."

Jake offered a short-lived pout in jest. "I'll go on Friday if Quinn goes."

Quinn rolled her eyes and huffed. "How can I say no now? But I got to get home. I can't keep my eyelids open."

The friends split up, Jake and Quinn heading north and Cash and Wynter following Main Street south. Despite what they had experienced over the past day and a half, none of them would remember their dreams tonight.

○

ANSON ENTERED THE station and caught Sadie's eye. He took off his hat to conceal himself and leaned toward her, speaking quietly. "Charges have been dropped."

"Really?" Sadie raised her eyebrows in surprise. "By the way, what *was* the charge?"

"Aggravated assault with a motor vehicle," Anson said. "There were four people in the other vehicle."

Sadie cast a momentary glance at Jezebel sitting in her cell. "Wow. I'm constantly surprised at what teenagers are capable of these days." Sadie shook her head. "She's lucky."

"That's for sure." Anson looked back at Jezebel cuffed to the bars. "Was she misbehaving?"

"You could say that," Sadie said. "I draw the line at indecent exposure in the jail cells."

"Yeah, she's got a *big* personality."

Sadie collected the booking paperwork from her desk and tucked it back into a drawer as Anson approached Jezebel and squatted.

"Looks like today's your lucky day."

Jezebel looked vacantly into the corner of her cell. "I want my phone call."

"You'll get it soon enough," Anson said. "Quinn has decided to drop her charges. But there's conditions."

Jezebel laughed.

"Four hundred fifty dollars for tire and rim replacement, and fender repair. Plus the standard fifty dollar fine."

"Five hundred?" Jezebel snorted and spat on the floor. "I don't have that kind of money."

"I think you'll find a way."

"Fuck that." Jezebel scowled. "That bitch ain't getting one penny out of me."

"Then an aggravated assault charge goes on your permanent record. Plus, you could face up to six months in juvie." Anson tapped on the bars and stood. "It's up to you, Miss Caine. I'll give you some time to think about it." He began to walk away when Jezebel piped up again.

"If I agree, can I get my phone call? And get these damn handcuffs off?"

"Okay to the phone call," Anson said. "If I unlock the cuffs, no funny business or I'll charge you with public indecency." He took out his handcuff key and uncuffed her. He looked at Sadie. "I'm guessing these cuffs are yours."

Anson handed her the restraints and picked up a phone from the adjacent desk. He walked back to the holding cell, running the extension cord along the floor, and held the phone handset to Jezebel through the bars. "Make it quick. I can cut you off at any time."

Jezebel punched in a phone number and pulled the handset to her ear, stretching the handset's cord to its maximum length through the bars.

She listened to the line trill. After the fourth ring the call picked up. "Rox, listen up. I—"

Her shoulders sagged. "Fuck." Jezebel waited for the beep. "Rox. Anson's got me locked up at the police station *illegally*." She daggered a look at him.

Anson returned her glare by shaking his head slowly and holding his finger over the cradle switch.

"Grab the 'Cuda and pick me up. I need to get out of this fucking dump."

Anson disconnected the call. "I don't like profanity in my station." Jezebel dropped the handset, the plastic rattling against the bars. He pulled it through and reseated it on the cradle. "Remember, no funny business."

Jezebel laid down on the bench. "Since the charges were dropped, you could just let us go."

"Or I could hold you until your ride comes, or until the morning," Anson said. "Whichever happens first. And there's no 'us.' Possession of a controlled substance is a class C felony." He pointed at Ransom. "He stays."

Jezebel groaned and draped her arm over her eyes, her elbow resting on the bridge of her nose.

Anson strolled back to his office.

In the adjoining cell, Monty shielded his mouth and lowered his voice. "Looks like your girlfriend's goin' to need some money, huh?"

Ransom looked at him with disinterest. "Let it go."

"Opportunity's knockin'." Monty backed away, palms raised. "That's all I'm sayin'."

"Say it somewhere else." Ransom slid down the bench to the common set of bars between cells. He settled his gaze on Jezebel. "What's the plan after you get out of here?"

There was no answer from Jezebel. She had fallen asleep.

〇

Monty watched the station fall silent. Ransom stared at the ceiling and tapped his fingers on his thighs as Jezebel snored quietly in the adjacent cell. Sadie sat at her desk reading through paperwork.

"Officer?" Monty waved at Sadie. "What's the time? There's no friggin' clock in here."

Sadie glanced at her watch. "Twenty-five after seven." She returned to her papers.

Monty groaned. "My lawyer is so goddamned slow."

"Language," Sadie warned without looking up from her work.

Monty directed a whisper toward Ransom. "She sure doesn't snore like she talks, huh?" He motioned at Jezebel.

Ransom looked at him. "Crap. Don't do it."

Monty furrowed his brow in confusion. "What?"

For an instant, Ransom's irises glowed bright blue, like a Christmas lightbulb about to blow. Then he vanished.

"The fuck?" Taken aback, Monty straightened his posture as his nose caught a subtle hint of ozone.

In the other cell, Jezebel sucked in a deep breath as if it were her last and sat bolt upright. She opened her eyes and found her gaze locked with Monty's through the bars of the cell.

As mysterious as it was, Ransom's disappearance just as Jezebel awoke was too much of a coincidence. The two had to be connected somehow. The criminal gears in Monty's brain began to turn, and he let a grin slide over his lips.

She walked across her cell to the common set of bars and hissed, "If you say anything about this, I'll fucking kill you."

Monty lowered his head and narrowed his eyes at her. "Jezebel's got a secret," he said in a sing-song voice. "And she needs bread. What to do... what to do?"

Jezebel gritted her teeth. "I swear. Don't cross me, asshole."

"I see Sleeping Beauty's back," Sadie said without looking up from her papers. "Remember, no shenanigans between you and—" She turned to look at Ransom. Her jaw dropped and her eyes widened when she saw Monty sitting alone in the other cell. "Shit! Anson. We got a problem."

Anson poked his head out of his office. "What's that?"

"He's gone." Sadie stood and backed away from her desk.

Anson stepped out of his doorway. "*Who's* gone?"

She looked back at Anson, her eyes wild. "The boyfriend."

Monty's cell was out of Anson's direct line of sight. He placed his hand on the butt of his gun, not because of what he might see in Monty's cell, but because of Sadie's reaction. She was genuinely spooked.

Anson crossed the station floor, more of Monty's cell coming into view with every step, until he saw what Sadie was talking about. "What the hell?"

Jezebel sat back down on the bench and thrummed her fingers on her thigh.

"Everything okay, Jezebel?" Anson gave her a quick once-over.

"I'm *fine*." She sneered at him.

Anson scanned Monty's cell. There was no sign of Ransom anywhere. Monty sat back against the wall with a smug and satisfied look on his face.

"Where is he?"

"Who?" Monty said. "Oh, you mean Ransom? I don't know, man. I was... sleepin'." He shot a look at Jezebel. "Woke up and he was gone. Thought you let him go."

Anson shook his head and turned to Jezebel. "Where is Ransom?"

Jezebel gazed at him squarely. "I don't know who you're talking about."

"Don't play this shit with me, Miss Caine."

"I can't tell you something I don't know." Jezebel stretched her legs out in front of her and stared at her feet. "I must have been really high or something when you brought me in 'cause I don't remember anything."

"There's only one way in and out of these cells." Anson pointed to the cell door. "And you need a key."

Jezebel let out a laugh. "You learn shit like that at the Police Academy, Sheriff?"

"Cut the crap, Jezebel."

"Miss Caine, if you don't mind." Jezebel kneeled on the bench and pressed her chest against the bars, stretching her T-shirt and accentuating her breasts. "I, like, barely know you."

Anson backed away from the cell bars and shared a frustrated look with Sadie. "People don't just vanish into thin air, Miss Caine."

Jezebel shrugged.

Anson's eyes shifted between Monty and Jezebel, anger rising in his voice. "No one saw anything, huh? Nothing at all?"

"That's what we've been fuckin' sayin', Sheriff," Monty said.

"You're so full of shit, Monty."

"I will not have you talk to my client that way," a firm voice spoke from the front of the station. A brunette woman dressed in a sharp navy business suit stood at the front desk, a briefcase in her hand.

Anson exchanged a knowing glance with Sadie, then strolled to the front desk and cleared his throat. "Miss Rockwell."

Rockwell acknowledged him with a curt nod. "Sheriff."

Monty waved. "Hey, Becca."

Rockwell motioned at Monty. "Hold tight. Say nothing more." She returned her gaze to Anson, letting her eyes linger on the lines of his uniform a little too long. "I understand you've been holding my client without probable cause."

"He was speeding," Anson said.

"Then why is he behind bars?"

Anson shrugged a smirk. "It's my job to keep Newhaven safe, and it's safer when good ol' Monty is in a jail cell."

"That kind of thinking will get you sued," Rockwell said. "Did you issue my client a speeding ticket?"

"Of course."

"Then you have no grounds to hold him. Release him immediately."

Anson looked at Sadie and motioned to Monty's cell. She walked to the cell door and unlocked it. "How much does he pay you?"

"You violated my client's rights, Sheriff." Rockwell locked eyes with Anson. "Do it again and I'll make your life very difficult."

"Is that a threat, Miss Rockwell?"

"It's a guarantee."

Monty strolled past Jezebel's cell, leaned in, and whispered,

"Sure hope I don't spill your little secret." He tapped his temple. "You need bread. I got rock to sell. Think about it."

Sadie grabbed Monty by his collar and pulled him back from the bars. She spoke low in his ear. "You saw something. I know you did."

"Whatever you say..." Monty squinted at Sadie's uniform. "Officer Buckley."

Sadie pushed him forward.

Monty rolled his shoulders and adjusted his collar as he approached Anson and Rockwell. "Sheriff, you gonna give me my sunglasses back?"

Anson furrowed his brow and tapped his lips with his index finger. "What are you talking about? I don't remember any sunglasses."

Monty's eyes darkened. "Oh, is that how you're gonna play this?"

"I can't give you what I don't have, Monty."

"Let's go." Rockwell took Monty's arm and led him out of the station.

"Wait." Monty yelled back at Anson. "Where's my car?"

"Try Far Gone Towing, out of Halston." Anson smirked at him.

Monty clenched his jaws. "You better watch yourself, Sheriff."

Rockwell gave his shoulder a whack. "Keep your mouth shut, *idiot.*" The two of them stepped out into the early evening air.

Anson reached into a drawer at the front desk and pulled out a pair of mirrored sunglasses. "I think Monty forgot these." He snapped them in half and dropped them into a nearby waste bin. "Oops."

Sadie chuckled and returned to her paperwork. "You got a mean streak, Anson. Wouldn't want to get on your bad side."

"I'll take that as a compliment." Anson returned to his office.

"Got anything to read in this dump?" Jezebel had reclined on the cell bench and was tapping her feet randomly.

Sadie could ignore a ticking clock, but Jezebel's tapping was like nails on a chalkboard. Instead of letting Jezebel know her irritation, she picked up the day's copy of the *Newhaven Register* and tossed it between the bars. "Get up to speed on your current events."

Jezebel collected the newspaper from the floor. "Nothing interesting happens in Newhaven," she said, "unless I make it happen."

"You've got a peculiar definition of 'interesting.' "

The evening dragged out. Anson sent Sadie home at nine o'clock. Jezebel bitched and complained the entire time. Shutting his office door couldn't shut her out entirely. By ten o'clock she had run out of grievances or energy and the station fell silent.

About half past ten the front door buzzed. Anson crossed the station to the front doors. Roxy stood outside, backlit by the moon. He unlatched the door and let her inside.

"I was wondering when you'd show up."

Roxy stepped into the station, wary of Anson's every move. "Is she mad?"

Anson relocked the door. "What do you think?" He led the way back into the station, Roxy following close behind. "Miss Caine, your ride is here."

Jezebel leapt up and gripped the bars with both fists like she intended to uproot the cell wall from its foundation. "About time, you fucking bitch. You realize how long I've been waiting?"

"Sorry," Roxy said. "I had a family thing."

"Sorry?" Jezebel's eyes turned black with anger. "Just wait 'til I'm out of here. I'll show you sorry." She redirected her rage at Anson. "Make it snappy, you sack of shit."

Anson pulled the keys to the cell from the lock box. "I could just as easily leave you here all night. Nobody'd be the wiser."

"You wouldn't dare."

Anson dropped the keys to the cell back into the lock box and closed it. "Try me."

Jezebel clenched her teeth and scowled, the tendons in her neck standing out in wiry strands.

"Please Sheriff," Roxy said. "Let her go."

Jezebel spun her head around, ready to attack Roxy, but Roxy held her hand up, silencing her.

"She promises to behave."

"Is that right, Miss Caine?" Anson tapped his fingers on the lock box, trying his best to be entertained by the situation.

Roxy locked gazes with Jezebel and for once, she won the standoff. She nodded subtly at Jezebel and motioned at Anson.

"Yes, Sheriff," Jezebel said, just barely concealing her anger. "I *promise*."

"Excellent." Anson retrieved the keys and unlocked Jezebel's cell door.

Jezebel kept her eyes on Anson as she approached the open cell door. She glanced at the revolver holstered at his hip, only for a second, but Anson noticed.

"You want my gun, huh?" He crossed his arms and shook his head slowly. "No chance."

"We're leaving, Sheriff," Roxy said. "Come on, Jazz."

Anson followed them out, keeping his distance. Jezebel slammed the latch to the door with her fist and pushed her way through.

Roxy stepped through the entrance and stopped. She looked back, opened her mouth to speak, but reconsidered, instead offering a look of contrition.

Anson considered that a win and nodded at her. If he could reach Roxy, even for a moment, there was a chance he could reach Jezebel. He held onto that hope as he watched the hellion and her sidekick descend the steps to the Barracuda parked nearby.

As Anson locked up the station and headed home, he found himself wondering how long it would take before he crossed paths with Jezebel again. Because Jezebel was nothing if not consistent.

○

JEZEBEL STEPPED TO the driver's side door and beckoned with her hand. "Give me the keys."

Roxy dug into her pocket and pulled out a key ring with two golden keys on it, the heads embedded with a clear plastic pentagon crystal. She unlocked her door and tossed the keys to Jezebel.

Sliding behind the steering wheel, Jezebel cranked the ignition and revved the engine. The entire car rocked in response. She turned to Roxy and grabbed the back of her shirt. "If you embarrass me like that again, I'll fuck you up."

"Get your hands off me!" Roxy pushed Jezebel's hand away, the ferocity of her voice surprising Jezebel. "I'm not your fucking *slave*."

"Ho-ly shit." Jezebel stared at Roxy, her astonishment melting into a grin. "Is Roxy finally growing a pair?" She threw the Barracuda into reverse and backed out onto the street.

Roxy's eyes glimmered with anger in the blue moonlight. "I didn't have to come tonight. The sheriff would've let you go in the morning."

Jezebel focused her eyes on the road. "For your sake, it's good that you showed up tonight."

Roxy narrowed her eyes at her. "What's that supposed to mean?"

"You figure it out."

Jezebel headed toward Main Street, the route she'd take if she was going straight home.

"Where are you going?"

Jezebel ignored her as she cruised down Main Street headed south.

"You're going the wrong way." Anger rose up again in Roxy's voice. "I don't want to walk home."

"Too fucking bad." Jezebel slammed on the brakes, screeching to a stop. "Get out."

Roxy looked at her, bewildered. "What? I thought we—"

"You thought wrong. Get the fuck out."

Roxy opened the car door. "I'm not going to forget this."

"Yeah?" Evil spread across Jezebel's face. "Here's something *I'm* not going to forget. You're the one who buys all my drugs and Monty'll back me up. Don't cross me."

Roxy stepped out of the car.

"Close the fucking door."

Roxy scowled at her. "Do it yourself."

Jezebel threw the Barracuda into park and reached across the console. "Don't cross me!" she yelled one last time before pulling the door closed and driving away, tires squealing smoke.

Roxy turned in the opposite direction and began her journey home. It wasn't the distance that bugged her. She'd be home in fifteen minutes. It was Jezebel's lack of respect, her way or the highway, and sometimes she took things too far. A good night's sleep would go a long way to smoothing things over.

A honk sounded from behind. At first, she thought Jezebel had had a change of heart. Roxy shook her head and laughed. Altruism had never, and would never, pass through Jezebel's brain.

Roxy glanced over her shoulder. Anson's SUV rolled along with her. She rolled her eyes and quickened her pace, wiping any trace of tears away from her eyes with a quick twist of her wrist.

Anson accelerated just slightly to match her pace and rolled down his window. "Hey Roxy. Need a lift?"

"I'm fine, thanks." She trudged along the sidewalk without looking back.

"Look, it's late," Anson said. "I'd feel better if I drove you home."

Roxy continued to walk without responding.

"Last chance. No wisdom offered. No questions asked."

Roxy stopped and looked at him. "Promise?"

Anson placed his left hand, three fingers out, over his heart. "Scout's honor."

"Okay." Roxy walked around to the passenger side and pulled herself into the cab, closing the door and buckling in.

Anson nodded and began the drive toward Roxy's house. True to his word, three minutes later he rolled down Mortimer Avenue, stopping one house before hers to avoid raising suspicion. He threw the SUV into park.

Roxy hopped out. "Thanks."

Anson returned a small wave and a nod.

She closed the door and ran across the street to her house without looking back. The SUV's headlights lit her way.

Anson waited until enough time had passed to allow Roxy to get inside her house safely, then drove past her house on his way home. He thought he had seen her silhouette in the front window when he passed but couldn't be sure.

But from the house across the street and directly behind where Anson parked, from the left-most top dormer window, Jake had watched the drop-off with interest.

# Against
# All Odds

Roxy slept most of Thursday away, reducing the day to a couple of bathroom trips and an excursion to the kitchen for food. She had pushed her seventeen year old body to its limit and her body had pushed back with a vengeance. Thursday may as well have not existed this week.

She had told her parents that she was coming down with a cold and they had left her alone, claiming they couldn't afford to take time off work. The sickness was partly true. Coming off a binge of Monty's shamrock speed had left her extremely fatigued and sleepy. There were no hot guys like Ransom in her dreams. Instead, her head had filled with an overall feeling of dread.

The doorbell woke Roxy on Friday morning. She rolled onto her side and squinted at the clock. Ten o'clock. Her parents had already left for work. She threw on her housecoat and shuffled downstairs to the front door.

She peeked through the side pane of the living room bay window and saw Jezebel standing on the front steps.

"What the hell?" In all the time that Roxy had known Jezebel, she had never rung the front doorbell of her house. On the rare occasions that Jezebel visited, she would usually just walk in using the side entrance. No knock, no nothing. If Roxy's parents had known, they would have totally freaked out.

Roxy unlocked the front door and peeked out. "What are you doing here?"

Jezebel pushed through the front door and held up a white paper bag with the logo for "Lucy's Burger Stop" on one side, the Coca-Cola logo on the other.

"Get dressed," Jezebel said. "Your breakfast is getting cold."

Roxy raised a brow. "Bennies?"

Jezebel nodded.

"Barbecue Bacon?"

Jezebel nodded again. "Let's go. I'll be in the car."

One of Lucy's breakfast specialties was a poached egg sandwiched between a toasted English muffin, with ham and plenty of Hollandaise sauce. Everyone said they were a rip-off of McDonalds Egg McMuffins, but there was no comparison. Roxy's favorite replaced ham with bacon and a spicy barbecue-style sauce.

Roxy bounded up the stairs to change. Jezebel wandered the foyer and spotted a small ceramic dish sitting atop a mirrored console table. She dug through it and pocketed the spare change and a pair of silver dangle earrings. She left the front door wide open and returned to the Barracuda, setting its engine rumbling.

Roxy flew out of the house a few minutes later, dressed for summer in denim shorts and a white and green horizontally striped T-shirt. She hopped into the passenger seat. Jezebel gave the Barracuda some gas and rolled down the street.

"Where we going?" Despite their argument on Wednesday evening, Roxy was bubbling with excitement.

"Ollie's."

Roxy smiled. "Of course."

Ollie's MovieTyme was a defunct movie drive-in on the outskirts of south Newhaven. Ollie's ceased operation in 1979 and the land remained undeveloped, unlike many drive-ins across America that closed and became strip malls or were consumed by urban sprawl.

Despite the torn and tattered appearance of the screen, the structure itself still stood. The storage shed behind the screen served as a popular location for teenagers to drink and get high. The more adventurous would climb the supports on the back side of the screen, giving them a view of Newhaven from a hundred feet above the ground.

Jezebel parked behind the storage shed. She pulled out a Barbecue Bacon Bennie and a sack of Tater Nugs and handed them to Roxy.

"Nugs too?" Roxy smiled. "You're the best, Jazz."

"Don't you forget it." Jezebel pulled out a double burger and a tray of Nugs for herself.

Roxy took a big bite and closed her eyes with a sigh. "So good." She chewed and swallowed. "Why are you doing this? You've never done anything like this before."

"You're my enforcer." Jezebel paused. "You're Bonnie to my Clyde." She turned and locked gazes with Roxy. "We're better together than apart."

Roxy studied Jezebel's face, looking for deception, but spotted nothing. There was no emotion at all. That would have been a red flag for anyone else, but for Jezebel it was business as usual.

"Okay," Roxy said and took another bite of her Bennie.

"Look at this." Jezebel leaned forward in her seat and pulled out a long black object from her back pocket. She pressed a button on the side and a double-edged blade shot out of one end.

"A switchblade?"

Jezebel drove the tip of the blade through the bottom of her burger, piercing through the top, then pulled it out. She placed the blade flat against her tongue and sandwiched it between her lips. The blade came out of her mouth clean.

"Not just any switchblade." Jezebel held the knife up and admired its clean lines. "Way better than my old one. The blade comes out the front. The button retracts the blade too. No fancy finger work needed."

"Can I try it out?"

Jezebel glanced at Roxy's hands. "Don't get any of that barbecue shit on it." She handed her the knife.

Roxy set her Bennie down on her lap and held the hilt in front of her. She slid the switch forward and the blade appeared as if by magic, glinting in the morning sun. "That's wicked." She jutted her arm back and forth like she was stabbing something, then retracted the blade and handed the knife back to Jezebel. "Where did you get it?"

"Monty had a connection."

"Is it legal?"

"Don't fucking care," Jezebel said. "Did you see the scratches on my fender?"

"Yeah." Roxy focused on her Bennie and Nugs. "It looked pretty bad."

"Like an idiot, Quinn dropped her charges against me. Good for me, bad for her." She engaged the switchblade and flipped the knife edge through the paper bag sitting on the center console.

Roxy watched the sides of the bag separate in two pieces. "Holy shit that's sharp."

Jezebel looked at her sneering reflection in the knife's blade. "We're going to take out Quinn and anyone else who gets in our way." She retracted the blade, slid the hilt back into her pocket, then took a big bite of her burger.

Roxy directed her eyes forward as she finished her Bennie and started on her Nugs. Take out Quinn? What did that mean, exactly? She assumed it was bad but was too intimidated to ask. Besides, she didn't want her Nugs to get cold. There was nothing worse than cold Nugs.

○

WYNTER COLLECTED HER purse and stepped out from behind the display case. She gave a wave at Hunter and Daytona. "Thanks for covering for me this week. You really helped me out."

Hunter nodded at her. "It's casual."

Wynter turned, walking backwards. "Hey Hunter. Guess what? I've got plans tonight."

"Wintergreen scores! Partying or what?"

"Starlite," Wynter said.

"Awesome. Maybe we'll see you there after work." Hunter looked at Daytona and grinned. "What do you say, babe?"

"Maybe. If you're good."

"Oh, I'll be *very* good." He scooted up behind her and kissed her neck. Daytona shrugged her shoulders and giggled.

"Later." Wynter turned to meet Quinn shuffling toward her from the main concourse.

"I'm so glad the day is over," Quinn said. "A few days away from here reminds me how much I hate it." She joined Wynter heading for the plaza exit.

"You should find another job. The summer's only half over."

"A job doing what, exactly?"

"I don't know." Wynter gave it some thought. "What about writing movie reviews for the Register? You'd probably get free admission."

"Cool idea," Quinn said. "I could probably do both jobs blindfolded... except the movie-watching part."

"And the writing."

Quinn chuckled. "That too."

"You could also convince Zain to let you give rollerskating lessons at the Starlite. He'd probably be all over that."

Quinn sighed and smiled dreamily. "I'd rather he be all over *me*."

"Don't think he's into jail bait."

Wynter laughed as they pushed through the exit doors and stepped into the warm early evening sunshine.

"I'd offer you a ride home but Blue Belle's still in the shop."

"I was going to walk, anyway," Wynter said.

"Swing by Finn's on the way for some sweet Cash?"

"No." Wynter blushed. "We're meeting the guys at the Starlite, remember?"

Quinn glanced at her sideways and smirked.

"Seriously," Wynter said.

"Seriously?" Quinn laughed. "You two need to get it on. *Seriously.*"

"We're just friends."

"You're still hung up on Ransom, aren't you?"

Wynter fell silent for a moment. "You don't understand. We're connected, Quinn. And when I saw him at the police station and how he looked at me, I know he still cares for me, and has feelings for me."

"I don't know, Bug. I hope you're right." Quinn stopped. "I better get going, but I'll meet you at your place at eight." She stepped up to Wynter and hugged her, then kissed her cheek lightly. "Later!" She broke away and headed north.

Wynter followed Main Street south. She could have easily dropped by Finn's to see Cash, but he was not on her radar. Quinn was right. She was still stuck on Ransom and she had to find a way to get him back.

○

JAKE PULLED OUT a couple of shirts from his closet and laid them on his bed. Dressing to impress was new to him and if anyone had suggested that he was trying to catch Quinn's eye, he would have denied it.

He decided to go as full *Back to the Future* as he could, with jeans and suspenders, a red T-shirt under a light plaid button-up, and a jean jacket over top. Jake didn't own a red down vest and even if he did, he would have left it at home. It didn't suit the summer weather. He was wearing enough layers as it was. Quinn would get it. He was certain of it.

He pulled on the T-shirt and began buttoning up his plaid shirt when he heard a familiar rumbling outside. Jake's eyes shot to the camcorder on his desk. He picked it up, powered it on, and pressed record before he even had a clear shot of the street.

He peeked over the sill of the dormer window and spotted Jezebel's black Barracuda idling just down the street, across from Roxy's house, just as he had expected.

"Jezebel's out." Jake raised the viewfinder to his eye, framed, and focused.

The car's horn blasted from below and a few seconds later Roxy ran across the street and hopped into the muscle car. Jake expected the Barracuda to peel out, but it pulled away from the curb and out of sight well within the speed limit and as quietly as the engine would allow.

Jake turned the camcorder on himself. "Eyewitnesses report that Jezebel and Roxy are on the prowl tonight, current destination unknown. The people of Newhaven have been asked to keep an eye out for anything suspicious. Jake Peterson reporting, Action Five News." He stopped recording and powered down the camera.

He noted the time: quarter to seven. Jake reclined on his bed and figured he could fit in one game of Donkey Kong since Cash had banished him from the arcade tonight. But time flies when you're saving Pauline and before he knew it, almost an hour had passed.

Jake had ten minutes to get to the Starlite. If he ran full tilt, he just might make it. He barreled down the stairs, pulled on his shoes, and tore down the street as fast as his feet would carry him.

THE BARRACUDA'S DASHBOARD clock read ten minutes to seven. Jezebel drove slowly down Quinn's street, passing yard after yard of green lawns without a weed in sight. "Seek and Destroy" by Metallica pumped out of the speakers. She turned the volume down on the tape cassette player. "I should collect all my dandelions and bring them here." She scowled. "Rich bastards."

"Watch it," Roxy said. "I'm one of those *rich bastards*."

"You're different. You're a psycho, just like me."

Roxy glanced out the passenger window to hide her discomfort with the psychopath label. The smell of freshly cut grass calmed her. "Why are you going so slow?"

"I'm scanning the street. You know, seek and destroy." Jezebel narrowed her eyes on the houses ahead. "You live in this so-called *paradise*. Which one is Quinn's?"

"That one there." Roxy pointed at a sprawling white house with a red brick foundation.

Jezebel pulled the car to the curb two houses down and parked behind several cars ahead of her. She stopped the tape and killed the engine.

"Damn, I liked that song." Roxy looked at her expectantly. "What do we do now?"

"We wait." Jezebel twisted her body to face her. "You're my enforcer."

"I know." Roxy eyed her hesitantly. "What?"

"Surveillance is one of your jobs."

"It is?"

Jezebel glanced up the street and pointed. "Hide in those bushes up ahead. It's almost right across from Quinn's."

"We can see fine from here."

Jezebel stared at her, darkness building behind her eyes.

"But maybe I'll see more from those bushes." Roxy stepped out of the car and slammed it shut. She grimaced and mouthed "Sorry" before crouch-running to the bushes and concealing herself.

"Jesus," Jezebel muttered to herself. "She couldn't *enforce* her way out of a wet paper bag." She slid down in her seat so her eyes just cleared the top of the dashboard.

By ten after seven, about the same time Jake was settling into a short game of Donkey Kong, the street remained quiet. Roxy ran back to the car and pulled open the door.

"Nothing's happening."

"It's only been about twenty minutes," Jezebel said. "Get back out there."

Roxy sighed and swung the car door closed. Jezebel gritted her teeth and prepared for the loud slam but Roxy remembered at the last second, grabbed the handle, and eased it closed.

"She can be taught," Jezebel said to herself.

Through the open driver's side window, Jezebel heard a door close from up the street. A house door. Roxy was halfway back to the bushes and heard the door as well. She dropped to the sidewalk and crouched behind a parked car.

A teenaged girl with glasses and black hair in a bob ran down the walkway from her house. She wore a trendy rollerskating ensemble.

*Quinn!*

Jezebel slid down in her seat even more. After a second, she eased back up and saw Roxy peering through a car window, watching Quinn cross the street.

Roxy slipped on some gravel and nearly lost her footing. She recovered and scrambled to the back bumper to avoid discovery on the sidewalk. She looked back at Jezebel and pointed, mouthing words that no one would be able to understand at that distance.

Roxy peeked out from the car's back bumper. Quinn continued walking away from her down the sidewalk, shrinking in the distance. Once Quinn was out of sight, she ran back to the Barracuda and jumped in.

"I know where she's going," Roxy said between excited breaths.

Jezebel glared at her, shaking her head. "Well?"

"She had rollerskates hanging off her shoulder." Roxy's eyes sparkled.

Jezebel nodded, a small devious smile growing on her face. "You did good, Rox." She meant it this time.

Her hand went to the keys in the ignition and with a quick twist of her wrist, the Barracuda rumbled to life. Jezebel rolled out onto the street and used Quinn's driveway to complete a three-point turn.

Jezebel rolled the Barracuda in the opposite direction as Quinn had walked. She pushed "Kill 'Em All" back into the cassette deck, pressed play, and cranked the volume. "Seek and Destroy" continued mid-song. "Next stop, Starlite SuperSkate."

Jezebel circumnavigated Newhaven, taking the 19th Street Bridge over the Interstate, and approached the Starlite from the west to reduce the odds of running into Quinn. The two arrived at their destination before Metallica had begun their next song. They had also beaten Quinn there.

As they approached the Starlite parking lot, Jezebel passed a familiar silver Fiat traveling in the opposite direction.

"Hey." Roxy pointed at the car. "Isn't that—"

More than the car, it was the mirrored sunglasses that confirmed who was driving.

"Shit. Fucking Monty. That's all we need." Jezebel looked back over her shoulder. "Did he see us?" She spotted the Fiat in her side mirror turning around to follow.

Roxy looked back through the rear window. "He's following us."

"Goddammit. That fucker." Jezebel turned into the Starlite parking lot, which was already filling up with vehicles. She found a stall in the back of the lot and parked. "I forgot to tell you. Monty knows about Ransom."

"Yeah, they almost got into a fight at the Shey-Inn."

"No, you fucking *idiot*. He saw Ransom *disappear*. When I was in jail."

Monty parked his Fiat directly behind the Barracuda, blocking Jezebel's only exit, and stepped out of the car.

Jezebel shot a look at Roxy. "Don't say *anything* about Ransom. Understand?"

Roxy nodded, still stinging from Jezebel's earlier insult.

Monty approached Jezebel's side of the car and leaned toward the window. "Evenin' ladies."

"What do you want, Monty?" Jezebel glowered at him.

"Just sayin' hi to my two best clients." Monty grinned ear to ear. Even with sunglasses on, he made no attempt to hide his ogling.

"You buy those *gay*viators in bulk?"

Monty ignored the insult. "Have you given any thought to my proposition?"

"I'm considering it," Jezebel said. "Now stop staring at my tits, you perv."

"Just appreciatin' beauty is all." Monty scanned the back seat. "Where's your friend?"

"What friend?" Jezebel tried to grab his sunglasses, but he stepped back just in time and grabbed her forearm.

"Don't play dumb, Jezebel." Monty squatted to look at Roxy. "It was the damnedest thing, Rox. One second, he was there. The next, poof, gone, vanished into thin air." He released Jezebel's arm, leaving white finger marks behind.

Roxy shrugged.

Jezebel rubbed her arm. "Scram, asshole."

"I'm onto you Jazz," Monty said. "You too, Roxy. *And* your friend... Ransom, was it?" He leaned in closer. "You're goin' to sell rock for me whether you like it or not. 'Cause your secret's safe with me, 'til it ain't."

"You done?" Jezebel glared at her distorted reflection in his glasses. "Who'd believe you, anyway?"

Monty raised his hands, palms out, then strolled back to his car and drove away.

Roxy craned her neck out the passenger window to make sure Monty had left. "So he saw Ransom disappear?"

"I woke and Monty was staring at me with that stupid fucking grin of his. Since he's trying to blackmail me, he probably knows."

"Everybody wants Ransom."

"Yeah, including me. Like, right now." Jezebel climbed into the back seat and stretched out. "Keep a lookout for that bitch. I got to go find my sex slave." She draped the crook of her elbow across her eyes.

In less than ten minutes, Jezebel was out, snoring softly. The parking lot had filled almost to capacity. Roxy continued her surveillance of the rollerskaters lined up at the door waiting to get in.

Roxy pulled a joint out of the breast pocket of her button-up shirt and lit it from a book of matches she had found in the glove box. She inhaled deeply and held the smoke in. Relaxation washed over her as she exhaled a plume of smoke out her window.

"Surveillance is easy." Roxy smoked the joint down to a nub and flicked it to the pavement. She fought to keep her eyes open, but the fight did not last long. Soon she joined Jezebel in dream land.

Across the parking lot, Monty sat in his Fiat and watched the Barracuda and its occupants. Surveillance *was* easy if you didn't pass out first.

◯

QUINN KNOCKED ON the door to Wynter's trailer at quarter to eight. She gazed at the cloudless sky while she waited. It was a perfect evening, not too warm. From within the trailer Quinn could hear the thuds of hurried footsteps.

The door swung open and Wynter stepped out. "Bye. Don't wait up," she called back.

"Have f—" Madeline's voice cut out as Wynter closed the door.

Quinn took in Wynter's outfit, raised a brow, and nodded. "Looking *hot,* Bug."

Wynter wore denim shorts and a white long sleeve button-up shirt. She had rolled up the hem and knotted it in the front, exposing a strip of her smooth midriff. Her cuffs were rolled up to her elbows and she had drawn her red hair up in the back with a thick white ribbon. Her purse and rollerskates hung from her shoulder.

"Just taking a page from your fashion guide," she said. "You look mega sexy, too."

"You remember what you called yourself the last time?"

Wynter thought a moment, then shook her head.

"A walking marshmallow," Quinn said. "Remember that?"

"Things have changed."

"They sure have. But I'll let you in on a secret."

"What's that?"

Quinn leaned in closer. "We could wear pillowcases and the guys would still drool over us."

Both girls laughed as they walked out the exit of the trailer park to the adjoining street.

"Do you think Ransom will be there?"

Quinn eyed Wynter with concern. "Do you want him to be there?"

"Yeah. I do."

"What about Cash?"

"He'll understand. He knows I need Ransom back."

Quinn kicked a pebble across the street. "He'll be crushed but he'll never admit it."

"You make me sound like I don't care," Wynter said. "I do, but not in the same way as I do with Ransom."

"I'm not so sure. Besides, if Ransom's there, then Jezebel and

Roxy will be there for sure." Quinn glanced at Wynter. "You still want him to be there?"

Wynter thought for a moment. "Yeah. I'll kiss him and we can run away."

"Jezebel will never let you get away with that."

A sneaky smile broke across Wynter's face. "That's why I'm going to need a little help from my friends."

"Going to be sly with some help from your friends?"

Both of them began to giggle as they attempted a mangled rendition of "With A Little Help From My Friends" by The Beatles.

Ten minutes later Quinn and Wynter strolled up the ramp to the Starlite's entryway. Cash leaned against the corner of the building, looking a bit too casual. Jake stood next to him, panting with his hands on his knees. When he saw Quinn and Wynter approach, he straightened himself up and tried to look cool. It didn't work.

Quinn whispered into Wynter's ear, "Is Jake sweating?"

"He's... something."

Both giggled before they approached.

"Hey guys," Wynter said. "Ready to skate 'til you drop?"

"Been looking forward to it all week." Cash tugged at his shirt. "Sorry I didn't dress better. My shift ended, like, half an hour ago."

"I'm glad you made it."

"But you look beautiful, Wynter." Cash smiled.

"Thanks." Wynter felt herself blush. She couldn't bring herself to meet Cash's gaze.

Quinn tilted her head and gave Jake a curious glance. "You okay, McFly?"

Jake managed a laugh and gave Cash a friendly tap. "Told you she'd get it." He looked at Quinn, his breathing settling down. "I ran all the way here. Didn't want to be late."

Cash tapped Jake back. "Tell Quinn *why* you're late."

"Uh…" Jake balked.

"He was playing Donkey Kong."

"Correction." Jake held up an index finger. "I was helping Mario save Pauline."

"Maybe you can save *me* tonight." Quinn winked at him and took Wynter's arm. "From boredom that is," she whispered. Both girls giggled and paraded into the Starlite.

"Did you see that?" Jake stared at Cash. "What does that mean?"

"I think it means you better not play any video games tonight." Cash smiled at him and tapped Jake's shoulder. "Come on."

The two of them followed Quinn and Wynter inside the building. Across the parking lot, Roxy woke with a start. Jezebel had brought back a guest.

○

SOMETHING KNOCKED THE back of Roxy's seat, waking her. She looked back and saw Jezebel squinting at the evening sun. In the footwell behind her seat sat Ransom. He smirked at her and wiggled his eyebrows.

"Hey, Roxy."

Roxy spun back around and checked the time on the dash: quarter to nine. Her eyes flicked to the entryway of the Starlite. The building's neon and flashing lights cycled through their programmed animation. The parking lot was packed to capacity but there were no crowds waiting to get in.

"Are they here yet?" Jezebel crawled into the driver's seat. "Rox?"

Ransom took a seat in the back and leaned over the center console.

Roxy scanned the parking lot as her mind raced to find a way to answer. After smoking an entire joint, she found she couldn't focus and her heart pounded in her chest as if she had just run a hundred yard dash.

Jezebel sniffed, her eyes going dark. She slapped Roxy's shoulder.

"What the fuck, Jazz?"

"Are you baked?"

Roxy put her hands to her face, then peeked through the cracks of her fingers at Jezebel and started to laugh.

"Save any for me?" Ransom asked.

"Shut up." Jezebel returned her glare to Roxy. "Are they in there or not?"

Roxy propped her feet on the glove box. "Fuck if I know."

Jezebel grabbed Roxy's shirt in her fist and pulled her across the console. In her other hand, she raised the hilt of her switchblade close to Roxy's neck and engaged the blade.

Ransom backed away as the two girls stared each other down.

"What you going to do, huh? Cut my throat in your precious Barracuda?" Roxy may have been high, but her eyes blazed with newfound confidence.

Jezebel let Roxy go, retracted the blade, and pocketed the knife. "You're on thin ice."

"Whatever."

"You guys are better than TV," Ransom said.

Jezebel glanced at Ransom. "And you're better if you don't talk." She opened the driver's side door and stepped out. "Let's go."

Roxy climbed out of the Barracuda, followed by Ransom. "So, we're going to walk right in? That's the plan?"

"Ransom sticks with me." Jezebel looked at him. "Got it?" She pointed at Roxy. "As for you, distract them until I can get Quinn alone. Then I'll smoke the bitch. Everyone else is a bonus."

"Your *plan* sounds a little half-baked," Roxy said.

"Got something better?"

"We go back to your place and party. Why waste time with these idiots?"

"Sounds good to me," Ransom said.

"They need to be taught a lesson." Jezebel gritted her teeth. "Especially Quinn."

"Why not wait and jump them later?"

Jezebel didn't answer Roxy's question. Instead, she focused on the Starlite's entrance, her jaw clenched in angry angles.

" 'Cause she wants an audience." Roxy's eyes found Ransom's. "Isn't that fucked up?"

"You better not answer that." Jezebel walked around the front of the car. "Or I'll keep you in my head."

"Jesus." Ransom took his place next to Jezebel. "Anything but that."

"Come on." Jezebel and Ransom headed toward the entrance of the Starlite.

Roxy hung back for a moment as she tried to mull over possible outcomes for what they were about to do. It all came back in a jumble, none of it good.

"Can't do this without my enforcer," Jezebel called back.

"Shit," Roxy said under her breath as she ran to catch up. "Just don't kill her, okay?"

Across the parking lot, Monty had watched the Barracuda's two occupants become three. And Jezebel held the key.

C

With all the coveted picnic-style tables taken, Wynter, Quinn, Cash, and Jake sat on raised stools around a small circular table, just big enough to hold their drinks, a large order of fries, and two condiment bottles.

"Cruel Summer" by Bananarama broadcast through the

speakers in the arena as rollerskaters traced circles to escape the summer heat.

Jake grabbed the ketchup and began squirting it over everything.

"Whoa, McFly." Quinn grabbed the ketchup bottle from his hands. "Not everyone likes *fries* with their ketchup."

"Sorry. I thought everyone liked ketchup." Jake blushed. "I can get another order if you want."

"I think we'll be okay for now," Cash said. "You okay, Quinn?"

"I don't know." Quinn smirked and wagged her finger back and forth. "That's strike one."

Jake swallowed hard. "Sorry, Quinn. I had no idea."

Wynter leaned across the table. "She's teasing. She wouldn't be smiling if she was pissed off." Wynter grabbed a fry and took a bite.

Jake recalibrated his thoughts as he loaded up a fry with ketchup. "Did you know Jezebel's out? Just before I left tonight, I saw her pick up Roxy. It was weird."

"What's so weird about it?" Cash took a sip from his cup of soda. Of the four of them, he preferred not to use a straw. "Quinn dropped her charges."

"I'm still wondering if that was the right decision." Quinn caught Wynter's look of surprise and shrugged. "I know that's not the point, but there's something appealing about sending that bitch to jail."

"The point being getting Ransom back, right?" Cash locked his eyes on Wynter. "Back in your head?"

Wynter nodded and hid her eyes behind a lock of hair.

Quinn took a french fry. "So what made it weird?"

"Normally, Jezebel likes to be seen," Jake began. "You know, 'Hey, look at me. Look how I can burn rubber and annoy everyone blah, blah, blah.'" Jake sipped from his soda. "Tonight, except for honking her horn once, she drove away silently. Like she purposely didn't want to draw attention."

Cash looked from Jake to Quinn and Wynter and back. "Okay, that's kind of weird. Maybe a two out of ten on the weird scale."

"Can we talk about something other than *Jezebel*?" Wynter grimaced when she said her name.

"I saw Anson the other night..." Jake realized the direction the conversation would lead and cut his words short. "Never mind. Not important." He regarded the others at the table. "So, what's our plan? If Ransom walked in right now?"

"First thing that comes to mind is divide and conquer," Cash said as he dunked his fries into a pool of ketchup in one corner of the tray. "Separate Ransom from Jez... uh, from *his host* and get him back with Wynter."

"Then what?" Wynter tapped a french fry on her napkin. "Run?"

Quinn raised the fry in Wynter's hand and bit the end off it. "You should kiss him, then kill him."

Jake sputtered soda over the front of his shirt. "What?"

"Think about it." Quinn leaned into the table and lowered her voice. "He drifts when he dies. Then he's back in Wynter's head. It's fast and easy."

"Easy?" Jake's eyes bugged out. "Maybe for you. I couldn't kill someone."

"Then I guess running is your only other option," Quinn said.

Wynter eyed Quinn cautiously. "I could hide. I'm sure Zain would help."

"You can't hide forever." Quinn took a long sip from her soda. "She'll eventually find you. Then who knows what she'd do."

"Looks like we're going to get our chance." Cash motioned to the Starlite entryway. "Déjà vu."

Jezebel had her arm snaked around Ransom's waist, and his around hers. She directed Roxy to the cashier to pay for admission and rentals.

"Let's hit the rink," Cash said. "Maybe we can catch them by surprise and jump Ransom. I feel like a sitting duck here." He grabbed a handful of fries and jammed them in his mouth.

"That's the thing about public places." Quinn found Wynter's eyes. "Nowhere to hide."

"Let's go to the opposite end of the rink and watch for them." Jake rolled to the rink entrance. "Like when the Reliant was chasing the Enterprise in *Star Trek II: The Wrath of Khan.*"

"Brill." Quinn followed him enthusiastically.

Cash looked at Wynter with a confused look, then shook his head. "They're made for each other. Take my hand."

Wynter looked back at Ransom. He was still at the admissions window, his arm around Jezebel's waist. He kissed her neck and laughed. Wynter returned her gaze to Cash.

"I know you want him instead of me. I get it." Cash smiled somewhat wistfully and motioned to the rink, hand outstretched. "You can't skate with the one you love, but you can skate with a friend who'll keep you safe."

Wynter grabbed Cash's hand and they joined the flow of skaters, pumping their legs to catch up with Quinn and Jake, who were already waiting at the opposite side of the rink.

"How about this?" Jake collected Wynter, Quinn, and Cash into an impromptu huddle with his arms. "Me and Cash get Roxy alone. Quinn, you sneak up on Jezebel and, like, trip her or something. Then Wynter can take Ransom somewhere and do whatever she needs to do."

"Yeah," Cash said. "That could work. If we're really lucky, that is."

"But where would we go exactly?" Wynter looked to the others for suggestions.

Jake shrugged. "The arcade?"

"Nah," Cash said. "Too crowded."

"It's not very romantic, but what about the bathroom?" Quinn looked at the others expectantly.

"Yeah, that's good," Wynter said.

"Oh shit. Speaking of bathrooms..." Jake pointed to the entrance to the rink. Jezebel and Ransom had joined the circling crowd. "Time to go. I feel the need..."

Quinn joined in. "The need for speed!"

The group of friends split up and set their plan into action.

○

JEZEBEL AND RANSOM sat on a bench tying up their rollerskates. "Do you see them?" She looked up at Roxy, who was standing at the rink boards surveying the passing crowd.

Roxy plopped down next to them on the multi-colored carpet. "Nope."

Jezebel noted Roxy's red-rimmed eyes. "It's a good thing you aren't skating. You'd probably crack your empty head open." She laughed and stood, stretching her legs a few times. "They're here somewhere. Distract them until I can get at Quinn."

Roxy held her hand to her forehead and saluted Jezebel.

"And get off the fucking floor." Jezebel nudged Roxy's knee forcefully with her toe stop.

"Bite me!" Roxy's eyes burned with annoyance. She pulled herself up and propped her forearms on the sideboards.

Jezebel took Ransom's hand and led him to the rink. As soon as the wheels of his skates hit the smooth floorboards, he spun around and twirled Jezebel under one arm, catching her with the other.

Jezebel blinked at him. "Holy shit. You can skate."

"Yes, I can." Ransom looked surprised by his skill but rolled with it. "One of my hidden talents."

"Well take me for a ride, boy toy." Jezebel raised her hand and waited for Ransom to lead. She turned and stuck her tongue out at Roxy. Roxy responded by shooting back both middle fingers.

Jezebel and Ransom merged with the crowd and danced their way around the rink.

"What a fucking show off," Roxy mumbled to herself.

"Who's a show off?" a familiar voice said from behind.

Roxy spun around to find Cash and Jake. "Um, hi." She glanced back at the rink for a moment, before returning her attention to the two guys in front of her.

"You're looking fine tonight, Roxy," Cash said. "Or is it Rox?"

"Whatever. It's cool."

Jake wiggled his nose and sniffed. He cast his eyes around the concession area and smiled. "I'll be right back."

"How come you're not skating, too?" Cash made sure to lock gazes with her.

"Um, I didn't feel up to it?" Roxy rubbed her palms on her pant legs.

Jake reappeared beside Cash holding a partially eaten tray of french fries with ketchup covering half. "They hadn't taken away our food yet, so I nabbed it. Fry?"

Cash tried to hide his disgust. "No thanks."

Jake plucked a french fry and took a bite. He presented the tray to Roxy. "Want some?"

"Sure," she said. "I'm, like, starving."

"Help yourself." Jake watched her take a handful. "So... Roxy. I saw you get out of Anson's car the other night."

"He was just driving me home." Roxy cast a narrow-eyed glance back at the rink. "Jazz forced me to walk home and—"

Yelling broke out at the opposite end of the rink just as Pat Benatar began belting out "Love Is A Battlefield."

Roxy turned to look, craning her neck. "What's going on?"

"Looks like someone fell," Cash said.

"Want some more fries?" Jake held out the tray.

"Sure." Roxy took a french fry and dipped it in the leftover ketchup. "I shouldn't be talking to you. Jazz is, like, going to kill me."

"The past is the past. Why can't we just be friends?" Jake smiled, his dimples popping, and Roxy appeared to wilt.

"Yeah, I mean I wanted to party. But Jazz wants revenge 'cause you guys scratched her precious car." Roxy scowled.

"Well, you did try and run us off the road," Jake said.

Cash opened his mouth to speak, but the only words he managed were, "Oh shit." Over Roxy's shoulder he saw Wynter fast approaching the entrance to the rink, Ransom in tow. Jake threw the fries into a nearby trash bin.

"What are you—" Roxy turned around just in time to see Wynter and Ransom shoot by her onto the carpeted foyer. She tried to follow their path through the crowd, but Cash and Jake blocked her view.

Roxy's eyes narrowed, her face flushed with anger. "You assholes *tricked* me!" She tried to push by Cash and Jake, but they held her back. "Let me *go!*"

"Sorry," Cash said. "All's fair in love and war."

"What the *fuck* are you talking about?" Roxy shoved Cash hard. He rolled sideways and lost his balance, toppling backward over the bench. She pushed past Jake and ran after Wynter and Ransom.

Jake offered his hand to Cash and pulled him up. "You okay, dude?"

"Yeah." Cash dusted himself off. "Nice move with the fries. She smelled like primo bud."

"Stoners like their munchies."

Cash cast his eyes back and forth. "Which way did Roxy go?"

"I don't know," Jake said. "Toward the bathrooms?"

"We better find out fast because here comes trouble." Cash motioned back at the rink. He rolled toward the entrance of the Starlite, scanning the crowd for Roxy.

Jake nodded and rubbed his hands together. He glanced back to see Quinn race toward the rink entrance, with Jezebel close on her tail.

C

WYNTER AND QUINN followed several feet behind Jezebel and Ransom, seeking cover from the crowd of rollerskaters between them.

"Is she having a good time?" Wynter matched Quinn's stride. "Because she's for sure not looking for us."

"She's probably leaving it all up to that idiot Roxy." Quinn shook her head. "Ugh. I hate her so much. Is it time? Tell me it's time."

Wynter took a deep breath, then cocked her head and smiled. "Listen."

"What?" Then recognition spread across Quinn's face. "Love is a Battlefield."

"It's a sign," Wynter said. "You do your magic and I'll grab Ransom."

The two friends worked their legs in unison, increasing their speed as they weaved around other skaters like a couple of hockey players.

A few feet ahead, Jezebel held Ransom's left hand with her right. A twinge of jealousy fluttered through Wynter's mind, but she calmed herself knowing that she'd have Ransom back by the end of the night. Everything would be right again.

"Ready, Bug?" Quinn's eyes sparkled.

Wynter nodded.

Quinn broke away, taking the lead. She crouched, extended her right arm out and hooked Jezebel's legs, pulling them out from under her. Then she darted quickly to the side and spun around.

Jezebel fell backward, landing hard on her backside and inciting a collision ripple effect. People toppled beside her as they scrambled to avoid contact.

Jezebel's eyes nearly popped when she saw Quinn pointing and laughing from the side boards. Her rage wasn't far behind. "You're *dead!*" She began the process of righting herself.

Ransom twirled on his rollerskates, facing backward, and tipped up onto his toe-brakes, stopping in an instant. He rolled back to Jezebel, hesitated, then extended his hand to help her up.

Before Jezebel had a chance to grab Ransom's hand, Wynter seized the moment of surprise and latched onto his hand instead. Wynter spun Ransom around, hand in hand, coming to rest facing him like they were slow dancing. Their eyes locked on each other.

"Come with me if you want to live," Wynter said.

Ransom smiled at once, but hesitated. Both Wynter and Jezebel had an effect on him, and he appeared to struggle with the choice. Finally, in a quiet voice he said, "I'm sorry."

"Save it!" Wynter took the lead and pulled Ransom toward the exit of the rink.

"Go, Bug! Go!"

In a moment, Jezebel was on her feet again. "I'm going to fucking *kill* you."

"Just like when you tried—and *failed*—to run me off the road?" Quinn laughed. "You'll have to catch me first." She spun around and tore across the rink. She focused on following Wynter and Ransom ahead of her. Any distraction would slow her down and allow Jezebel to gain an advantage.

Quinn hit the foyer, her wheels slowing on the carpet.

"The bathrooms!" Jake called out as she passed by.

Quinn returned a thumbs up.

She navigated to the corridor that led to the bathrooms and ran smack into Roxy. Quinn pivoted on one foot, swung her free leg around, and swept Roxy's legs from under her, knocking her to the ground.

But Jezebel was hot on her trail, pushing through the crowd in the foyer. Quinn fled down the corridor and faced a choice.

*Shit. Which bathroom? The boys' or the girls'?*

They hadn't decided. The plan was moving too fast.

With Jezebel passing Roxy at the beginning of the corridor, Quinn had a split second to decide. What would Wynter do? She pushed through the door to the girls' bathroom.

"Bug?" Quinn's whisper echoed in the small space as she listened for an answer.

○

Wynter pushed through the door to the boys' washroom. Ransom rolled in after her. The bathroom door made a slow arc, its hinges creaking as it finally closed.

She pushed Ransom against the wall and kissed him long and hard, not waiting to catch her breath. Time felt as if it had stopped, despite the urgency of their escape.

"I've been waiting, like, forever to do that." Wynter laid her head against Ransom's chest. "I've missed you."

"I've missed you too," Ransom said.

She looked up into his blue eyes, burning brightly. "Why Jezebel?"

Ransom sighed. "She paid attention to me. You pushed me away."

"You were going too fast," Wynter said. "I wasn't ready."

Ransom nodded, remorse instead of happiness on his face. "I see that now. I'm sorry. For everything."

"I'm sorry, too." Wynter interlocked her fingers with his. "Come back to me? Be my guy?"

"Yeah." Ransom nodded his head, his smile returning. "I'd like that."

Wynter rolled her feet up on her toe-stops, held Ransom's face in her hands, and kissed him again. "I love you, Ransom."

"I love you, too, Wynter."

"Let's get out of here." Wynter smiled at him, then eased open the bathroom door. The corridor was clear. "Come on."

The two of them slipped out of the boys' bathroom and rolled toward the entrance of the Starlite. The bathroom door creaked closed behind them.

○

JEZEBEL ROLLED OFF the rink into the foyer, spotting Cash and Jake as she passed. "You're next, motherfuckers." She pressed through the crowd, trying to keep Quinn in her line of sight. "Get out of my fucking way!"

Jezebel saw Quinn knock Roxy off her feet and disappear down the corridor to the bathrooms. She looked down on Roxy sprawled on the carpet. "Some enforcer you are. Fuck. Get my shoes. Can you handle *that?*"

At the end of the corridor, Jezebel saw Quinn step into the girl's bathroom. "I've got you now, bitch."

She rolled to the door and shoved it open. Quinn stood at the opposite wall facing her, holding a string mop in her hands. The door swung closed and Jezebel pulled the garbage can in front of it. It wouldn't stop someone desperate to get in, but it would buy some time.

The bathroom had three enclosed stalls and a large mirror that faced two sinks. The air held the stink of cheap perfume with overtones of bleach.

Jezebel scoffed at the mop. "The only thing that's going to be good for is soaking up your own blood." She pulled out her new knife and engaged the double-edged blade with a click.

"You're a fucking psycho." Quinn secured her feet in a "T", one heel pressed into the arch of her other foot to make sure her skates wouldn't roll, and swung the head of the mop at her.

Jezebel avoided the mop head with ease and took a roll

forward. Her lips curled into a wicked grin. "Compliments will get you nowhere." She tried to grab the mop with her free hand.

"I shouldn't have dropped the charges." Quinn waved the mop in a wide arc, overshooting Jezebel by a few feet. The weight of the mop made it difficult to control. "Your ass belongs in jail."

"But you did," Jezebel said. "So, *suck* it." She rolled forward and grabbed the mop head and tried to yank it from Quinn's hands.

Quinn pushed back just as hard and Jezebel almost lost her balance. She retracted the knife blade and slid the hilt back in her pocket. With both hands free, Jezebel grabbed the mop handle, twisted it, and pulled backward.

Quinn let go of the mop and Jezebel fell to the tiled floor. Quinn began to laugh and point.

Jezebel's eyes darkened with anger, but her face displayed an element of confusion.

"You're so stupid." Quinn picked up the mop again.

Jezebel cocked her head. The sound of creaking hinges from the corridor filtered through the door and she realized she had been tricked. Her head shook slowly. "You fucking bitch." She stood and rolled to the bathroom door, pulling it open and sending the garbage can sliding toward Quinn. Then she was through.

"RUN WYNTER!" Quinn tossed the mop aside and glided to the door to follow Jezebel.

○

ZAIN PULLED CASH AND JAKE ASIDE. "Guys! What the hell is going on?"

"Sorry, Zain," Cash said. "Whatever happens—"

"Or will happen," Jake added.

"We're sorry," they said in unison.

Zain scrunched his brows in confusion. "What's that supposed to mean?"

"Sorry, gotta go!" Jake spotted Roxy at the lockers, digging out her key. He approached her from behind and snatched the Starlite-branded fob from her hand.

"Hey, give that back!" Roxy reached for the key, but Jake's rollerskates plus his natural height gave him a good eight inches on her. He held it above her head, jingling the key to taunt her.

Behind Zain, Cash saw Wynter and Ransom skate from the bathroom corridor to the front entrance.

"Jake, we got to move," Cash called back. "Now!" He turned to Zain. "I'll explain later. Again, we're sorry." He rolled and weaved around other skaters in the foyer and stopped beside the entrance to the corridor. Cash peeked down its length. Jezebel was hot on Wynter's trail.

"Here you go." Jake tossed Roxy's key to the far end of the lockers. The key bounced under a bench. She set off after them, yelling obscenities as she went.

Cash waited until the last second before sticking his leg out across the corridor. He caught Jezebel's feet and she rocketed forward, falling flat on her face.

"Jake!" Cash called back.

"At your service," Jake said, standing next to him.

Quinn arrived at the beginning of the corridor, marveling at Jezebel on the floor. "That's the third time tonight she's kissed the pavement."

"Great. A new record. Let's go!" Cash skated toward the front doors of the Starlite.

Quinn took Jake's face in her hands and kissed him firmly. "For luck."

"A Star Wars fan, too?" Jake swooned.

Cash held the door open. "Move it!"

Quinn took Jake's hand and raced toward Cash, and in seconds all three were outside following Wynter and Ransom.

"Hey!" Zain ran to the doors. "Those skates are rentals!" But Quinn, Jake, and Cash were already out of earshot. He turned back toward the foyer and saw Jezebel rolling toward him. A crowd of spectators were gathering behind her. "You can't take those skates."

Jezebel pulled her knife out, locked the blade, and thrust it toward him. "Fuck you." She bent over and ran the knife over the tongue of each rollerskate, cutting the laces open all the way to the toe. She kicked off the boots.

Roxy appeared by her side with Jezebel's shoes. "He threw the key—"

"Shut up." She slipped on her shoes. "Move!"

Jezebel and Roxy ran out the front door, heading for the Barracuda.

Zain gathered the remains of Jezebel's rollerskates. The frayed laces hung in tatters. "Could've been worse," he muttered to himself.

He picked up the phone at the admissions window and dialed. The call connected within seconds. "Sadie? Is Anson around?" Zain waited for Sadie to transfer him. "I got some rogue rollerskaters... Yeah, the usual suspects." He explained the situation as best he could and hung up.

"Show's over, folks," Zain said to the crowd. "The party's out there." He pointed to the roller rink.

But the show wasn't over. Far from it.

# The Winner Takes It All

Hand in hand, Wynter and Ransom raced down the ramp to the Starlite parking lot and made a sharp turn toward the exit. The evening sky spread out above them in oranges, blues, and purples as the summer sun dipped toward the horizon.

At the exit, Ransom tugged Wynter right, in the direction of the trailer park. If they positioned themselves in just the right spot, the neon from Sven Dwarfs shone above the rooftops and through the trees like a beacon to safety.

"No." Wynter pulled Ransom in the opposite direction. "That's where they'd expect us to go."

"But we're so close."

Wynter shook her head. "It's too dangerous."

"Where are we going then?"

Wynter continued left with Ransom by her side. To anyone watching, they looked like two friends going for an evening skate. A regular sight on a clear summer evening.

"We'll take the bridge and hide out in Windspeaker Park."

"Only if you're sure." Ransom looked at her, unable to hide the concern in his face.

"I am." Wynter returned his gaze. "I've never been more sure."

The two of them pumped their legs in time, rolling over cracked asphalt and past ramshackle houses, locked together by the hands that refused to let go of each other.

○

CASH HELD THE door to the Starlite open for Jake and Quinn, then followed them out. One after another, the three friends rolled down the ramp next to the stairs in front of the rink.

Being a much better rollerskater, Quinn led the way out of the parking lot.

"Come on!" Quinn slowed enough to grab Jake's hand and help him along. They turned right, heading straight for the trailer park.

Cash rolled to the parking lot exit and followed in the direction Quinn and Jake had headed. But his gut told him that something was off. Wynter wasn't that fast. He glanced backward and spotted Wynter and Ransom far ahead, rollerskating in the opposite direction.

"Quinn! Jake! This way!" Cash reversed direction to follow Wynter's chosen getaway route.

Quinn stopped and looked back. "What are you doing?"

Cash stopped, managing to stay on his feet, and called back. "They went this way." He pointed at Wynter and Ransom, now almost specks on the road ahead.

"Makes sense," Jake said. "Take the road less traveled."

"I hope you're right." Quinn gripped Jake's hand and set off after Cash. "This road is going to destroy my wheels."

"I'll buy you a new pair." Jake smiled and tried to put on the charm between harried breaths. It didn't work. Quinn was focused on reaching Wynter and Ransom.

After a few minutes they overtook Cash.

"Eat my dust," Jake said as he flew past.

Cash struggled to maintain his speed, but his legs were not

used to the sustained exertion needed to catch Quinn and Jake. "Nice guys finish last."

"We'll see about that," Jake called back.

Cash couldn't see Wynter and Ransom any longer and the distance between himself and Quinn and Jake increased with every stride. But he forced himself to continue as fast as he could manage. He wasn't about to let Wynter down now.

○

JEZEBEL BURST THROUGH the doors of the Starlite. She scanned the parking lot, fuming, her eyes boiling with rage, then bolted down the steps toward the Barracuda parked at the back.

Roxy followed not far behind but kept her distance. Jezebel's demeanor reminded her of a werewolf in search of prey and she knew not to get between her and the thing she wanted. In this case it was Ransom, then revenge against Wynter and her friends.

Monty stepped out from behind a van parked next to the Barracuda. "Goin' somewhere?"

Jezebel gritted her teeth and tried to push past him. He matched her attempts, blocking her path. "Jesus Christ, asshole. Not now." She stared at herself in his mirrored sunglasses.

Jezebel deked left, running around the Barracuda's trunk. Monty matched her move and ran around the hood of the car, but she was too fast. She unlocked the door and pulled it open. Monty pushed it closed.

"Fuck, man. What do you want?"

"Your *nowhere* man. Ransom." Monty took off his sunglasses, revealing eyes that were deadly serious. "I want him on my team."

"Selling *shit* for you?" Jezebel pulled open the door and reached under the driver's seat. She held up a crowbar, the short curved end pointing forward. "No chance. Fuck off."

Monty raised the hem of his stained T-shirt and revealed the butt of his .38 snubnose tucked into the waistline of his jeans. "It's only a matter of time before I get what I want."

Jezebel eyed the gun. A flicker of fear showed in her eyes. "I'll think about it. But it's not going to matter if I don't get out of here. *Now.*"

"Do more than think about it." Monty dropped his T-shirt and backed away from the car.

Jezebel hopped in, dropping the crowbar behind her seat, and unlocked the door for Roxy. She started the engine and backed out of the stall. With short bursts of speed and squealing tires, she navigated to the exit and turned right, heading toward Sven Dwarfs Trail'r Park.

Monty laughed. "Stupid bitch went the wrong way." He strolled across the parking lot to his car, started the engine, and drove out to the street. He parked by the curb and switched on the radio. "You've Got Another Thing Coming" by Judas Priest rocked through the Fiat's cheap speakers.

"Fuckin' perfect." Monty hung his left arm over the car door and tapped his hand to the beat. It was only a matter of time.

○

JEZEBEL FLOORED THE GAS, rocketing the Barracuda down Jones Avenue, focusing all her rage on the neon sign to Sven Dwarfs. She dug the switchblade out from her back pocket and tossed it at Roxy. The knife bounced off Roxy's leg and landed next to her feet in the passenger footwell.

"Get ready to use it." Jezebel shot her a doubtful look. "Don't fuck up—"

"I won't fuck up, *alright?*" Roxy picked up the knife and engaged the blade a couple of times.

"Don't wear it out."

Roxy scowled and peered out the open window. "Just drive."

Jezebel passed the trailer park and turned left toward the Main Street Overpass. "Where the fuck are they?"

"They sure can skate fast," Roxy said.

Jezebel rolled her eyes and pulled a U-turn right before the overpass.

Roxy looked through the back window. "What are you doing? You might miss them."

"They're not *that* fast." Jezebel pulled over, idling at the corner, the trailer park just ahead. She looked past Roxy, back down Jones Avenue to the Starlite. They could be at Wynter's trailer already but what were the odds of that? Besides, Jezebel would never be able to get Ransom alone if they were already home.

"Fuck it." She turned right and shot back down Jones Avenue toward the Starlite.

Roxy sat forward. "Hey, isn't that Monty's car up ahead?"

The angular lines of Monty's silver Fiat were visible on the street, next to the Starlite.

"Jesus, that car is ugly." Jezebel slowed and rolled up next to the Fiat.

Monty turned down the volume to the radio, slouched over his car door, and grinned at them through the Barracuda's driver-side window. "Lookin' for somethin', ladies? Or *someone?*"

"Cut the crap," Jezebel said. "Where did they go?"

"Everything has a price."

Roxy held up the switchblade and engaged the blade. "Spit it out, asshole."

Monty took one look at the knife and laughed. He ignored Roxy's empty threat. "You know what I want, *Jazz.*"

"Alright," Jezebel said. "Just tell me where they went."

Monty slid his glasses down and narrowed his eyes on Jezebel. "If you're lyin', you're goin' to regret it."

"I'm not lying."

Monty reset his sunglasses on his nose. He pointed his thumb backward. "Down the street and right on 19th."

Jezebel gunned the engine and peeled toward the end of the street, leaving behind a strip of melted rubber and a cloud of blue, acrid smoke that hung around Monty's car like a bad omen.

"Gnarly." Roxy twisted in her seat to watch the Fiat shrink in the distance.

"Is he following us?"

Roxy squinted through the tire smoke. "No. He's just sitting there. Probably waiting to sell drugs."

Jezebel's face darkened with malice. "Good. We don't need his shit. He just better be right."

Roxy glanced at Jezebel, uncertain. "You're not going to sell drugs for him, are you?"

"I don't know," Jezebel said. "Maybe. If the money's good." She turned right onto 19th and zoomed down the street. Ahead the Barracuda's headlights revealed a lone rollerskater on the side of the road.

"It's going to be like shooting fish in a barrel," Jezebel said as the distance closed between the car and her first target.

○

MONTY CHOKED ON the smoke left behind from the Barracuda's tires. The still evening air did nothing to help dissipate the bitter miasma. Even his attempt to wave it away with his hands had little effect.

He placed his hands on the keys, ready to start the engine, but stopped himself. Through the windshield he spotted a new complication: a familiar white Chevy Suburban was headed toward him. He decided to play it cool.

Anson rolled up next to the Fiat. "Evening, Monty." He sniffed and recoiled at the smell of burned rubber. "You know there's no parking on the street, right?"

"I was just goin' to move, Sheriff."

"Good." Anson noticed the slow-moving tire smoke. "But before you do... seen anything strange tonight?"

Monty looked up at him and responded deadpan. "Nope."

Anson looked past the hood of the Suburban. The vehicle's headlights illuminated a pair of tire tracks stretching toward the end of the street. "Nothing at all, huh? Sure about that?"

Monty shrugged and nodded.

"Well, you'd best be on your way, or you might find your car impounded."

"Sure thing, Sheriff." Monty started the Fiat's engine, popped it into gear, and headed east toward Main Street. In his rear view mirror, he watched Anson drive to the end of Jones Avenue and turn right onto 19th Street, headed north.

He might have made some good money at the Starlite tonight, but Monty had his sights on something, or *someone* else. And there was more than one way to get to 19th street.

○

ROXY SQUINTED INTO the distance and held up her hand to block the setting sun from her eyes. "Who *is* that?"

"Who gives a shit." Jezebel gunned the engine. "Get ready to cut them."

Roxy clicked the switchblade. The double razor edge glinted in the orange sunlight. "What if I cut them bad?"

"SO? That's kind of the point, idiot." Jezebel shook her head. "Jesus, do I have to do everything *myself?*"

"No. I'll do it. I just don't want to kill anyone."

Jezebel grimaced at her. "You're spineless."

The last hundred or so feet were laid out in front of her like a red carpet. The Barracuda consumed all the gas Jezebel gave it, and in return the vehicle practically flew over the asphalt. At the last second, she steered toward the rollerskater.

"It's Cash!"

"More like *smash*." Jezebel held the steering wheel steady.

Cash turned his head, locking eyes with Jezebel just for a second, then jumped toward the ditch. Roxy leaned out of the passenger window, hooting and hollering, and clipped his shoulder with the knife. The blade cut easily through his shirt and the skin beneath. He tumbled and rolled into the ditch.

"Got the bastard!" Roxy held up the switchblade. Cash's blood coated one side of the blade.

"Forty points," Jezebel laughed. "Feels like I'm in *Death Race 2000*."

"Look, up ahead. There's two more! Who is it?" Roxy leaned forward in her seat as if that would help her see better.

Instant recognition. "Quinn." Jezebel spoke in a low growl. "It's about fucking time."

"Quinn and *Jake*," Roxy hesitated for a second before she took her spot at the window, switchblade in hand, Cash's blood still wet on the blade.

"You think I can take them both out at the same time?"

"Most definitely!" Roxy called back excitedly.

Jezebel revved the engine and accelerated toward her next two targets. There was no stopping her now.

C

QUINN PUMPED WITH HER LEGS. Jake contributed as best he could but his inexperience rollerskating combined with the consequences of a relatively sedentary lifestyle impeded his stamina. Quinn was the powerhouse in this scenario.

"Cut me loose," Jake said between panting breaths. "I'm just slowing you down."

"Not a chance. Wynter needs us. Both of us." Quinn kept her

eyes forward, scanning the road for Wynter and Ransom. "Stay on your feet, soldier."

Jake beamed. "*The Terminator,* right?"

Quinn shot back a smile. "Possibly."

Even with smooth rubber rollerskate wheels, the cracked asphalt and loose gravel rattled their legs and feet with every push.

A different rattling rose up from behind them. No, not quite a rattle, but a rumble. A growl.

Jake managed a quick look behind. "Ah, shit."

"What?" But as soon as Quinn asked the question, the answer was in her ears, the engine sound she had grown to hate.

*Jezebel and her Barracuda.*

Quinn tried to ramp up her efforts, but she didn't have much more to give. She squeezed Jake's right hand in her left. "Get ready to jump for it."

The black car was upon them in seconds, leaving them no time to react and nowhere to go. At the last moment, Jake pushed Quinn to the right, launching her into the ditch beside the road. At the same time, he jumped, clearing the Barracuda's front bumper and rolling over the hood and air intake. He slammed into the windshield, cracking it, and sailed over the top of the car to the opposite side of the road.

Roxy leaned from the passenger window and swiped with the switchblade, missing Quinn by inches. She leaned her head back and laughed maniacally even though she had inflicted no injury.

Jezebel kept her foot on the accelerator and off the brake, leaving Quinn and Jake behind in a cloud of dust, backlit by the setting sun.

"Jake!" Quinn scrambled out of the ditch on all fours. She could see his crumpled form on the opposite side of the street, and he didn't appear to be moving.

Steadying herself on her rollerskates, she stepped over the gravel shoulder and glided over to where he lay. She could see his chest rising and falling, but his laboured breathing caused her the most concern. "Jake! Are you okay?"

Jake groaned and blinked up at her. "I don't think so." He grimaced. "My leg is broken... breathing hurts."

Quinn set down on one knee to stabilize herself. She scanned Jake's body and saw that his left leg was bent at an unnatural angle. She shuddered and looked away. "What can I do?"

Jake pushed himself up to a sitting position, wincing every time his left leg shifted. "Those bitches tried to kill us. Go after them."

"No, I'll stay." Quinn eyed him with concern. "You need help."

Jake grabbed her arm, his grip gentle yet firm. "This isn't a game anymore, Quinn. I'm not sure it ever was. Wynter needs you now more than me. I'll be fine."

"Are you sure?"

Jake nodded. "But don't you forget about me."

Quinn smiled. "*The Breakfast Club*. Simple Minds." She leaned toward him, caressed his jawline, and kissed him. "I'll be back... most definitely." She stood and was off like a shot, racing in the direction Jezebel had headed.

"*The Terminator.* Again!" Jake laughed. "I love you, Quinn." The words were out but Quinn was already beyond earshot. He watched her nimble body disappear around a bend in the road.

◯

CASH HAD SECONDS TO REACT. He looked over his shoulder to judge the Barracuda's speed and distance. If his timing was off even by a second, it could mean painful injury or death.

The world seemed to slow down and speed up at the same time. Cash met Jezebel's eyes for just a moment, enough time to see that there was nothing behind them except hate. And Roxy hung out of the passenger window, waving her arm and yelling like a psychopath.

He bent his legs in preparation, loading them with as much energy he could muster.

*Now!*

Cash leaped toward the ditch but the wheels on his rollerskates rolled out from under him, sapping most of the power from his jump.

He cleared the Barracuda's bumper and felt the fender brush past his legs. A searing pain opened across his left shoulder as he sailed into the ditch. Cash landed hard on his right side and rolled three times before coming to a rest on the opposite incline of the ditch.

He wanted to lie there and regain his strength but there was no time to lose. He was alive and Wynter needed him. He was still of use.

Cash worked his way out of the ditch, now very aware of the pain in his left shoulder. He went to rub it and pain shot down his arm. His hand came away wet with his own blood.

"The bitch cut me."

Cash contemplated taking off his rollerskates. He could have run faster than skating, but the asphalt would tear his feet to shreds in no time. He steadied himself on his eight rubber wheels and began to skate, one stride after another. He found his rhythm, and his speed and confidence grew.

The wind generated by Cash's forward momentum teased at his hair and cooled his face.

*This ain't half bad. Except for the blood.*

His left arm had a sticky red streak from shoulder to wrist and he cast a trail of blood droplets on the asphalt every time he swung his arms in sync with his stride.

Cash raced toward the low-hanging sun and saw a figure on the side of the road. As he drew near, his guts filled with dread. "Jake?" he said to himself.

It took a few more strides to confirm it. Jake, in his Marty McFly inspired outfit, sat on the opposite side of the road, slumped to one side.

"JAKE?"

Jake looked up and forced a smile, his eyes clouded with pain. "Cash. Dude."

Cash crouched and tipped himself onto the road next to Jake. "I still don't know how to stop on these things."

"I just drag my fingernails on the ground." Jake tried to laugh at his own joke, but his injuries held him back.

Cash gave Jake a once-over. "Jezebel get to you too?"

"Yup." Jake shifted his position, hissing his way through the pain. "Went right over the Barracuda. Pretty sure I broke the windshield. And my leg. Maybe some ribs." He eyed Cash's bloodied arm. "What about you? That looks bad, dude."

"Roxy cut me." Cash shrugged. "It's just a flesh wound."

Jake nodded, wincing through his words. "*Monty Python and the Holy Grail*. Nice one."

Cash scanned the road ahead. "Where's Quinn?"

"Jezebel missed her, thank God," Jake said. "She went after them. You should too."

"But you need help," Cash said. "I'll go knock on someone's door."

Jake shook his head. "Look at me and believe me. Wynter needs you *more*."

Cash studied Jake's eyes in the waning sunlight. He did believe him. "You sure about this?"

Jake nodded.

"Okay." Cash stood. His legs felt like rubber but he thought he could still get some use out of them.

"Hey, guess what? Quinn kissed me, dude. Right before she left."

"Excellent." Cash gave him a thumbs up. "You guys were made for each other."

"Totally." Jake waved him away. "Now get going."

Cash nodded at him, turned, and resumed his pursuit.

Jake watched him go and felt a brief pang of fear go through his heart. For a moment he wondered if he had made a mistake sending Cash away, but it was the best decision. There was no sign of the Barracuda or Quinn, and soon Cash disappeared from view as he followed the bend in the road.

Jake looked to the sky. "At least it's a beautiful evening."

The sound of a truck approaching caught his attention. A white Chevy Suburban zoomed toward him from the direction he had already traveled. It was a vehicle he knew well. Jake gritted his teeth, held both hands up, and waved.

The Suburban skidded to a stop opposite him in the other lane. Anson leaned out of the window and aimed a flashlight at him.

"Jake... Peterson?"

Jake shadowed the bright light from his eyes. "Sir, yes sir!"

Anson flipped on his light bar, washing the surrounding road and foliage with rotating red and blue light. He shifted the Suburban into park but left the engine running. Anson threw open the door and ran over to Jake. After a cursory once-over, he said, "Can you move?"

"No, sir. Broken bones."

"Who did this to you?"

"I'll give you a hint. She drives a black—"

"Barracuda." Anson shook his head. "Jezebel. Goddammit. She's leaving a trail of carnage tonight." He motioned with his head in the direction Cash went. "Carried on that way, I take it?"

"Yes, sir."

Anson rubbed his beard in thought. "Look. Stay put. I'll radio for an ambulance, but it might take an hour. The hospital's in Halston." He ran back to the Suburban, grabbed the radio handset from the dash, and relayed the details to dispatch.

"Sheriff?" Jake's pain came through in his voice.

"What is it, Jake?"

"You got anything in your car for pain?" Jake winced. "An hour's a long time."

Anson nodded. He flipped open the tailgate, pulled out a first aid kit, and ran back to Jake.

"Tylenol is going to have to do for now."

Jake nodded. He was sweating profusely. "Can I have three? I'll take two and keep one in reserve."

Anson dug through the first aid kit and shook three white tablets into Jake's hand. He recapped the container, returned it to the first aid kit, and zipped it closed. He paused, his hands on the kit. "On second thought, I'm going to leave this with you, just in case." He ran back to the Suburban and closed the tailgate. "Hold tight. An ambulance is on its way."

"Thanks, Sheriff." Tears rolled down Jake's face.

"Just call me Anson from now on, okay?"

Jake tried to smile. "Okay, Anson." He placed a tablet on his tongue and swallowed it dry, grimacing at its bitter taste. "I hope you throw that bitch's ass in jail for good."

Anson hopped into the SUV. "So do I, Jake. So do I." He threw the vehicle into drive and sped off after Jezebel.

Jake swallowed the second Tylenol and watched the sun set from the side of the road, wondering if his friends would be alright.

He held up the remaining Tylenol tweezed between his thumb and index finger and shrugged. "What the fuck. Make your move, Jake," he whispered to himself. He popped the last pill into his mouth and thought of Quinn. She would have caught the *Risky Business* reference. He hoped it wouldn't be his last.

C

Anson floored the gas, propelling the Suburban down the road. The vehicle's headlights captured a rollerskating figure ahead and he slowed, pulling into the left oncoming lane.

He craned his neck to get a good look at the teenager as he passed by. "Cash?" Anson drove ahead and pulled over to the shoulder, shifting into park.

He threw open the door and stepped out. "Cash?"

Cash rolled toward the back of the Suburban, stopping himself with his arms on the tailgate. "Anson," he said, breathless.

Anson hooked a thumb at the back door. "Get in."

Cash didn't argue. He stepped carefully over the loose gravel on the shoulder and pulled himself up into the back seat, closing the door after him.

The overhead light of the cab acted like a spotlight on Cash's injury. "Jesus, Cash. Your arm."

"Compliments of Roxy," Cash said. "But the important thing is Jezebel missed me."

"Put some pressure on that." Anson shifted into drive.

"Thanks, but I think it's stopped."

Anson resumed pursuit. "You said Roxy did this to you?"

"She hung out the window with a knife." Cash found Anson's eyes in the rear view mirror. "Did you see Jake?"

"Yeah. Ambulance is on its way," Anson said. "Why are Jezebel and Roxy after all you guys?"

"It's all Jezebel. Roxy just does what she says." Cash began to untie his rollerskates. "Jezebel wants Wynter's boyfriend."

"Who would that be?" Anson asked. "I always thought that was you."

"I did too at one time, but no such luck." Cash pulled off one rollerskate. "It's this other guy. His name is Ransom."

Anson furrowed his brows, then made a brief glance over his shoulder as if to make sure he had heard Cash correctly. "Ransom? He's the one that disappeared from my jail without a trace. You know anything about that?"

Cash directed his gaze to the darkening countryside moving past his window as he pulled off his other rollerskate. "No."

"What the hell?" Anson slowed the vehicle.

Cash followed Anson's sight line to see another rollerskating teen up ahead. "It's Quinn."

"Jesus, this is one Friday night I won't soon forget." Anson pulled into the left lane and matched Quinn's position and pace. Through the open passenger window he called, "Quinn! Get in. I got Cash in the back, too."

Relief broke on Quinn's face. She leaned left, rolled to the front passenger door of the Suburban, and grabbed the door and side mirror. Anson slowed to a stop.

Quinn pulled open the door and slid into the front passenger seat. She looked to Anson, her cheeks flushed with exertion mixed with concern. Dried tear tracks stood out on her face. "Thank God you're here." She looked back and saw Cash and panicked. "Where's Jake?"

"Couldn't move him but an ambulance is en route." Anson picked up speed and grabbed the radio handset. "Sadie. In pursuit of two hit and run suspects, north on 19th towards Main. Stand by."

Sadie's voice on the radio crackled back. "Copy, Anson."

"He pushed me out of the way." Quinn hung her head and burst into tears. "Jezebel would've mowed us both down if it hadn't been for him." She balled her hands into tight white-knuckled fists and pounded her thighs. "This is so fucked up."

Cash's eyes found Anson's in the rear view mirror. Words escaped him. Instead, he reached forward from the back seat and placed his hand on Quinn's shoulder. She took his hand immediately and squeezed it.

Silence descended on the cab of the Suburban. Anson floored the gas and propelled the vehicle forward, the cooling evening air whistling by the open windows.

The 19th Street Bridge loomed in the distance. The Barracuda sat askew across the median and four figures cast silhouettes against the sky.

Anson pulled over. "Stay in the vehicle."

The instant Anson's words were out of his mouth, Quinn's hand grabbed the door handle and pushed it open. Her rollerskate wheels hit the asphalt and she rushed toward the Barracuda as fast as her legs would carry her. "BUG!"

"Shit." Anson shifted his gaze to Cash in the back seat. "I don't suppose you'll stay put either?"

Cash shook his head. "Sorry."

Anson clenched his jaw and nodded. "Okay. Just stay behind me." He grabbed the radio handset. "Sadie, suspects found, 19th Street Bridge. Approaching with caution. Backup requested if available. Stand by." He tossed the handset onto the driver's seat.

Anson emerged from the Suburban with his hand on the butt of his gun. Cash followed in sock feet and together they approached the standoff.

○

JEZEBEL'S PERSISTENCE HAD PAID OFF. Ahead of her Wynter and Ransom rollerskated hand in hand, mounting the subtle incline to the 19th Street Bridge together. Rage coursed through her veins as she pulled to the side of the road.

"Wait, what are you doing?" Roxy alternated her gaze between Jezebel and their ultimate prize. "Why are you stopping?"

Jezebel focused all her thoughts and energy into the task that lay ahead. There could be no screw ups. She gripped the steering wheel with white knuckles and revved the engine.

"Get ready with that blade." Jezebel spoke quietly through clenched teeth. "I want her fucking *dead*." She turned to Roxy. "You hear me?"

"It's going to be hard," Roxy said. "She's on the inside."

"Just do it." Jezebel slammed her feet on the brake and the gas at the same time. The back wheels screamed and spewed a dense cloud of smoke. She could see Wynter and Ransom stop, look behind them, then stumble forward.

"See that?" Jezebel eyed Roxy wildly. "They're scared." She lifted her foot off the brake and the Barracuda fishtailed forward, picking up speed instantly. "I want her dead."

"But we can't kill her." Roxy rubbed the switchblade's hilt with her thumb. "He's linked to Wynter. If you kill her, he'll—"

"Bullshit. You don't know what the fuck you're talking about."

"He *told* me. He's Wynter's creation."

Jezebel shook her head, blinded by hate. "He's a liar. Get that knife ready."

The Barracuda barreled down the road, the gap separating Wynter and Ransom from the front of the car closing fast.

Jezebel's vision tunneled on Ransom and Wynter like a rifle scope. Soon she'd have Ransom back and Wynter would be out of her life forever. She stomped on the gas, but the pedal was already flush with the footwell.

The speedometer inched past fifty-five miles an hour. Two hundred feet turned to one hundred, then fifty. The hit would be glorious.

"It's going to be beautiful, Rox!"

Ransom leaned toward the guard rail of the bridge and curled his body around Wynter. The Barracuda's right side mirror clipped his backside, propelling them further toward the rail.

Roxy swiped with the switchblade, missing Ransom's broad back by inches. Jezebel slammed on the brakes a second too late. The front bumper hit the guard rail and split it along its riveted seam. The Barracuda stopped with a jolt, its right tire hanging off the edge of the bridge. Friday night interstate traffic zoomed back and forth beneath, the drivers unaware of the mayhem above.

"Did you get her?"

Roxy glanced back at Jezebel, her expression speaking for her.

"Fuck!" Jezebel screamed. "You fucking *bitch!*"

"Fuck you! I couldn't reach."

Jezebel threw the Barracuda into reverse, but the bumper had snagged under the guard rail. She saw Ransom and Wynter pick themselves up and skate around the back of the car.

"Get out!" Jezebel revved the engine to try to dislodge the car.

Roxy looked at her, blinking a mixture of surprise, confusion, and anger.

"Don't let them get away *again*." Jezebel spat her words at her. "GO! I'll cut them off."

Roxy pushed open the door only a foot before it banged against the guard rail, but it was enough to squeeze out. She ran around the back of the Barracuda and raced after Wynter and Ransom, switchblade in hand.

Jezebel shifted into reverse and pumped the gas to get the Barracuda rocking back and forth. "Come on you *stupid piece of shit!*" As if the car had heard Jezebel's curse, the bumper snapped free of the guard rail and the vehicle shot backward. She skidded to a stop, shifted to drive, and floored the gas pedal again, angling away from the rail.

The rear tires shrieked on the asphalt, spitting a familiar smoke cloud from behind. The car accelerated toward Wynter and Ransom, with Roxy in hot pursuit and gaining.

"At least she can run." Jezebel roared past Wynter and Ransom and pulled the steering wheel hard left. The Barracuda responded and skidded diagonally, drifting across the median. She slammed the Barracuda into park, popped open the door, and armed herself with the crowbar she had stowed behind her seat.

Wynter attempted to stop and reverse but caught her rollerskate wheel in a crack in the road. She fell down hard, breaking her fall with the heels of her hands. Sharp pebbles worked their way under her skin and caused her palms to bleed.

Before Ransom could reach down to help her, Roxy pushed

him aside. He stumbled, lost his footing, and landed on his backside.

Jezebel hooked the crowbar handle across Wynter's neck and pulled her to her feet. Wynter choked for air as she grabbed at the bar, but her bloodied hands could not maintain a grip.

"Don't hurt her!" Ransom scrambled to his feet and advanced on Jezebel.

Roxy stepped between them, switchblade raised. "Not so fast, hot shot."

"What do you want?" Ransom shouted.

Jezebel laughed. "What do you think? I want *you*. You're *mine*."

Ransom scowled. "I'll never be yours. I may have screwed around, but Wynter will always have my heart."

Jezebel's jaw tensed. "Have it your way." She increased the pressure on Wynter's neck.

"Wait!" Ransom rolled forward and Roxy swiped the switchblade at him, stopping him in his tracks.

"Back the fuck up," Roxy said.

Half a block away Anson pulled his Suburban to the side of the road. Quinn burst from the vehicle and skated toward the standoff. "BUG!" she cried.

Anson and Cash followed.

"Quinn, stop!" Anson held one hand cautiously over the butt of his gun as he approached the scene. "Weapons down. Miss Caine, let Wynter go."

Roxy shot an uneasy glance at Jezebel. Their entire plan was derailing fast.

"Back the fuck away," Jezebel called back. "Or I'll kill her."

That got Quinn's attention. She glanced backward and saw that Anson and Cash had stopped their advance. With the crowbar pressed against Wynter's throat, Jezebel had the upper hand. Everyone knew it.

Quinn held her hands together just under her nose as if she

was praying. "Oh, Bug. I'm so sorry," she said, choking back tears. "Please don't hurt her."

"You don't get to make demands, *bitch,*" Jezebel said.

"Everyone take it easy." Anson raised his hands, palms forward. "Just drop your weapons and we'll talk this out."

"Fuck you, Sheriff." Jezebel faced Ransom. "You know what I want."

"Okay." Ransom cast his eyes at Anson and sent him a subtle nod. "Take me instead of Wynter. Just don't hurt her."

Jezebel eased the pressure on Wynter's throat.

"No, Ransom. Don't—"

Jezebel cut Wynter's words short. "Shut up."

"Stop!" Ransom's face went vacant. "This ends *now*. Take me instead."

Jezebel nodded toward the open door of the Barracuda. "Get in. Slowly."

Ransom nodded and rolled toward the door. He pushed the seat forward and sat. "Now let her go."

"Easy now, Miss Caine," Anson said.

Jezebel's eyes swept the scene, moving from Cash, to Anson, and settling on Quinn. She removed the crowbar from Wynter's throat and kept it in her right hand.

"Drop your weapons," Anson said.

Wynter coughed and rubbed her neck. Quinn took a rolling step toward her.

"So long, *bitch*." Jezebel gave Wynter a hard push.

Winded and afraid, Wynter fought to keep her balance, but her feet rolled out from under her. The guard rail struck her just below her knees and she toppled backward over the edge.

"BUG!" Quinn sprang toward the guard rail.

"No!" Ransom leaped from the back seat toward the spot where Wynter had fallen, his arms outstretched as if he could somehow reach her.

Jezebel swung the long end of the crowbar up and drove it

through Ransom's body. The chiseled end pierced his sternum and exited high on his back. Blood cascaded over her hands.

"Wynter..." Ransom gasped, his hands searching, his eyes staring where Wynter had stood moments before.

"No." Jezebel held his face in her bloodied hands and kissed him. "Jezebel. Always Jezebel." She scowled and let him collapse onto the road. "Rox, in the car."

Roxy retracted the switchblade, stuffed it in her pocket, and moved around the back of the Barracuda.

"Don't move." Anson drew his gun and aimed it at Jezebel. "Stay right where you are," he said, anger and concern in his voice. "There's no coming back from this." He ran backward to the Suburban, keeping his aim on Jezebel.

Cash pushed the image of Jezebel's kiss to the back of his mind. Without hesitation, he raced back to the embankment where the bridge began and hopped the rail, shredding his socks as he controlled his slide through the dirt to the Interstate below. Quinn rolled after him. Instead of removing her rollerskates, she scooted down the embankment on her backside.

"Get in the car," Jezebel repeated.

"But what if he shoots—" Roxy shifted her line of sight nervously between Anson and Jezebel.

"He's not going to shoot you." Jezebel stepped over Ransom's body toward the driver's seat. "He's never shot his gun in his life. He's a fucking pussy."

"I said *don't move!*" Anson reached for the radio handset on the driver's seat. "Sadie, injuries at the scene. Divert ambulance to I94, at 19th Street Bridge. Suspects attempting escape. Standby."

Sadie's voice crackled back a response but Anson had already dropped the handset. He kept his aim steady as he ran back toward Jezebel.

"Don't move!" Anson focused his attention on Jezebel.

Roxy backed herself around the rear of the car.

"I think you're going away for a while this time, Miss Caine." Anson steadied his aim on Jezebel.

"For what? It was an accident," Jezebel said. "*Whiner* lost her balance. I have witnesses."

Anson shook his head slowly. "You pushed her. If Wynter dies, you're looking at manslaughter, minimum. There's at least one count of felony hit and run. But you murdered—"

Jezebel kicked the crowbar across the asphalt. Ransom and the expanding pool of his blood, as well the blood on Jezebel's hands, were gone, as if they had never existed. The rollerskates sat toppled to one side where his feet used to be.

"What in the hell..." Anson's aim faltered as his brain tried to reconcile what he had just seen. At some point during his call to dispatch, Ransom had disappeared.

"Looks like you got no evidence, Deputy Dipstick." Jezebel gripped the steering wheel and swung herself around into the Barracuda. Roxy took Jezebel's cue and jumped into the passenger seat.

Jezebel threw her head back and laughed as she shifted the Barracuda into drive and peeled off toward the north end of town.

The sound of screeching tires pulled Anson out of his confusion. He aimed at the evading Barracuda and managed to fire two rounds at the car's tires. Both missed their mark and struck the asphalt.

On the opposite side of the bridge, Monty ducked next to his Fiat parked on the shoulder. Now his sunglasses hung from the collar of his T-shirt. As Jezebel drove past, the Barracuda's headlights revealed his steely gaze. He made a gun sign with his finger and thumb and pointed it at her.

"Fuck you!" Jezebel called out and raised her middle finger out the window.

The Barracuda's headlights aided Anson's identification of Monty's Fiat, but it was the Fiat's pop-up headlights that gave him away. Monty stepped around the Fiat to the guard rail and looked down.

"You better get the hell out of here, Monty," Anson yelled as he holstered his gun. He picked up the crowbar and rollerskates and ran to the guard rail. Looking down, he saw Wynter sprawled on the grass, close to the westbound lanes of I94. Cash kneeled beside her, holding Wynter in his arms. Quinn stood next to him, choking back tears.

Anson threw the crowbar and rollerskates into the Suburban and slammed the door closed. He ran to the embankment and slid to the highway below. A moment later he joined Quinn and Cash by Wynter's side.

Cash looked at Anson, his face flushed with anxiety and concern. "Do something," he whispered, barely audible over the traffic noise.

"Ambulance is on its way," Anson said. "Best not to move her."

Cash's eyes glistened with tears. "I... I can't let her go."

"Then don't." Anson gave Cash's shoulder a gentle squeeze.

Minutes felt like hours. Soon the sounds of sirens rose above the din of the highway, and with it a fleeting hope for survival.

◯

MONTY TOOK OFF his sunglasses and hung them off his collar. He had no intention of injuring himself in a car accident at night, despite how cool he looked.

He had picked the right spot on the bridge. Across the angled hood of the Fiat, he could see everything. Jezebel had a crowbar against Wynter's throat and Roxy had Ransom boxed in. Anson had his gun trained on Jezebel.

He could only imagine their conversation, being too far to hear anything of substance.

Monty slipped his .38 snubnose out from behind his belt and

tossed it into the glove box. He didn't need any more reasons to be arrested again. When he looked up Ransom had entered the back of the Barracuda and Jezebel had released Wynter.

"Teenagers," Monty said to himself. "All a bunch of fuckin'—"

Jezebel shoved Wynter backward and sent her over the edge of the guard rail. Ransom sprang from the back seat of the Barracuda, his hands reaching for Wynter. Jezebel's crowbar burst out of Ransom's back.

"Holy fuckin' shit." Monty pushed open the car door and ran to where the guard rail of the bridge began. Wynter lay on the grass below. He looked back at Jezebel kissing a limp Ransom impaled on the sharp end of the crowbar, blood all over her hands.

"She's goddamn insane." Monty grinned, but as soon as the words were out of his mouth, Ransom disappeared in a flash of blue energy. The crowbar rang out in the night as it struck the asphalt.

Jezebel threw herself into the Barracuda and sped past him. Two gunshots rang out, the bullets glancing off the asphalt beside the car. Monty ducked beside his Fiat and made a gun with his hands, aiming at her as she drove by.

"You're workin' for me now, Jazz. You just don't know it yet," he said to himself. Jezebel laughed and flipped him off as if she had heard him.

Monty cast his mind back to the Newhaven Police holding cell he had shared with Ransom two days ago, where Ransom had disappeared just like tonight. Having an associate that could disappear into thin air had serious advantages. No jail cell could hold him. But how? The pieces of the puzzle were all in front of him, but he didn't know how they fit together.

Monty looked over the edge of the bridge and trained his eyes once more on the frantic scene below. It was obvious that Jezebel was involved but what was Wynter's role in this mystery? Finding out was his top priority.

○

WYNTER FELT THE guard rail hit the back of her calves as her feet rolled out from under her. The setting sun and the stars mixed with moving headlights from the highway traffic in a spiraling blur.

For the second she was in free-fall, it felt like all her other falling dreams. Disorienting, scary, and exhilarating all rolled up into one. But it wasn't a dream. The heat of a bruise spreading across her throat tugged at her consciousness. Jezebel had restrained her with a...

*What was it?*

One second wasn't enough time to figure out the answer to the question.

In one second Wynter's world stopped as quickly as it had flipped upside-down. She landed on her back moving twenty-five miles per hour. A wash of white light blinded her, like being unprepared for a flash photo in the dark.

She couldn't move.

She couldn't breathe.

*Am I dead?*

The white dissolved to black and Wynter could see stars salting the sky. Some stars danced.

Then a familiar face. Light from highway traffic backlit his head like a halo. His eyes looked like pools of stars. "Cash?"

Air found her lungs, but it hurt to breathe.

"Oh God, Wynter." Cash leaned in and lifted her into his arms. His tears mingled with hers as he kissed her forehead, setting his lips afire with a warmth he had never experienced before. "Don't die." He repeated the words like a mantra.

"Cash." Wynter found his face and locked her gaze with his. "Cash."

Cash leaned close, positioning his head close enough to feel her lips brushing over his ear.

"Find me," Wynter whispered. "Find me and bring me back." She looked up and saw a black figure standing at the edge of the overpass, blacker than the night sky. "Promise me."

Cash sat back, his eyes bewildered. "What do you mean?"

Wynter smiled at him ever so slightly. She closed her eyes and her body fell limp.

"No no no no. I love you, Wynter. I promise." Cash wrapped his arms around her and convinced himself that as long as he held her, Wynter would be safe. "I promise," he whispered again into Wynter's ear without any idea how he would follow through.

Cash refused to let go until help arrived, even after Quinn and Anson had joined him. He prayed it wasn't too late.

*June 7, 2021*
*Victoria, BC, Canada*

How will Cash fulfill his promise to Wynter and keep her safe at the same time? With Jezebel on the loose, anything could happen. And what if saving Wynter means she reunites with Ransom... for good? Find out in "Lucid Revenge," book two in the Dreamwaker Saga.

*LeeGabel.com/dreamwaker-saga*

*__Note from the author:__ If you liked this book, may I ask three things?* __First,__ *please rate this book. I appreciate your opinion and what I focus on next depends on you, the reader.* __Second,__ *please consider joining my reader group at LeeGabel.com/join. Once a month I share little details of my life (the fun stuff, that is) and keep you informed of future books. Plus, I'll give you a* __25% discount__ *on all my ebooks.* __And third,__ *if you liked this book, please recommend it to your friends. You can also ask your local library to order it for you if they don't have it yet. My sincere thanks.*

__One more thing:__ *This book features music from the 1980s and earlier. For a playlist of all music referenced, please go to: LeeGabel.com/music*

# *Afterward*

**Like it? Rate it. Share it.**

If you enjoyed *Lucid Bodies*, please rate it and spread the word. With your rating, you take part in this book's success. If you're interested in joining my Reader Group for fun chit-chat and advance notice of upcoming releases, please sign up by going to LeeGabel.com/signup.


**Note from the author**

Whew. What a journey 2021 (and part of 2022) was. I began this three-book saga in January 2021, smack in the middle of the COVID pandemic. The idea of lucid dreaming had remained in the back of my head for a number of years. I've tried to direct my dreams and have never been able to. But the few dreams I remember are usually quite vivid and I thought, "What would it be like if I could make a dream real?" I refined the idea further by focusing on making a single person from a dream real. It seemed like a cool idea and, if really possible, probably one that would get me into a heap of trouble. Perfect story material. The Dreamwaker Saga was born and it represents my seventh, eighth, and ninth novel.

I decided to write all three Dreamwaker books back-to-back, unlike writing and publishing stories one at a time, like my earlier books. Stories change as they're written, although the Dreamwaker Saga did stick largely to my outline. Writing the books back-to-back allowed me to refine details in earlier books to reflect the minor changes that had worked their way into the story later on.

The Dreamwaker Saga takes place over the summer of 1986 and contains many pop culture references. I give sincere thanks to the many creators of the film, television, music, and magazines of the era that helped enhance the fictional world I constructed for this story. I hope you enjoyed the indirect ride down memory lane. I certainly did.

I am eternally grateful for my wife and editor Sheila. I couldn't do this without her, nor would I want to. MJ Mumford, while spinning your own time travel suspense novels, your eagle eyes and honest feedback elevated this book to a higher level. And I owe a debt of gratitude to David Hoselton for his feedback on my earlier work as a screenwriter. He helped me gather the courage to take on this novel writing journey on my own. Watch David's work on *The Good Doctor*, which airs on ABC. And to my family and friends who supported my decision to quit my job to write full-time, you were right. I am your number one fan now.

**About the author**

Lee reads practically any genre. Plus, he's a movie junkie. That's a dangerous combination. Traditionally trained as a screenwriter, Lee moved to writing multi-genre books in 2016 and is the author of nine novels.

Lee once walked 63.5 kilometers in thirteen hours. Why? Ask him. He loves to hear from readers. Past lives include working within the visual and dramatic arts landscape as a graphic designer, illustrator, visual effects artist, animator, and screenwriter. In 2005, he contributed to an Emmy award (LOST; "Pilot; Part 1 and Part 2") for Outstanding Special Visual Effects for a Series.

In reality, Lee lives on an island in the Pacific Northwest with his wife and son. In his head, he lives wherever his characters are.

**Find Lee on the Internet:**

Want to join Lee's Reader Group or find out more about Lee and the books he writes? Please go to: LeeGabel.com/links

*An infestation of supersized vermin with a hunger for raw meat? CHECK.*

*An estranged son staying for the summer? CHECK.*
*An intense fear of rats? DOUBLE-CHECK.*

Sam Shaw's life has flipped upside down. Pets and tenants in his Bronx brownstone begin to disappear. Left behind is a wake of carnage.

All evidence points to a hybrid colony of vicious white-tailed rats that has moved into the basement – genetically superior with intelligence to match.

When his ex-wife dumps his son Bradley on his doorstep, Sam must switch into protection mode, if his son will let him.

Faced with impossible odds, Sam hires Bertha O'Connor from Detest-A-Pest Exterminators Inc. She runs the only outfit brave enough – or crazy enough – to take the job.

*With help from the Detest-A-Pest crew, Sam must face his fears or the white-tailed mutants will eat him alive. Because this horde of super-rats are smarter than anyone had bargained for...*

*Detest-A-Pest #1 (304 pages)*

*Spiders. Over 35,000 species. Every person on Earth eaten in one year. Now there's one more... a ravenous eight-legged hybrid thousands of years in the making and bigger than a dozen burritos.*

After a summer of exterminator training in New York, Bradley returns home ready to face his senior year with renewed confidence. But fate gets in the way of his grand teenage plans – especially when eight legs attack instead of four.

And these aren't your typical, everyday spiders. Their newly acquired taste for raw meat has them casting a wide net over Bradley's sleepy San Fernando suburb. It doesn't take them long to scramble up the food chain.

Add a vengeful ex-girlfriend casting a web of lies into the mix, and things get downright sticky.

But Detest-A-Pest can't resist a challenge. Sam and O'Connor rejoin Bradley and his inventive friends as they wage war on an infestation of spiders poised to swallow not only the high school, but the neighborhood and everyone within...

*Detest-A-Pest #2 (504 pages)*

*A playground for the rich. A genetic mutation a thousand years old. A relentless hunger for human flesh. What could go wrong?*

Harry Harcourt has a problem. People are dying at exclusive golf resort Mar-A-Verde. As head greenskeeper, it's up to him to "fix" the problem and keep the course open... or face termination. But it's not one problem, it's a vast network of vicious problems, all under the turf.

As bodies pile up, resident doctor Daniela Trejo joins Harry in the fight. Together, they capture a creature unlike anything on Earth – acid skin and razor-sharp fangs with agility that matches its appetite. But the creature escapes.

Outmatched and outnumbered, Harry seeks outside help. No one wants to touch the job – no one except Detest-A-Pest. O'Connor, Sam, and Hope hit the road for what looks like an easy payday in a tropical paradise. What awaits them is a journey through hell that has gruesome death hiding in every shadow...

*Detest-A-Pest #3 (340 pages)*

*A family in crisis. An impossible choice. A race against time.*

An unplanned pregnancy turns the lives of Deanna, her husband Max, and her teenage son upside down. But there's something else wrong...

After baby David receives a cancer diagnosis, Deanna drops everything to focus on finding a cure. Max has other ideas.

Based on his own troubled past, Max challenges Deanna to consider quality of life versus quantity. Their opposing opinions throw their marriage into chaos and Deanna seeks treatment options alone.

Caught in the middle, Alex must navigate this family crisis on his own. An unexpected friendship with a cancer survivor may offer the perspective he needs.

With the clock ticking, Deanna stops at nothing to save baby David's life... but her relationship with her family may not survive the process.

*David's Summer (310 pages)*

*Two sisters. One wants in. One has a plan. But gang loyalty cuts family ties...*

Jess works, spends time with friends, and earns good grades in school. But she's also sole provider for her drug-addicted mother... And she hates it.

Her sister Nova holds a high-profile position in the Dynamite Queens. Within her turf Nova enjoys fame, fortune, freedom, and respect   at a cost of family life.

But Jess wants what Nova has and is willing to do anything to get it. After one explosive argument, Jess joins a rival gang, a decision that leads her down a path of brutal consequences.

South Central L. A. erupts with violence as two gangs – two sisters – wage war on each other. For the winner, victory could be unforgiving...

Tied is a fast-paced look at family, friendship, betrayal, and revenge through the lens of tough Los Angeles girl gangs.

*Note: This novel contains strong language and gang violence.*

*Tied: A Street Gang Novel (316 pages)*

*"Get snipped," they said. "It will solve all your problems," they said. Unfortunately, Ted listened...*

Five years ago, it was love at first sight. Now, it's life on autopilot as tumbleweeds roll through Ted and Iris's bedroom. Their lackluster love life is driving Ted nuts. Iris's solution to their bedroom blues: get snipped.

Kunal and Ray, Ted's best friends and sworn enemies of Iris, agree with her for once. All roads seem to lead to a surgical solution, but Ted's not going there... until an explosive argument changes everything. A vasectomy seems like Ted's only play to win Iris back.

The antics of his precocious next-door neighbor complicates matters. Ted's ill-conceived decisions jeopardize everything important in his life, including his nuts.

But life was about to throw Ted a romantic curve-ball aimed straight at his heart...

*Snipped: A Cutting Comedy (300 pages)*